THE CRUISER

THE CRUISER

DAVID POYER

ST. MARTIN'S PRESS
New York

THE CRUISER. Copyright © 2014 by David Poyer. All rights reserved. Printed in the United States of America. For information, address St. Martin's Press, 175 Fifth Avenue, New York, N.Y. 10010.

www.stmartins.com

The Library of Congress Cataloging-in-Publication Data is available upon request.

ISBN 978-1-250-02058-1 (hardcover)
ISBN 978-1-250-02059-8 (e-book)

St. Martin's Press books may be purchased for educational, business, or promotional use. For information on bulk purchases, please contact Macmillan Corporate and Premium Sales Department at 1-800-221-7945, extension 5442, or write specialmarkets@macmillan.com.

First Edition: December 2014

10 9 8 7 6 5 4 3 2 1

He who wishes to serve his country must have not only the power to think, but the will to act.

—Plato

THE CRUISER

1

Italy

THEY'D been in the air for two hours from Spain when the copilot made her way toward him, bracing a hand on the back of each seat. "Coming up on Naples, Captain," she murmured over the hum of the engines. As the wing of the vice CNO's private jet lifted, she bent over him to point outside, giving a flash of cleavage at the neckline of her flight suit. "There's Vesuvius, sir. Harbor's coming up on your right."

The immense double mounds of the volcano barricaded the sky. Below stretched miles of roofs, streets, apartments, their windows flashing flame-orange in the winter sun. The air was hazy with mist, or maybe smoke. What must it be like, living in the shadow of a volcano? The very volcano—if he remembered correctly—where Hephaestus had forged the weapons of Mars, the god of war.

Then a great glittering rose-silver arc rolled up into view, and Dan leaned into the seat belt, shading his eyes. The pilot kept the wing depressed, as if to give his only passenger the opportunity for a long look down.

Captain Daniel Valentine Lenson, U.S. Navy, traced the tracks and roads that edged the sweeping concavity of sea that was the Bay of Naples; the inner harbor; the stone moles, spidery thin and knobbed as a movie alien's fingers. Cruise ships lay alongside the Mussolini-era passenger terminal, deck on deck shining in the sun like white steel wedding cakes.

A cliff of masonry, the fortification that had guarded the city in days past, frowned half a mile south of the inner harbor. Two hundred yards short of it lay the gray wedge of a Ticonderoga-class cruiser. A tug was nudging a barge alongside; smaller craft sketched foamy orbits around it. Those would be force protection, small boats guarding the helpless giant.

"Can you see it?" The copilot, leaning even farther over him. Blond hair swung forward, wafting a perfume he hadn't caught before. "We can notify Traffic Control and circle. Get you a better look."

"No, thanks." One glimpse had seared it into his retinas. The orange of spill-containment booms. The blues and greens that paled abruptly to shoal water a third of the way back from the stem. USS *Savo Island* was hard aground. That much was clear, even from five thousand feet.

"We'll be wheels down in ten, then. Is your seat belt secure? Just let me check—"

"I'll snug it up, thanks." Dan scratched his chin. He wore two rings: the heavy gold Annapolis one, and the thinner, traditional Navy wedding band, with stars and anchors. Glancing at his hand, she opened her mouth, as if about to say something. Then seemed to think better of it, and headed back to the cockpit. Still, he could appreciate the curve of her receding ass, firmly outlined by the tight-fitting flight suit.

The turbines whined up, then down, and dust floated and sparkled in the sunlight slanting through the window. No wonder Admiral Barry "Nick" Niles had diverted his personal aircraft to get a newly promoted surface line captain here as quickly as possible. An Aegis cruiser. The envy of other navies worldwide. Yet now she lay helpless on a shoal everyone knew was there, that was plainly shown on charts and even marked with a warning buoy.

How could it have happened?

And what was he going to do about it?

HE descended the deplaning ladder feeling like a member of Congress, carrying his briefcase and with his notebook computer slung over the other shoulder. Into hot exhaust and chilly, smoke-smelling wind. Down the line, airliners nuzzled a glass-walled commercial terminal. The U.S. Naval Support Activity, Capodichino, shared the runway with Naples International Airport.

A tall, eager lieutenant in khakis. "Captain Lenson? Lieutenant Mills. . . . Matt. It's a real honor."

He returned the salute awkwardly, and the junior officer relieved him of the computer. "I need to see Commodore Roald as soon as possible," Dan told him.

Mills glanced up from Dan's ribbons. He swallowed, looking intimidated.

"They don't make me any different from anyone else, Lieutenant. The commodore?"

A fresh blast of exhaust swept over them. Turning away, Mills yelled, "Right, sir. She, uh, told me she didn't need you until tomorrow, sir."

"My orders were to report to her."

"It's a legal issue, sir. She can't meet with the relieving commanding officer until the decision's made that the outgoing CO is actually outgoing. As I understand it."

That made sense. Niles had insisted that he see Roald the instant he arrived. But Nick Niles wasn't here. Mills was ushering him into a small room with a plush brown suede sofa, a low table, and a modernistic, chromed Italian coffeemaker. "This is our distinguished-visitor lounge, sir. The head's through there. We'll get your luggage and bring your sedan around."

"I may not need a car. Where's the court being held?"

"Court of inquiry's in Admin Two. That's further down the Spina. Or I can just take you to your quarters."

Dan sank into the sofa. "So. Matt, is it? What do you do for Commodore Roald?"

"Actually, I'm the Aegis go-to guy on the DesRon staff. Did my previous tour on *Anzio*. Why she sent me to meet you, I think."

"Can you give me any background? I know the investigation's still in progress. . . ."

Mills closed a door Dan assumed led to the main passenger area. "I can tell you what I heard from the Port Ops guys. But I can't vouch it's true."

"Always good to hear the scuttlebutt."

"Yessir. Long's you know I'm not exactly the burning bush . . . *Savo* went aground day before yesterday. Coming in early, in the rain, bound for anchorage A4. What I heard, the quartermaster chief noticed they were coming in off bearings. The navigator told the conning officer she was coming in too fast and to change course. She—the conning officer—she thought she was right, and the CO backed her. The navigator tried to relieve her, and the skipper told him to, quote, 'shut the fuck up,' unquote. Then ordered him off the bridge."

Mills glanced at the door. "At that point—and again, this is secondhand—kind of an argument-slash-clusterfuck broke out. Suddenly the castle looms out of the rain. The bo's'un sounds the collision alarm. The captain takes the conn, but they lose steering or maybe engine control, and when he orders the anchor dropped, the deck gang can't get the brake released in time."

A shiver harrowed Dan's back. A concatenation of errors and failures leading to disaster. "How fast did they hit?"

"Fifteen, sixteen knots."

He winced. "How bad's the damage?"

"They're still looking at it. A team from Surflant's down there. And, um, a lot of Italians." The aide's cell went off. "Excuse me, sir. . . . Yeah . . . yeah, he's here, in the DV lounge. . . . Yes ma'am. I'll tell him." He snicked it closed. "She says you might want to go down and take a look. I can drive you, if you want."

Dan wavered, torn between waiting for Roald and wanting to see the ship that very soon might be his own. Then took a deep breath, and nodded.

FIVE or six demonstrators pumped placards as Mills flashed his ID at a police barrier between crumbling ancient bastions. Some of the signs were in Italian; others, English. One read NO TO SHOCK AND AWE. They were waved through, though a car that tried to follow them in was surrounded by the shouting crowd. They rumbled over a concrete causeway, past a marina. A tunnel yawned in a looming pile of decaying volcanic stone. "The Castel dell'Ovo," Mills said. Dan assumed they were headed for the tunnel, but instead the road zagged and they skirted the massive sloped buttresses until the Mediterranean, blue and soft as a newborn's eyes, opened ahead.

Police and fire vehicles were jammed bumper to bumper. They had to pass three separate cordons. The first two were Italian; city police, then the federal carabinieri. The last was U.S. Navy, in helmets and black Kevlar and shorty carbines with black web slings. Guards examined their IDs, listened to Mills's explanation of who Dan was, and directed them to where they could look out over a final barrier of tumbled riprap crusted with barnacles and drifted plastic bottles and lost beach sandals.

The exposed mud smelled like a sewage treatment plant, but probably wasn't as ripe as it would get in summer. The cruiser lay motionless. Heat shimmered above the stumpy aux exhaust riser aft, but as far as he could tell, the main turbines weren't lit off. The sheer of the hull, the towering bluff of the superstructure, echoed the ramparts inland, though its horizon-blending haze gray was lighter than the ash-gray volcanic tuff of the medieval fortification. Tugs lay alongside, and the barge he'd noted from the air had been joined by another. Dan guessed they were taking off fuel, water, and lube oil, starting the laborious process of lightening ship. A third barge with a crane hovered some distance off.

A chief in tac gear saluted. He was in charge of force protection; could he be of any help? Dan nodded toward the ship. "I may be relieving her skipper. Depending on the investigation. What d'ya know about how she went aground?"

"Not much, sir. My team's out of Civitavecchia. We're just helping the locals maintain the perimeter." He glanced seaward. "I got tac comms with our RHIB, though. Want to take a look?"

Dan considered. "Can I borrow a helmet?"

"Certainly, sir. Spare in the boat." He spoke into a Motorola, and one of the circling inflatables broke from orbit and turned a blunt nose for them.

They boarded from a floating pier at the boat basin. Not far away several yacht owners were talking rapidly in Italian, gesticulating contemptuously toward the grounded warship. Dan settled Kevlar on his head as the rigid inflatable purred back out into the smoky wind, the light chop.

The cruiser grew as they neared. It towered vertical, clifflike, unclimbable, with a lack of motion that struck a sailor as unnatural, although the steady roar of blowers and machinery, the mingled smells of exhaust and fuel and cooked food, were familiar. The overlofty, topheavy-looking superstructure was canted slightly to starboard. Aluminum, Dan remembered, and the whole class had been reporting cracks. A seaman in dark blue coveralls watched from the boat deck. Dan noted the colors had been shifted aft.

His gaze rose. Aloft, flags fluttered, the surface search radar rotated. Flat squarish panels with truncated corners, not quite octagons, were set like badges on the superstructure. They were the ship's reason for being; in many ways, her main batteries, though ranks of missiles were hidden beneath hinged flush covers fore and aft.

Those bland panels were SPY-1 antenna arrays. The Ticonderogas had been designed around them, mating a Spruance-class hull and propulsion to the most powerful radars ever put to sea. Within a radius of three hundred miles, an Aegis cruiser could detect, track, identify, and reach out with missiles to destroy any aircraft threatening the massive carriers that centerpieced U.S. or NATO battle groups.

"So, Lenson," Nick Niles had rumbled four days before, slapping his desk, "I keep my promises. Still want a ship?"

Dan had stood by the window of the vice CNO's temporary office at the Buchanan House, looking out toward the Pentagon. The offices he and Niles had staggered out of together, through burning fuel, under collapsing ceilings, over torn-apart bodies, were being gutted and rebuilt.

"Yes sir," he'd murmured. Niles had stalled his career, blocked his promotion, spread the word that the most highly decorated officer in the sea services was a hothead, an individualist, reckless, cavalier, unaccountable. He seemed to have changed his mind after 9/11. Somehow he'd engineered Dan's fourth stripe, though his fingerprints were nowhere to be seen. But Dan was still wary of African-American admirals bearing gifts.

"You made captain. Sure you don't want to cash in your chips? Take a medical retirement on those wheezy lungs, go make some real money?"

He didn't answer, and a hollow boom quivered the air as a big palm walloped the desk again. "Okay. A command? I got one. You might actually be a good fit. Your background with missiles. Think about who you can cherry-pick from TAG to take with you. Fill in the holes."

"Well, I—"

"But you won't have long." A sausagelike finger had boresighted him. "I can't wait for results. She's out there on a national-level mission. If this ship doesn't turn around, and I mean on a dime, I've got another O-6 with his bags packed. And tread light this time, Lenson. No more *Gaddis*es. No more *Horns*."

"What's the mission, sir?" Dan had asked.

And Niles had told him.

"We can look at the far side, sir," said the coxswain, beside him in the boat. Dan nodded. Binoculars flashed from the bridge wing; he turned his collars up to hide his rank insignia. On the port side the red antifouling coating rose several feet above the waterline. "The screws seem to be in deeper water," Mills yelled, and Dan nodded again. That'd be a plus, if the shafts and screws weren't damaged. He could borrow fins and take a look, if that wasn't beneath the dignity of a skipper. Still, the sonar dome, all the way forward, looked as if it had been driven right up onto the shoal.

He took one more long survey, stem to stern, all 570 gray humming, roaring feet of her; at men and women standing about on the fantail, gazing longingly at the city that stretched away into the hazy distance, climbing the slopes of silent ominous peaks. Then said to the coxswain, "Thanks for the look. You can put us ashore now."

DRIVING back to the base, Dan remembered coming here as a lieutenant (jg), aboard USS *Guam*. Naples had been a grim, depressed city of blowing trash and sullen crowds and wash hanging from shabby tenements, with too many people and far too little employment. In those days every bullet-chipped wall had been plastered with Communist posters, and sailors on liberty had been warned to travel in groups.

There was still trash back in the alleys, and the streets were no wider, but the Terminale Marittima had been freshly repainted and the cars they idled behind were new. The shops were all open, with bright signs and fully stocked windows. The women who crossed in total disregard of whether or not the lights said to walk swung along jauntily in glossy leather boots and stylish coats, and the men looked far more hopeful. Italy seemed to be doing well, even in what had always been one of its least-advantaged cities. Maybe the protection of the U.S. Navy had helped it get there. He liked to think so, anyway.

Mills was slowing the sedan at the entrance to the base when Dan noticed another crowd. The guardhouse lay at the end of a cul-de-sac walled off from the main terminal by blocks of warehouses and trucking garages and the concertina wire surrounding the Alitalia repair shops. A line of cars waited to enter, but between them and the guard shack a chain of demonstrators were waving signs, gesticulating, and marching back and forth. Their shouts echoed down the cul-de-sac, amplified by the concrete walls.

"What's going on up there, Matt?"

"I'm not sure. Work disagreement, I think. There's always a strike someplace in town."

"That hasn't changed."

"Usually it's pretty tame. They even announce the time it'll be over, when they strike the train lines. So everybody can plan. It's pretty civilized." Mills touched the pedal and the sedan edged up. He slid out a sign that read AUTOVETTURE DI SERVIZIO—US NAVY and propped it on the dash.

Dan lowered his window for a better look. Unlike the demonstrators down by the waterfront, all these were male. Some had beards, which he hadn't seen on any Italians in the streets. They were dark-skinned. A squad of police, shields and helmets stacked at their feet, were joking and smoking, leaning against a warehouse wall.

The brake lights of the SUV ahead flashed as it reached the throng. As the police yelled at the demonstrators, it pushed slowly through. Some of the crowd screamed back, parting sullenly. Others ignored it, haranguing the gate guards, who stood with gloves on pistols. A reaction team watched from a Humvee. The noise level was building.

Dan pressed the switch. The window was humming upward again when a green projectile hurtled up out of the mob, whirled in the air, and plunged. It burst on their windshield with a crack of shattering glass, spattering pinkish liquid, which, an instant later, burst into flame. His window was still closing as it hit, and some spurted in, filling the cabin with gasoline fumes. Time slowed as he watched the flame outside propagate along the fume-line, jump the gap just as the window sealed, and ignite on his shoulder and in the rear seat.

"Holy shit," Mills said, hitting the accelerator. Dan twisted away from the flames, beating at them frantically as they lurched forward.

They crisped his hair, and a choking plasticky smoke filled the interior. Flailing at the fire, feeling his skin start to burn, he only dimly sensed their acceleration forward, then an abrupt brake that slammed him into his shoulder belt.

A thick white cloud blasted windshield and hood, instantly extinguishing the flames that roared and licked there. Tiny volcanoes of blistered, smoking paint vented gas and then sagged, stiffening as frost coated them. The door jerked open and an icy howl enveloped him, stopping his breath, instantly freezing his skin. But the flames doused as if by incantation. The rush of frigid gas moved on, to blast first over Mills, hunched at the wheel, eyes squinched, then shifting to the backseat, to quell the last stubborn pools of fire back there.

Gloved hands seized his belts, sawed, and yanked. He stumbled out in a gush of smoke and white vapor, flakes of which drifted around him before sublimating into invisibility. He nearly fell, but other hands steadied him, and he coughed hard, his 9/11-scarred trachea nearly closing. He swallowed, and grabbed the mask tubed to a green cylinder someone held out.

"Matt, you okay? —Matt?"

"Okay, sir," Mills said, sounding shaken, but looking unhurt. "You burned?"

"Just my . . . mainly my uniform, I think."

As a medic led him toward an emergency response van Dan glanced back. A steel mesh barrier and a solid line of troops barred access to the base. Red and blue strobes hurtled across still-smoking asphalt. The Italian police were in among the demonstrators, pushing them to their knees, handcuffing them. Some fought back, and the cops blocked the blows with their shields. Black batons rose and fell as, down the narrow street, sirens seesawed and more police vehicles turned in toward the scuffle.

He coughed hard, and sucked another hit of oxygen. If he hadn't gotten that window closed, the gasoline would have gone all over him. A fucking Molotov cocktail. Was he the target, or just a random victim? His damaged throat spasmed again and he closed his eyes, trying to breathe.

"Sit down right here, sir," the corpsman said. Filipino, by the look of him. "Got a problem with that airway?"

"No. No . . . problem."

Shrewd brown eyes examined him. "Looked like you might have. Just need to have you lie down here, then. And I'm going to give you a little injection, all right? Just to help you relax."

Still fighting to catch his breath, Dan only nodded.

THAT night, in his suite, he looked through a book someone had left in the lobby bookcase. It was by Freya Stark, about Rome's long struggle to maintain its eastern frontier against first Mithradates, then the Seleucids, and then the long struggle with the Parthians . . . who seemed to be related, in some way not quite clear, to the Pathans or Pashtuns he, Dan, had fought in Afghanistan. The Persians seemed to be involved too, but later in the story.

Eventually, trying his cell every few pages, he managed to get through to Blair. His wife sounded depressed. She'd been fighting the blues for a long time now, after being injured in the Twin Towers collapse. She'd gone through bone infection, burn problems, and trouble with the autografts to her face and ear. "How's it going, honey?" he said. "It's me."

"I know. But why's your voice so raspy?"

He debated telling her about the firebombing, but decided that would serve no good purpose. His skin still itched where the corpsman had applied an antibiotic ointment. He shivered. After getting badly burned on *Reynolds Ryan*, and so narrowly escaping from the Pentagon on 9/11, he was really starting to fear fire. "I don't know. Do I sound different?"

"Maybe not. Where are you now? Italy?"

"Correct. Naples."

"I'm sitting here watching them start another TV war. Are you aboard your ship? *Savo Island*, you said?"

"No, I'm at the Navy Lodge. I can't take over until they relieve the previous CO."

"I wish you didn't have to go."

He lay on the bed, BlackBerry pressed to his ear. The news was on the television, an Italian channel, sound muted, but a long shot panned the length of a beached and helpless warship, lingered on the U.S. flag, then pulled back to show the harbor. A commentator spoke in the foreground, ending with a smirk and a shake of the head. Dan closed his eyes. "So, how's the ear?"

"Looks horrible, but the swelling's going down."

"And the fund-raising?"

"I feel infected after every meeting. But Checkie says it's got to be done. He's been a big help. He advises me before every sit-down."

"That's good, hon. But I can't believe you need much hand-holding." Checkie Titus was her father, a retired banker. Blair was from one of the oldest families in Maryland, and a former undersecretary of defense. Dan didn't think she'd actually have much trouble raising enough cash to run for Congress, though he wasn't sure he wanted her to win. That, of course, had to go unvoiced. Like maybe a lot of things between husbands and wives.

"I wish you didn't have to deploy again."

"I wish I could be in two places, hon. How about this. Maybe you can take a break and fly over. How's Crete sound? The ruins of Minos. Or maybe Athens?"

"I've been to Athens, but Crete . . . hmm. That'd be new." Her voice changed, gained what sounded like anticipation. "Can you let me know your schedule?"

"Not sure just yet. And I couldn't tell you over the phone anyway. I'll give you the name of the port-calls guy at Surflant."

When he hung up he lay watching the muted images flicker shifting shadows on the ceiling of the darkened cavelike room. He hadn't seen his daughter in nearly a year. Wouldn't see his wife for months. Neither would any of the others aboard the ship he might shortly call his own.

Why did they do it? When they could all make more money ashore? Be with their families. Have actual lives. Instead, they were part of a crew.

Part of a crew.

Yeah.

Maybe that was explanation enough.

2

THE next morning Mills took him to the Spina, a bricked court-
yard with a Subway, a Navy Federal Credit Union office, and a
Navy College storefront. Admin Two's long, wide, light-filled corridors smelled of cappuccino. They were floored with glossy white
callacatta veined with writhes of cinnabar. The slick hard marble
felt strange underfoot; he was used to buffed tile or terrazzo.

Across a desk, a woman who'd always made him nervous was
giving orders over her cell. They'd shaken hands when he came in,
her small palm slightly sweaty; then her phone had chimed. In-
tense, skeptical Jennifer Roald, a small-boned, sharp-faced brunette
was only a little older than he. She'd directed the White House Situation Room when Dan had worked in the West Wing. They'd
stayed in touch, and now and then she'd been able to extend a helping hand, or pulse the Old Girl Network on his behalf. She'd obviously hit wickets and punched tickets since; now she was ComDesRon
26, *Savo Island*'s squadron commander—and thus, his putative
direct boss, at least for manning, equipment, and administrative
matters.

Studying her, he wondered if *she* could have been the one who'd
gotten the promotion board to throw out its initial recommendations. Probably not. They hadn't been *that* close. Coworkers, no
more. Only Niles had the clout to swing a board his way. And the
cunning to make sure no one would ever be able to prove it.

Snapping the cell closed, Roald focused a dark gaze on him. "Dan,
good to see you again. That was the NCIS. They're helping the Ital-

ians with the case. The police are working their way through the demonstrators. They want to know if you got a look at who threw the bomb."

"It wasn't a bomb. Just a bottle of gasoline. Green, maybe a wine bottle. I only got a glimpse. And I didn't see who threw it. It flew up out of the crowd, then hit our windshield. I smelled gas, and whoosh—it ignited."

She pushed across a paper slip. "Call this number. The agent's name's Erculiano. Italian name, but he's American."

He said he would and Roald glanced at a notebook screen. "Okay. Where we stand on the grounding . . . Sixth Fleet convened a JAG manual investigation, came down with a six-man team. They'll wrap at noon and present their conclusions to Admiral Ogawa. You know him?"

"I don't think so. No."

She frowned. "He seems to know you. Or of you. Anyway, he'll hold mast at 1400. I can't anticipate the results officially, but between us, I think he'll fire several people on the spot. Captain Imerson will be one. The base master-at-arms is over on *Savo* packing their seabags. They'll go from mast to the barracks and we'll fly them back to CONUS tomorrow."

"They're not going back to the ship?"

"There's some concern there might be, um, physical violence." She nodded at his raised eyebrows. "Yeah, that bad . . . Some things here for you to read. The last Insurv report. The Command Climate Survey. But right now we have to talk about where *Savo Island*'s going from here."

He nodded and took out his BlackBerry, but she gestured to put it away. "Let's make this off the record. To tell the truth, I was surprised to see your name on the message. I asked for a forceful backup, but I thought you were . . . off the board, somehow." She smiled. "That doesn't mean I'm not glad to have you."

"Uh . . . thanks."

"What have they told you? Well, first. You've XO'd an Aegis, haven't you?"

The XO was the executive officer, the second in command. "Actually, no. *Horn* wasn't Aegis capable. My XO tour was on a Knox."

"But you have missile experience? Computer background?"

"With the Tomahawk program. Computers, yes. And as far as conning goes, I'm pretty confident on the bridge."

"If you mean you wouldn't have put her aground, I certainly hope not. From what I've heard, it was a real monkeyfuck, the last few minutes before they hit. But we'll read all about that in the investigator's report."

"You don't want me at the admiral's mast."

"Absolutely not. Stay out of sight." Her cell chimed again and she flipped it open, listened, said, "Make it so," and oystered it. "Okay, what'd they tell you before you got on the plane . . . never mind. I'll start from square one. You know *Savo* just went from a baseline 7 Aegis to something new."

"Theater ballistic missile defense."

"TBMD's a new mission for us. Up to now it's been an Army responsibility, from the old Sprint to the Patriot. But if the Navy can do it without boots on the ground, shore installations, and host-country complications, this could be a Surface Force breadbasket for the next fifty years. We've grown the Standard missile with a higher-energy booster and a lighter proximity-kill warhead. So you get the range and altitude for a midphase intercept. Dahlgren rewrote the operating system with addendum units and took out the software stops they built in back in the seventies. With me so far?"

"I think so, but I'd want to get down in the weeds with some people I'm bringing over from TAG."

"I'm glad you have additional personnel resources. You've got a tech rider aboard from Johns Hopkins. I can break you out a couple bodies from my staff, too. Gap fillers only; I'll want them back."

"Thanks. So—this mission?"

She glanced at the door, and dropped her voice. "You'll be loosely associated with the Med strike group that's hitting Baghdad with Tomahawks and manned strikes. But you, yourself, will be defense of Israel. That's why Sixth Fleet's hair is on fire over this grounding. It was supposed to be an overnight in-and-out, to fuel, pick up the last shot for the anthrax inoculations, and head straight for station off Tel Aviv. Instead, she's high and dry in full view of every TV network in the Med. The Israelis are screaming, and I can't blame them a bit. We promised them a missile shield, and we're not delivering."

She glanced at her watch and he took the cue. "Okay. What are the personnel redlines? Any you're aware of?"

"Yes, I am *aware* of some," Roald said, in a voice that said *Do not accuse me of not knowing the status of my own units.*

"Sorry, didn't mean to—"

"Forget it. You're billeted for 299 enlisted and thirty officers. That's not counting the air det. They're lily-padding up from the Gulf of Aden. If this mast goes like I expect, you'll be down eight to ten bodies. A big hit. The command master chief. Even worse, your combat systems officer."

"Holy smoke." He'd already discussed candidates back at the Tactical Analysis Group, his last duty station; guys he'd worked with before. But they'd need time to get up to speed. The personnel Roald had just promised from her own staff could be hot-runners, or they could be bottom-blows. All too often, what you got from another source, even a well-disposed one, were no-loads who weren't pulling their weight in a current billet. "Do you think—will the XO go too? Or stay?"

"Admiral Ogawa'll decide that based on the report of the investigating board. Right now I can't say. I won't tell you what I think of him. The exec, I mean. Let you form your own opinion." She looked back at her screen. "The other issue I wanted to surface is material condition. Form your own opinion on that too, but keep an eye on your engine controls. All the consoles, the back plane wiring, where they run Chip A to Chip B, it's grounded. Not a good design, in my book."

"That can shut the engines down when you don't expect it."

She nodded. "And cascade—take the next engine down too. Actually, that might have been a contributing factor to the accident. That Main Control reset without notifying the bridge, or the bridge didn't quite register the reset, with all that shouting going on, so the throttles were full ahead when the engines came back online. Then suddenly they get this huge surge of power and don't react in time."

She spread her hands. "But like I said, I'm out of the loop, and rightly so. It doesn't exactly come across as career enhancing for me, either." She frowned, glanced at her cell, as if the fact it hadn't rung in the last couple of minutes puzzled her.

Dan got up. "I don't see how it can hurt you."

"Mud has a way of spattering." A closed-mouth bend of the lips that this time wasn't really a smile.

"Thanks for the briefing. I appreciate your support, Commodore."

She bent to fish in a black sample case. "That's my job. Here're the reports I told you about. Go someplace quiet and read them. Call NCIS about the gate incident. We'll sit down again when we find out who's going and who's staying. Discuss specifics."

Her cell chimed again. He left her frowning into the distance as she listened.

HE found an empty meeting room and read through the files. The Insurv report first, the ship's last board of inspection and survey. It was like a marine surveyor's appraisal, or the inspection you ask a mechanic for when you're thinking of buying a used car. Every mechanical and electronic system, its status and shortcomings and how well the records reflected that, which told you whether the crew were gundecking their maintenance. He read the engineering plant section with particular care, noting the control system grounding problem Roald had alluded to.

The next document was the Command Climate Survey. This was a new report sailors completed anonymously via the Internet. It rated their perceptions of how fairly they were treated, any instances of discrimination, whether the command played favorites, and so forth. There'd been a lot of strife over it, the hardshells complaining that giving the crew power to rate their commander was inverting the chain of command. But as he read it over, flipping back and forth to the unit sitreps on psychological problems, DUIs, and administrative separations, an unsettling picture emerged.

Something had been deeply wrong aboard. And of course, whatever the problem, the skipper was ultimately responsible. As Roald had said, heads had to roll, and Imerson's would be the first.

But this would be only one of a rash of recent DFCs, detachments "for cause." What was happening to the fleet? His unease grew as he recalled a *Navy Times* piece that had said cuts in crews and training funding had left some Aegis units in a low state of readiness. Was *Savo Island* one? If so, he might be getting issued a real can of worms. Especially if the people he lost included the strike team, the very officers and sailors he'd need most in combat. He was glad now he'd talked to Donnie Wenck and Rit Carpenter before he'd left TAG.

Wenck could be a real help. Carpenter, probably, too, although the older man had baggage Dan wasn't comfortable with. He'd talked to Monty Henrickson, but the civilian analyst had been less than enthusiastic about a months-long deployment.

He went to the Subway for a six-inch turkey, light on the mayo, then back to the second deck of Admin Two. He was rereading the Insurv report when a civilian in slacks and sweater looked in. "Captain Lenson?" Italian, by her accent. "You are Lenson? Admiral Ogawa will see you now."

COMMANDER, Sixth Fleet, wore rimless spectacles and had buzz-cut hair the color of weathered asphalt and a receding chin that did not seem to diminish his command presence. His name was Japanese, but he didn't look markedly Asian. Another officer—the deputy chief of staff, Dan guessed from his rank—nodded as he entered. Ogawa pointed to a chair. "Grab a seat, Captain. We haven't met, but I've heard about you. From Steve Leache, Vince Contardi, among others. Seems like you really leave an impression—either one way or the other."

"Um—thank you, sir."

"How's Blair doing? She was in the South Tower, wasn't she?"

"That's right, sir. She was burned. And broke a hip. But she's recovering."

"We met in Ukraine, the negotiations for Black Sea porting rights. Impressive woman. Well, I'll make this quick." Ogawa tapped a blue-bound document. "I've reviewed the report of the investigating board. I'm relieving Captain Imerson this afternoon. Have you inspected the ship?"

"I haven't been aboard. I did a waterline inspection as she lies."

The admiral skated another file toward him. "Damage report. Preliminary, but it'll give you an idea what you have to work with. I'm convening mast in half an hour, as soon as my jaggies can set it up. I'll listen to the defendants, but unless they can change my mind, the following will go: commanding officer, command master chief, two E-8s, two E-7s, and an O-3—your combat systems, unfortunately.

"You, Captain, will take command. I expect you to bring the ship back up to full proficiency as soon as possible. This will be a wartime deployment on a national strategic mission, executing a presidential directive. We've committed *Truman* and *Roosevelt* battle groups in the Med. *Abraham Lincoln*, *Constellation*, and *Kitty Hawk* strike groups in the Gulf. *Bunker Hill* and *Cowpens* will launch from the Red Sea. You'll be our goalie, in case Saddam decides to hit Israel. He threatened that during the Gulf War—"

"Yes sir, I know. Actually I—"

"Oh, yes, I heard about that. Captain Roald has volunteered people from her staff to help you out."

Dan cleared his throat as the deputy thumbed away at a tablet, trying to wrap his head around the geopolitics and at the same time figure out what he needed to ask for. What had Nick Niles himself said, back when they'd handed him a cruise missile program that was about to crater? *I've been handed a sick program. What I ask for, I'm going to get. Let's take advantage of that.* "Sir, I'd like to pluck some folks from TAG I've worked with before. And maybe a civilian contractor, to help us over the hump."

Ogawa's eyes narrowed. "I don't favor contractor support in a war zone."

"I didn't mean a corporation, sir. Individual augmentees. A sonarman, retired Navy, and a PhD I've worked with before. And an E-6, who's real sharp on digital systems—"

"Talk to Carl here. We might be able to, if we don't have to advertise it. Out of my back-pocket fund. Carl?"

"We might could." The deputy made a note.

"Your TAG guys, they're what? Officer, enlisted?"

"One enlisted, one retired enlisted, one civilian."

Ogawa fluttered a hand. "Sure that's all you want? You'll be at the tip of the spear. Carl, get their names and cut the orders. Call Mickey if you have to."

Dan liked how this guy operated. At fleet commander level, things he'd always considered tough to arrange apparently became minor details, to be flicked aside for a staffer to sweat over. He cleared his throat. "Can I get an augment to my OPTAR? If there are material problems—"

"Cut him an extra half million," Ogawa said, and Carl made another note. "Anything else? I know you don't know yet what you'll need. But when you do, shoot me a message."

"Aye aye, sir."

"This won't be easy. From the looks of the report, there are some real problems sitting out on that mudbank. And maybe today's housecleaning won't be the last. But Nick said Dan Lenson could turn it around. I hope this works out better for you than *Horn* did. I'm depending on his judgment here. And on you."

Great, Dan thought. USS *Thomas Horn* still lay alongside a fenced-off pier at the Norfolk Naval Shipyard, with WARNING; DO NOT APPROACH; RADIOACTIVE HAZARD signs hanging over bow and stern as she half-lifed toward being cool enough to scrap. But aloud he said only, getting up as both Ogawa and the chief of staff rose, "I'll do my best, sir."

HE wondered where he should be—standing by, or headed down to the waterfront—but since he still didn't have hard orders, he finally stayed. He called Erculiano from Mills's office, since he couldn't seem to get a cell connection again, and gave him what he could about his attacker, which wasn't much. The NCIS agent said he'd be going down to the police station that afternoon to help sort through the demonstrators and see if they could identify the bomber, and that he'd like to have Dan with him. Dan said, "I have to stand by for the admiral, but if I'm done by then, I'll go along. For what it's worth."

He hung up and checked the corridor, but the double doors to where Ogawa was holding mast were still closed. He consulted his watch, corrected for the time difference, and called TAG, back in Norfolk.

His former CO didn't sound pleased at the idea of letting go of Donnie Wenck, but seemed happy to give him Rit Carpenter. "You sure you want him?" he asked, and Dan said yeah, the old sonarman would be okay once they had him sealed aboard ship. He was less cooperative at the idea of letting go his chief analyst. "I'm not sure we can do business without Dr. Henrickson," he said.

"For two months?"

"You're guaranteeing it's only two months?"

Dan said reluctantly that no, he couldn't make that promise. He wanted to add what Ogawa had told him about this being a national-level mission, but the line was not secure. He leaned out to eye the doors again; still closed. "Uh, I think you'll be getting something from ComSixthFleet. To clarify what we've got to do out here, and how much I could use him."

"Well, we have to support the operating forces. Then, too, I don't know if I shared this with you before, but there's some stuff coming down the pike about possibly shutting the doors here."

Dan rubbed knitted brows. Shutting the doors? The Tactical Analysis Group developed tactics and doctrine for surface warfare battle. "I don't understand. I know, teeth to tail, but they've already gutted the schools. If we don't train people and develop doctrine, we're eating our seed corn."

"I hear you, but it's in the draft POM." He seemed to cut himself off then. Maybe remembering too that they were on a nonsecure line. "Anyway, I'll talk to Monty. Since it's you, he might go. When're you relieving?"

"Not sure. Tomorrow? The mast is still in session."

"Well, let me know. And walk light. Relieving a skipper can really wreck a crew. They're going to be devastated."

"I've been looking at the stats. There are underlying problems, that's pretty obvious. And they just came out of four months in the yard. So maybe this will actually turn out positive for them."

"But when you get hit, the bruise doesn't show for a while. You need to stay on top of that. Ask for what you need. Stay close to the squadron commander—"

Dan leaned out again, to see the doors opening. "Gotta go, Dick. Court's adjourning, I mean, mast's adjourning."

"Good luck."

HE stood watching as they filed out. They staggered, as if unused to dry land, or as if they'd lost blood and were in shock. Their gazes slipped past his or dropped to the marble deck. Chiefs, a lieutenant, petty officers. He wondered if he should close his door. Let them pass unseen. He'd been a defendant himself. Once you'd gone through it, the experience was demystified. Yet still it felt strange watching each man emerge; orient himself, as if lost; then depart, soles scuffing away down the empty hallway. At the far end two marines waited, fists on hips. The escort to the barracks, from whence they'd be flown back to the States. Not even to return to the ship to pack.

Last out was a shaken-looking man with silver shining at his temples like the chromium eagles on his collar. He was fingering the gold star and anchor on his left breast that meant he'd held command at sea. He looked as if he were walking toward the electric chair.

Then his gaze rose, and Dan read the sentence in those blank eyes. Misconduct, improper performance of duty, improper hazarding of a vessel; the precise wording of the specifications hardly mattered. The man's career was over.

The former commanding officer of USS *Savo Island* blinked. His gaze registered the eagles on Dan's own collar. His lips tightened. "They needed a scapegoat," he murmured bitterly.

"Excuse me?"

"They needed a scapegoat. Make sure you're not the next one."

Then he was gone, striding with steady paces down the bright echoing corridor.

"Captain Lenson? The admiral will see you now."

He took a deep breath, squinting after the departing figure as it vanished into white light. Then checked his gig line, rubbed his mouth, and crossed the hall.

3

T HE next day, as tugs chuffed and strained alongside in brilliant winter sunlight, Dan climbed the boat ladder to the main deck. A boatswain's whistle trilled from the gray ramparts. A bell gonged, and the 1MC intoned hollowly, as if from the belly of a brazen idol, "*Captain, United States Navy, arriving.*"

Savo Island rolled beneath his feet. A smoky haze above the city linked fingers with a mist over the water. The hills marched along with them as the tugs churned her stern-first toward an outer anchorage. As he reached the quarterdeck a blast of diesel exhaust blew across, rasping in his throat. A double line of chiefs and officers in blues snapped to attention, swaying in a buffeting wind. Dan right-faced aft, saluted a streamed-out flag, and nodded to the officer of the deck. "I have permission to come aboard."

"Very well, sir."

The OOD's arm snapped down. He looked apprehensive. No one in the double line of sailors Dan paced between was smiling either. Another gust, and a white hat flew off, hit the deck, and rolled into the scuppers. The now-bareheaded sailor, whose name tag read Benyamin, winced but held his salute, lips paling, as dirty water darkened the bleached cotton. Dan ran his gaze along one rank, then the other, noting not so much the details of uniform as the faces.

He dropped his salute, and a ragged line of arms snapped down. He wheeled out of the wind, into the quarterdeck passageway that led from one side of the ship to the other.

A slight, balding, painfully thin commander in khakis hovered beside the watertight door that, if the layout here was the same as it had been aboard *Horn*, led to Officers' Country and the wardroom. Moisture sparkled on his forehead. He murmured, "Captain, welcome aboard, sir. I'm Fahad Almarshadi. Your exec."

Dan eyed the tentatively extended palm, but didn't take it. "I understand there's a temporary OIC. From the DesRon staff."

"Yessir. He sent his respects, but said he had to stay on the bridge." Almarshadi retracted his palm, smoothed slicked-back hair with it, and swallowed. "Shall I—shall I take you up there now?"

"That'd be best." Dan took the lead to show he knew his way. Outside the wardroom the decks were torn up; their footsteps crunched on rusting metal. "What's all this?"

"Sir, Captain Imerson didn't like this old blue terrazzo. He wanted it chipped up and replaced. I've got the—"

"How many man-hours have you wasted on that?"

Almarshadi sucked air but didn't answer, falling in behind Dan as they reached a ladder up. The climb seemed longer than on *Horn*, and he remembered the two additional decks an Aegis cruiser had. Decks crammed with radar equipment, transmitter rooms, and a much larger combat information center. Sailors gaped as they hove into view, then faded into side passages.

A watertight door thunked open, and they emerged onto a wide-windowed bridge filled with sunlight and thronged with uniforms. Conversations stopped. The faces turned to him were appallingly young, unlined, apprehensive. He pushed through a nearly tangible web of quickly dropped glances to the centerline of the pilothouse. Shading his gaze against the glare, he swept the harbor. Peered down at the anchoring detail, who were standing about in yellow hard hats down on the forecastle. Then paced out onto the wing to check aft. He didn't much like leaving port stern-first, but there didn't seem to be anything he could do about it at the moment, since the tugs had her in hand.

The officer in charge introduced himself and offered a few terse sentences. *Savo Island* was in a lightened condition. The barges alongside held her fuel. All potable water had been pumped into the harbor. The six hundred five-inch rounds forward had been walked aft to raise the bow. Dan asked about damage. The OIC said the ship's damage-control teams had found no leaks or sagging bulkheads. A port engineer from Norfolk and a combat systems engineer from Surflant were aboard. *Savo* was proceeding to anchorage Bravo 4, where divers would inspect the shafts, screws, and hull. "You might actually get off without a dry-docking," he finished.

Dan said, "That'd be nice. How do you want to handle the turnover?"

"Ready when you are. Here and now, if you want."

"Got the keys?"

"Firing keys? Right here." He lifted them off over his head, on a glinting steel-bead neckchain, and handed them over.

When Dan settled them around his own neck they still felt warm. He searched around the harbor again, glanced astern. "Thanks, I've got it.—Who has the conn?"

"I do, sir." A woman's voice. A lieutenant. Raven hair, black arched eyebrows, the profile of a Hindu goddess. "The pilot's on the starboard wing."

He went out and introduced himself. The pilot, a cigarette stuck to his lip, looked him up and down, grimaced, then went back to instructing the tugs in rapid Italian on his handheld. Dan studied the distant double hump of Vesuvius, a powdery purple against the glorious gold morning light.

Usually there was a ceremony. The crew was mustered with traditional pomp to witness the turnover of command. But he didn't have an outgoing skipper present; there would be no briefings by the man he was relieving, and by now every man and woman aboard knew he was here. Probably his official bio was being circulated on the LAN, and anyone who knew anyone who'd served with him was regaling his shipmates with embroidered Dan Lenson sea stories.

So . . . forget the ceremonials. As, he vaguely recalled, Ernie King had done without, when he'd left *Lexington* back in the thirties. Maybe what they needed most was just to know someone was in charge. "Shipwide circuit. All hands," he told the boatswain's mate, who flicked switches and bent to the mike, fitting his pipe to his lips. An earsplitting shriek echoed from every speaker on deck and rebounded from the slowly receding castle walls. The forecastle team flinched and looked up.

Dan gave it a second, then took the mike.

"This is Captain Daniel V. Lenson, United States Navy, speaking.

In the next day or so I hope I'll have the opportunity to meet each of you. I will now read my orders.

"'Proceed to the port in which USS *Savo Island* may be and upon arrival, report to your immediate superior in command, if present, otherwise by message, for duty as commanding officer. By order of the Chief of Naval Operations.'"

He lowered the paper to find everyone on the bridge looking away. When their gazes swung back, something had altered in them. Infusing them with a new wariness. With . . . foreboding? Suspicion? Respect? It was difficult to say exactly, but it was plain; some invisible barrier now stood between him and every other person on the bridge.

The dark-haired woman cleared her throat. "Captain, this is Lieutenant Singhe. I have the conn. We're under way cold iron, en route to anchorage B4."

"Very well."

"Do you have any orders for the conn?"

"The standing orders will remain in effect until further notice." He stood waiting, but no one said anything. After a moment more, he went out on the wing, to consult again with the grimacing pilot.

HE told the XO he'd meet with the wardroom that afternoon. When the anchor was down and holding and the divers' barge was alongside, Almarshadi called the bridge to say they were ready. Dan glanced down a ladderway on his way aft to see a steady stream of sweaty sailors hustling along the main deck passageway. Curious, he called down. They were coming back from up forward, where each had dropped a five-inch shell off at the forward magazine, then headed aft for another.

Standing in the torn-up passageway, he examined the maze of pipes and ductwork in the overhead. Noting dust, flaking paint, the evidence of too-casual maintenance, but not really thinking of that yet. Mulling, instead, how he was going to roll in, and fighting a gut-worm of nerves. Shit, you'd think he'd have gotten over this by now. But apparently not.

He'd taken on troubled ships before. *Gaddis. Horn.* But *Savo Island* was a major command, the kind of unit the Navy expected to be forged of hardcore blackshoe haze-gray steel through and through.

Instead something had infected and dispirited her crew. He hoped they could avoid a dry-docking. That'd get them under way faster, and a ship under way was happier and tighter.

But fixing a damaged crew could be harder than repairing a damaged hull.

He remembered Imerson's tortured glance, and his muttered, "They needed a scapegoat." Had *Savo*'s last skipper been the victim of a deeper problem? Or had he *been* the problem?

He wouldn't have long to make that determination, and figure out what to do about it.

"Attention on deck," Almarshadi shouted. Twenty men and women around the long blue-leatherette-covered table and in the lounge area started to their feet. A few he'd already met, the major department heads, as they'd come up to the bridge that morning. Cheryl Staurulakis, from an old Navy family, was his operations officer. Hermelinda Garfinkle-Henriques was the supply officer. Ollie Uskavitch was Weapons. It turned out he already knew his chief engineer. Bart Danenhower, a black-mustached Baylor grad, wore a blue-striped locomotive driver's cap along with his ragged coveralls. He'd gained weight, and Dan recognized him only with difficulty; he'd been the repair officer on *Horn*. Almarshadi—his exec—was standing off to the side, wringing his hands.

They all looked so very damn *young*. Even the lieutenant commanders. How savvy and grizzled his own department heads had seemed, back when he'd first joined the aging and foredoomed *Reynolds Ryan*. Which lay now deep in the Irish Sea, some of those same men sleeping with her.

He shook his head, dismissing those memories. The glances of these young officers were all pinned to his chest. To the racks of ribbons that signified that, like the Cowardly Lion, he'd once or twice been brave.

Forget that, too. He started to gesture them to sit, then left them standing. "Good afternoon. I'll make this brief. I'll be putting my guidance out in detail in the form of a printed command philosophy and changes to the operations and regulations manual. But I wanted you to hear a few things from me personally.

"First of all, and above all: I believe in you. I've looked over your records, and this is a solid wardroom. As far as I'm concerned, those who fouled up have already paid. I'll trust you, and I expect you to trust me."

He paced, then stopped himself. A bad habit picked up from too many hours on the bridge. "Our destination is the East Med, a combat deployment on a national strategic mission executing a presidential directive. I can't share what that directive is yet. But my philosophy is, the more you know, and the more our crew knows, the better. At the same time, I trust you to keep classified information within the skin of the ship. I'll be discussing ways and means of doing that with the Comm-O.

"We'll have to be combat ready again in as short a time as possible. I depend on you to do your jobs and do them well. If you feel that for any reason you can't manage that, come and see me and I'll arrange your transfer before we leave Naples."

He looked from face to face. "I'm dead serious about that. If you don't want to be aboard, or feel you're being tasked beyond your capabilities, you don't belong on *Savo Island.*

"I expect you and the chiefs' mess to set high standards. Listen to your people; keep them focused; emphasize safety. Let me worry about the big picture. I want you obsessed with the details.

"Above all, I believe in meeting our operational taskings. Mission accomplishment has to come first. That's what we're sworn to do, and that is what we *will* do.

"But balanced against that is the welfare of the crew. All too often, we in the Surface Navy are tempted to meet our commitments at the expense of our people. And we can, for short periods of time. They understand. But if we keep shortchanging them, eventually our readiness bleeds away.

"So if you have a problem that affects combat readiness, bring it to your department head's, or the XO's, attention. But also if it's an issue of crew safety, or crew health, or even elementary fairness, and you don't think it's being addressed adequately, or we're not cutting someone the slack he or she deserves, come and see me personally. Night or day."

He paused. What else? There was so much. Jimmy John Packer's remarks about command. Old Captain Ross's story of the three envelopes, when Dan had taken over *Horn* from him. No, he wasn't interested in blaming anything on Imerson. That was in the past. Yeah, he'd beaten that to death.

But maybe those were the important things. Get her afloat—check. Get her inspected and under way—that was next. He coughed into his fist and glanced at the door. A curious face lurked outside the porthole, squinting in. "So, get ready to get under way. And once again, if you want off, see me today. After that, I'll expect everybody to be on the team."

He nodded once, curtly, and the exec darted like an alert starling to open the door.

HE climbed to the bridge again and ate lunch in his chair, looking out over the bay. His steward was named Longley, a pimply young mess crank who seemed tongue-tied in his presence. The anchor watch spoke in whispers. Around 1400 Danenhower, the chief engineer, came up to hand Dan his combination cap, which he'd left in the wardroom, and to report that the forward pump room was flooding. Either the grounding or the retraction had torn off the pit sword, a tube that sensed flow past the hull and thus speed through the water. His guys were pouring a patch, and they expected to have it under control in a couple of hours. Dan asked if he saw any problem getting under way without a pit sword; they could get speed off the GPS. Danenhower said he agreed, they could replace it later. Dan told him he wanted a full-power run if they were cleared to get under way and to start setting up for it. Danenhower nodded as if he'd expected it. He seemed to be the kind of chief engineer a skipper appreciated: not too creative, despite the locomotive engineer's hat, but detail oriented and, above all, candid. You didn't want any surprises from the engine room.

No one came up to ask to leave. He hadn't expected anyone to, but the offer was on the table until midnight.

At last he climbed down and strolled aft along the weather decks, looking out at the harbor, then examining the horizon. The seas marched in from the open Med, and the wind was bracing but not so cold he wanted a jacket. He paused at the vertical launcher, rows of hatches set flush just aft of the helicopter hangar, and discussed

VLS readiness with the groom team. No problem there, at any rate; both launchers were fully loaded out and ready to go.

Fahad Almarshadi was on the fantail, shivering as he discussed the inspection with a dripping wet-suited diver amid tanks and suits and regulators laid out on a sheet of green canvas. He fell silent as Dan came up. Dan looked over the side, down into turbid green water. Should he borrow a set of fins? Mask? No, they knew what to look for. "How's it going?"

The dive supervisor nodded respectfully. "Captain. So far, you've got some little cracks on the leading edge of your blades on number two."

"How serious?"

"Well, hard to say. We'll finish the inspection, then get out of the water while you turn your screws at low speed. If there's no vibration, there might not be major damage."

"How about the sonar dome? I know we snapped off the pit sword."

"Well, mostly what you got on your dome is scraped paint. She must have come in right between two bumps in the bottom. There might be damage we can't see, though."

"What's your recommendation, Chief?"

"Well, sir, the safe thing would be to dry-dock, check everything out."

Both men fell silent, watching him. Almarshadi fidgeted, almost dancing in place. Dan looked up past them at *Savo*'s towering superstructure. High on it the shieldlike SPY-1 arrays stared aft. They didn't rotate, like conventional radars; their powerful beams were steered electronically, one array to each ninety-degree quadrant. "I need to get under way. Not spend two weeks in the yard."

The diver looked away. "Well, sir, you're the skipper. Way it works, I make my report, you decide what it means."

"Okay, that's fair. But if you don't find anything worse than what you just briefed . . . Fahad, I want to get under way tomorrow at 0800."

Almarshadi blinked. "Yes sir, but we're still fueling. And we're going to need to load food. They're holding that for us. And a couple of days' liberty for the crew would be—"

"We don't have time for liberty. And we can get our loggies replenished from the strike group. I want a full-power run tomorrow. If no problems surface, we'll press on toward our patrol area." Dan looked at the radars again. "Which reminds me, do we have any superstructure cracks?"

"Cracks? No sir. Not that I'm aware of."

He pointed up. "That's an aluminum-magnesium alloy. Over time, salt water leaches the magnesium out. Once we're under way, I want a structural-integrity inspection on everything from the main deck up. I also want some kind of steel plates fabricated—armor—around all our deck machine-gun mounts. There are four or five other safety and readiness items I want taken care of right away. I'll do messing and berthing inspection with you tomorrow."

Almarshadi nodded, hand trembling as he jotted rapidly in a green wheelbook. Dan thanked the diver, took a last look over the side, and headed forward again.

THE Combat Information Center smelled like the inside of a brand-new refrigerator. It looked strange with all the lights on and a seaman in blue coveralls rearranging dust with a push broom. *Savo Island*'s CIC was much larger than *Horn*'s had been. Four long lines of seats and consoles funneled toward four large-screen full-color flat-panel displays to port.

The overheads dimmed as Dan strolled toward the displays, flicking off one by one. He stood before them for some time, examining the presentations as a steady rush of icy ventilation stirred the hairs on his nape.

One showed hundreds of green lines pointing in seemingly random directions, superimposed on an outline map of central Italy. Air activity from Florence, to the north, to the Strait of Messina, to the south. A second displayed video from a camera installed, as far as he could judge, on one of the Phalanx mounts. The other screens were blank.

Above the large screens a dozen smaller text readouts presented the status of the various combat systems, a weapons inventory, unit daily call signs, and computer status summaries. The older displays were flickering green on black or orange on black. The newer ones had larger screens in full color and didn't shimmer.

He leaned his weight on the back of the padded leather reclining chair that would be his during general quarters. The days of watching the horizon for an enemy ship, of hours spent maneuvering for tactical advantage before the guns roared, were long gone. Ticos had more armor than the Spruances they were based on—spaced, hardened steel, sandwiched with Kevlar spall liners—but antiship warheads, like armor-piercing shells, were designed to penetrate before exploding. If an enemy ever got in sight, he would most likely already be dead, along with most of his crew, blasted apart, drowned, burned alive, or sliced into ribbons by flying metal.

A twenty-first-century cruiser's main mission was to shield higher-value units. To knock down all the incoming weapons she could, until her magazines were empty. And then, to position herself between the carrier and the threat, and look as much *like* that carrier as she could. To absorb the last missiles, and go down, if necessary, protecting the centerpiece of the task group.

There'd be a hell of a lot of information to take in, and he'd have to react fast. Imerson had probably gone through Aegis training as part of his command pipeline. He himself would have to learn on the job, and very quickly indeed. He'd told Roald he had no doubt of his ability to maneuver a Tico-class cruiser. And he didn't. But as far as *fighting* her . . .

He took a deep breath. He couldn't show his misgivings. No one else felt confident if the CO showed self-doubt.

Survivor guilt, the civilian shrink had called it. Part of what he felt, maybe. But the trouble was, Daniel V. Lenson had always wondered if he was good enough. Sometimes he'd done all right. Sometimes he hadn't, and the faces of the dead and the accusations of being a modern-day Jonah had corroded like acid. Did every commander have to wall off this doubt and fear? Maybe he *was* some kind of imposter. Just faking the role of Naval Academy grad, surface line officer, Medal of Honor winner, commanding officer . . .

"Hey, Dan."

He turned to confront Donnie Wenck's bland smile and slightly insane-looking bright blue eyes. The first class's blond cowlick was sticking up, as usual, and as usual his hair pushed the boundaries of the regs and his blues looked as if he'd slept in them. Dan had worked with him on classified missions to Korea, the Philippines, and the Gulf. Sometimes it was difficult to get through to him. But his aw-shucks demeanor and occasional spaciness disguised a mastery of arcane software fixes, and in a tight spot—such as being trapped by the whole Iranian navy beneath the calm blue Gulf in a stolen submarine—no one remained more coolly riveted to the task at hand.

Behind Wenck, in winter blues, stood a clean-shaven white-haired civilian in suit and tie, and Lieutenant Mills, in khakis. They were reef-knotted around a female second class in the blue one-piece ship's coveralls, who hunched at a console behind and to the right of Dan's own battle station. On her screen, four evenly spaced flame-orange spokes clicked around the compass. They didn't sweep smoothly, like the radar repeaters he was used to, but snapped ahead in minuscule increments, refreshing several times a second. The display was deeply hypnotic and somehow unsettling. He had to tear his gaze away from it back to Donnie. "You're out of uniform, Chief," Dan told him. "And you'll need to call me 'Captain' again."

Wenck frowned, and the hollows beneath his eyes deepened. "Not a chief . . . sir. You know, the board turned me down."

"And you're on my ship now. Which means I can jump you a rate. A command promotion."

The blue eyes blinked. "Ooh! Goat locker's not gonna like that."

"The other chiefs? They'll live. So don't give me any grief about it." Dan leaned in to mutter into his ear, "You're just gonna have to leave the fucking Game Boy in your duffel, all right? I *don't* want to see it in CIC."

"Well, I brought you something too." Wenck nodded toward a large gray trunk with the kind of snap locks that meant electronic equipment. "Power-supply cards, signal-processing cards, crossfield amplifiers, IFF cards. The high-failure items."

Dan traded glances with Mills. "I won't ask where you got those, Donnie."

"Good, 'cause I already forgot." He bent to unspool bubble wrap from porcelain and metal. "And two of these. This is what actually turns your panels on and off. Don't let 'em clink together, they'll break."

"Switch tubes," breathed the second class. Even Mills looked impressed.

Dan turned to the civilian. At last, someone older than he was. He stuck out his hand. "Sorry, we didn't get introduced. I'm Dan Lenson. You'd be our VLS groom guy?"

"No. Dr. William Noblos, from Johns Hopkins Applied Physics Lab."

Uh-oh. "Sorry, my mistake. Doctor. That's right, the commodore told me you were aboard. The Aegis expert." He gave Noblos's hand an extra pump, added a pat to the shoulder. He didn't want to get off on the wrong foot with this guy. "I'm very glad you're with us. You have a stateroom, right?" Noblos nodded. "Wenck and Mills and I can use some high-level help. Have you and Donnie met?"

"Just getting acquainted."

He looked down at the woman at the console. "And this is—"

"Fire Controlman Second Terranova, sir." A soft voice, nearly inaudible under the whir of ventilation and cooling. When she glanced up lank brown hair framed a chubby face and chipmunk cheeks. "I'm ya senior SPY tech. They call me 'the Terror.'"

Dan looked her over doubtfully. The work-center leader for the most vital piece of equipment aboard looked like she should be playing the trombone in a high school band. He started to ask how old she was, then decided he'd rather not know. And no way was he going to call her "Terror." "Uh, good to meet you, Petty Officer Terranova. Is that New Jersey I hear?"

"Yessir. Just outside 'a Newark."

Dan cleared his throat. "Don, did you see Rit yet? And Monty?"

"Rit's still out in town. Monty didn't make the plane."

This wasn't good, about either Henrickson not coming, or Carpenter being loose in Naples. The old sonarman had caused an international incident in Seoul, caught banging a fourteen-year-old Korean girl on the grave of a British soldier in the UN cemetery. "We need to get him aboard. Now. He got a cell?" Wenck nodded. "Call him. I want his ass aboard in two hours, or he can buy his own ticket back to Norfolk. —Doctor, can I quiz you for a couple minutes? I hear you've been riding us for a while—?"

"Since Rota."

He'd read as much as he could find about the TBMD upgrade before leaving Washington. Years before, the Navy had started a program called LEAP Intercept, for low exoatmospheric antimissile projectile. It was designed to uprate Aegis and the Standard missile to the point they could shoot down Scud-type ballistic missiles in the midcourse phase, prior to atmospheric reentry. If it proved out, the Navy would have a new mission: protecting allies from the new missiles North Korea, Iran, and China were deploying. They'd also have a sturdy shield for U.S. operations overseas.

"Uh-huh. Well, can you background me on where we stand? Or—first, I guess, how about weapon loadout?" he asked the rider.

But Mills answered him. The lieutenant—originally on Roald's staff, now seconded to *Savo*—nodded toward one of the overhead readouts. "Captain. That screen shows four SM-2 Block 4A theater missile defense missiles in your vertical launchers, along with Tomahawk, Harpoon, and Asroc." It was carefully phrased, as if this were a diplomatic reminder; that Dan really knew all this.

"Okay, I see the callouts for those. But . . . there are only four Block 4As? The antimissile rounds?"

"The first four off the production line," Noblos put in.

"I see. . . . So, what's our system status?"

The white-haired scientist said, "Well, to background you, Captain . . . that would take some hours to do properly."

"We can sit down later. And I want to. But give me the broadbrush now."

"Well, you have a long-range surveillance and track function added to your AN/SPY-1. I'm assuming you're familiar with the earlier baselines? The downside is, your install is a preproduction model. Not even really a beta version. So far the program's had only two successful intercepts in five attempts. Also, several of your radar parameters are degraded and the rest are nominal."

Dan glanced at Terranova. There was no greater insult to any sailor than to say his equipment was poorly maintained, and the stereotype of a typical shipboard fire controlman was one of a fairly temperamental person, both extremely intelligent and something of a prima donna. Essentially, a grossly underpaid Silicon Valley software geek. Surely there was no way she'd let such a direct insult go unchallenged.

But to his surprise the girl did not object, respond, or even look up. She just made a slight adjustment to a knob that did not seem to alter the display as far as he could see. Noblos too had paused, as if for a rebuttal, but now went on. "Mr. Mills and I can get into that, your transmitter power out versus your phase/frequency band. Along with Petty Officer . . . with Chief Wenck. But to summarize, your maintenance has not been kept up and your operator proficiency does not seem to be where it will have to be for a successful intercept."

Dan looked at Terranova again; they were criticizing her; but still she didn't respond. "Can we get up to those spec and proficiency benchmarks fairly soon? Or is this the kind of problem where I need to send a CASREP?" A CASREP meant that the ship's capabilities were degraded; that it might not meet its assigned commitments.

Noblos cocked his head. "Well, it's inherently a tough problem, hitting an incoming missile at a combined closing rate of over twenty thousand miles an hour. In my opinion—and this is not Johns Hopkins's, just mine—this capability is being fielded too soon. It needs additional testing, and additional development. Which I gather is ongoing, aboard USS *Monocacy* at the Pacific test range.

"So the most accurate answer may be, I don't really feel able to answer your question. At least, as specifically as you may want."

Dan rubbed his face, getting a bad feeling. Just as he'd feared, the system was new and buggy. Maintenance was lagging, and his lead fire controlman seemed unwilling even to defend herself, let alone the ship.

Wenck said, out of nowhere, "Is it possible there's a virus in the system?"

Noblos frowned. "A virus? No. That's not possible."

"That would degrade the parameters."

"No. It's just poor tuning, shoddy maintenance."

Dan looked back at the readouts, remembering a ship that'd once had a virus. USS *Barrett*. Everyone had said that was impossible too. "Donnie, why do you bring that up? Do *you* think there's a virus?"

"Hey, I ain't even got my seabag unpacked, sir. But I'd like to make sure."

"Wasted effort," Noblos said.

Terranova just stared at her screen.

"Three hours." Wenck held up a thumb drive. "Just to start with a clean slate."

"I'd go with it," Dan said, his tone making it not an order but a suggestion. Noblos shrugged and turned away, and just like that, he knew he'd gotten on the rider's bad side.

He looked around the dim, chill, nearly empty space. Its ranks of vacant seats in front of unlit consoles were like the rows of seats in a theater before a play. He tried to relax, to rub the doubt off his face.

If this ship was really going to war, they all had a lot of work to do.

4

The Tyrrhenian Sea

TWO days later, leaning back in his chair on the bridge, Dan surveyed an untenanted horizon beneath a cloudy sky. Far to the east, long out of sight, the coast of Italy. A hundred sea miles northwest, the rocky coast of Sardinia. And an equal distance south, Sicily. He'd asked the senior watch officer to prune back the warm bodies in the pilothouse. But there were still twenty people up here. What had happened to "reduced manning through automation"? Navigation was computerized now, with a console instead of paper charts. But they still had to keep a paper track, in case the computers went down. Which meant you had double the people on watch.

Don't be cynical, he told himself. You're where you wanted to be: back at sea.

But sometimes it was hard.

The day was white, a pale sky over a smoky sea. But not dim; on the contrary, it glowed from within, as if beyond that frosted vault some master craftsman welded with a colorless flame. The wind was piercingly cold. The seas were parkerized steel, marching in low ranks from the west, barely three feet, at most. Just enough to make *Savo Island* surge slowly beneath him, a deliberate, gentle heave like the slow, steady breathing of a resting horse. He was still getting used to the ship, but as far as he could tell, she liked being back in harness.

"Ideal conditions," he told the chief engineer.

"Yessir." Danenhower looked haggard, unshaven, mustache askew, but the chief engineer had gotten his department ready in forty-eight hours, in a ship that two days before few had thought could have gone to sea at all. "We're ready to start the run, Captain."

"That's good work, CHENG. Appreciate the effort."

"What we do, sir."

"I also appreciated what you did back when *Horn* got nailed."

"It was the repair locker team leaders, Captain. They're the ones saved us from taking a long swim."

"Guess you've got that right. Have you kept track of Lin Porter? What's she doing now?"

"Last I heard, she had a Burke-class. *The Sullivans*, I think."

"She got a command? That's great. Well, what about this panel-grounding issue on the engines that I keep hearing about?"

"Think we've got a handle on that, sir."

"Is it a design issue?"

"It is, but there's drawbacks to an ungrounded system, too. We had an intermittent, but I think we've got it nailed. It takes attention. But we're on top of it."

Dan started to ask if he liked the Harry Potter book he'd glimpsed on his bunk when he'd passed the engineer's open stateroom door, but did not. It might sound patronizing, or as if he were making fun of the guy's reading matter. Instead, he cleared his throat. "Navigator, what's our draft?"

"Forward, twenty-two feet six inches. Aft, twenty-two three."

"Make sure that's logged. Along with the water depth at both turn points."

"In the log, sir. 3190 meters here."

That was good and deep. He raised his voice. "Confirm, clear to the east?" They'd run that way for an hour at flank speed, then turn and tear back through the same water. That would zero out any effects from wind and sea, though with today's conditions such influences should be negligible.

The officer of the deck lifted her head. The Indian-goddess profile he'd noticed the first day aboard belonged to Lieutenant Amarpeet "Amy" Singhe. Like the rest of the crew, the strike officer was in blue one-piece belted coveralls. But she made them look elegant. Deep black eyes met his. "Yes, Captain. Clear as far as the radar can see."

He stared blankly, noting the tautness of blue cloth over her breasts, the glossy black curl of twisted-up hair.

In the eternal pot-stirring of the Navy Uniform Board, sailors no longer wore dungarees at sea. The surface fleet had taken over coveralls as a working uniform from the sub force. And since all hands wore it, officers were distinguished from enlisted by the color of the web belt—blue for enlisted, khaki for chiefs and officers—and, of course, collar insignia. It was comfortable, but he wasn't sure yet how he felt about having everyone look so much the same.

"Sir?" Danenhower said.

"Let's go," Dan said. Danenhower hit the 21MC and relayed the order down to Main Control, then left the bridge.

"Right standard rudder, come to course zero nine zero," Singhe said.

"My rudder is right standard, coming to zero nine zero true . . . steady on zero nine zero, checking zero-eight-eight." The first number was the true course, by the gyrocompass; the second, by the magnetic compass. The phrases, even the cadence, were familiar, traditional, yet it sounded different. Maybe because both voices, the OOD's and the helmsman's, were female.

"Permission to start full-power run, Captain?"

"Soon as you're steady on course, Amy."

"Aye, sir. Bo's'un, pass the word."

BM2 Nuckols reached for his whistle and leaned to the 1MC. An earsplitting, endless call. Dan had never understood why it was a point of pride with boatswain's mates to break every eardrum on the ship. Nuckols intoned hoarsely, "Now commence full-power run. All personnel stand clear of the fantail and aft of frame 315."

Singhe said, "Log commencing run. All engines ahead flank three." The helmsman answered up. In the old days there'd been a lee helmsman, too, separate controllers for course and speed, but now both steering and engine commands were executed at the same console. Yeah, they'd saved one body there.

He strolled out to the wing, into the icy wind, and leaned on the bulwark as *Savo Island* gathered speed. The acceleration was perceptible, but not exactly enough to knock you off your feet. After thirty or forty seconds, though, she was charging through the chop, sending a turbulent bow wave veeing out into the grayblue sea. The turbines rose to a whining roar. The wind did too, shifting to blow from ahead, buffeting him. He grabbed his cap just as it blew off, and tucked it into his belt.

Singhe stuck her head out. A loose strand of midnight hair whipped in the wind. "Flank three, sir. Hundred and seventy rpm."

"Very well." He stood there until he was chilled through, alone except for the starboard lookout. Just watching the rapidly passing sea.

HIS at-sea cabin, one level below the bridge, was snugger and less opulent than his inport suite two decks down, where he could host meetings, or welcome dignitaries for an intimate dinner. This small vibrating closet held only a bunk, a steel hanging locker, a desk and computer, and his own chair and one for a visitor.

And Master Chief Tausengelt, in that extra chair.

The command master chief was the senior representative of the enlisted. This too had originated with the submarine force, where the chief of the boat stood second only to the CO as the source and fount of authority. Master Chief Electrician Tausengelt wasn't exactly grizzled, but he was older than almost anyone else aboard. He was lean as a smoked beef stick, with deep furrows down both sides of his mouth. His thin, light hair was only fuzz in front and not much thicker behind. He wore both the enlisted surface warfare water wings and enlisted aviation wings, and below them the heavy oval brass badge of the command master chief. Tausengelt was from Roald's staff, like Mills. He'd replaced the previous CMC, who'd gone down in the purge.

But the CMC wasn't just a mouthpiece for the crew to the skipper. He was also an inside track for the captain to find out what the crew really thought, before an abscess got to the point of bursting. Dan wanted to make him even more than that, to actually make the senior enlisted a stakeholder in the command team. Not quite a triumvirate—CO, XO, CMC—but as close as he could get. So that now Dan had no problem asking, "Well, Master Chief, you've had a chance to canvass the crew. And the chiefs' mess. What's your call? We over this, or not?"

The chief took his time answering, but finally said, "Basically, I'm not sure."

The steady roar of the turbines, conducted through the steel of the superstructure, made them both raise their voices. "Not a real informative answer, Master Chief."

"All I can give you right now, sir. Tell you one thing. This is the most suspicious goat locker I've even seen. Real closemouthed. If there's some under-the-table there, they're not giving it up."

Dan thought about this. Wenck had said the same, but he'd chalked that up to the more senior chiefs resenting a newly fleeted-up E-7, plus the natural distrust any organization had toward someone a new leader brought with him. "How do they feel about losing the old CO, the previous CMC, all those people?"

"Basically, I won't deny there's grumbling. Some say the good went overboard along with the bad."

"Probably not totally untrue. Collateral damage."

"What's that, sir?" Tausengelt cupped his ear. "It's goddamn noisy in here."

"Nothing. Yeah, it's pretty loud in here at full power. How's that command philosophy going? XO seen it yet?"

"Got a draft, sir. Should be in your mailbox."

Dan half turned and brought it up on his screen. He scrolled down it, gaze snagging on clichés. *Mission accomplishment first. Make your own quality of life.* But he couldn't fault a Navy document for clichés. The shorthand might sound tin-eared or repetitive to outsiders, but it conveyed concepts in efficient, almost digital bursts. "I'll look it over and get back to you. How's the junior enlisted feel?"

"I don't get much of a sense either way from the deckplates. Basically, they're focused on their jobs. Your inspection—that shook them up. You got into places Imerson never went."

"Or Almarshadi?"

Tausengelt remained diplomatically silent.

"The first-class lounge?"

"Pretty much the same."

"The JOs?" Strictly speaking they weren't Tausengelt's business, but an experienced chief knew what the junior officers were thinking. Usually, before the JOs knew it themselves.

Tausengelt took his time. Dan waited, hoping he didn't start his next sentence with "Basically."

"Basically, sir, there might be a problem. One of the lieutenants. She was on the bridge when the ship hit."

"Really? Who?"

"The Indian girl . . . woman. Lieutenant Singhe."

"Really? I didn't know that."

"She was the officer of the deck. But you notice, she didn't get shitcanned."

He rubbed his chin. Yeah, that was strange. Even personnel who hadn't been on the bridge were gone. But the examining board, and the admiral, had exonerated the OOD? "What's the story there? Do you know?"

Tausengelt shook his head as the ship leaned. Something creaked in the bulkhead. Dan tilted his watch. They were halfway through the first hour of the full-power run. "Basically, no idea, sir. But the chiefs, the other JOs—they all clam up tight when she walks in. I've seen it. It's weird."

"Okay, well, thanks." Dan slapped a palm on his desk, realized only after he'd done so that he was unconsciously mimicking Niles. Not a pleasant thought. "Thanks for coming up. I'll get back to you on the command philosophy."

"I'll look for it, sir."

His guest was standing, about to let himself out, when a tap sounded at the door. "Come in," Dan called.

"Lieutenant Uskavitch, Captain."

"I remember you. Come on in, Ollie." The weapons officer had to be the largest man aboard; he filled the doorframe and looked down even on Dan. Right now, he looked tense and reluctant. "The master chief was just leaving. Whatcha got?"

"Maybe he should hear this too. Not good news, sir. We're missing a firearm."

Dan sat back down. "Please tell me somebody saw it go overboard."

"Not gonna be that easy, sir. Seaman Downie was the messenger of the watch, on the quarterdeck, while we were aground. He left his sidearm on the log table for a couple of minutes, while he got relieved. When he came back, it was gone. We tore the quarterdeck apart. Interviewed everybody we can identify who went through there. No joy."

Dan shook his head, mood going even darker. Of all the paperwork nightmares, losing a pistol was about the worst. Not to mention the fact that an unsecured, unaccounted-for firearm could now be floating around his ship. "Goddamn it. Tell me about Downie."

"I don't think he's got it, sir. Downie's no rocket scientist, but he's a pretty dependable dude. We tried to handle this at the division level. He gave us permission to search his locker." Uskavitch raked his fingers back through spiky short hair. Perspiration glimmered at his hairline. "We had a lot of people going on and off during the grounding. Divers. Italians—customs, the garbage scow people, all those dudes on the barges we offloaded fuel and oil to, all the deliveries. I'm worried one of them happened through the quarterdeck just then, saw an opportunity, and dropped it into his tool bag."

Dan shook his head. He didn't need this. At all. "We're going to have to hold a shipwide search. Right away, this afternoon. As soon as we secure from full-power run. Sid, can you organize that with the chief master-at-arms?"

"Will do, sir."

"And Downie?" Uskavitch said hesitantly. "I'm not sure he's really at fault here—"

"What? Of course he's at fault, Lieutenant. He's going to have to stand mast. That's just negligence, leaving it unattended. And lack of training." The weapons officer winced. Dan nodded curtly, trying to master his anger before he said something he didn't want to. "If it doesn't turn up by evening meal, start drafting the messages."

They nodded and, after a moment, let themselves out.

HE caught up on his e-mail, though nothing was high-precedence. Anything flash, of course, would come in hard copy, hand-carried to the bridge or his cabin by a radioman with a clipboard. Routine material came into Radio, was automatically scanned for keywords, and was routed to a distribution list on the ship's network. A secure intership high-level chat function was also accessible at his battle station in CIC. One message was from the squadron supply officer, informing him of an additional $459,000 in his quarterly operating fund account. Ogawa had come through. That lightened his mood a little. Could it be he'd actually have some cash to spend on nice-to-haves?

He logged off and the screen blanked. He made sure he had his stateroom key and locked the door. Turned toward the ladder up, out of habit, then thought: Better show your face in the engine spaces.

HE slid down one ladder, then another. Aft, past the smells of cooking meat and seething grease, the clatter and bustle of the mess attendants setting up. Reminder to Self: Talk to the supply officer and the chief messman about how they could bump up the quality of the meals. Better chow was the fastest way to improve morale, especially on long stretches under way. Maybe he could put some of those extra bucks into food. Desserts, especially—young sailors loved fancy desserts.

Down another ladder, and the decks turned to painted steel and the air smelled not of soup and bread but of fuel and lube oil. When he opened the door faces turned. Someone yelled, "CO's on deck."

Dan remembered when Main Control had been in the engine room, 120 degrees as soon as you stepped out from under the blower vents, with the paint worn off greasy bronze fittings and valves by hundreds of hands. This space was brightly lit and air-conditioned, with comfortable chairs where the electricians and enginemen watched screens. Interestingly, the screens showed digital representations of analog gauges, dials, and valve handles. There was even an icon of red fluid perking in a glass tube. "Carry on, guys. Where's my EOOW?"

"Here, sir. ENC McMottie."

"How's it going, Chief?"

"Okay so far, sir. Had a frequency blip from generator number two, but she's back in spec now. All temps and pressures in the green."

Instead of sweaty dungarees and rags wrapped around forehead and hands, McMottie looked natty in pressed coveralls. One thing that was the same, though, was the racks of samples in glass tubes against a light panel on the bulkhead. They shone clear and yellow or reddish gold. All but one, which was cloudy, like fouled urine. Dan pointed to it. "Problem there, Chief?"

"Keeping an eye on it, sir."

"What's that sample from?"

McMottie pulled the tube and held it to the overhead light. "This is from the starboard CRP."

CRP was short for controllable reversible-pitch prop, the nine-foot-diameter screws that were driving them through the water at thirty-plus knots right now. Dan said, "That should be clear."

"Right, Cap'n. Should be piss-clear. Trouble is, we run it through the purifier and it comes out clean. A day or two, it's cloudy again. Thought at first it was condensation from the fuel oil tank, next to it. But we heated that tank and it didn't clear."

"How long's it been like that?"

"Long as I've been aboard, sir. We had the yard birds check it out, last yard period. They didn't have any brilliant ideas."

"Shall we take a look?"

"Uh, sure, Skipper. Stant, can you take the captain down? I'd take you myself, sir, but I got the watch. Commander Danenhower's back in ER 1. You might run into him."

"How are we on parts? The loggies taking care of you?"

"Well, that's a sore point, sir. This just-in-time system . . . we don't carry the spares we used to, when I was a engineman seaman. I know, inventory costs money, but when you need a part, you need it right then. Not at your next port visit."

"I hear you. Let me look into that." Dan gave it a beat, then lowered his voice. "Anything else I need to know about?"

"What's that, sir?" McMottie glanced at the others at their consoles.

"If there's anything you or anyone else wants to bring me, I meant what I said in the chiefs' mess yesterday. Bring it to me. If I don't know about it, I can't fix it."

McMottie's gaze dropped. "I'll remember that. The EN2 will take you down to the ER, sir."

THE engine room felt more familiar. White-painted insulation on pipes and uptakes, rattling steel gratings slicked with the oil that seemed to ooze out of the atmosphere. Ticos were powered by gas turbines, not the steam plants he'd grown up with. Which meant the air was dry, but still hot, and the never-ending clamor of pumps and generators and reduction gears followed them from upper to lower level, growing to an eardrum-numbing roar as they approached the turbines, now at full power.

He checked the Hydra radio on his belt, making sure he hadn't lost comms with the bridge. The second class's shaved head bobbed as he slid down a ladder, showing off, and slammed steel-toed boots into metal with a rattling clang. Dan followed more cautiously, gripping the slick smooth handrails. The space was huge. You could hide something small . . . like a pistol . . . down here, and no one would ever find it. As they hit the deckplates Danenhower bustled out of a side alley, locomotive engineer's cap askew, barking into his own Hydra. Of course, McMottie had called him at once with the word the skipper was poking around the engine room. As was perfectly proper. They huddled to discuss the CRP. "It's clearly moisture," Danenhower shouted. "But we don't know where it's coming from."

"Is this a major problem, Bart? Where you have water, you get corrosion."

"I don't think so, sir. Not if we keep cycling it through the purifier. This is the hydraulic oil that runs through the center of the shafts, to operate the prop pitch and reversing system. Annoying, but it's not going to rust anything. Not at the levels we're seeing."

"Okay. If you're not worried, I'm not." Dan looked around, up, down, at the terra-cotta-painted bilges beneath the gratings. He didn't see any rust, nor trash, nor torn insulation, nor the other signs of neglect or cut corners. Whatever problems *Savo Island* might have, they didn't seem to be in her engineering department.

Danenhower looked up from his watch. "Leg's almost over, Captain. We're ready to go to the crashback phase."

"I'm going to observe that on the bridge. You be down here?"

"I'll be here, Skipper."

THE air was icy when he let himself into the pilothouse again. "Captain's on the bridge."

He nodded to the OOD—still Singhe—and eyed her again, wondering how you could escape a grounding board and an admiral's mast when everyone around you got flushed. But maybe that was it; the process had to stop somewhere, and probably the board had considered her lack of seniority and let her go. She caught his look and smiled over one shoulder, and he immediately averted his gaze. It's in the past, he reminded himself. You told them that. So act accordingly.

But why had she smiled that way? And why were those dark eyes so riveting?

"Sir, three minutes left on this leg."

"Hm. Very well, Lieutenant. Just let me look at the training package." An hour at flank three, then a crashback to full astern. Back for fifteen minutes, then reverse from full astern to flank three again for fifteen minutes more. At that point, they'd finish with a full left and full right rudder at full power ahead, then the same rudder test, going full power astern.

The 21MC said, *"Bridge, Main Control. Standing by for crashback."*

Another earsplitting whistle. Dan couldn't help it; he had to plug his ears with his fingers, though he caught amused glances. "All hands stand by for crashback," grated the boatswain. Singhe reminded the aft lookout to retreat to the 01 level, to get off the fantail.

Dan looked to the navigator, who held up ten fingers, then began counting down one by one.

"Remember, one fluid motion," Singhe said to the helmsman, that cryptic smile still curving her lips. "Don't jerk it back. All the way from ahead to astern in one smooth pull. Ready? Stand by—*all back full.*"

The turbines whined down the scale, then respooled up. He clung to the jamb of the starboard wing door, looking aft. The ship seemed to shudder—if ten thousand tons of metal could be said to shudder. The quivering was slow, but it ran up his legs and shook his guts under his diaphragm. Past the leveled barrel of the aft 25mm a white flood tide churned up, crashed down over the fantail, then surged forward as the stern, quaking as if in a seizure, began to back over their own wake, gathering speed as the propwash turned the sea sliding by beneath the wing to a turbulent cold chartreuse-and-cream.

A soft, persuasive voice beside him. "Sir, I'd like to talk with you sometime. About our enlisted leadership program."

He blinked. Suddenly recalling where he'd seen the name Amarpeet Singhe before. "You wrote an article for *Proceedings.*"

"*Defense Review*, sir." She glanced aft, then back up at him. "I've been trying to put some of those initiatives into practice. Flattening the management structure. It's standard procedure in corporate management. But the previous CO . . ."

"Liked things the way they were?"

"Pretty much. I guess so." She glanced aft again, then ducked back inside to bend over the radar screen. He blinked after her, absently noting blue cloth stretched tight over all-too-easily imagined curves and indentations. Where could moisture be coming from in the CRP shaft? No doubt Danenhower and McMottie were right; it was minor. But a full backing bell for fifteen minutes would surface any problems. Better to have it break now, than when they were on station, responsible to CentCom.

Which was odd, come to think. He massaged his forehead, blinking down into the jade and cream that seethed below. He needed to read his orders again. Jen Roald had passed them to him in hard copy; they were locked in his safe, along with the 9mm Beretta he'd checked out from the gunner's mates.

Every Navy ship, whether deployed with a task force or on an independent mission, had three masters. The first was her type commander, who levied requirements based on maintenance, repair, manning, and logistics. The second was her operational commander, in his case Sixth Fleet, which reported to EuCom—European Command—more specifically, to Commander in Chief, U.S. Naval Forces Europe. The third was her tactical commander, usually the commander of a strike group.

But *Savo Island*'s orders for Operation Stellar Shield specified that CTG East Med—in effect, Dan himself—was assigned *not* to EuCom, but to Central Command. CentCom's area of responsibility was the Mideast. Confusing, for it divided his responsibilities in a way he'd never seen before and wasn't sure he liked.

Not that liking it had much to do with it. That was why they were called "orders," after all.

A quarter hour later. So far, no reports of damage. The gently heaving sea lay void all around them. Across the bridge, Singhe was head

down in the radar again. He averted his gaze from her shapely der-
riere under the cotton coveralls.

The 21MC said, *"Bridge, Main Control: coming up on comple-
tion of fifteen-minute flank three ahead."*

"Very well," Singhe said. She dipped back into the radar, then
looked around. Located him, and smiled again. "Captain, next on
the training schedule is Event 0124, rudder trials. Nearest contact,
skunk papa. Range, twenty thousand yards. Bearing, two two zero.
Course, one four five, speed ten. Past CPA and opening. No other
contacts. No failure or lube alarms from the engine room. Permission to conduct rudder trials."

He shaded his gaze out to starboard, remembering Ike Sundstrom's nagging insistence that someone always go out and look
in the direction you were going to turn. He'd seen his share of
crotchety COs. Actually, more than crochets. But you picked up
what seemed good from those you served under, and tried not to
copy what didn't. Passing the best practices on to your juniors.
One contact, away to the southwest. From the speed and course,
a coaster, plodding its way from Cagliari down to Sicily or Malta.
He checked in with Danenhower on the Hydra. The engineer said
everything sounded fine at his end. Do the rudder tests, and it'd be
a wrap.

"Permission granted," he told Singhe. "But make sure someone's
out on the wing, or check there yourself, before you put that rudder
over."

She sent the junior officer of the deck out, a fresh-faced ensign
named Eugene Mytsalo. "Clear to port," he reported back.

The pipe shrilled. *"Commencing rudder tests. All hands stand
by for heavy rolls."* Dan took his fingers out of his ears and felt for
his seat belt. Snapped it closed, and braced an elbow against a steel
ledge. Around the bridge, men and women sought nooks between
the helm and the remote operating console for the 25mm, or reached
up to the woven bronze cable that stretched across the pilothouse,
a handhold when the world tilted far out of vertical.

"Speed?"

"Thirty-five knots, sir," said the navigator from his position over
by the chart console.

"This really fast as we go, Bart?" Dan said into the Hydra. "No rocket boosters you can kick in?"

"This is it, sir. Do it now, while we got everything cranked up."

He nodded to Singhe, who grabbed the overhead cable. "Hard right rudder," she ordered.

"Hard right rudder . . . my rudder is right hard, ma'am."

For a long second *Savo Island* did not seem to respond. She plunged ahead at the same velocity, seemingly unaffected.

Then she began to lean.

Dan tightened his grip, unable to discontemplate the hundreds of tons of weight the additional decks in the superstructure added, and what that meant for stability. For a moment the deck under him seemed to lean left. Or maybe he was just braced for it. If she leaned *out*, that was bad. *Very* bad. If she leaned *into* the turn, she'd be fine.

Then the incline began, the rudder digging in, the deck tilting faster and faster to starboard. Pencils and small objects rolled and clattered to the deck. The helmsman, a small spare woman with blond braided hair, clung grimly to the console. Dan nailed his gaze to the clinometer. Forty degrees. Forty-five. Forty-seven. A rushing roar came through the starboard door, and he glimpsed past Mytsalo a rolling roar of seething sea. The bow wave, crowding into a jostling welter of foam as the bow turned into it.

Fifty degrees.

They clung and watched. The needle hung there, and then, all too deliberately, retreated. The cruiser rolled back upright and Dan relaxed. "Speed?"

"Two-niner by GPS, Captain."

Right, they didn't have a pit sword. "Very well. —Bart, everything cool down there?"

"Rudder bearings're fine. No vibration. No indication of stress."

"Make absolutely sure. If we had any damage from the grounding—"

"Everything's okay so far, sir. Tell you for sure after the port turn."

He nodded across the slanting air to the woman whose almond-eyed smile sought his, and Singhe sang out, "Rudder amidships. Steady course three four zero."

The helmswoman was echoing the order when a bell cut loose on the bulkhead. Sudden. Peremptory. Strident. At the same moment a detonation shook the ship's fabric. A soft one, not that distant, and not that loud. A second later, a ghostlike waft of pale smoke breathing out from the ventilators brought the dense, chemical stink of an electrical fire.

5

ENGINES stop!" Singhe shouted, just as Dan opened his mouth to give the order himself. Smoke was blasting out of the ventilator, thicker, whiter. The stink of burning insulation and something else, acrid and poisonous, filled the bridge.

"On the bridge: Don gas masks. 1MC: Set damage-control status Zebra," Singhe shouted, her tone slicing through the chatter and hubbub like a cleaver. "Sound general quarters."

"Belay that," Dan snapped. Then, as the helmsman reached for the throttles, added, "Not the all stop—but stand by on the general-quarters alarm."

Nuckols had reached up and secured the ventilation; both wing doors were open; the smoke was streaming outside, thinning. Singhe glanced at Dan through the lenses of her mask; then stripped it off and stuffed it back into its case. *"Fire, fire, fire,"* came over the 1MC. Not from the bridge; from Damage Control Central. *"Class Charlie fire in SPY-1 equipment room, compartment 03-138-1-C. Fire, fire, fire. Repair Two provide."*

Dan leaned to toggle the 21MC. "Combat Systems, bridge: captain. What've you got?"

"Electrical fire, Captain. Equipment Two. The Combat Systems rover opened the door and it's a sheet of flame in there. We're securing power." With the last syllable the bridge powered down. Fans whirred down the scale. Screens went blue, then blank. Silence welled up from wherever it had lurked all this time. The ship . . . creaked. The wind sighed. Something topside went *clunk*.

Equipment Two was a couple decks down. Dan tried to dismount from his chair but got hung up on the seat belt. Unstrapped, he headed for the ladderway. The door was dogged. He hesitated; placed the back of one hand against it. The steel was cool. He barked to Singhe, "Shift to sound-powered circuits. Shift to manual backup. Keep those lookouts alert." Then sucked a deep breath, heeled the dogs free, and jerked the door open.

A puff of white smoke welled up. He slammed and dogged it again and stood shaking, trying to regain control. But . . . but . . . No. He did *not* want to breathe that. Icy sweat broke across his back. The nav team regarded him curiously. He shot a glare at them, then instantly looked away, not feeling proud. In fact, deeply shamed.

"All right, then. General quarters," he said.

AN hour later he stood in the passageway outside his sea cabin. Contemplating the fact that if he'd been in there, he'd have been trapped. The firefighting team had used water fog to fight their way into the radar compartment, and CO_2 to douse the flames. Fortunately they'd contained the fire. The repair team leader stood panting and smoke-stained, mask dangling, sooty gloves tucked into his belt, talking to the Combat Systems watch officer. Past them, through a half-open door with a wavy, melted plastic warning placard that read CAUTION DO NOT ENTER VOLTAGE DANGEROUS TO LIFE, equipment steamed and smoked. "A coolant hose," a chief missile fire controlman named Slaughenhaupt was saying. "We've got six megawatts of power out through here. As much as your typical shoreside power plant. So there's a lot of heat generated. At an incredible voltage. Come in here while it's operating, it's like standing in the presence of Zeus."

Dan asked him, "And it's water cooled?"

"Yessir, the system runs chilled water through the chassis plates. You've got a seawater loop and a secondary distilled-water loop. Looks to me, the hose worked loose. So when we took that heel, it comes off. Shoots water all over, and *bam*—major-league fireworks."

Dan leaned in. Steam eddied up from scorched metal. It stank of pyrolysis and what smelled like burnt chicken feathers. "How long will it take to get everything back in operation?"

Slaughenhaupt glanced away as Donnie Wenck joined them. Lifted his shoulders, then dropped them. "Don't think that's gonna happen, sir. See that silver stuff all over the deck? That's solder. This is gonna take a complete rebuild."

Dan sucked air, looking down at the smoking pools of hot metal. "So we can't radiate."

"Well, not true, sir. This is one driver-predriver. We got six. Three forward, three aft. You need two to operate a transmitter at full power. You leave the other in standby; that's your backup."

"So we can run the forward radar?"

"Yessir. We just don't have the backup"—he nodded at the steaming equipment—"in case another DPD goes down."

Dan frowned. "But we've got two arrays forward. Port and starboard. Are you saying we can only operate one?"

The chief said patiently, "No, sir, you don't pulse both arrays at the same time. We shoot one beam at a time from one array at a time."

"So we're, basically, down a sixth of our radar capacity. How about the cooling system? How do we run without that?"

The chief said they had redundant cooling, too. "I'm telling you, sir, we can run degraded. Everything's got a backup."

"Well, maybe for air detect-to-engage. What about BMD?" He caught uncertainty in the other's eyes, and pressed in. "Let's say we get degradation in one of the other predrivers. Can we detect-to-engage on an incomer? Out to three hundred miles? Or will our power-out not be enough?"

A hesitation told him all he needed to know. He turned to find Almarshadi teetering a step above on the ladder. "Commander? Can you shed some light?"

The little XO looked uncertain. "Who we really need is Terranova. What do—"

Dan cut in: "Have you been listening, Exec? How much degradation is losing one of our predriver groups going to inflict on us? How much capability can we lose before we're out of the missile defense business? And what kind of maintenance lets a coolant hose, a *coolant hose*, get so loose a fifty-degree angle makes it let go? Those are the first questions I'd like to have answered. If you have the time, that is."

"I . . . believe I'll have to get back to you on that, Captain."

"Good, do that. Within an hour." Dan nodded once, to them all. He didn't need to make his expression any harder than it probably already was. And he was already sorry he'd unloaded on Almarshadi. He almost added a word of apology, then thought savagely: Let him take it. He'd certainly had to, when he'd been Jimmy Packer's second in command. "Where's Lieutenant Mills?"

"CIC, Captain."

"I want him in my inport cabin too. No later than 1400."

AS he was powering up his computer in the large bare captain's suite down on the main deck level, someone knocked. "Come in," Dan yelled.

"Lieutenant Mills, sir."

"Come on in, Matt. Get a look at the equipment room?"

"Yessir. CASREP's on the LAN. You should have it."

"Is Hermelinda coming?" The supply officer. Mills nodded. Dan said to the screen, "We need to make some decisions. Higher needs to know our capability's degraded." He glanced at Mills, unsure if the newly arrived officer would be able to help with what really concerned him. Namely, how could they go to war with a system that wasn't just experimental, but now significantly degraded vis-à-vis their primary mission. "My question is: How badly? I'm getting conflicting opinions."

Another knock, and they filed in: Almarshadi, looking even more apprehensive than usual; Donnie Wenck; the supply officer, Garfinkle-Henriques; and the chubby-cheeked petty officer from New Jersey, Terranova. Wenck was still in a first class's dress blues. Dan was pointing to chairs when his Hydra clicked. *"CO, Bridge."*

He unclipped it. "CO."

"Sir, Lieutenant Staurulakis."

"What'cha got, Cheryl?"

"The chief engineer reports full power and rudder trials completed satisfactorily."

The 1MC said, *"All masters-at-arms muster in the mess decks with the executive officer."* That would be the shipwide search beginning for the missing pistol. His Hydra said, *"We need to know where to head from here, Captain."*

"You have the course plotted."

"The course for the eastern Med, yes sir. We're still executing that—?"

"Until further notice," Dan said. "I'm going to report the radar casualty and see what kind of parts support we can finagle."

The Ops officer said she understood and signed off. He clicked off too and looked around the table. "Okay, we're down one DPD. That leaves one spare, aft. What's next? Repair? Replace? Terranova?"

The pudgy-cheeked little FC twisted her braid, not meeting his eyes. He still couldn't believe she was his senior tech for the most advanced radar in the Navy. "Sir, we have eight different kinds of microwave power tubes and CFAs and TWTs in the DPD. We have spares for all of them and Petty Officer—I mean, Chief—Wenck brought us some more. But our real problem's the chassis. It's burnt, melted, the solder joints are gone, all the cooling channels are distorted. The simplest thing to do would be to strip it down to parade rest, test the TWTs and Mark 99s and SDRs, keep the ones that are in spec and survey the others. Then plug in all the components into a totally new chassis."

Dan nodded. "Okay, how fast can we do that?"

Mills said, "We can start pulling tubes as soon as the space cools down. Though some of them have radioactive components. So we'd need to do a survey before we send people in. Problem is, we don't carry spare chassis . . . chassis-es."

Dan raised his eyebrows at the supply officer. "Hermelinda?"

"Matt's right, sir. Unfortunately, they're custom-fabricated for each ship set. So they're not in the supply system."

"You checked that?"

"Wouldn't say so if I hadn't, Captain."

"Okay, good. That's what I like to hear."

"I have a message out to the original equipment manufacturer, seeing if they have any in inventory. But I wouldn't expect it."

"How about Dahlgren? They're the Aegis capital, right? Would they have a chassis set, maybe even a complete driver-predriver, that they could let us have?"

"I'll get a message out," Mills said.

"Make it immediate priority. But a caveat. Everything that goes out of here about this is classified top secret," Dan said.

That stopped them. Garfinkle-Henriques especially looked puzzled. "Top secret," Dan repeated, before they could ask why. "All right, let's get to it. Matt, you stay. Oh, and Hermelinda, is there a stock number for the chassis?"

The supply officer said patiently, "If it was in the supply system, it would have a stock number, sir. But since it isn't—"

"Okay, okay, I get it." He looked at his LAN screen. "I've got your CASREP. But before I put it in, I'm going to make a call."

He'd thought about doing this via the new high-side chat function. But he distrusted chat. There was no paper trail. There wasn't even, if he understood it correctly, really an electronic trail, or at least one he trusted to be secure.

Because he didn't want this to get out. It was bad enough they were degraded. To let it become public knowledge would mean they didn't even have a deterrent value. Like letting another boxer, your opponent, know you had a broken right hand. There was no paper trail on the red phone, either, but at least it was a secure circuit.

He'd have to make three calls, though. To Commodore Roald, first. Then to Sixth Fleet, and to the commander of TF 60, the task force he'd be joining, at least temporarily, on his way to his ultimate station. Or should he depend on the message traffic to keep them in the picture? He'd ask Jen. She'd know.

A few minutes later he had her on the red phone, and everyone had left except Mills. The STU-3 was warm in his hand. Roald sounded the same as she had when he'd called her once from Korea. Deliberate. Cool. Almost remote. *"You're still operational, though. Correct?"* she said.

"Affirmative . . . but without the reserve DPD. Over."

"How was your effectiveness before that?"

Dan recalled Dr. Noblos's sour assessment. Where *was* Noblos anyway? He hadn't seen the civvie rider since they'd put to sea. "I'd have to say . . . the jury's still out on that. Uh, over."

"Can you continue the mission?"

He started to say "I think so," but that didn't sound so good. He cleared his throat and started over. "Yes. But we need help, specifically on repair parts. The message will give you more detail. It's going out now. Over."

"*What's your ETA at Point Hotel? Your rendezvous with the task force?*"

"Just altered course for it. The full-power run went fine, by the way. I'll get you an ETA by message."

"*You understand there's no other unit in the Med, or in the pipeline, with your capability, Dan. And we're going in. Not for attribution. But there's no question. So you have to find a way to stay operational. More than that. To be ready for the worst. Over.*"

"I understand. Over." But he didn't feel that confident about Terranova's troubleshooting and maintenance. And he obviously didn't have enough spares allowance. "Uh, but this current problem . . . it's the symptom, not the disease. I get the impression the ship—by that I guess I mainly mean the previous CO—depended too much on tech support, and not enough on growing own-team skills. Over."

Roald said she wasn't the first cruiser skipper she'd heard this from. "*But it's not a problem that developed in a day, and we're not going to fix it in a day, or a week. Also,*" she added, "*I want you to keep all your CASREPs close hold. Please ride herd on that. Over.*"

"Already made that clear on this end. Any reference to our capability, or lack of same, is TS."

"*Good. That's maybe even as vital as actually making sure you have the capability.*"

Dan couldn't help raising his eyebrows. "Even if we're only a marker on the board?"

He must have sounded sardonic, because she shot back, "*Politics is just as real as operational readiness, Captain. Maybe more so. I should think, with your experience, you'd realize that by now.*"

"Appearance is reality? Over."

"*Sometimes, Dan. Sometimes it is.*" The secure circuit beeped and hissed as she let up on the sync key, then beeped again. "*I recommend setting EMCON on all your ship-to-shore comms. And 'River City' on your Internet and e-mail. I'll move heaven and earth to get you that chassis. That will be my staff's number one priority. In return, keeping a lid on your problems is yours. Over.*"

"I need to notify Sixth Fleet. And TF 60. Over."

"*No you don't. I'll call Admiral Ogawa myself. Tell me what else you need, if your techs find more shortfalls. Stay on it, Dan. And get down to Point Hotel as soon as you can."*

"Copy all," Dan said. His gaze met Mills's. They both looked away. He said, "Over," and waited.

But heard only the hiss of a circuit with no one on the other end.

6

Strait of Messina

UNIDENTIFED *sonar contact, bearing one-one-zero, range eighteen thousand yards. Suspected Kilo-class submarine."*

"Hard right rudder, steady course zero nine zero. Engines ahead one-third. Bo's'un, set antisubmarine condition two."

Dan sat kneading his forehead in CIC, listening to two circuits at once and watching the symbology pulsing across the displays: circles for friendly, squares for unknown, triangles for enemy. He knew this geography, a narrow, island-littered passage, all too fucking well, thank you. So far this afternoon, fighter aircraft had suddenly broken out of a commercial air route, and been queried, warned, then destroyed. He'd also fought off a short-range attack from what had appeared to be a small fishing trawler carrying a battery of Silkworm-type cruise missiles.

He'd managed to knock the missiles out of the sky and sink the trawler. Now, though, to judge by the submarine contact, plus the pop-up of more small, fast air contacts over the landmass to the east, it looked as if he was going to have to deal with simultaneous air and subsurface threats.

To his right the tactical action officer, Cheryl Staurulakis, spoke rapidly into her boom mike, the words coming through his headphones too. "TAO, all stations: Commence area defense detect-to-engage. OOD: Bare steerageway. Come to course zero nine zero to maximize non-battleshort-enabled illuminator coverage. Disable all doctrine statements."

"CSC: Doctrine disabled."

"CIC, Bridge: Steady on zero nine zero. Standing by to comb torpedo track."

"TAO, Air: Vampire, vampire, vampire! Fifty nautical miles, altitude sixty feet, speed six hundred knots, inbound to own ship."

"Vampire" was the proword and warning an antiship missile was on its way. Staurulakis leaned forward, sneezing suddenly into a fist.

"TAO, RSC: New track, 0034, bearing one eight five, range forty-eight nautical miles. IFF negative. Unknown, assumed enemy."

"Very well. Correlates, sir," Staurulakis told him, without unlocking her gaze from the displays. "Recommend we ID as hostile."

Dan nodded. "Concur."

"All stations, TAO: ID'ing track 0034 as hostile." She hooked the contact, and the symbol on the big screen changed to a vertical red caret.

Dan rubbed his mouth, evaluating the scramble of tracks and callouts that Beth Terranova, with Donnie Wenck sitting close behind her, was putting online. In the center pulsed the blue cross-in-a-circle that meant Own Ship. Surrounding it, nearly obliterating the landmasses that crowded in, glowed the arcane tracery of dozens of friendlies and passing merchants . . . and hidden among them, fast-moving enemy boats that could change in seconds from innocent transients to mortal threats. Aegis had been designed for the open ocean. For the U.S. Navy, gutter-fighting in crowded, narrow waters was like forcing a falcon to fight a rat in a cage too small to spread its wings in.

"Track 0034, range thirty nautical miles, six hundred and fifty knots, inbound."

"TAO, MSS: Manually engage when firm track is established."

"TAO, ASWO: Subsurface contact classified hostile bears one eight seven, range seventeen thousand yards."

"TAO, EW: Track 0034 correlates to emission spectrum of DM-3B mono pulse radar, Iranian Noor antiship sea skimmer."

"Permission to engage Goblin track 34 with SM-2, Captain."

He recognized a scenario from his nightmares. The numbers on the weapon inventory screen were dropping. They were attriting the enemy, but their own magazines were almost empty. He had one

Standard left. Save it, and accept the risk of missing the incomer with his close-in weapons? Or use his last long-range round? The right answer depended on how long the engagement would continue. How much longer the enemy could keep taking losses. Staurulakis broke her fixation on the display and glanced at him, pale eyebrows lifting as she coughed.

"Kill track 34 with Standard," Dan said. He closed his eyes and found the red switch marked FIRE AUTH by feel. To his right Staurulakis typed rapidly, echoing the command as computer code, a backup for switch failure or battle damage.

"Birds away." A bright symbol detached from the circle-and-cross and winked into a blue semicircle rapidly tracking outbound. It curved, then steadied on a collision course with the red caret. No one around him spoke, though back in the curtained alcoves of Sonar murmurs testified to the slow deadly wrestling match of the antisubmarine battle going on at the same time deep beneath the sea.

The two symbols neared, then flashed. When the flashing stopped one had vanished. Dan shook his head; it had been their missile, not the incomer.

"No kill, no kill."

"Three-four is leaker, leaker!"

"TAO, Sonar: We have tube opening sounds from Kilo. Torpedo firing imminent."

"Fuck," Staurulakis murmured. "Mount 51, engage."

"Tell the bridge to come right, unmask mount 52 as well," Dan told her. "But remember to minimize your radar cross section." He told her to prosecute the submarine contact with torpedoes, and to stand by to fire their two antisubmarine-rocket-launched torpedoes out of the vertical launchers if the fish failed to connect. They had no more missiles; the next layer of defense was guns, and last, the rapid-fire automatic 20mm of the Phalanx. If the enemy sub put a torpedo in the water, the situation would become desperate. She nodded tersely and snapped into her boom mike, "Batteries released, mount 51 and 52, mount 21 and 22, arm CIWS and deselect hold fire."

"System in high power."

"Range, fifteen miles and closing. Speed seven hundred."

"Watch for a pop-up maneuver at five miles. Reduce your radar cross section. Stand by for jamming. And don't forget chaff," Dan told her. She nodded without replying.

"PASS loaded . . . RCS control . . . AAW autoselected."

He leaned back and combed fingers through hair soaked with sweat despite the blast of icy air. Behind him and stretching back into CIC the tactical team squinted into screens, each intent on his own lines in the drama. An occasional cough was the only sound, and now and then a murmur into a voice circuit, though most of their interaction was via the keyboard.

There was, of course, no submarine, and no supersonic missile turbojet-howling toward them yards above the waves, its silicon brain fighting off *Savo Island*'s jamming. The missile firing keys didn't hang around his neck on their beaded steel chain, but were in the weapons safe in his at-sea cabin. There *was* an aircraft, a Falcon configured to emulate various enemy missiles. Out of NAS Sigonella, for two hours of area/own-ship exercise. The contacts and landforms on the right three displays were a virtual-training scenario, carefully firewalled from the actual surface and air picture on the leftmost screen: the slowly passing coast of Sicily and the crooked, horned toe of the Italian boot at Capo Vaticano.

The scream of a jet engine outside. *"Playmate, mark on top,"* someone said in his headphones. He took them off and massaged his eye sockets with the heels of his hands. Someone had said you could reset eyestrain by doing that.

"Dinner, Captain." His steward slid a napkin-covered tray in front of him and snatched away the napkin like a conjurer. "Wednesday's slider day."

"Sliders. Great." For some reason this had become the Navy word for burgers, conjuring an image of pink patties skidding in hot grease when a ship rolled. The fries were still warm, and there was even a shaker of salt on the tray. "Thanks, Longley."

"What I'm here for, sir."

He ate slowly, one eye on the screens. The ship's tactical action officer sat atop a reporting pyramid. Below him or her was the antisubmarine-warfare coordinator, the antiair coordinator, the antisurface coordinator, and the bridge team, all feeding information and recommendations. The TAO controlled the ship's weapons and radars, fighting in concert with friendly, "blue," forces in his or her area. The TAO actually fought the ship; if he or she was skilled, the CO's can in the next seat was nice, but not essential.

Dan was using this exercise to evaluate his three school-qualified TAOs, Mills, Staurulakis, and Almarshadi. So far the operations officer would be his first choice in actual combat. Petite, pale-haired, sharp-faced, unflappable, Staurulakis tended to be faster on the trigger than he liked, but she read a scenario quickly and her solutions were as good as his own. A few more hours together and they'd be one dangerous beast with two brains.

Savo Island was still headed east, but he hadn't wanted to arrive at Point Hotel without a firm idea of just how sharp was the blade that had been thrust into his hands. So far, Engineering had reported no problems, and his bridge team seemed to be on top of things. Their test would come late that night, as they transited the Strait of Messina, a choke point dreaded by everyone since the Greeks had ventured to challenge Scylla and Charybdis.

"Captain?" He looked up at Fahad Almarshadi, who was slightly bent, smiling radiantly. The exec's smile lessened as Dan didn't return it. "The, uh . . . thought I'd give you an update."

"Cheryl, I'm going offline, talk to the XO. —What have you got, Commander?"

"The results of the sonar self-noise test you asked for." He swallowed visibly. "It's . . . not as good as I'd hoped."

Dan flipped through the report. "Why's our throughput so low?"

"One thought is, there might be water vapor in the transducers."

Which could trace back to the grounding damage; his decision to bypass a dry-docking might be coming home to roost. He grimaced. "We checking it out?"

"Yessir, the STGs are doing that."

"Rit Carpenter made it aboard, right? He on it?"

"He's down there with them, sir. A big help, from what I hear."

"Good. Have him come up and . . . no, belay that. What else?"

Almarshadi went over their progress on testing the other cooling hoses in the electronics, then on how the Aegis team was doing against their proficiency milestones. When he paused, Dan lowered his voice. "No joy on finding that missing pistol, I take it?"

"No sir. It just . . . disappeared. I've got the loss report ready for you to sign out."

Great. "Fahad, why exactly do I get the impression that, like, something's not exactly *right* aboard this fucking ship?"

The exec's dark brown eyes slid off his as if Teflon-greased. "I'm not sure I . . . understand what you're referring to. Captain."

"I went over the records. We had liberty misconduct in Gibraltar. The Command Climate Survey . . . it's pretty obvious there was a hostile work climate in some of the departments. I also saw that the commander master chief, I mean, the previous one, not Tausengelt, had a request in for transfer. How did all that connect to what happened coming into Naples? That's a symptom, not the cause. Or am I pissing up the wrong rope?"

"I wasn't on the bridge then, Captain."

"Which leads to the question, why were you below decks, Fahad? Why was the XO not on the bridge, coming into port in poor visibility?"

Another visible swallow. "Captain Imerson did not like me in the pilothouse when he was there."

Aha. Dan put his next question in the least judgmental phraseology he could think of. "I see. Okay. And why do you think he felt that way?"

Almarshadi seemed to grab his gaze and steer it, consciously, like a radar beam, back up into Dan's face. A spark of—anger? resentment?—flared in those dark pupils. "I believe it might have had to do with my being an Arab."

Dan contemplated this, along with the gold cross he'd glimpsed underneath Almarshadi's T-shirt. There were a lot of Christian Arabs, although the uneducated didn't seem to grasp this. It was true, a few individuals didn't leave prejudice behind when they put on a uniform. On the other hand, he'd run into his share of minorities who played the race card when they were just plain incompetent.

He let the silence rubber-band, not meeting the XO's gaze, just staring up at the display. Staurulakis was cat-and-mousing three Houdong-class patrol boats. Houdongs were Chinese-built, part of the progressively closer alignment of that country with Iran. They were filtering in, jockeying for the classic noon, four, and eight o'clock positions. Faced with that, she'd fight at a disadvantage, since warding off an attack from one sector left her vulnerable in the others. He realized Almarshadi was still gazing at him expectantly. "Uh, okay. Anything else?"

"No sir. That is about it. Oh, and Lieutenant Singhe has requested to see you. When it is convenient."

"Amy Singhe? What's it about?"

"She didn't want to say."

"Uh-huh. Okay." He checked the TAG Heuer that Blair had given him as a wedding present. "I'll be in my at-sea cabin after evening meal if she wants to come by."

Almarshadi stood, pocketing his BlackBerry, but Dan snagged his sleeve as he turned away. "One second."

"Sir?" The XO turned back quickly, as if startled.

"I'm not sleeping that well. I thought tonight . . . we'll be headed through Messina between 01 and 0300."

"Yessir?"

"I need to get my head down awhile, so I want you on the bridge. Back up whoever's OOD."

Almarshadi seemed to grow an inch taller. His head came up. "Yes sir," he said. "I will be there."

HE told Staurulakis to drill the other Condition Three sections and continue the tracking exercise until they ran out of aircraft time. And to continue after that with the canned Hormuz scenario. He stopped at the equipment room to find the cleanup progressing, with Dr. Noblos hovering. Dan asked how the reduced redundancy would hurt their tracking abilities. Noblos said it wouldn't help, but the effect would depend primarily on the geometry between the launch area and their patrol area. The rider seemed less prickly than the first time they'd interacted, so Dan kept it short. Let whatever had irked the man heal. He'd need Noblos when they got on station.

He climbed to the bridge and rode his chair for a while, seemingly intent on his message traffic, but actually observing the bridge team from the corner of his eye. Four contacts were in sight, with five more over the horizon, being plotted on the radar and on the contact board. Nearly all were headed south, probably for the strait, the narrow bottleneck between the Tyrrhenian and the central Med.

The wintry light glinted off flinty waves. The sun peered out only now and then through a scrim of high cloud. Other clouds, lower, fluffier, lay far off to the east, marking the mainland of Italy.

The Falcon made another low pass, its roar rising as it neared, dwindling as it parted. Motors whined as the tapered tube of the five-inch swung after it, its slow elevation, quivering indecision, then sudden whiparound as it crossed the zenith somehow comical. The 21MC said, *"Bridge, CIC: Event 0265 complete. Falcon 03 requests permission to take it to the barn."*

He nodded. The jet waggled its wings and banked away, shrinking to southward.

Dan swung down. He called the quartermaster over and pulled up their track on the nav screen. Through Messina, then south and east past the cow's-udder peninsulas and islands of Greece. They'd pick up the task force south of Crete. He sketched an adjustment, and the QM, a reedy deliberate fellow whose accent said Jamaica, said he'd take it from there. "Have the navigator see me when you get it laid out," Dan told him. "What's our first course? For the strait?"

The quartermaster set it up on the screen. "One one three, Captain."

"One one three, and pick it up to twenty knots." The OOD echoed the command, passing it to the helm, and *Savo Island* came around to the southeast.

AFTER dusk, after dinner. The porthole in his cabin was moon-dark. He was unbuttoning his shirt, contemplating reading a few more pages of *Rome on the Euphrates* before some serious bunk time, when someone tapped at the door. "Come in," he called.

"Lieutenant Singhe, Captain."

"Oh yeah. Almost forgot. Come in, Amy. Uh—leave that cracked, please."

Singhe took the chair two feet from him with a fluid motion. Her boots were polished glassy, which was not really required at sea, and her coveralls fitted as if tailored. Only at the knees did they look even slightly worn. She wore a khaki belt with the *Savo Island* belt buckle: bronze field, the outline of Ironbottom Sound in silver, and the silhouette of USS *Quincy* superimposed in gold. Below it was the ship's motto in black enamel: *Hard Blows*. Not one he cared for, but not worth the effort of changing. Her coveralls were open at the throat; that glossy hair was pulled back, and she brought some scent with her, sandalwood, at the same time clean and exotic.

He wrenched his mind back from wherever it was headed. "XO said you wanted a word," he opened.

"Yessir, if you have time."

Someone tramped past the slightly open door, and footsteps rattled on the ladder. The passageway illumination winked off, then on again, a deep scarlet, for the dark-adapted eye. He reached up and slid the darken-ship curtain across his porthole. "Turn that overhead off? Thanks."

With just the desk light on, only the blue glow from his desktop screen, and the fainter jade-green illuminations from the gyrocompass and radar repeaters above his bunk, relieved the darkness. That and the ruby glow that seeped past the jamb, limning her silhouette in carmine. She nodded toward his bunk. "Good book?"

"Huh? Oh . . . just ancient history."

"You're interested in history, sir?"

"Just something I picked up." He cleared his throat. "What's on your mind, Lieutenant? I mean, Amarpeet?"

"I wanted to talk about something I've been trying to initiate aboard, since my piece on leveling military management came out."

"I read that. Good article," Dan said. "Thought-provoking. You wanted to apply certain, uh, modern principles to the Navy."

"It fits in better with how the world does business now, sir. Communication at the speed of light. The drive toward reduced manning. Most of all, the professionalism of today's enlisted. Our command structure was set up for a small educated class and a large group of unskilled and more or less unwilling draftees. But the old, hierarchical information-flow model . . . it's dead. It's *wasteful*. And quite frankly, it turns our best enlisted off."

Dan considered this. She was absolutely right about the way the Navy was designed. How had Herman Wouk described it? "Designed by geniuses, to be run by idiots"? But the idea of cutting midlevel management didn't thrill him. The one time he'd had to—trying to run a ship without a flag in the China Sea, without chiefs and department heads, basically just himself, a worthless exec, and a ragtag crew no one else wanted—hadn't worked out well. "Uh—did I see you have an MBA?"

"Yes sir. From Wharton."

"We don't see many people with those kinds of degrees in the Navy. At least at the JO level."

"I'd like to make that count, sir. Is there any possibility we can do an experiment aboard *Savo Island*?" She reached to the small of her back, bending forward as she did so, and he had to avert his gaze. "Here's a copy of my proposal for reorganizing the chain of command."

"Well, hold on a sec, Amy. There's more to this than management. There's also leadership."

A shadowy form paused outside, might have looked in at them, but then continued aft.

"Leadership's just another word for charismatic management, sir. If we want to get hard-nosed about it."

"The core tenets: unity of command, chain of command, the ability to verify a command—"

"Again, irrelevant to the way we actually do business. Where do the guidelines for our most important decisions reside today, anyway? In computers. Doctrine's preset now, in hardware and software, not in top-down relationships. And as computing power proliferates—"

"I guess we could argue that both ways," Dan said. "And there are legal issues . . . UCMJ, Navy Regs, laws of war . . . but I don't want to sound negative." He flattened the still-warm pages under his hand. Cleared his throat. "But I'll offer a caveat up front, Amarpeet."

"Amy."

"Amy. A personal warning. I've seen JOs who don't have good relationships with their chiefs. Not only do they screw up their divisions, they get ostracized within the wardroom. Since they don't have the technical expert backing the stuff they say. And it's hard for them to get deckplate compliance without support from the chiefs. Uh . . . that said, I'll be happy to look this over. With an open mind. And then discuss it further.

"Any other issues you're aware of aboard, Amy? Seeing as how this is the first time we've had a chance to really sit down together."

Hands on knees, she'd started to rise, but sank back. "Well, sir, you may be aware that, just like you said, there's some pushback from the chiefs' mess."

"I'm not sure I know what you mean. What kind of pushback?"

"Maybe not so much even that, as a certain mind-set. I hear what you're saying, about making things difficult for myself. But these men really don't understand their sailors. They know their technical fields—most of them, anyway—but today's young sailor is foreign to them. Even more so, the women. Also, I'm convinced 'don't ask, don't tell' will be repealed soon. They're not ready for it. At all. And speaking of men, have you noticed, we don't have a single female chief?"

Dan blinked. "I hadn't, but you're right. But can you point to a specific example? Any chief in particular?"

"Actually, one of the worst was the former command master chief."

"The one who got D/S'd with Captain Imerson."

"Yessir. But by no means was he alone. I don't want to name names. And I don't think you meant to put me in that kind of spot—" She stretched an arm around the back of her neck to massage her nape. Grimacing, as if it hurt. "So I'll sort of slide past that question." She made as if to rise again. "Is that all, sir?"

"I guess so." He lifted the paper. "I'll read this. And thanks for bringing it to my attention. Especially about us needing a female chief. I'll ask Sid Tausengelt to look at our E-6s, see if we can identify a candidate."

"Yes sir; I'll be glad to provide input. Want me to close this door? Oh, and one last thing . . . I do a yoga class Tuesdays and Wednesdays, back in torpedo stowage. If you wanted to join us, you'd be welcome."

He said thank you, he'd keep that in mind, and the ribbon of ruby narrowed, shrank, vanished. He sat alone in the near darkness, still enjoying her scent. For a moment he imagined shaking that dark hair down over what were, by the way she filled out those coveralls, all too evidently more than adequate . . . *no.* He took a deep breath and let it out. God. He even had an erection.

Chill, Lenson. You're twenty years older than she is. Well, maybe not. Maybe eighteen. Still, old enough to be her father.

What about her ideas? Think about that, not her tits. "Flattening management." His initial reaction was skeptical. But hadn't he felt exactly the same when he'd been her age? Enraged at the iron-rigid hierarchy of seniors who all too often seemed incompetent, if not, occasionally, clinically nuts? More serious was her charge about the goat locker. But received wisdom in the fleet was that a sure route to big trouble was to bypass or downgrade the chiefs and senior enlisted. They ran the ship, after all.

The muted shriek of the J-phone. He snatched it off the bulkhead. "Captain."

"OOD, sir. Sorry to wake you—"

"Wasn't asleep. Whatcha got?"

"Sir, we're at course one one four, speed fifteen. Entering the Strait of Messina. Twenty-four contacts on the screen. Crossing contact, Skunk Bravo Lima, range eight thousand yards, bearing one three zero. Closest point of approach, time three zero, bearing zero nine four, two thousand yards—"

"Is the XO up there?"

"Yessir, Commander Almarshadi's here. Did you want him on the line?"

Dan closed his eyes. Remembering how it had been with Crazy Ike Sundstrom. Whatever else, the Commodore from Hell had taught him what *not* to do. The commander bore the ultimate responsibility. True. But he had to trust. He *had* to trust.

He took a deep breath. "Not necessary. Log this: Commander Almarshadi is in charge. Maneuver according to his instructions. Call me only if we're in extremis."

A moment's astonished pause, behind which he heard the crackle of the bridge to bridge; a warning going out. "Aye aye, sir," the young voice said at last, its tone falling, as if doubting. But acknowledging the order. "I'll log that."

He hung up, figuring he wouldn't get any more actual sleep that night than he would if he were in his bridge chair. But he had to build up his XO's confidence. Where they were going, he'd need someone he could depend on for backup.

But Singhe. Hard to stop thinking of her. Was he too susceptible to an attentive young woman? He didn't think so. She was ambitious. Hard-charging. Innovative. All the things that were supposed to rank JOs in the top 1 percent in their fitness reports. All the things he was supposed to nurture. As her commanding officer.

He felt around on his desk for the papers she'd left. When he lifted them to his face, he could still smell sandalwood.

7

Point Hotel
Latitude 33° 36' N,
Longitude 28° 35' E
The Eastern Mediterranean

C APTAIN, your presence is requested on the bridge." Two days
later Ensign Mytsalo, chubby cheeks glowing bright pink at
actually speaking to his CO, held the J-phone up. Looking uncertain,
as if unsure of the ceremonial involved in passing such a request.

They were in the wardroom. Dan blotted his lips, looking regret-
fully at the steaming tomato bisque, the hot turkey sandwich on
white-and-blue Navy china before him. "Uh . . . ask if it's urgent."

"XO says the task force is in sight, sir."

"Range?"

"Just on the horizon . . . closest unit twenty-three thousand yards."

"Tell him I'll be up in three." He'd have time for soup, at least.

He savored a spoonful, but it soured as he remembered another
time, on another ship. He'd been on the bridge, and they'd been making an approach on a carrier battle group. But the carrier did an
unannounced 180. The result was that instead of approaching from
the stern, they'd suddenly found themselves on a collision course
with upwards of seventy thousand tons of steel coming down the
ship's throat at a combined closing rate of seventy miles an hour.

"Excuse me," he said to the assembled wardroom. They started to rise too, until he motioned them back down. "Don't get up. Ops, Nav, and Training, how about joining me on the bridge when you're done with your meal. Don't hurry. I'll be up there awhile."

HE'D kept *Savo Island* at close to full speed. Past Greece and then, to the north, Crete. Point Hotel, their rendezvous with the task force, was about 170 miles south of Rhodes and 150 miles north of Egypt. Halfway between Europe and Africa, in the empty reaches of the central Med.

So far, there'd been no significant problems with shafts, props, or plant, and the rest of the coolant hoses had checked out. In CIC, Wenck and Dr. Noblos had been drilling the team by tracking the commercial airlines that arched between Europe and the east Med: Beirut, Haifa, Tel Aviv, Cairo. Noblos admitted they were shaping up. "But they're still marginal," he'd grumbled. Marginal was better than substandard, but Dan had asked him to keep pressing.

The bridge door opened on an opalescent glow. "Captain's on the bridge," the boatswain sang out.

"Good morning, Captain. I mean, good afternoon." The OOD saluted, binoculars in his other hand. "We're on zero niner niner, speed twenty-five. GTM 1A and 2B on the line. Eighteen contacts on the screen—"

"Thanks, good. Resume your watch. The XO can update me." Dan bent to the radar scope, noting the cluster of bright pips ahead. Noting, too, the absence of chatter from the Navy Red and Fleet Tac speakers above his head. Ten years before, the ether would have been loud with voice comms as the destroyer screen maneuvered within their sectors and the carriers sought the wind. Now most interaction had gone to satellite-mediated chat.

He swung up into his leather-covered chair, reclined it, and let Almarshadi bring him up to speed. The day was bright with a curl of high cirrus. The seas were heavier, five to six feet, but the air was clear and hard as sharp ice. He sat with ankles crossed and boots propped, musing as one by one masts and upperworks porcupined the distant rim of sea. Destroyers. Frigates. Closer to the center of each formation, the cruisers, like *Savo Island* herself.

Last, slowly lifting deck on deck, majestic, broad, implacable . . .

the carriers. Twelve miles apart, but he could see both at once, far to left and right, looming like gray islands. He glanced from the call-sign board to the formation diagram Almarshadi handed him, then out the window, trying to match names to distant specks. To port, *Theodore Roosevelt, Anzio, Cape St. George, Arleigh Burke, Porter, Winston Churchill*, and *Carr*. To starboard *Harry S Truman, San Jacinto, Oscar Austin, Mitscher, Donald Cook, Briscoe, Deyo, Hawes, Mount Baker*, and *Kanawha*. Three submarines were also attached to Task Force 60, though, of course, they weren't showing on radar. Point Hotel was at just about the deepest part of the eastern Med. No doubt carefully selected, to give the subs the best sound channels. His gaze returned to the oiler; they'd be going alongside shortly.

As mast after mast grew around him, as he penetrated to *Savo*'s station aft of the tanker, he couldn't help feeling proud of the country that could send such power halfway around the world. This assemblage of gray ships, these aircraft, missiles, guns, and those who knew how to use them, assured peace. Or as much of it as the world would know in this twenty-first century after Christ. For sixty years now, inheriting the task from the Royal Navy, the U.S. Navy had stood guard between the continents. For sixty years it had deterred and influenced, backing the word of the U.S., the UN, and international law. For what was law without power? What was justice without out the means to enforce it, or compassion without the means to discipline those who massacred whole populations?

Not to mention guarding a trade that undergirded and sustained that world. He'd heard a man say in a bar once—some loudmouth drinking a Dutch beer, cooled by a Japanese air conditioner, no doubt wearing clothes made in Thailand or China and driving a truck fueled by Saudi crude, and wearing the logo on his jacket of one of the biggest exporters of American agricultural equipment— "Why the hell do I have to pay taxes for a fucking navy? I live in fucking Kansas."

". . . scheduled to go alongside at 1430," Almarshadi finished.

Dan cleared his throat, retrieving the last few sentences from memory. "Are we ready to go alongside?"

"I believe so. First Division is laying out the gear. I'll inspect it with the first lieutenant."

"Safety," Dan said, though he felt stupid having to say it. "Safety is para . . . I mean, did Captain Imerson practice emergency-breakaway procedures? When's the last time we unrepped?"

"The week before Naples. We reviewed emergency breakaways, but—"

"Reviews are good. But from now on, we'll end every refueling with an emergency breakaway. So everyone knows it cold. Hard hats and life jackets at all times. Safety observers. Muster the boat crews, make sure the RHIB's ready to lower, and test our comms with search and rescue aboard the carrier." He lowered his head to peer out at the sky. "Next item: the helo folks'll be coming aboard right after the Vertrep brings their heavy gear over. We're ready for them, berthing, messing, watch bills?"

"Yes sir. I inspected their spaces, made sure they were clean."

"FOD walkdown? On the flight deck?"

"Did it this morning with the helo PO."

"Okay, good, XO. You're ahead of me. Oh, and also . . . something else . . . how often do we lift the hatches on the vertical launch systems?"

"Uh, I think we cycle 'em once a month."

"You think. When was the last time we definitely did it?"

"Uh, I'll have to find out from—"

"If it's longer than three weeks, do it again. Check the gaskets. And the timing. The last thing we want is to try to fire a bird and find the hatch is locked down, or leaks, or sticks halfway."

Almarshadi thumbed busily on his BlackBerry. "Aye, sir. Should we . . . should we not be reporting in?"

"Jesus! Good point." Dan sucked air, a jolt of Annapolis-instilled panic; then relaxed. A couple of minutes late in a routine formality, that was all. Still, first impressions . . . He spun the dial at his elbow to the Command Net, double-checked—it did not do to make your report on the wrong channel—and verified his and the task force commander's call signs on the board. Again, this was a satellite net, and he felt uneasy again. The Navy was growing all too dependent on its servants in the sky. If they went down, or fell silent . . . He depressed the Transmit button and waited for sync. "Iron Sky, this is Matador. Over."

"That's for us," the OOD said, and Almarshadi wheeled, correcting him even as the junior officer of the deck was making for the phone. Mytsalo jerked his hand away as if it were red-hot.

The overhead speaker: *"This is Iron Sky. Over."*

"Iron Sky, Matador actual. Reporting in and conveying respects. Over."

Another, different voice. Either the admiral or the chief of staff. *"Dan? Good to have you with us. We've got priority freight for you after your unrep. That'll come via Vertrep before dusk. Report to the screen commander and antiair coordinator for night screening station. How long do you plan to steam with us? And is there anything we can do for you while you're here?"*

"Sir, thanks for the welcome. I could benefit from some tactical exercises. But as soon as possible after refueling, my orders have me heading farther east. Over."

"Roger, copy. We've got a Mayfly tonight we can slot you into. That should help with your divtacs. Possibly can break you out a couple of F-18s if you need air services. Anything else?"

"No sir, that should do it. Many thanks. Heading in to unrep."

"Iron Sky, roger, out."

"Matador, out." He rattled the handset back down, looked around the horizon; then focused on the stern of the tanker, looming larger and larger as they slid into their slot astern.

SAVO put in the remaining hours until dusk refueling and replenishing, first alongside *Kanawha* for an hour, drinking down forty tons of JP-5. The sky got cloudy and the seas came steadily in, the same dark bluegreen as spruce boughs, as they headed into the prevailing wind. Dan sprawled in his chair, watching the black rubber hose sway between the rolling hulls. When refueling was complete, he ordered the emergency breakaway.

Well clear, *Savo Island* took station five thousand yards to the south. The vertical replenishment—by helicopter, from the carrier—took considerable time, as there were quite a few netted loads for them, equipment boxes, fresh stores, spare parts and equipment for the SH-60 bird that was coming aboard later that day.

Meanwhile he studied the twenty-page letter of instruction, scenario, and tasking message for that evening's exercise. "Mayfly" was a generic proword, or shorthand, for at-sea missile-firing exercises. Tonight's was called VANDALEX. He'd already reviewed the standing OPGEN for the battle group's general warfighting guidance. For the most part, it followed the Med readiness standards and procedures he was familiar with from *Horn*'s deployment.

Scenario T-03 was based on Country Orange attempting to seize an island chain from Country Green. Scenarios no longer used real nations' names, though usually they were fairly transparent. But he couldn't quite see who this one was designed to emulate. At any rate, the task force commander had fragged *Savo Island* in place of *Oscar Austin* as the assistant fleet antiair warfare coordinator. This meant he'd be the fallback in case of any equipment failure or damage. His station was twenty miles east of the main body, making *Savo* part of the outer screen—those units most likely to be engaged first.

Which meant he and Cheryl Staurulakis had to have these twenty pages essentially memorized by midnight. *Arleigh Burke* was designated firing ship, an artificiality, but you had to have some sort of setup when playing with live targets. Which they would be. The Orange navy was being simulated by a mixed force, two Turkish subs currently some sixty miles to the southeast, and a surface action group of two Dutch Provincien-class frigates to the north.

He flipped through the red-bound references, then through the heavy blue volume of *Jane's*, mentally marking the frigates for a Harpoon strike, if they ventured close enough. His main worries were the two German-built Type 209 submarines, and the Kormoran antiship missiles that Turkish F-5 fighter-attacks out of Izmir, playing the Orange air force, would be carrying.

In the dimly lit confines of Sonar, an oddly spacious compartment just off CIC, the lead sonar technician, Albert Zotcher, was coughing into a tissue when he looked up from the display. He grabbed the armrests and started to rise before Dan pressed his shoulder down. "Got a copy of tonight's scenario, Chief?"

"We're running tapes on 209/1400s now, Captain." Zotcher, a studious-looking little guy who Dan thought looked like old pictures of Grossadmiral Karl Doenitz, nodded at the sonarmen on the stacks. They glanced incuriously at Dan, then back to the patterns that played spellbindingly before their eyes, like ripples on tangerine silk. "We'll have to watch them. There's a fifty-mile danger circle on the Sub-Harpoon."

Dan pinched his lower lip between thumb and forefinger. Cruisers weren't traditionally that hot at the antisubmarine skill set. Usually stationed close to the carriers—the "1 shell," if the carrier was the nucleus and the screening ships were electrons—their primary responsibility was stopping air threats. But once on her lonely station to the east, *Savo Island* would be on her own. For sheer self-defense, he wanted the ship as sharp as possible in every area. Unfortunately, looking over the last combat systems assessment report, he hadn't been impressed. *Savo Island*'s ASW gang had graded in the bottom 30 percent.

"What's this the XO's telling me about water vapor in the transducers, Chief?"

"Could be, sir. It's not easy to tell."

"Could that be grounding damage?"

Zotcher said, "It might be, sir. Then again, it might not."

O-kay, Dan thought. "Is Rit Carpenter any use to you? Where is he anyway?"

"Should be up in an hour, sir. Yes, he's pretty . . . old-school, right?"

"That's one way of putting it. Yeah."

"Like the crusty old guys I learned from. But he knows his way around a sonar stack."

Dan nodded. "Yeah, he does that. And how about . . . Lieutenant Singhe?"

He got a dull-eyed glance. "How about her, sir? What do you mean?"

"She seems to have some new ideas. I wondered if you had an opinion on them."

"I'm not sure I get what you're asking me, sir. She hasn't discussed nothing with me."

"Okay, just thought I'd ask. What can I expect for detection ranges?"

They discussed mixing layers and propagation for some time, doing several runs on the sonar mode assessment system, before Dan felt he had a solid fix. The two U.S. subs attached to the TF, both Los Angeles–class nuke boats, would be running submerged, at slow speed, ahead of the task force. It was plain they'd have to depend on them, and ASW air from the carrier, for long-range detection. Dan rubbed his forehead. "What're we getting from the array?"

"The TACTAS? I'd like to stream it as soon as we can, Captain."

The towed array was a mile-long cable studded with very-low-frequency hydrophones that spooled out of the stern. Deployed, it not only could pick up a sub's pumps, motors, prop, and flow noise from many miles away, but could even provide an approximate range. Once it was trailing, though, the ship's maneuverability was severely restricted. More than one skipper had forgotten it was out there, turned too sharply, and cut the tether, irretrievably shitcanning four million dollars' worth of microphones into the tender custody of Davy Jones. But not using it wasn't cost-effective either. "I thought it was out there already. That should be standard operating procedure in ASW play. Check with the bridge and let's get it deployed. You'll need to stabilize and background before COMEX."

Zotcher nodded, fingers kneading a tissue as he sniffled, already back into the patterns the sea wove before his eyes. Dan watched him for a minute, then another. And at last, realized the man had nothing further to say.

HE watched from the hangar as the helo lined up, grew, hovered above the slowly tilting flight deck, then finally settled to squat its tires nearly flat as the turbines whined down. The lead pilot and detachment commander, Lieutenant Commander Ray Wilker, nicknamed "Strafer," introduced himself and his crew. Dan showed them their spaces and gave the "welcome aboard" talk. The SH-60B, call sign Red Hawk 202, had as its main mission the extension of its host ship's sensor range. They had night vision and electronic eavesdropping equipment, sonobuoys, and a data link, along with a limited selection of weapons. Dan felt reassured having a helo aboard. It would be a definite boost to his own-ship protection capability, once they were close inshore.

HE grabbed a green tray, trying to remain impassive amid the curious glances of those around him in the serving line.

"You go on ahead, Captain," one young man said, waving him on into the mess decks. His dark hair was cut very short on a bumpy, long, rather unattractive skull. His coveralls, of the exact same fabric as Dan's, were worn sky blue at the knees; his rolled-up sleeves showed the pale blotches of lasered-out tattoos. A ripple went down the line to the steam tables as one sailor after another turned to see what was going on. Every word Dan said in this line would be over the ship by morning.

"That's all right. I'm in no hurry." He pushed out a hand. "Dan Lenson."

"Oh. Yessir! DC3 B-Benyamin," he stammered.

Dan kept smiling, recognizing now the man whose cap had blown off as his new captain was being piped aboard. "That's right, I remember you. So, how's it going in Repair Three?"

Benyamin gaped. "You know I work in . . . ? Sorry, sir . . . I was just surprised to hear you . . ."

"Relax. I see your name every day in the POD. Junior sailor of the month? Too bad that reserved parking space isn't doing you any good in the Med."

"Yessir. Uh, nosir." Benyamin looked right and left, as if seeking someone else to step in and help him out. None of his shipmates did. "Uh, where'd you serve before, sir?"

"My last ship was USS *Horn*. Then I was at the Tactical Analysis Group before coming out here."

"*Horn*," someone murmured, and the name fizzed down the queue like a burning fuze. The faces changed, as if confronted by some figure they'd considered up until now mere legend—the dog-wolf of Minnesota, or Vlad Dracula himself.

He wondered exactly what they'd heard. But no one seemed to want to ask anything more, and if they had, he couldn't have elaborated. So he just nodded in what he hoped was a friendly way and slid his tray along stainless rails. Mexican day: chicken fajitas, enchiladas, beef and bean burritos, Spanish-rice-and-tortilla soup. He carried his meal out into the dining area and found a table at random, noting the mess decks master-at-arms heading his way. A flash of memory: the first day in junior high, or maybe high school, looking for a place in the clattering shouting throng. A metaphor for life itself, maybe. Each man and woman had to . . . not so much find, or discover, or be given that spot in the world, but rather elbow and pry one out from amid the seething multitude of those already here.

"Mind if I join you?"

Startled faces looked up. "Captain," one sailor said. Benyamin hesitated, then put his tray down opposite.

A heavyset black man muttered, "Come down to sample the chow, Skipper?"

"It's exactly the same in the wardroom, Seaman Goodroe. Except cold, since they have so far to carry it up." He started on the enchilada. Not bad.

The master-at-arms set a glass of bug juice the color of brake fluid beside him. Dan nodded thanks. Benyamin murmured tentatively, "They say, Captain—they say you have the Medal of Honor."

"That's what's in the official bio," Dan said, trying to make a joke out of it. "But I still can't walk on water."

The buzz of talk, the jangle of silverware, gradually welled up again to fill the low compartment. Up in front a row of crewmen watched satellite-televised basketball as they ate, abstracted gazes six thousand miles distant.

A slight pale kid with the beginning of a mustache cleared his throat. "So, Captain, I hear we're gonna pull into Haifa for a week."

"Really? Guess it's possible, but there's nothing like that in the schedule."

"Can't you put in for a port visit?"

"It doesn't work that way, exactly. Not with the . . . op schedule the way it's looking."

A pixie-faced Hispanic-looking girl said, "Is it true we're attacking Iraq?"

He shrugged. "Above my pay grade, seaman . . . Colón. Our job's to be ready if we do."

"But it's a possibility? Sir?"

"Looks more like it every day. But like I said, we're only going to know once we get the tasking."

"Captain Imerson never told us shit," the heavyset seaman said. "We're out there on the deck, and we don't know where we're going, or how long we'll be out, or what we'll have to do. Is it gonna be like that the rest of this deployment, sir? Any way we could sorta get, like, more in the picture?"

Dan felt ashamed. Amid all the things he had to catch up on, he'd overlooked including his shipmates. Who did the work. Whose blood would pay the price if he screwed up, made a wrong decision. "That's a great suggestion, Goodroe. Tell you what: I'll get with the XO, see if we can have him do a daily ops brief over the 1MC." He got out his BlackBerry and made a note, their gazes following his finger.

"Hey, let's let the skipper eat his lunch, dudes," the master-at-arms suggested. From that point on the talk subsided, though the side glances continued; and all that was heard was the murmur of conversation at the other tables, the rattle of crockery and silverware, and the clatter from back in the scullery when he pushed his tray through the opening and met the startled gaze of the aproned, bespattered mess crank immured back there in heat and steam and stinks. To him too Dan gave a solemn nod of recognition and thanks, and received it back with a graceful inclination of the head.

LONG after midnight, in CIC, he nursed yet another paper cup of sonar shack joe, fighting a headache and blinking tiredly at the large-screen displays.

COMEX—commence exercise—had been promulgated three hours before. The Orange surface action group had kicked off with a Harpoon attack on the northern screening units, followed by a Tomahawk salvo targeted on *Roosevelt*. They were overwhelmed by a Blue missile and air counterstrike, but Dan figured that if anything, this first attack was a diversion. Trying to anticipate the land-based threat, he'd moved *Savo* up to the outboard edge of her station and concentrated his team's attention on the northeast quadrant, letting his gun-laying radar handle the all-around watch.

For half an hour nothing had developed. He'd begun to wonder if he'd been suckered out of position when the F-5s had suddenly popped up, not out of Izmir, where Terranova had been looking, but low and fast out of the mountains of Caria. "They're trying to hide in among the islands," the FC had said, hooking three pulsating squares and turning them to carets. "But see how clearly the Doppler lock picks them out?"

"Range?"

"Hundred and ninety miles."

Dan leaned closer, marveling. The vibrating spokes of the radar clicked around as if escapement-driven. For each of the hurtling contacts a profile read off elevation, speed, course, and electronic identification. "We can do an alert script," the FC2 murmured. "Write it into the doctrine from the console. Specify elevation, speed, and course, and the system will alert and track automatically. You get the buzzer if it classifies hostile. In self-defense mode, the system takes it from there through firing. Once we tell it what we want to guard against, Aegis doesn't actually need us in the loop anymore."

For some reason this reminded him of what Amy Singhe had said in his cabin the night before. "Doctrine is preset. It resides in our computers." He scratched his head, turning this over like some clumsy piece of tool-flint with a brain designed hundreds of thousands of years in the past. He'd watched commanders dither. Try to sort dozens of variables, match them against doctrine, and all too often make bad calls. Or at least suboptimal decisions. Against supersonic threats, a mistake left no second chance. Maybe they had to depend on silicon and code, then. But it still didn't sit well.

"I think we want to be," he said. "In the loop, that is."

"Sir, that's your decision as CO. But Captain Imerson had no problem running everything in automatic."

"Let's not go through that again," said Matt Mills. The lieutenant had come in and stood by now to take over on the nickel-and-dime, five-on-and-ten-off schedule the TAOs were standing. "Evening, Captain."

"Matt. Say, you run into Dr. Noblos? Haven't seen much of him the last couple of days."

"The good doctor's got some kind of respiratory infection. Corpsman said he needed rest more than work."

Dan reflected. According to the last report from the Johns Hopkins consultant, both *Savo*'s SPY-1 system and its team's watchstanding skills were still marginal. "He's, um, really sick?"

"What I heard."

"I'll check on him. Okay, sorry to interrupt your turnover."

"No problem, sir."

The F-5s angled west, and the antiair coordinator assigned them to *Arleigh Burke* for the live-fire exercise. One of the Turkish fighters would launch a drone target. But all units were warned to stay alert; a second wave was likely, and would probably strike from a different quarter. As Mills and Staurulakis started the turnover, Dan noticed the rumpled blond back of Donnie Wenck's head at another console. He strolled over to stand behind him for a while, glancing back from time to time at the large displays. At last, he leaned over his shoulder. "What you running there, Donnie?"

"Diagnostic subroutine."

"Did you ever check for that virus you mentioned?"

Wenck sighed. "Oh yeah. System's clean. But it's really clocking slow. I'm still not sure why. I was on that new high-side chat last night. We were getting deep into Linux. Good stuff. You know, we were always so isolated trying to fix things at sea, but now you can go brain to brain with the other FCs and really get to pick somebody's neurons who's maybe way out in PacFleet. I actually got to talk to the system supe aboard *Monocacy*, you know, our follow-on ship? That's out there testing, out of Kwaj? And he says we're due an upgrade."

"Hardware, or—?"

"No sir, software." Wenck explained that *Savo Island*'s system was baseline 7. NSWC Dahlgren had written a patch for the ballistic missile defense mission, called ALIS, which optimized long-range scan and took out speed and altitude stops that had been built in back when the system had first gone to sea. "That was a real dinosaur. Baseline 2.10. Rugged, but not a lot of computing power—eighty-megabyte ROM-based memory. Reel-to-reel tapes. Those old UH-3 disk packs."

"I remember them from when I was with Joint Cruise Missiles. We used 'em for Tomahawk targeting."

"Uh-huh. Well, they had to build in those stops back then, or the radar would be tracking the moon. But your Scuds and M-11s and such are operating in those regimes. Also, we got another slight problem. Or maybe not so slight. In fact, it could fuck us royal."

Dan glanced at the vertical screen. Where the hell were the Turkish subs? "Okay, hit me. But, you know, Donnie, try to keep it . . ."

"Officer-comprehensible?"

"You got it."

Wenck smoothed his cowlick, but it sprang up as soon as his palm left it. "It's like, interoperability? You know we got Patriots in

Israel. I was going over the defended-asset list. You know, what we're assigned to cover?"

Dan lowered his voice. "Tel Aviv, primarily."

"Right, but it gets more specific than that." Wenck rattled the keyboard and a simplified map of Israel came up. He rattled again and a carpet of symbology overlaid the topography. "See this? Patriot battery at Ben Gurion Airport. Here's their coverage arc. See how it underlies ours? Shorter range, but—"

"Patriot's terminal defense. They don't fire until the last minute or so before impact."

"Right, but it starts earlier than that. We're gonna get our—"

The air was growing very cold. Dan shivered and drifted a few steps away to rest a hand on Mills's shoulder. "Check with Sonar, see if they have anything from TACTAS."

"Just heard from them, sir. Still no joy," the TAO murmured into his boom mike.

"Sorry, Donnie, go on. I'm listening."

"I was saying, three ways to receive cuing. Either our own SPY-1, download from AWACs, or else from the satellite—infrared detection of the booster plume."

"That's the Obsidian Glint?"

"Right. Problem is, Patriot's a semiactive tracker—the missile, like, navigates to impact listening to the radar emissions reflected off the incoming projectile."

"So're our Standards."

"Right. Exactly! Their signals are from a phased-array radar not too different from ours. So, let's say we pick up a cuing, and fire. And at the same time that radar at Ben Gurion's out there scanning. Now suddenly there's two missiles out there for them to home in on: the real target, and our Block 4. That's what I'm leery of."

"That it'll shoot down our missile, you mean?"

"I guess it *could*, but we'd be at the ragged edge of its intercept envelope, and heading away by that time—it'd be trying to catch up on a tail chase—I ain't no Patriot expert, you know? I'm more worried, there's two birds active out there, we'll decoy the Israelis off the real one. Then if we miss, everybody's fucked. That Scud, or whatever it is, is gonna get through."

Dan wondered how exactly to put this without sounding like,

well, like an *officer.* "Uh, Donnie, I think that's something to look into. But there's three pieces to having us out here. A warfighting piece, a deterrence piece, and then there's a political angle, too. Ideally we'd have all three in place—we can shoot the missile down, the other side knows we can, and the Israelis see we can."

Wenck frowned. Just as Dan had figured he would. "You're saying, we don't actually have to have a P-sub-K of—"

"Yeah, yeah, we want to two-block that figure, but the point I'm making, if the guy who's thinking about firing that missile figures we'll just shoot it down, he might not hit the button. And even if he does, and we miss, and it hits an orphanage, at least we tried. We stood by our ally."

The chief's shoulders lifted, then sagged. Signifying either total lack of interest, or incomprehension. Dan waited, then went on. "Anyway, how do we fix it? This interoperability thing?"

"Like I said, I'm working it, and one of the guys thinks he can get a Patriot dude up on chat. There was an op-test called Coral Talon, but I haven't been able to get an e-copy yet. What would really help is if we had, like, freqs from the Israelis. Or better yet, some way to talk to them direct, instead of going up through all the political bullshit architecture and then down again." He pointed to a tall console farther down the aisle. "The EWs are picking up what they think's the Ben Gurion battery, but it's gonna freq-hop like crazy when it goes into battle mode."

Dan glanced plotward again. Where the *fuck* were the Orange subs? *Arleigh Burke* had two lines of helo-laid sonobuoys out, but no contact. Could the "enemy" 209s already be *inside* the barrier? It seemed unlikely. But it was unsettling that they'd disappeared. Which of course was exactly what subs trained to do, but still . . . "Look, I'm gonna have to get back to this exercise, but keep working this, okay? Anything you need to get my signature on, or approve a message asking for that study or whatever, let me know. Okay?"

Wenck's head was going up and down, but his attention was already a million miles away, back in the lines of code scrolling across the screen.

Dan was turning back for Sonar when the overhead speaker crackled to life. *"Vampire, vampire, vampire! Bearing zero-eight-eight, range twenty, tracking left."*

Vampires were submarine-launched missiles. From the *east*. And *close*. He hurled himself toward his seat. On the display, the just-emerged missile was already hooked and blinking. It was crossing *Savo*'s beam, five miles off, at an extremely high angular velocity. Not an easy target, and headed directly for the carrier.

A second pip bloomed behind it. Then a third, from a different azimuth.

A coordinated attack. How had *both* subs evaded the screen? He grabbed for a handhold on the datalink console as the cruiser heeled, coming around to unmask batteries. He jammed on the headphones and his hand found the Fire button by feel as the engagement litany picked up velocity.

"Lock on."

"Ready to fire. Select—"

"Holy shit, they're *really* firing!" Mills yelled. Dan tensed, before the lieutenant continued, "Uh, sorry, belay that . . . my mistake. Exercise-generated imagery. Sorry. Won't happen again. Sorry, Captain, sorry."

Dan eased out a breath. "Eye on the ball, Matt. It's only an exercise. Knock them down. They're homing on the carrier. EW?"

"*Jamming*," came over the phone circuit from the SLQ-32 console. "*No visible effect.*"

Before they could fire, the dry voice of the anti-air warfare controller crackled over the net, assigning the inbound vampires to a destroyer in the inner screen. Dan cursed; *Savo* had missed her chance. She heeled again, this time reorienting to take on the subs. Voices rose from Sonar and the tracking table as they lined up for a shot. Dan toggled the ASW display on the leftmost screen, squinting. The screen flickered. Then he saw.

"Range, thirty-eight thousand, bearing zero eight zero. Stand by to fire Asroc."

"Negative!" Dan shouted. "Check fire, check fire! He's too close to the fucking dog box."

Putting a torpedo in the water there would endanger one of the Blue subs, the friendlies, scouting out ahead of the force. Apparently, due to layer depth, or whatever low cunning the Turkish sub commander had employed, the Blue sub hadn't detected him.

However he'd done it, the Orange sub was using the Blue one like a hostage shield, leaving Dan unable to attack. He keyed the 21MC, then let up on the lever as Mills passed the command he'd been about to give. "Bridge, TAO; come left—"

"Remember you have the tail streamed," Dan put in.

"Yes sir. —Come left, no greater rudder than fifteen degrees; steady three two zero; go to flank." He was repositioning *Savo*, placing the cruiser, as a shield between the enemy and the carrier. Blocking the next missile salvo. The hum of the turbines rose to a whooshing scream. The superstructure began to vibrate. A deckplate buzzed like a cicada.

Dan pressed his mike switch. "Sonar, CO: Do you have a solid contact?"

"Bridge, Sonar: Contact tracking one eight five, speed nineteen. CO, Sonar, did you copy?"

"Copy," Dan snapped. Nineteen knots: top speed for a submerged 209, and not one its batteries could maintain long. One boat was sprinting south. Attempting an end run? Or trying to seduce them off its partner? "Source of that datum?"

"TACTAS, sir. Mainly flow noise, sounds like."

"Keep an eye on that bearing," Dan told Mills. "As soon as they clear the dog box, I want an Asroc in the air."

"TAO aye." Mills switched to the ASW circuit, and Dan half overheard his side of the conversation as they made ready to fire. He switched back and forth on his headset, watching chat click up his desktop screen, seeing *Arleigh Burke*'s Standard splash the drone fifteen miles from *Theodore Roosevelt*, the exercise opening like a flower on the big flat-panel displays. He switched and keyed. "Aegis, CO: Keep an eye peeled up toward Antalya. They could launch a second strike out of there."

Terranova's Jersey-accented soprano: *"Aegis aye."*

He switched back just in time to catch "TAO, Sonar: Lost contact."

"What the *fuck* is going on back there?" Mills muttered. "Sonar, TAO: What do you need to regain? . . . Okay . . . okay, but we're right at the edge. . . . Yeah. Yeah, we can do that. Bridge, TAO: Left turn, steady up on one eight zero and drop to ten—"

Longley, at his elbow. "Coffee, Captain? And we got, hey, we got oatmeal cookies tonight. Really good."

Dan blew out, trying to keep his temper. He didn't want more coffee . . . but he needed more . . . *so* fucking tired . . . but his stomach churned. He grabbed a cookie and wolfed it. Typical big, chewy U.S. Navy mess deck cookie. Not much you could find fault with, actually. He chased it with a slug of coffee that turned out to be so scalding he would have spat it back into the cup if both Mills and the steward hadn't been watching him. "Holy *smoke*, Longley, did you brew this with a blowtorch?"

"Ran that straight up from the galley, Captain. Know you like it hot."

His tongue felt flayed. Dan clicked back to the antisubmarine circuit, wondering why he wasn't hearing anything from Zotcher. But then snapped the dial back to antiair when another voice said, *"TAO, Sonar: Regained contact. Range twenty thousand. Bearing one zero five."*

"Christ, at last," the CIC officer muttered, on Mills's other hand.

The exercise lulled. Dan stretched, tried to fight his eyelids up again. Shivered, and resolved to bring a sweater the next time he came up here. Checked his watch: 0413. Considered calling Almarshadi to take it, but didn't. The XO needed sleep too.

Finally he stood, and stretched again, touching the overhead with the tips of his fingers. He bent and snagged his toes a couple of times, just to get the blood moving again. Something popped in his back. He glanced over at the Aegis display. Past Wenck and Terranova, their heads together, the electronic warfare consoles flickered a weird graveyard green. It might not just be that the Patriot battery could mistake *Savo*'s SM-2 for the incoming Scud. Could there also be mutual interference, from the Patriot's and Aegis's own radar guidance? Had anyone ever thought to deconflict the spectra between the Army's antimissile system and the Navy's? They freqshifted, sure. But would the *bands* they swept overlap? It sounded all too much like the kind of thing no one in either service had bothered to check out, and that you'd find out too late. He'd have to ask Noblos. Investigate—

"Datum: Bearing two seven three, nine thousand yards."

The red diamond of a hostile sub ignited on the screen. At the same instant, the cool tones of the exercise coordinator murmured in Dan's headphones, *"Simulated Orange Vampire launch, two seven zero, nine thousand."*

"Vampire, Vampire, Vampire!"

On the chat screen: *SJC TAKE TRACK 7895*

Frozen, Dan watched as USS *San Jacinto* veered left to place herself in front of the carrier, locking on the rapidly nearing sub-launched missile. "The fucking sub's in the inner screen," Mills said, incredulous. "His little buddy went south to fox us. We had him all the way. But how in the hell did the *other* bastard sneak past us?"

Dan slammed down his headset and stormed back through Combat. *Savo* slanted, hard, as she slewed around again. If the sea had been pavement, rubber would have been smoking. He slammed his shin into the steel frame of a chair and ripped the blue Sonar curtain aside.

In here the darkness was almost total; the only lamps were the wavering orange curtains on the screens, a Northern Lights cat's-cradle that wound the gaze seamlessly into them. He put a hand out to avoid any stray stanchions. "What the hell's going on back here? We can't track a nineteen-knot sub at nine miles' range?"

No one answered, though one of the sonarmen flinched. The other was just as hypnotized as before. To Dan's astonishment, though, Zotcher's head was back against his headrest at an awkward angle. And . . . he was *snoring*.

When he seized the man's shoulder and shook it, he might have been rougher than he meant to be. Zotcher's head snapped forward and back. His eyes jerked open; he blinked groggily, sniffling. "Goddamn it, Chief! What the hell do you think you're doing!"

Zotcher flinched and rubbed the back of his neck. "Oh—ah—sorry, Captain. Just resting my eyes—"

"Resting your eyes, hell! You were asleep! On watch, in the middle of an exercise." Dan lowered his voice with an effort. "We're not up to standard in our ASW readiness. And now I see why."

Zotcher seemed to realize what was going on. He struggled out of the chair. "Sir, you got to understand. I don't feel—"

"I don't want to hear it. Who's your relief? The off-watch sonar supervisor?"

"Sonarman First Skelton, sir. But I don't—"

"Call him. When he gets here, brief him. Then I want you out of the sonar shack, Zotcher. You're restricted to the chiefs' mess until I decide what to do about you."

The chief grimaced, still massaging his nape. "You hurt me, sir. Hurt my neck, when you did that."

"Oh, really? Well, I don't give a—"

He halted himself, suddenly aware of other faces at the ripped-open curtain, of a murmur outside, men and women looking in. Suddenly remembering the anger of other captains, and how it had spread fear instead of confidence. A commander without self-control had no control.

"Chiefs' quarters, until further notice. Call your relief." He spun on his heel and walked out. Back to the air-conditioned cool, the gossip-whisper of ventilation, the muted prattle of keyboards. Smoothing his hair, blotting sweat from his scalp, he sank into his chair once more. Blinking at the never-sleeping screens streaming with new data, and trying to force his weary mind back to the problem at hand.

8

East Med

DAWN, and still without sleep. He felt twinned from reality, stuck in a parallel universe that existed on some separate brane from the one he was probably supposed to be in. Exhausted, yet jittery from too much caffeine. "We should've had 'em both cold," he muttered, shifting in his bridge chair. The newly risen sun burned like a forest fire directly in their path. Low clouds mounded like foam in a bug-juice cooler, orange and cotton-candy pink, while blue heaving swells tore apart into a salmon froth on either hand. They'd detached, and now southeasted over a lumpy sea toward the arced sector where they'd take station. Awaiting the starting gun . . . He kneaded his stomach; was that sensation hunger, or something else? He grabbed his freshly charged Hydra and slid down.

"Captain's off the bridge." The hollow pressed steel of the bridge door thump-clanged closed. He dogged it, then slid down the ladder, gripping handrails polished glossy-smooth by a decade of horny-palmed sailors. Enlisted in coveralls stepped aside as he slammed down, spun the corner, vaulted down the next ladder.

"Attention on deck!"

"Seats." He took his place as the rest of the officers found chairs. Apparently the previous CO had preferred the head of the table, the traditional arrangement, but he liked the center. It was less intimidating, and he could talk to more of his JOs face-to-face. Still, it took a few minutes before the ensigns and jaygees resumed discussing whatever it was they'd been talking about. He checkmarked the slip for eggs and bacon and rye toast. Pushed away the coffee the attendant put beside him. He had to relax. Detoxify. Maybe today he could get back to the weight room—

As he forked the first bite the J-phone beeped. The mess attendant said, "Captain, for you."

Dan rattled the handset out from beneath the table. Mumbled through a full mouth, "Cap'n."

"Sir, Radio here. We have the quick-look report on last night's VANDALEX. Do you want it in your in-box, or—"

"Hard copy to the wardroom."

"Aye, sir, on its way."

As he scanned the clipboarded message, the junior officers stood and excused themselves in muted voices. He grunted, skipping the boilerplate, looking for the name of his ship. At last he found it. *Savo Island* had let the Orange sub through the outer screen, and two hits on *Theodore Roosevelt* had reduced the carrier's strike capacity to 70 percent. He all but snarled aloud. He scribbled his initials, and slammed the clipboard on the table. Then snapped his Hydra on. "XO, you up? Fahad? You there?"

"Yessir, on the bridge."

How had he and Almarshadi missed each other? "Have you seen this quick-look? From last night?"

"Um, no sir, I—"

"Are you reading your traffic? Look it over. Or, wait, I'll send the messenger up with the hard copy. Read it. Then call me back. I found our sonar chief sleeping on watch last night. I want to—" He caught the mess attendant's wide-eyed gape and cursed himself. *Shouldn't* have said that. "Anyway, call once you've read it."

The exec said he would, and Dan hung up. He exhaled, and drank half the cup of coffee before realizing what he was doing. Slammed it down, just in time for a heave and roll to splatter it over the table-cloth. He sucked at a tooth, trying to sort through it. He was disappointed. Dissatisfied. Yet the anger felt *good.* . . .

A tap at the door. Tausengelt stuck his head in. "Skipper? A word, sir? After you're done?"

"I'm finished." He crammed half a piece of buttered toast, jammed his napkin into the ring. Tilted his head at the rear of the wardroom, where a settee and bookcases around a central table gave at least the illusion of privacy.

An ensign poring over a coffee-table book on the *Titanic* got up hastily and excused himself. Dan waved the elderly command master chief to the sofa. "Want some coffee?"

"No thanks, sir."

"What's on your mind, Master Chief?"

"Basically couple problems, sir. First off, I think, is what happened this morning."

"This morning?"

A quizzical glance. "Al Zotcher, sir. You and him. In Sonar. Here's the version I have so far. Basically, Chief Zotcher's hard down with a respiratory bug. He was thinking about putting himself on the sick list when he got the word about the exercise. Knew that was important, so he took the watch. You came in, found him with his eyes closed, and jerked his head back. With considerable force. Now he's got whiplash, maybe some kind of disc problem."

Dan snorted. "That's what he's saying? He had his *eyes closed*? He was fucking *snoring*, Master Chief. He's sea-lawyering both of us."

"Well, sir, that does put a different light on it. But, basically, he's still got neck issues. Were you planning on taking him to mast?"

Dan thought about this, wishing he felt more alert. "You restricted him to quarters," Tausengelt prompted. "Threw him off the watch bill."

"Yeah, yeah, I remember. His inattention let a sub past us. I didn't know he was sick. But that isn't germane; he's either on the sick list or he isn't. And if he's on watch, he's got to be alert and in charge."

"Absolutely, sir. No one's arguing that." The older man was respectful but firm. "I'm just trying to see if there's any middle ground here, okay? He's willing to admit he wasn't doing all that great a job last night. Problem is, this allegation you pulled his head back. Basically, I'm thinking of you now, sir. That could get sticky, any of the legal eagles got word of something like that. The way things are getting these days."

Dan stifled a yawn, not meeting the other's gaze. Recognizing what wasn't actually being said, though it *was*, and very clearly. Knowing too the senior enlisted adviser was right; a commanding officer laying hands on a subordinate, causing injury, would be cause for instant relief. He didn't care that much, as far as his career was concerned. Whatever happened, he'd go out a captain, with the Medal and full retirement. As well as the Navy Cross, Silver Star, Navy and

Marine Corps Medal, Bronze Star, and the rest . . . not that many end-of-tour awards, but not a bad career.

But this wasn't about Dan Lenson. *Savo Island* didn't need another failed skipper. And Jen Roald, and Ogawa, and the U.S. Navy, and, yeah, the residents of Tel Aviv, didn't need a ship that couldn't meet its commitments, when a war was slated to start in days.

To balance against that: his authority as captain. He needed the senior enlisted. Without their cooperation, nothing would improve. But giving them the idea you were a rollover was never good.

But was admitting you were wrong actually a rollover? He cleared his throat. "I appreciate the heads-up, Sid. How's the chiefs' mess taking this?"

"Well, sir, basically, you know how it is. They're a good bunch. They support the command. But right now I'd say they're . . . divided. This happens just once, well, we can keep it inside the tent. But you don't want to get a rep for going off on a hair trigger, sir. Or putting your hands on people. You really don't."

The Hydra buzzed. *"Skipper, Bridge. You there, sir?"*

Dan reached down. "I'm in the wardroom."

The officer of the deck reported a contact that would cross their bow close aboard. Dan made sure he had it visualized, then told him to increase speed to put the closest point of approach behind them. "Check my solution. If it doesn't look safe, call me back."

"Aye sir. Bridge out."

Back to the unsmiling chief across from him. A friendly warning, from a peacemaker? Or a threat? It sounded like both. He decided to take the extended hand. "Okay, I admit, I flew off the handle last night. But he *was* asleep. You really think he's sick?"

"Looks like it to me, sir. You can go down and see him. He's in his bunk right now. And, you know, Captain, the guy's got three Good Conduct Medals."

"He does? And . . . well, never mind. Okay, you made your case. I'm willing to lift his restriction."

"Will you hold mast on him? For sleeping on watch?"

"Not this time. Just formal counseling. But, for the good of the ship, I don't want him back in Sonar until he's certified fit for duty. Carpenter can take his watch section; he's more than qualified. If I catch him napping again, though, I'll bust him to seaman. That's a guarantee."

"Fair enough, sir. Let me take that back and see if we can arrange some kind of modus vivendi there."

Dan raised his eyebrows. "'Modus vivendi,' Master Chief? Nice." The roar of an electric motor; the mess attendant was vacuuming the carpet at the far end of the space. He looked at his watch—*sleep?*—dusted his trousers, got set to rise. "That all?"

Tausengelt grinned apologetically. "Not quite, sir. One other issue. Lieutenant Singhe."

"What about her?"

"Have you seen what she's doing on the chat function? On the LAN?"

The LAN was the local area network, the ship's hardwired internal network. He knew it included a chat-room function, but hadn't checked it out yet. "No. No time. What?"

"Basically, she's organizing work-center quality circles."

"Uh . . . okay. Is that a problem?"

"Some of the guys don't like it. At least, not the way she's setting it up."

"You mean, some of the chiefs?" Tausengelt nodded. "What don't they like?"

"It's just basically turning out to be bitch sessions for the no-loads. The dudes who work, they don't have time to sit around and *discuss* working. She's encouraging the seamen to come up with better ideas. That doesn't square with the senior enlisted. They already know how it should be done."

Dan frowned. No, a lot of the enlisted khaki wouldn't like it. Not after they'd spent ten or fifteen years learning the right way, or, anyway, the Navy way. But how else would you come up with innovation? "Well, I'm not sure she's not right, Master Chief. Sometimes the best ideas come from the deckplates."

"We already got a way to do that, sir. The Bennie Sugg. Pass it up the chain. She's chairing these discussion groups. Bypassing the goat locker. Like, they don't know where she's going with this."

"Are they participating?"

"The chiefs? She doesn't want them in the chats. Blocked them, in fact. To 'encourage free discussion.'"

That didn't sound good. "I wasn't aware of this, CMC. Have they taken it up with the XO?"

"The commander doesn't get involved that much, Skipper."

"Have you discussed it with him?"

Tausengelt glanced away. "No sir."

Dan leaned back. "Well, look. Amy's a hard charger. She's got some bright ideas from business school she wants to try out. Unless it's actually hurting readiness, even if there's some steam being let off on these chat boards, I don't see it as a major issue yet. Let's let her run with it for a while and see where it ends up." He hesitated. "Unless you don't think that's wise."

Tausengelt's face was unreadable. "You're the skipper, sir."

HE checked with the OOD on the Hydra while climbing the ladder to his at-sea cabin. The contact to port had a left-bearing drift now; it would cross in their wake, three thousand yards astern. Dan told him to maintain thirty knots and keep a close eye on it until it was clear. He switched channels and talked to the navigator as he let himself in, unbuttoned his shirt, and fell into his bunk. They'd reach their patrol area tomorrow at noon. He called Cheryl Staurulakis and got the ops officer started on their reporting-in message.

Then lay staring at the overhead while the decisions he'd just made buzzed around inside his skullcase like trapped wasps.

Any choice a skipper made could lead to disaster under the right circumstances. Screw up the geometry on a closing ship, and it could cut you in two. He'd seen that happen, aboard USS *Reynolds Ryan*. One wrong rudder order, and almost two hundred men had died.

So . . . Zotcher. Had he come down too hard? Or not hard enough? Knuckled under to the chiefs, or just shown them he was reasonable?

Was Singhe really ambitious, hard-charging, innovative? Or was there something suspicious about the way she was bypassing the chiefs and the senior enlisted adviser? He didn't think she had anything malevolent in mind. But blocking the ship's middle management from online discussions didn't sound like a good way to advance a serious agenda. Of any kind.

He remembered dark eyes studying him, and seemed to smell sandalwood again. Then, somehow, he was asleep.

* * *

THE buzzer jerked him out of a confused pursuit through endless corridors. It had seemed to be the Pentagon, but in some hotter, less affluent country. The windows were boarded up, and through those endless refuse-strewn passageways something stalked him. He had a pistol, but when he tried to use it the trigger malfunctioned, again and again, as he struggled to keep the sights on a shape he couldn't clearly see, that shifted identity and appearance even as it pursued him.

The buzzer went off again, and he rolled over, flinging an arm out. The back of his hand hit the brass lever and tore skin. "Captain," he grunted. What time was it anyway? Apparently he'd missed lunch.

"Sir, OOD here."

"What you got, Bird?"

"Sir, corpsman called a minute ago to report a man dead in forward berthing."

He rolled out and put bare feet on the chilly deck. "Say that again."

"It's Seaman Goodroe. In Weps berthing."

A heavyset, truculent man in coveralls, hunched over a mess tray. "I . . . dead, how? I saw him on the mess decks just yesterday. Talking about . . . *Dead?* From what?"

"Sir, I didn't get the impression the chief corpsman was real sure."

"Forward berthing? I'll be down right away. Does the XO know?"

"I'll notify him soon as I get off, sir. Figured you ought to hear it first."

Dan told him he was right and hung up. Dressed as quickly as he could. The blue coveralls were a forgiving uniform, though he didn't care for the way they showed a corner of your skivvy shirt. He pressed his pins into his chest with the palm of his right hand and let the door lock click behind him.

FIVE decks down, in the muzzy humidity of the berthing compartment. When he'd first joined the Navy, these had been pipe bunks, metal frames four high, a thin pallet and a worn fartsack sagging on a crisscross of webbing. Now each sailor had his own nook with reading light and curtain. Not exactly roomy, with fifty men in a compartment, but there was some privacy, at least.

The man who lay in bunk 24 was past privacy. The face, immobile

as dark wax, and staring eyes told him that. The corpsman, Grissett, looked up from ballpointing notes. An astringent smell edged
the air. Grissett wore thin blue latex gloves. A transparent tube lay
on the bunk, still sealed in plastic. Behind him stood Chief Toan,
the master-at-arms, badge glittering, hands behind his back. They
both swung as they caught sight of Dan. A very slight, ugly young
man with a dirty tee, scuffed, torn boots, and coveralls peeled
down to his waist hovered a few feet away. "What happened?" Dan
asked.

"Morning, sir. I mean, afternoon. The Troll here—"

"The Troll?"

"Sorry—the compartment seaman, here. He called the master-at-
arms when he couldn't get Goodroe up." The corpsman nodded at
the body. "Cold. No pulse. He's been dead awhile."

Dan looked the corpse over. By no means the first he'd seen, but
definitely one of the most peaceful-looking. The heavy-jawed face
was expectant, as if at a joke just heard but not yet fully grasped.
The nude chest was covered with thick curling black hairs that
shriveled to stubs as they approached the beard line. A trace of what
might be dried foam at the corner of bluish lips. He bent closer; a
hint of brown in it? Started to reach out, then, at a cautionary flinch
from the corpsman, retrieved his finger before touching anything.
"Is that blood? At the corner of his mouth?"

"Take a sample in a minute, sir. Downie here"—the compartment
cleaner grinned, then sobered—"he says he, I mean Goodroe, felt a
little down and had a cough. He was off watch, so he turned into his
bunk. That's all."

Usually you looked for an off-watch sailor in his work center during the day, but the era when all hands were expected to turn to at
daylight was long gone at sea. These days, a sailor off watch, and
not feeling well, might well decide to turn in for a Tallerigo. "What'd
his work-center supervisor say?" Dan asked the CMAA.

"On his way down, sir. He knew Goody was in his rack, but didn't
know nothing else."

"Any history? Anything . . . Any idea what's going on here?"
Dan scratched his head. He'd been talking to the man, what, just
yesterday? A young, husky, jock-type guy. Maybe a little . . . antag-
onistic, with his remarks about how the crew needed to be in the

picture more. But he hadn't seemed ill. "Is this a natural death? Or what?"

The corpsman frowned. "A lot of possibilities right now, sir. You know most of our guys are strong, healthy specimens of testosterone-filled manhood. So the first thing, you look for signs of strangulation, or beating. But I don't see any. Could be a drug OD—"

"I've seen those," the CMAA murmured.

"—or poisoning, accidental or deliberate. He could've had underlying valve disease. A heart murmur they let go, or didn't hear, when he enlisted. If he got septic in the night, maybe endocarditis—the infected valve sends emboli to the rest of the body, like fingers. But, bottom line, this is gonna be a coroner's case, sir. We got to handle it by protocol, and get the body to the medical examiner ASAP."

"Okay, I get it. Anything in his record?"

The chief corpsman slipped a file folder from beneath a clipboard. "His last entry's the final installment of the anthrax inoculation. That we got in Naples."

Dan scratched his head again. He'd had a course of what he assumed was the same vaccine, experimental then, during the Gulf War. "This vaccine. Is it, I don't know, ever dangerous?"

"It's a mandatory inoculation." The chief shrugged. Flipped pages. "A three-shot buildup and booster. No record of any adverse effects to the first two shots. No, wait . . . he reported fever and swelling after the second. Two days later, follow-up, he's fine."

"Good records. When'd he get the booster?"

"Two days ago. I gave him that myself."

"This is the AVA stuff, right? Is this a documented side effect? Sudden death, I mean?"

"Anthrax vaccine adsorbed, yes sir. No sir, there's no such warning on side effects."

"So what killed this apparently healthy guy? Best guess?"

"Captain, I just can't give you an informed opinion right now. If we had an MD aboard, maybe, but I doubt he'd want to come out and tell you something that might turn out to be a hundred and eighty wrong either." The chief snapped the latex on one glove, then tore open the plastic wrapping on the flexible tube. He peeled down the corpse's boxers, dug out the slack flaccid penis, spread its meatus, and began threading the tube into it.

Dan said, "Uh, what exactly are you—"

"Drug screen. Gotta catheterize him. And we're gonna have to take lots of photos, at the highest resolution we can."

Dan got Almarshadi on the Hydra and told him to get the ship's photographer down to forward berthing, and then to meet up with him. "Okay, do the protocol," he told Grissett. "By the book. Then body-bag him, and back to the reefers until I can get direction on disposition. Can you decontaminate, I mean, disinfect the rack? Would that be something we'd want to do?"

"Yes sir, that wouldn't be out of the ordinary. Once we get him out of the compartment. I can use an alcohol solution. A spray bottle. And take his linens to the laundry in a separate bag, do 'em in super-hot water."

"Good. Anybody else touch him? Uh—Troll?"

A flinch; a grin. "No sir, I didn't touch him." Then a frown. "Well, yeah, I did. To sort of shake him. To, uh, wake him up."

"I'll get his hands disinfected too, just in case." The corpsman studied the body and snapped the glove-rubber again. "You didn't touch your face afterward, did you?"

Dan left them there, gathered around the drawn-back curtain like a nineteenth-century tableau: grave visages around a sickbed, silent and respectful in the unexpected, yet never faraway, presence of the Dread Leveler.

ALMARSHADI caught up as he was letting himself out on the main deck. Dan wanted to get some fresh air; the old-socks-and-deodorant man-reek of the berthing space seemed ominous once associated with death.

They stood by the lifeline, buffeted by a cold wind, as sailors ducked into the breaker—the covered walkway, almost like a highway tunnel, that led from the port side midships up to the forecastle. The sea roared as Savo ripped through it, peeling off curving chunks of whitecap that toppled to either side like dump-truck loads of shiny pale green and white marbles, and now and again she rolled and the wind tore a spatter of spray across them, the scent and taste sharp and refreshing. At intervals, when the sun broke through, crystalized salt sparkled on the bulkheads by the refueling station, on the chocks, bitts, life rails, the davit socket, like gypsum deposits in a cave.

Dan allowed himself ten seconds to stand in silence, swaying with the roll, one with the morning and the wind and the endless topple of the bow wave. Communing, for just a moment, with the ancient sea, the mariner's eternal mother and eternal enemy. Then told Almarshadi to report the death to CTF 60 and request instructions.

"But we outchopped . . . right?" The smooth dark face was uncertain; the black hair ruffled in the breeze. Dan smelled cigarette smoke. Red coals glowed in the dimness of the breaker. The best execs were shadow selves, masters of detail within the skin of the ship. They freed the commander, instead of continually pulling him in, as this sparrowlike Arab seemed to do all too often. But he'd had worse seconds. Remembering Greg Juskoviac, his totally worthless XO aboard *Gaddis*, he could appreciate Almarshadi a little more. At least the guy was trying.

"We're not under his tactical command, no, but he's the closest force commander. So let's see what he can do for us. Meanwhile, I've told Grissett to clear out one of the freezers. And not to let anyone else touch the body."

The exec inspected his boots. Scuffed the nonskid. "Do we want to slow down? In case they want to offload it?"

Dan frowned. "No. I want to reach station as soon as possible."

Almarshadi kicked at a scupper. "Okay, sir. Oh. By the way. I think you did the right thing. About Zotcher."

Dan looked aloft, at the snapping flags atop the signal bridge. A lookout was studying them from the wing, decks above; when he caught his captain's eye he swung his binoculars out again to sea. The barrel of a machine gun pointed in the same direction. "Glad I have your confidence. What about Amy Singhe? Am I picking up bad blood between her and some of the chiefs?"

"Amarpeet doesn't get along with them. Considers them beneath her, I guess. You know she's got an MBA from Wharton?"

"Yeah, I knew that. You call her Amarpeet? Not Amy?"

"That's her name."

Dan looked aloft again. "Not a smart attitude. Looking down on the chiefs, I mean."

"I'll counsel her."

"Okay. But first check on how they're doing with Goodroe. And get that message out."

HE walked the deck yearning to try to nap again, but knowing he wouldn't. The immobile heavy-jawed visage, its last sight on earth probably the stained underside of the next mattress up, haunted him. One day joking on the mess decks. The next, in olive plastic, being slid into cold storage.

You expected death in battle. And going to sea in ships crammed with explosives and fuel and heavy machinery was always danger-ous. You lost people overboard, or sucked into turbine engines on carriers, or from smoke inhalation, or asphyxiation in voids. But what killed healthy young men in their bunks? Cocaine? Didn't that stop the heart? But there'd been no sign of a coke problem in the Command Climate Survey, and it usually showed up either there or in the urinanalysis program. Navy drug use was way down, and Goodroe'd had no record. Heart attack? The man had been in his late twenties; it seemed unlikely.

He dropped down a deck and strolled the length of the ship, step-ping over knee-knockers, absentmindedly noting the condition of firefighting stations, dogging mechanisms, repair-party lockers. Putting a hand up now and then to check for dust on the top of the insulated ducts that ran along the overhead, painted cream-white and stenciled every few yards with black arrows denoting direction of flow. A knot of men and a blond woman stood around by the bar-bershop, nearly all the way aft. Navy didn't salute inside the skin of the ship, but they came to their feet, nodded, murmuring, "After-noon, Captain."

"We doing okay? How's the service here?"

"Turbo Mouth, he does okay. Talks pretty much nonstop, but he does a good haircut."

"Price is right," another sailor said. "Go on ahead if you need a trim, sir. We can wait."

"Thanks, maybe tomorrow."

The woman asked, "We keep hearing rumors on the news, sir. We gonna invade?"

"Seems to be a possibility."

"I hear they're threatening that if we attack, they won't limit the war to the Mideast. What do you think that means?"

"That's a good question. It might be why we're headed where we're going. But all I can really say is, we just need to be ready. Just all do our jobs and stand by."

They didn't look satisfied, but there weren't any more questions. Strange that they hadn't gotten the word about the death yet. Or maybe they had, and were just wary about bringing it up. He'd ask the corpsman to put something out, to all hands, before the scuttlebutt started to fly.

He looked into torpedo stowage, had a short discussion with the leading torpedoman, then ambled forward again up the port side. Halfway to the mess decks his radio crackled. *"Skipper, XO."*

"Go, Fahad."

"Got that message done, about Goodroe. Waiting for your chop."

"Run it past Chief Grissett."

"Already did, Captain."

"Okay, good."

"There's a message from DesRon in your in-box. They want to schedule a red phone call at 1500 local with Two Six Actual."

Jen Roald. His commodore. He checked his watch. The sea; the ship, the crew. And the captain. Like the old game played for decades with dice and drinks. Did they still play that, in officers' clubs, in petty officers' clubs, in what had once been Acey-Deucey clubs? Or had it too gone, another tradition eaten by the locusts? "Okay, XO, thanks. I'll take that in CIC."

HE got there at 1445 and logged in at his chair. The vertical displays were blank, all but the central one, which showed the Global Command and Control picture. A lot of air traffic to the east. To the west, far behind now, glowed the bright pips of the battle group. He found Almarshadi's draft message about Goodroe, went through it, started to correct a phrase, then shrugged and hit Send. Too many skippers wasted time massaging text. If it said what it meant to say, without having to be read twice, so be it.

The news summary carried press speculation that operations against Iraq were about to start, but there was no confirmation in the official traffic. A Chinese general had made threats against Taiwan. "Kill one rabbit, to scare the monkeys," he'd said. A message slotted to both Matt Mills and himself from Naval Weapons Center Dahlgren, Network Systems Directorate, caught his eye. The header: SPY-1 Flight 7 Upgrade. He opened it.

Referring to the request Donnie Wenck had sent, it turned down *Savo Island*'s request for new software. The upgrade was in Open Architecture Computing Environment (OACE) Category 3 infrastructure, which had not yet been approved for fleet issue due to considerations of operational security.

Which, he guessed, frowning, meant they were unsure it was hardened against hacking. Everybody wanted open architecture, but the easier programming was to write and change, the more vulnerable it became. He started a reply, then saved it to his draft folder.

As usual with Jennifer, she called five minutes early. "Commodore," he said, then released the button on the handset.

"Dan. I guess you saw the response to your message to Dahlgren."

"Yes, ma'am."

"You made a good case, but you might want to hold off on pressing that issue. You're handling an emergent tasker. You don't want to degrade your system right now. Believe me."

"I was thinking along those lines. Any, uh, idea when the balloon goes up?"

"You know as much as we do. I called my relief at the Sit Room and he can't shed any light."

Dan rubbed a bristly chin. Ought to shave soon. "Uh, apropos of that, we may have mutual interference, with the Israeli Patriot battery at Ben Gurion. Our geographic sectors overlap and our freq bands are real close. We've asked for a copy of a Patriot/Aegis interoperability test they did at White Sands, but we haven't been able to break that loose. It'd be good to have some kind of direct channel to the Israelis too. To be able to deconflict in real time."

"Sounds reasonable. I'll take that for action and get back to you. Otherwise, how's it going? Over."

"I had what seems to be a natural-causes death this morning." He gave her the details, and ended, "I just hit Send on the full report. I'm requesting an autopsy. There's just not too much my chief corpsman can pull out of his—tail. Other than that it might be a vaccine reaction."

Her voice sharpened. *"To AVA? The anthrax vaccine?"*

"Correct. Over."

"That'll involve Bethesda. You'll be getting calls from Clinical Investigation. Has the family been notified? You did what's right, right? Over."

"My XO looked it up in the manual and did the death report and the next-of-kin notification. You and your N4 are info'd on those. Over."

"Okay then . . . keep me in the loop on that. Anything else you need?"

"Those parts for the chassis rebuild we requested. We got some of them helo lift from the TF, but there's still outstanding requests."

"My loggies are working it. Oh, and by the way—almost forgot— NCIS identified the guy who threw the gasoline at you, at the gate. Over."

This was news. He pulled his consciousness out of the phone, checked the display, checked his own personal six. Then wondered what he was looking for, in the chill, darkened, equipment-packed space. The shapeless void-thing that had stalked him in the corridors of dream? "Really? They got him? Over."

"Well, identified him. Unfortunately, the Italians had already let him go by then. And don't seem to be able to find him again—no surprise, I guess. Anyway, want to know who he worked for?"

"Uh . . . yeah."

"There's an al-Qaeda link. Maybe not directly, but we're pretty sure they pulled the string."

Dan thought of several things he might say, but the one that came closest to actually getting voiced was: *And I know why.*

After 9/11, at first, no one had known for sure who was responsible. Then they had, but hadn't been able to locate him.

But TAG had been able to retask a modeling agent framework, originally intended to data-mine a littoral environment to locate submarines, into a program that integrated communications, intelligence, and social relations to predict the location of a unitary actor. Such as bin Laden. Dan, Henrickson, and Wenck had taken CIRCE active at Bagram Field, Afghanistan, and had nailed Osama's location closely enough that a SEAL team had come within an ace of taking him out.

Now, with a titanic conflict impending, maybe OBL was taking the opportunity to settle his books.

Or was that simply megalomania? To think a randomly thrown bottle had been aimed at him? Surely he wasn't that important, in the great scheme of things. He grimaced. No, they'd seen an official car, and thrown a firebomb. That was all.

"Dan? You there?"

"Yeah. That's interesting. An asymmetrical response."

"Or something like that. Okay, we're up-to-date, right? Info me on your on-station message. I'll keep working on this end. Out."

He signed off and resocketed the phone. Looked once more at the display, at the symbology and overlay and now, coming into the picture on the right, the east, the curved-bow shape of the most fought-over land on earth. Next year in Jerusalem. Next year in Al-Quds. The Holy Land of the Crusaders and Salah ad-Din. Israel. Palestine.

He took a deep breath and let it out. Toggled to the next screen, and started his on-arrival message.

9

Oparea Adamantine

NOW *flight quarters, flight quarters. All hands man your flight quarters stations. Stand clear topside aft of frame 315. Flight quarters.*"

The echoes of the 1MC died. Dan sprawled in his bridge chair, boots up, foul weather jacket zipped snug to the throat, gazing out over an uneasy sea. As *Savo Island* nosed around to face the wind she rose, then plummeted, picking up a deep creaking pitch. The air had turned chill again, and all was gray; charcoal clouds pressing down on a sea like a herd of stampeding elephants, ruffled with streaks of white foam like dust blown off their great heaving backs.

No mark on that ever-changing, ever-unchanging surface testified to it, but they were on station at last. A misshapen arc thirty miles north to south and slightly narrower east to west, centered west and south of Tel Aviv. He watched the rounded neon numerals of the Fathometer rise with each flicker: 998; 1010; 1023. Crossing the thousand-meter line. The navigator and the chief quartermaster, Van Gogh, were having a muted argument at the far end of the bridge. A petty officer murmured into his handheld next to Dan. He was there to relay word from the helicopter control station aft, an armored, fireproofed mini–control tower set to one side of the squared-off flight deck.

"*Bridge, Helo Control. From the pilot: Can we come fifteen to twenty degrees left. He's got turbulence across the deck. We're just about at the wind limit.*"

Dark eyes gave Dan a level look; a sleek head inclined. Crossing to stand beside him, Lieutenant (jg) Noah Pardees murmured, "Skipper, range is clear to port. Closest contact fifteen hundred yards and opening. No other threatening CPAs."

Pardees, the deck department officer, was even taller than Dan, and so West Coast laid-back and so very meager he seemed barely to inhabit his coveralls. Dan nodded. "How about that fuel-pressure caution light? And will we still be within ship motion limitations if the wind increases?"

The petty officer said, "They say they got that addressed, Captain. The caution light. Green board, ready to fly. On ship motion: remember they go by their onboard gyros, not ship's inclinometers."

"Okay . . . I guess. If they're happy. What about this rain? Looks as if it could close in."

"Scattered showers. And no problem if the wind comes up another ten knots. After that, could get dicey."

Pardees murmured languidly, "That's not in the fleet weather prediction, sir."

"Bridge, Helo Control: Request green deck."

Dan resisted the impulse to get down from his chair and check the radar one last time. Pardees had his binoculars up, peering out to port. The junior officer of the deck, little apple-cheeked Gene Mytsalo, was out on the wing. He had to trust. Trust the weather prediction, the pilots' judgment, the mechanics who'd repaired the fuel pump or pressure switch or whatever had triggered the caution light. He was the captain, not God. The OOD lowered the glasses and shot him a glance. He nodded.

"Helo Control, OOD: Deck *is* green," Pardees said into his Hydra.

"Green, aye . . . stand by."

Dan gripped the arms of his chair, then made himself relax back into it. Feign serenity, at least, if he couldn't actually achieve it. He'd seen a helicopter explode once, on its approach to the deck. Not a Sea Hawk; one of the older aircraft, a Sea Sprite. A good bird, despite the accidents, but the Navy had retired them when it got rid of the last Knox-class frigates.

At last the rising roar from aft, shifting to starboard, testified to the launch. "Red Hawk 202 away," the petty officer relayed.

Red Hawk was the squadron name, 202 the airframe number. The slate-gray minke bulk of the aircraft, tilted slightly forward, swept past, vibrating the heavy shatterproof windows. A ghostly smoke-trail spinnereted behind it, pressed down by rotorwash but not dispersed. It shrank slowly, outbound, then banked left and tracked across their bow, in and out of the low scud of clouds.

"Navigator recommends continuing left to course one seven zero, and reducing speed to ten knots to commence port leg."

"Very well," Pardees said, turning away. "Left fifteen degrees rudder. Come to course one seven zero. Engines ahead two thirds; indicate fifty-five rpm at eighty percent pitch for ten knots."

The orders and responses came and went, ebbing in the endless litany that had never, probably, been interrupted since the Phoenicians had begun voyaging across this very sea. Dan squinted, followed the aircraft until it became a speck, winking into and out of existence, until he couldn't be sure he was actually seeing it any longer or only imagining it. Then it was gone.

And Goodroe with it. The iced-down remains were headed back to the task group, which would do a preliminary investigation—they had an MD and a fairly sophisticated operating room aboard the carrier—then ship it onward, via Italy and Germany, back to the States. He hadn't heard any rumors about bad luck. Maybe the superstitions of the sea were vanishing along with so many other taboos; women aboard ship, for one thing. More and more, life at sea reflected life ashore. But sometimes he wasn't sure that was an improvement.

His reflection stared back from the slanted bulletproof glass. He shook his head and bent to the morning traffic.

He'd signed off on the arrival message at 0600, assuring both Cent-Com and EuCom, and the subordinate commanders in the chain, including Jen Roald, that *Savo Island* had taken station at Ballistic Missile Oparea Adamantine. Now he looked at a response to that message—or no, its originating date time group meant it had been drafted before. It was from CentCom, a frag order—a modification to a previously issued op plan. Instead of operating alone, commanding officer *Savo Island* would command Task Group 161, made up of his own ship and a Los Angeles–class nuclear submarine, USS *Pittsburgh*. The sub would join tomorrow. Which meant it was speeding toward them now.

He flipped pages to the *Early Bird*, the daily Pentagon news summary. He'd asked Radio to print it out each day, and to forward it to

Almarshadi to excerpt for the crew. Iraq had threatened again that if the U.S. attacked, the war would spread. This was getting to be old news. He'd heard it before, during the Gulf War. But as it turned out, it hadn't been a bluff. Not then. He and a small team of Marines had only barely managed to abort mass destruction in the final minutes, deep beneath Baghdad.

He shook that memory off and read on. China was claiming several islands that up to then had been considered Philippine territory. A three-star Army general had been indicted for contract fraud. Two more Navy COs had been relieved. The reasons weren't released, but he guessed sexual harassment or misconduct, since no collisions or groundings were mentioned. Terror attacks in northwestern India had killed seventy-five and wounded hundreds. The terrorists had been identified as Pakistani nationals, with an al-Qaeda–affiliated group in Waziristan. India had promised retaliation—

The bridge J-phone went off. Mytsalo flourished the handset. "Captain. Mr. Danenhower."

The chief engineer wanted to know how long they'd be at this speed. "I'd like to water-wash one of the turbines, sir."

"How long will you have it down?"

"Two hours to cool, maybe an hour to do the washdown and checks. Three hours?"

Dan searched the horizon. "We're out here by our lonesomes, Bart. Be poking around this track for a while, I imagine. Do your maintenance. Leave one engine on each shaft." He squinted across the pilothouse to see Pardees listening. He hoisted his eyebrows; the Californian nodded casually. "I notified the OOD. Go ahead."

"Will do, Skipper."

He hung up and leaned back again. Revisiting once more just why they were out here, and what he could expect.

Was it a bluff? Their presence here argued *someone* thought it wasn't. The Iraqis had been under international sanction. But no one knew how far their military rebuilding had progressed. The administration thought they possessed weapons of mass destruction. That, after all, was the rationale for the attack. You could argue the ethics of preemptive war if you wanted, but he didn't feel like it. As far as he and *Savo* were concerned, their mission was clear. Difficult . . . but clear.

He reread an article excerpted from *Foreign Affairs*. It pointed out that this invasion aimed to do something no government had ever tried before: destroy a regime that possessed weapons of mass destruction. In 1945, of course, only the United States had actually developed nuclear weapons. In the two cases since, where countries with WMDs had engaged in hostilities, both had been only skirmishes: China versus the Soviet Union along the Ussuri River, and India and Pakistan over Kargil. Both had been limited, and in neither case had a regime's existence been threatened, as Saddam's would be following a Coalition victory.

He frowned. If the administration feared whatever WMDs Iraq supposedly possessed enough to attack it, presumably its enemy would have no scruples about using these weapons when actually attacked.

Put that way, it made eminent sense to have *Savo Island* on guard.

He only hoped precautions were in place to protect the continental U.S., too.

"Good morning, sir." Almarshadi, looking hangdog, as if he had to muster all his courage to speak at all. Dan returned the exec's salute and accepted the papers he offered. He wished he could buck the XO up, give him whatever it was the guy was missing. The morning reports were summarized recaps of equipment status, what was broken and repair-time estimates. He flipped through, asked a couple of questions, then focused on the DSOT.

The Daily Systems Operability Test was a series of checks the computers ran on the missiles stowed beneath the hinged hatches of the vertical launch system. For a short period each day they were awakened and quizzed. The module they lived in was locked and sealed; no one entered alone, or without an officer present and a "screamer," a CO_2 detector, on his belt.

He'd looked into both the forward and aft modules during his initial inspection. The entryway was doored with heavy fireproof steel. The interior of the "cell" had two levels, with spidery metal catwalks between the missiles themselves. Dim and claustrophobic, it smelled of metal and rubber—unlike the gun magazines, with their heavy odors of alcohol and powder. The narrow gratings, so insubstantial one could look down past one's boots to the bottom of the cell far below, labyrinthed banks of metal canisters packed so closely a fat man would have had to turn sideways to slide through. Harpoon, Standard, Tomahawk, Asroc, nestled in eight-celled miscegenation, their somnolent brains wired with black rubber-coated data and power cables. Those umbilicals were a primary point of failure. If their connections came loose, human beings lost comms with the missiles. And without comms, the proper firing permissions, they wouldn't, of course, launch.

Failure to launch, when an enemy missile was coming in . . . he didn't like to think about that. But the chief gunner's mate had assured him the connections were tight. And any discontinuity or intermittent would show up on the daily tests. He hoped.

"It looks good. All rounds check out," the XO offered.

Dan glanced at him, looked around: the same gray sky, the same featureless sea. "Okay, but what's this? The SBC system?"

Almarshadi brightened. "That's the space-based calibration system. See, we use Aegis to track space junk to calibrate the sensors."

"And it's down?"

"Not completely, but the signal rate return isn't up to par. They're checking it out."

"And how about this . . . this flow rate sensor in the chill water system? I didn't see that under engineering. It's under Aegis too."

"Yessir, that part of the chill water system cools the signal processor."

Dan hitched himself erect in the chair. "*Another* cooling problem? I thought we checked all those systems out."

"The hose connections, yes sir, we did. This is a flow sensor. Different issue."

"Have we got people on it?"

"Yessir, the HTs. I'll go down right after this, check on progress."

Dan went down the list, not really reassured. Between software problems, the less-than-great Aegis team performance against their benchmarks, and the reduced redundancy because of the fire, he was less than confident *Savo Island* was fit for her mission, if called on to execute. No skipper wanted to fumble the ball. But failure in this case wouldn't be like blowing an exercise. If he couldn't goalie, civilians would die. "Have you talked to Dr. Noblos about our intercept team performance?"

"Uh, no sir. I know he's been under the weather—"

"For how long now? I'd like to get our heads together. How about 09? In the unit commander's cabin. I'd like the FCs and strike team there too. Let's take this whole thing through the cleaners."

Almarshadi said he'd set it up. Dan hesitated, still looking off to where he'd thought for a moment he'd seen a dash of white, like a periscope feather, breaking the surface. The sonar was still crying out every few seconds, but after their performance in the exercise he had less confidence in their ability to detect any subsurface threat. Still—and this lifted his spirits—having *Pittsburgh* around would give them more protection. Yeah, whoever had organized that, he was grateful.

"Okay, let's get to it," he told Almarshadi. He looked around one more time; at a gray sea, a spatter of rain that crackled across the windows. The boatswain went around turning on the wipers.

With a last glance at the lowering sky, he went below.

HE winced. The earsplitting shrill of the boatswain's whistle had caught him in his cabin, logging on to high-side chat. *"Now set the BMD watch,"* the 1MC crackled. *"Now set the BMD watch."* He hesitated, then closed the log-in and powered his terminal down. Pulled his foul-weather jacket off the hook where he'd hung it after coming down from the bridge. Stuck his pisscutter cap in the pocket, slid down two ladders, and cranked open the door to Combat.

All four large-screen displays were lit. The icy-aired, darkened space creaked as it pitched. Voices murmured as the first watch section took their seats.

Cheryl Staurulakis had drawn up a rubric for how they'd view graphic information for the antiballistic-missile mission. The surface plot, surrounding the ship close in, was up on the leftmost display. The air picture glowed in the center, reaching out three hundred miles into Syria, western Iraq, Jordan, Israel, Saudi Arabia, and Egypt. Cyprus, that queerly shrunken simulacrum of the continental U.S., glittered to the north. A glance told him commercial air traffic was way down. "Business as usual" was coming to an end.

The rightmost display reproduced the outputs on the Aegis consoles. He watched the by now familiar above-the-horizon search beams clicking around. They passed over the flat sea without return, probed a clearly delineated coastline, then etched an eldritch green strewing of mountains. The elongated, depressed shadow of the Dead Sea curled like a fava bean. Past that glowed more mountains. Then the splotches disappeared; the beams flew straight, searching out over the featureless desert. An abyss from whence nothing returned, not even the strobing blips of commercial aircraft. Mordor.

He ran his attention over the displays, checking weapons inventory, combat systems summary, surface summary. On the far right, the summary of summaries, the System Availability. It was green across the board: SM-2s up, guns up, VLS, TLAM, Harpoon up, Phalanx up. A pip throbbed on the leftmost screen. Red Wolf 202, on its way back from the task force. "ETA on the helo, Matt?" he asked Mills, in the TAO's seat.

"Estimate feet dry time five-zero."

About twenty minutes. Dan sat watching for a few seconds more, then logged in to the high-side chat room for the task force. Most of the chatter seemed to be coming from the screen units. Only now and then did the carrier come up.

DCK CIC: showers coming your way
DYO CIC: haul over all hatch hoods
DCK CIC: ;)
PBG TAO: DYO pls lk at track 8934—see anything suspicious about that
DYO TAO: no looks like com air. Do you not have squawk??
TMN AO: let us know if you want a cap vector

A far cry from the clatter of signal lamps, the flutter of flags as they went up a hoist. He toggled among rooms; the task force, Sixth Fleet, then found what looked very much like the strike groups for Iraq. How different this was from the previous isolation at sea. Oddly enough, though, neither CentCom nor EuCom seemed to be up on chat.

Mills leaned over. "Permission to go into mode, sir."

"Do it."

Terranova's all-too-youthful voice in his headphones. "All stations, Aegis control. Stand by for BMD mode . . . shift to BMD mode."

Dan sucked air and sat up.

Wenck and Noblos and Staurulakis had all told him, and it made sense in terms of system resources. But seeing it suddenly bottleneck down on-screen was much more sobering.

Although the left two screens stayed the same, in a blink-fraction of a second the rightmost—Aegis's view of the world—suddenly keyholed. From 360 degrees, they now had a cone of awareness maybe 5 degrees in width. Brawny as the SPY-1 was, the theater ballistic defense mission sucked down so much power that over 90 percent of the screen had just gone blank. Only a shade still echoed from the north-south mountain chain, fading as distance increased from the searchlight beam. He felt as if he'd been struck blind. "I don't like this," he murmured to Mills. "We're losing all our long-range surveillance."

"Yes sir. But we still have the gunlaying radar, and our surface search radar."

Great, they were back to 1945. If a swarm of kamikazes attacked, they'd be peachy. A Syrian MiG-29 or Su-24, though . . . he could be clobbered from behind before they knew what hit them. He fidgeted in his seat, then got up and went over to Chief Wenck, at the console. "Donnie, there's no middle ground? We're just about totally fucking blind everywhere but where you're looking."

Wenck blew a lock of too-long blond hair off his forehead. He didn't look disturbed. "Wussywug."

"What?"

"What you see is what you get, sir. Only so much wattage to go out, so much processing power in the blades. We got Sea Whiz looking, right?"

"Yeah. And the gun. But everything else is shut down."

"What you see," the tech said again, a shrug in his voice.

Big help. Dan took another deep breath and sighed it out. Shit, oh dear.

"Flight quarters, flight quarters," the 1MC announced as he was pulling on his jacket. Followed a moment later by the air-side controller calling out, "Helo control reports: Red Wolf 202 inbound, four souls onboard."

It took a moment before this registered. He swung on his heel and stalked to the far side of the space, where the air picture consoles kept track of, among other things, their own helicopter. "I heard *four* souls," he asked the petty officer, who removed one of his headphones politely.

"Yessir, Captain. That's what the pilot reported."

"There were three outbound. Pilot, ATO, sensor operator. And . . . well, three live souls. Why's it four coming back?"

"I dunno, sir. I asked, but didn't get an answer."

"Tell them it's me asking this time."

"Helo in final approach," the 1MC announced.

"Uh, I'd wait a couple minutes, sir, if it's okay with you," the controller said. "He's got a lot on his plate right now. The pilot, I mean."

"Sure. As soon as he's got both wheels on deck."

When Dan got back to his seat he realized he'd left his classified chat screen up. He'd been only a few steps away, but he logged off quickly, before anyone could notice. Then examined the rightmost display again. Damn. That eye could see so far, but only in such a narrow slice; all else was obscurity. Like the Norse god—Heimdall, Hendall, something like that—who could see a hundred leagues and hear the grass growing. Guarding the gates of Asgard, waiting to announce the battle that would end the world with a blast of his horn. Funny, how whenever any religion contemplated the End of Days, there was always a horn involved. Looking back at the Aegis display, he couldn't shake his apprehension, as if something bad had to be lurking in that huge pie of unsearched space.

"Helo on deck. Secure from flight quarters. Now commence XO's messing and berthing inspection."

The helo control petty officer. "Sir, pilot on the horn for you. Click to thirteen."

Dan fitted the headset on again, adjusted warm plastic, snapped to 13. To hear a voice he didn't recognize. A young-sounding, eager male voice, with maybe a touch of somewhere in New England. *"Captain? Is that you?"*

"Yeah, this is Lenson. Who's this?"

"Adam Ammermann, Captain."

He blinked and massaged his forehead. Then checked the dial, wondering if he'd wandered in on some other frequency. "I'm sorry. Am I on the line with Red Hawk 202?"

"We're shutting down, sir. Please secure that," someone said in

the background, maybe the copilot; and the voice said, *"I've got to get off, I'll be there shortly."*

Dan stared at the handset, then slowly put it down.

A tall, round-cheeked man with a slash of dark hair above an oval, open face swung down out of the chopper. He wore a Mae West over a blue blazer with a white button-down oxford shirt and a maroon tie with a repetitive pattern of small red . . . seals? His smile lit up the flight deck as he bounded toward Dan, palm outstretched, lurching as the deck tilted. "Captain Lennon? Dan Lennon?"

"The name's Lenson." Dan freed his hand as soon as he reasonably could and waved toward the hangar. "Let's get clear of the flight deck, okay?"

"Right, right, *Lenson.* Adam Ammermann. Just call me Adam, please. Or, my friends call me Jars."

Inside the hangar the maintenance crew stared. Dan led the guy out of the way as the hangar door clanged and began powering upward. *Jars?* "Look, Mr. . . . . Ammermann, there's obviously been some mix-up. This is a U.S. Navy warship. I assume you're a reporter, or—"

"Oh, no." Ammermann's wide innocent face fell. He needed a shave. "They told me they'd notified you—you'd know I was coming. They didn't? Look, I—"

"Who's 'they'?" Dan interrupted. It might not be the guy's fault, but he didn't have time for the press. He got the Hydra off his belt. "Bridge, this is the CO, back at the hangar. I need the master-at-arms here, right now. —Sir, I don't mean to be unwelcoming, but we're not exactly open to drop-ins. So I'm going to ask you to stand by here until we can get this aircraft refueled, and then—"

But Ammermann had drawn a paper from the blazer and was holding it out. Dan accepted it reluctantly. The letterhead was familiar: dark blue serifed font under the impressed seal. He looked up reluctantly to a forthright grin, teeth so perfect they had to have undergone long-term orthodontia, so white they must be capped. Only the five o'clock shadow marred the impression, and a whiff of sweat mixed with cologne. "The White House."

"White House staff. Right."

"You're what . . . military?"

"Oh, no. *You* were military staff, right? Dr. Szerenci said you were."

"You know Edward Szerenci? The national security adviser?"

"Oh, yeah. I've met him several times. At least."

The master-at-arms, out of breath. "You wanted me, Skipper?"

"Yeah. Just stand by a minute, Chief. —This letter doesn't say anything about *Savo Island*, uh, Adam."

"That was in the message. You didn't get a message?"

Dan blew out. "Let me check. Meanwhile just stand by, all right? Go back aft, back there, out of the way."

The crew chief. "We refueling, sir? Or putting her in the barn?"

"Just stand by. —Chief, escort Mr. Ammermann to the ready room." He turned away, tried to shield his ears from the noise, and failed. He slammed the starboard door behind him and stalked forward along the main deck, until the engine whine receded enough so that he could get through on the Motorola. He asked Radio if there were any messages about an incoming political visitor, an Adam Ammermann.

"When would it have come in, Captain?"

"I don't know. Can't you do a global search or something?"

The radioman came back within sixty seconds. "Nothing under that name, sir."

Dan pivoted on his heel.

Back in the hangar he nodded to the civilian, but spoke to the chief. "Chief, there's obviously been some mix-up. Mr. Ammermann here must have been slated to go somewhere else. Somehow, the carrier put him on our helo. We've got a maintenance hold on the bird, so I'm going to place him in your custody until we figure out where he's supposed to go and how we can help him on his way. That okay, sir? Sorry about this, but this kind of stuff does occasionally happen. In the Navy, like everywhere else."

But Ammermann said earnestly, "Sure, but this is *Savo Island*, right? And you're Lennon—I mean, Lenson? This is where I'm supposed to be."

Dan studied him again. He didn't look like anyone who ought to be drifting around the fleet. Or maybe, just like one of the young profs you occasionally saw in the College Afloat program. "What exactly are you supposed to be doing here, Adam?"

"Jars. Please. The message explains it. But since you don't have that yet, well—I'm your liaison."

The MAA looked from one of them to the other. "Liaison with who?" Dan asked.

"With you. Office of Public Liaison. I've got an ID."

Dan scratched his chest as he examined it. He vaguely remembered Public Liaison from when he'd worked in the West Wing. They were fervent and ambitious but inexperienced and sometimes too full of themselves, and the military staffers had tried to avoid them whenever possible, especially since they tended to look down on anyone in uniform. Or at least they had during the previous administration.

"You're absolutely sure it was *Savo Island*? Well, if you knew my name . . . Look, I'll stash you in a stateroom until we figure this out. Okay? But until we do, I'm going to ask you to stay there. Don't leave that cabin. We have a lot of high-voltage equipment and this is an industrial environment. We're busy and we're on a . . . Anyway, I just want you to stay put for the time being, okay?"

Ammermann said sure, absolutely, whatever Dan said. A crewman hustled over carrying an expensive-looking leather suitcase and a hanging bag. Dan drew Chief Toan aside. "Take him to the unit commander's suite, and put somebody you trust on the door. I don't want this dude wandering around. We still don't really know who he is."

"Gotcha, sir."

"Be courteous. Get him coffee, put a movie on for him, but don't let him roam unescorted. In fact, don't let him out of the stateroom." The chief nodded, and Dan forced an Official Smile at Ammermann, who was standing by his luggage. The staffer kept glancing from the suitcase to the chief. Only when it was perfectly obvious that no one else was going to pick it up did he make a little quirk of the mouth and bend for it. As he did so pens and a smart phone fell out of his jacket, bouncing away over the nonskid. The crew chief was on it in an instant, yelling, "FOD alert! Get this shit off the deck, ASAP!" and slamming a boot down on the phone as Ammermann winced and plastic cracked.

Dan almost smiled. But not quite. Then he was out of there, mind snapping to the next item on the day's agenda.

* * *

THEY assembled in his in-port stateroom. Longley had coffee and doughnuts ready and Dan gestured everyone—Noblos and Wenck and Mills, Singhe and Terranova and Staurulakis, the major players in his Aegis team—to seats. Dr. Noblos looked worn and held a handkerchief to his nose; he sniffled. Terranova smiled down at the table with that inwardness, that passivity, he'd noted before, and grabbed for a doughnut. Wenck was humming to himself, some inaudible ditty that bounced his head back and forth as he plugged in a power supply and set up a notebook. Not for the first time, Dan wondered if there might be a touch of autism, Asperger's or something like that, there. Mills blinked into space. He'd just come off watch and looked as if his head were still in Combat. Staurulakis sat pale, calm, composed, compact, ready for anything. While Singhe, perfectly pressed, perfectly coiffed, smiled at him, deep brown eyes seeming to convey more than any whisper could. Sandalwood perfume drifted across the table. The strike officer wasn't really part of the TBMD team. But maybe the more brainpower they poured on this, the better.

He cleared his throat. "All right, I asked everyone here to iron out any hard spots now that the watch is set in ABM mode. I guess I'll ask Chief Wenck . . . or, maybe better, Dr. Noblos to start the recap."

The physicist coughed. He said in a hoarse voice, "I assume you're calling this to check our timelines and geometry?"

"Maybe start with an overview, Doctor."

Noblos smiled tightly. "I'll make it as . . . simple as I can, then.

"*Savo Island*'s mission is to maintain station once hostilities begin, in surveillance and track mode, ready to intercept any ballistic missile fired within a radius of three hundred miles. The obvious enemy is Iraq, the extended-range Scud they call the Al-Husayn, though Iran's also on the threat axis and within range. If the firing point is from western Iraq, we'll have a near zero angle of attack on the incoming missile from here.

"We'll probably acquire either via handoff from AWACS or cuing from Obsidian Glint. Aegis will develop a track, compute intercept trajectory, and initialize. We have a limited inventory. Four Block 4A Theater Defense rounds. The missile will perform a built-in system test, match parameters, and fire itself. This must occur no later than eight minutes after the target launch."

The scientist coughed. "After firing and in flight, the SM-2 establishes communication with the ship. The booster will burn out, and separate. The solid-fuel dual-thrust motor will ignite. Aegis keeps transmitting midcourse guidance through the third-stage motor burn, taking the warhead above the atmosphere. The kill vehicle will apogee three hundred twenty-five kilometers up at approximately fifteen thousand miles an hour. Terminal long-wave infrared guidance will take it to final impact.

"If, that is, all goes as planned." Noblos blinked bloodshot orbs at the overhead. "Limiting factors are the low round loadout, marginal crew training, marginal software function, and limited backup amplifier and power-out equipment. I have to be honest. The best possible outcome would be if we never have to fire. Because I don't think you're ready to detect, track, and discriminate well enough to achieve mission success."

Dan said as evenly as he could, "Thanks for the recap, Doctor, and for keeping it . . . comprehensible. Matt, what can you add?"

Mills spoke through his hands, which were clamped over his face. "Well, Dr. Noblos has pointed out most of the hard spots. But the cooling system and the calibration are question marks too. I have more confidence in Donnie and the Terror's tracking team than the Doc seems to. But the geometry's going to govern everything, and it's the one variable we can maybe get some more traction on. So I printed this out."

He passed out pages, and Dan studied his copy. A map of the Levantine, with a blurry infinity or sideways figure-eight pattern overlaid between the east Med and western Iraq. The left lobe of the lazy eight was much smaller than the right.

Mills said, "Over here to the left is our assigned box. You can see we have a pretty small footprint to jockey around in. We're going to have to watch the intel very closely. If we get launch indications farther south in Iraq"—he rocked his fingers in a seesaw—"we'll want to move north. And vice versa. The more we can minimize the sideways velocity vectors, the bigger the error basket we give ourselves."

"Bigger, or smaller?" Dan asked. "I'm not sure I—"

Staurulakis said, "Think of it as a funnel, Skipper. The narrow end's what we have to get the missile into. That's the error basket. The kill vehicle has its own little steering thrusters, once the infrared seeker locks on. That's the open end of the funnel. But there's only a limited amount of maneuverability after burnout."

Mills added, "Don't forget, it's going two miles a second by then. We have to get our bird into that funnel, as Cheryl calls it, so the seeker can track and discriminate for a hit-to-kill. The closer to a nose-on meeting we can manage, the bigger that basket will be, and the better chance we'll hit it."

Dan said, "Okay, let's assume we hit the, uh, the error basket. What's P-sub-K after that? Probability of kill?"

Noblos took that one. "For the warhead itself, if it gets out there and is positioned right, and the target's within its maneuverability envelope, P-sub-K will be around .8. Or so. But that's to impact. Actual P_K on an incoming warhead also depends on what kind of target we get, unitary or separating. If the airframe detaches from the warhead, for example, as reentry starts, you get two targets and possibly other debris as well. There's some discrimination built into the seeker, but it's not foolproof."

"Overall?" Dan asked quietly.

"Probably about .5."

He sucked air. Even odds were not so good when you had only four missiles. They could look, shoot, look, shoot, but at a closing rate of fifteen thousand miles an hour they'd have no time for a second try. "Can we fire two-round salvos?"

"Depends on the geometry." Noblos's grin was diabolical, until he grabbed a napkin and sneezed.

Nobody else said anything, and after a moment Dan nodded to Wenck. "Okay, Donnie, you're coming in at this pretty much from the outside. What're you seeing that we've all missed?"

The newly minted chief had been riffing on his keyboard all through the discussion. Now he rotated it to display a chart of the eastern Med. A sea-tinted teardrop faced its blunt end toward Damascus. The tapered tail extended far to the west, almost to Greece. He drawled, "A little different take on what Mr. Mills just presented. This blue patch is our defended area, against a missile from western Iraq." He pivoted the screen so all could see in turn.

"According to that, most of the area we can defend is behind us," Dan said.

"Right, but there's nothing we can do about that. It's just the way the intercept geometry works. Actually our optimal location would be about a hundred miles inland. But it means two things. First, we have a real narrow footprint we can launch from, to have much chance of making an intercept. Second, we've got to push that footprint in as close to shore as possible. The closer in, the better we can cover our defended area. However, we have to stay fairly far north, too. Unfortunately—"

"That puts us very close to Syrian waters," Staurulakis finished.

Wenck nodded. "Yes ma'am. The closer inshore we get, the bigger the hoop on that basket we're trying to hit. But you're right."

The operations officer murmured, "The Syrians are trying to figure out which way to jump in this war anyway. We probably don't want to be their excuse to jump the wrong way."

"Hey, if they do, we'll just lick their shit too," Wenck put in.

Dan winced—it was an unfortunate choice of words—and glanced at him. "Donnie, that's good. Clarifies the problem. Anything else? Any way we can make things easier for our tracking team? Give them some kind of advantage?" He made sure not to look at Terranova as he said this.

Wenck blinked and pushed his cowlick back. "Hey, everybody seems to think there's a bunch of dummies on that console. It's not Beth's fault. This is a new system. New software. But the training package is all old shit; all she got was the beta development notes. Wanna know why? Some dickhead in the missile-development agency cut their funds off. They need billions for some supersmart kinetic-energy warhead, so they cut all the funding for training. The Terror here, she had to make half of it up herself."

Noblos started to object, spluttering; Dan held up a palm. "Okay, okay! Maybe a little less finger-pointing and more listening here? We have a lot of constraints and not much wiggle room. Two things worry me, and they're related. What Cheryl pointed out—Syria considers the area where we'd most like to be, to successfully intercept, as its territorial waters. Allied to that is ship self-defense. Petty Officer Terranova told me, but it didn't really hit home until today, how vulnerable we are in BMD mode."

Mills said, "We're really almost blind against other threats."

Dan nodded. "Right; such as antiship missiles fired from Syria. Or by Hamas or Hezbollah, from Lebanon. Intel says they might have some Iranian C-802s."

Staurulakis murmured, "C-band search radar. Seventy-five-mile range. Sea skimmer; possible midcourse correction via data link; radar terminal homing."

Dan said, "Mount one of those on a truck, and that could be a real headache, if we're not looking right at southeast Beirut when they launch. We need to be ready to either jam it, decoy it, or shoot it down."

Wenck looked up with that dreamy stare he got sometimes. "What?" Dan asked him.

"If it's got a data link, maybe we could convince it it's off course. Send it someplace we aren't."

"Spoof it? Good, look into that. And we haven't even mentioned the problem with the Patriot battery at Ben Gurion."

"Plus there's Israel's own ABM system," Noblos said.

"Right . . . Arrow. If both Aegis and Patriot lock onto an incoming missile, and Arrow, too, we could all jam each other up good." Dan told the table at large, "I've kicked that one up to the commodore, but we still don't have any coordination with the Israel Defense Forces."

A sharp double rap; they all looked toward the door. "Come in," Dan called. It opened on the chief radioman, carrying a clipboard. He grinned uncomfortably. "Just a sec," Dan said. "I want to finish my train of thought here."

"Captain, this is the message you wanted."

Dan frowned; what message had he "wanted"? Unless it was a personal from Blair. But he'd cut off e-mail to the crew; he could hardly stay in contact himself. Unless something had happened at home. "Just a sec," he muttered. Then went on, turning back to their expectant expressions. "So, serious challenges. I want us to concentrate on those two things. One, how do we defend ourselves while Aegis is focused on looking inland—Matt, Cheryl, see what the two of you can work out. Two, how do we minimize interference with the Israelis, both Patriot and Arrow. Donnie, you and Bill work that issue."

"Freq-hop at the lower end of their spectrum, maybe," the chief said.

"Look into it. I need a recommendation. Petty Officer Terranova, brief me on your watch setup and any way we can destress your watchstanders. We could be out here awhile. I want them to be able to sleep. They've got to be fresh when they're in front of that screen. The rest of the ship's here to support them, so I don't want them pulled off for any other duties." He started to slap the table, but caught himself.

Noblos rose first and made for the door. The comm chief brushed past him and came toward Dan, holding out the clipboard. "The message you were looking for, sir," he said again, not meeting Dan's eye. "Sent late yesterday. Marked routine. So it didn't actually come in until just now."

Dan ran his eye down the headers, to the text.

PARA 2 (C): WH STAFFER ADAM ALONSO AMMERMANN ENRTE USS SAVO ISLAND. PURPOSE: SHIP VISIT AND LIAISON WITH CTG 161 IRO CURRENT OPERATIONS. NO HONORS. SAVO ISLAND PROVIDE BERTHING/MESSING 0-7 EQUIVALENT.

He lifted the Hydra to his mouth. "Chief Toan, CO here. —Hey, Matt, can you stand by a second?"

"Sure, sir." Mills halted by the door.

"CMA here, sir. Over."

"Mr. Ammermann. In the in-port commander's stateroom?"

"Yes sir. With one of my boys on the door. Just like you said."

"Okay, good. Tell him—tell Mr. Ammermann his clearance message came through. Take the guard off, and tell him he's welcome in the wardroom for evening meal. But we're going to have to talk about access, and so on."

He remembered more now about Public Liaison. They'd been mainly young campaign workers, or sons or daughters of major donors and political confidants. After a short orientation, the White House chief of staff, or at least someone in that office, sent them out to embed in various federal agencies. They weren't actually appointees, since they weren't subject to the confirmation process. He wasn't even sure they were paid. You could see them as sort of political commissars, but that might be taking them more seriously than they warranted.

* * *

Minutes later he was in the unit commander's suite pouring coffee for Ammermann, who'd taken off his tie and was half-reclining on the settee reading the message. When he looked up Dan said, "Apparently somebody made an error, sent it routine. and it got delayed en route. That happens sometimes, when there's a lot of traffic. I apologize."

"A lot of message traffic? Why's that?"

Dan started to explain, then hesitated. Could he really not know? And if he didn't . . . "Look, that says you're on your way, but it doesn't give me a clearance level. And we're . . . pretty busy right now, meeting our operational commitments. What exactly is it I can do for you, Jars?"

The staffer's expression went earnest again, the way it had been on the flight deck. He threw the clipboard aside. "Apology accepted, Captain. I'm not the kind of guy who stands on ceremony. But it's not what you can do for me. I'm here to help *you*. Direct liaison between you and the White House."

"Um, correct me if I'm wrong, but my chain of command goes up through the CNO. Then the Joint Chiefs, since Goldwater-Nichols, anyway. Then to the SecDef."

Ammermann nodded eagerly, as if Dan had just made his main point for him. "And that takes how long? Ages, right? And this is an important mission, as I understand it."

Dan said carefully, "What exactly do you understand about our mission, Adam?"

"You're here as our first ballistic missile defense deployment. To protect Israel when the war goes hot."

Dan noted the *when*, not *if.* "No chance of a settlement? I was reading about some kind of ultimatum."

The staffer shrugged. "We're giving him forty-eight hours to leave, but he's not going to. We're going to liberate the Iraqi people, and destroy Ba'athism forever. It won't take long. Their generals are already reaching out to us." He took out a pack of Salems and a black Zippo. Offered them. "You smoke?"

Dan shook his head. "Outside the skin of the ship, please. Most of our smokers go up in the breakers. That's forward, port and starboard on the main deck."

Ammermann looked at the pack, clicked the cover on and off the lighter a couple of times, but at last set them aside. "I have some news you might find useful, Captain. About this war we have to fight. Iraq has an uprated missile. Two days ago, DIA told seventy-five senators in closed session that Iraq can attack the Eastern Seaboard of the U.S. with biological or chemical weapons."

As Dan poured himself the last dregs of warm coffee a darkness like an advancing thunderhead shaded his mood. Remembering the bioweapons his team had found during the Signal Mirror mission. Most of that team hadn't come home. Of those who had, some had died from the virulent strain of smallpox Dr. Fayzah al-Syori had weaponized. If the Iraqis had regenerated stocks of that virus, and built even one missile with intercontinental range . . . He didn't want to imagine the consequences. Still . . . "Just having a supposedly up-rated missile doesn't mean a weapon's operational."

"We don't want to take that chance. I know you're married to a member of the former administration, Captain. And you served in the White House under Bob De Bari. Your sympathies may not be with this political team. But you have to believe we've got the best interests of the country in mind."

Dan rubbed the old scar on his ear. A souvenir of Saddam's Mukh-barat. He couldn't argue with that; if any regime could be trusted with such a weapon, Iraq's brutal and reckless dictatorship wasn't it. But he wasn't convinced he needed "help"—which usually translated to questions, objections, guidance, and second-guessing—from the political side. "If that's true, what're we doing here? We should be on station off Atlantic City."

"Because that's not your mission, Captain. We have that taken care of." Ammermann leaned back, put the cigarette in his mouth, but didn't light it. He smiled.

A brief silence, interrupted by a beep from Dan's Hydra. The bridge reported a crossing contact. Electronic intelligence identified it as a merchant. Dan told the OOD to maintain course, but to slow and let the other ship pass ahead. He signed off and met Ammermann's gaze again. "So you're my liaison. With the president, you say."

"Exactly right, Captain. Whatever you need, I'm here to help."

"Well, I'll have one of my people get with you about some spare parts. At the moment, though, that's the only thing I can think of you can help with. Also, Adam, we just don't have a lot of room, or ex-cess personnel to escort you around. Or, to be frank, the command attention—from me personally—that I'm certain you deserve. I'm going to berth you in here. This is where the commodore stays when he's aboard . . . or she. It's the best accommodation I have. But I'm going to ask permission to offload you back to the task force, or to a safe location ashore, at the first opportunity."

Ammermann cocked his head, still smiling. "You're the captain. The way it was explained to me—well, the president himself, if he was aboard, you'd still give the orders."

"Okay then. Let me know if you need anything else." Dan got up. Ammermann jumped to his feet too, held out a hand. Dan had to shake it. Only as he was closing the door did he catch the soft rasp of the cigarette lighter behind him. And the soft breath of a relaxed exhalation.

10

T HE bonging went on and on, echoing the length of the ship. The boatswain leaned to the 1MC. *"Now general quarters, general quarters, all hands man your battle stations. General quarters traffic route, up and forward to starboard; aft and down to port. Set material condition Zebra throughout the ship. Now general quarters!"*

The pilothouse burst into a frenzied bustle. Watchstanders grabbed for GQ gear, bowing to tuck and tape the cuffs of coveralls into socks. They pulled heavy padded flash gear, hoods and gloves—standard issue since USS *Horn*'s nuclear destruction not far from these waters—on over the coveralls, leaving only eyes peering out. They strapped gas masks rigged for quick donning on their thighs. Petty officers broke out sound-powered phones, in case comms went down. They passed out the same heavy steel helmets the Navy had issued in World War II, and banged open lockers of flotation devices and emergency breathing gear.

Dan was out on the wing, polishing his binoculars with lens paper, when the officer of the deck brought him out his helmet. The letters CO were stenciled in red on the front. He settled its weight on the crown of his skull. The wind gusted cold. Dawn was just breaking, a dull illumination that barely limned a charcoaled horizon, hardly distinguished sea from clouded sky. The stern light of a cargo ship glowed like a distant comet. *Savo Island* rolled slightly, charging through wind-ruffled onyx swells at twelve knots. Not all that fast, but he had to balance a desire not to present a stationary target with the need to conserve fuel.

Yeah, fuel. He frowned. Need to get with Bart Danenhower about that. He had no idea how long they'd be out here, and the Navy might not want to risk a tanker close inshore during a hot war.

Which might start any day. Any hour.

"Time: plus one minute," the 1MC announced.

So he'd decided on an old-fashioned general quarters drill. From the expressions around him, especially on the faces of the younger troops, they hadn't heard that pulse-pounding gong often since the last week of boot camp. But if *Savo* was as vulnerable as he feared, every man and woman aboard had to be ready to survive blast, flooding, fragments, and fire. As he glanced in at them through the window, for just a fraction of a second memory intruded.

He'd been looking away when it had happened. Fortunately. But even looking away, everything around him—sea, steel, cloth—had turned the brightness of the noon sun. The starboard lookout had screamed, dropping his binoculars, clutching his eyes. But the dreadful, burning light had gone on and on, as if someone had opened the scuttle to Hell.

Dan hadn't actually thought about what was happening. Drill alone had driven him across the bridge, slamming into the chart table, to shove the quartermaster aside and shout into the mike, "Nuclear detonation, brace for shock!"

The deck had jolted upward as he'd crashed down onto it, whiplashing him back up into the air. Dust and paint chips had leaped out of cable runs to fog the pilothouse. An instant later the windows had come in on them with a crack like lightning tearing an oak apart. Only the sound had gone on, and on. . . .

He came back now to find himself staring white-eyed into his own reflection, kneading his neck. The old fracture. Then, as he blinked, his gaze suddenly plunged through, past the wing window he was looking into, to meet the puzzled eyes of a slight young seaman manning the remote operating console for the port 25mm. The squished-together, almost toothless-looking old man's face was familiar.

Downie. "The Troll." The goofball who'd left his pistol unattended on the quarterdeck just long enough for it to be stolen. The compartment cleaner who'd discovered a corpse cold in its bunk. They stared at each other for what seemed like a long time. Then Downie half-grinned, dropped his gaze, and squatted to adjust his gas mask carrier.

Almarshadi bustled up in flash gear and flotation vest, carrying a rolled-up sheaf of bond. Dan beckoned him closer. Trying to control suddenly ragged breathing, a racing heart, reaching for the cool impassivity everyone expected of him. Trying to forget *Horn*, and what had happened to all too many of her crew.

Under his command.

"Fahad, good morning. Fine Navy day, right?"

The exec shivered. He cast a doubtful eye at the clouds. "Absolutely, Captain. Spectacular Navy day."

"Built the training package?"

"Bart and I got it written up last night."

"Good. Couple of issues on the bridge team. I want protective goggles for them too. Have them wrap a pair in the flash gear hood so they get them on at the same time as the hoods. Second, aren't they supposed to have flak jackets? Do we have those?"

"Hermelinda might have goggles in stock. And we . . . not flak jackets . . . we have, um, ballistic protection gear for the boarding party."

"Move it up here. We won't be doing any opposed boarding. I'd rather have the bridge team ready to keep fighting if we take a fragmentation hit."

"Time: plus two minutes."

The OOD leaned out. "Captain, XO: General quarters set. All stations report manned and ready. Time, two minutes and fifteen seconds."

Dan gave Almarshadi the gimlet eye. With a ready time like that, someone had leaked the drill. He got a shamefaced grin back. "All right," he told the OOD. "Have the bo's'un pass, 'Work center supervisors, now carry out EBD and emergency egress drills.'" Almarshadi waited, tapping the rolled-up papers against his thigh. Dan looked aft, then up, giving the crew a few more minutes to get set. But something was missing. After a moment he realized what. "Get our battle colors up!" he yelled into the pilothouse, and added, to Almarshadi, "And leave them up, as long as we're on station out here."

"Aye sir. Goggles, ballistic vests, battle colors."

A quartermaster—there were no signalmen anymore—double-timed to the flag shack and began breaking out the oversized Stars and Stripes. When it was snapping free against the gray sky, huge and bright and crackling in the cold wind, he looked up for a long time. Filling his sight with red and blue and white like some essential nutrient he'd been short on for too long.

Reynolds Ryan was gone. *Van Zandt* was gone. *Horn* was still radioactive, but he'd brought her back. Less than half as many ships out here now as when he'd stepped aboard his first destroyer so many years before. But the U.S. Navy was still on station.

Still on station. . . .

He took a deep breath, wondering why he was suddenly fighting tears. Fuck. *Fuck!* What would happen to these kids? Was *Savo* doomed too? He'd *just left* the Navy command center when Flight 77 had punched through the limestone skin of the Pentagon, blasting the space and everyone in it with fuel-flame and razor-sharp metal, turning everything in the C ring into fire and collapsing concrete.

Niles, and the others who'd called him a Jonah, a curse, a doom—were they right?

No. They couldn't be. He'd never have taken this command if he'd really believed that.

So why was the imp of self-doubt still whispering in his ear that he wasn't good enough, wasn't competent enough? That when the chips were down, he'd lack what it took.

He'd always come through before, true. *Oh, sure,* the imp sneered. *But one of these days. . . .*

A clearing of the throat beside him. Dan looked down from the streaming colors to find the XO regarding him. He dragged himself back into the present, into the bite of a frigid wind. And told Almarshadi, "Okay, that your drill schedule there? No, I'm sure it's fine. Take charge, Fahad. Go ahead and take charge."

"CAPTAIN'S in Combat" passed mouth to mouth. The lights were dimmed. Every seat was occupied. Everyone in CIC was in flash gear too, but their helmets lay on the deck beside them. He'd told Cheryl she could relax her battle dress if she wanted, once she was satisfied.

He settled into his command seat with a sigh, unbuckled his own helmet, and set it aside. His neck, injured in that nuclear whiplash aboard *Horn*, was grateful for the lessened weight. He kneaded it as he took in the screens. They shifted as Staurulakis tested inputs and cameras. Only the Aegis picture stayed constant. A gimlet gaze, but so exquisitely honed that as the spokes clicked back and forth, refreshing forty times a second, every desert wadi and ridge glowed green and gold.

Fractured neck, scarred airway, burn tissue in one shoulder from a hellish night in the Irish Sea . . . his body was a palimpsest. Niles had offered medical retirement. He could still run a mile in nine minutes, but he could envision a day when pelting through a ship, sliding down ladders, would be just too much.

What would he do then?

Agonize about that later, Lenson. Just now his ship, *his* ship, throbbed and whined around him. The turbines buzzed through the rubber-coated steel under the flight deck boots he wore for GQ. The ventilation whooshed, and keyboards clattered. The high lilting whalesong of the sonar trilled through alloy before hurtling out into miles of chilly sea. His elbow jerked and a paper cup of coffee he hadn't noticed being placed there spilled over the gray metal deskshelf. He mopped the keyboard with a paper towel that Staurulakis, eyes narrowed, handed him.

You are in fucking command, boy, he told himself. Get a grip.

He skimmed his message queue, reading the header on each, then either deleting or filing it. CTF 61 had acknowledged last night's question, about backloading Ammermann at the first opportunity. It wasn't an answer, just acknowledging receipt. The *Early Bird* carried Iraq's defiant response to the forty-eight-hour deadline. In the next article, Israel's prime minister announced that if attacked with WMDs, his country would retaliate in kind.

Dan forwarded those to Almarshadi for the daily news summary, then studied the fleet weather forecast. Up to twenty-knot winds and high seas for the rest of today. A high-latitude ridging event over Germany could lead to cyclogenesis over the east Med. A cold air surge over the region could drop temperatures to 10°C, and bring high winds and heavy snow. Snowfall-affected regions could spread out from southern Turkey to the coast of the Levant.

"Shit," he muttered. They really didn't need bad weather just now. Well, maybe it'd miss them.

He blotted surreptitiously at the now icy-cold remnants of the spilled coffee that had dripped down onto his crotch, and pulled up the message he'd started to draft the night before. It was to both his "masters"—CentCom and EuCom, info to CNO and State.

"Captain?"

He looked up at Bart Danenhower's broad, blank face. The engineer nodded, taking off the locomotive driver's cap and wiping his forehead on one sleeve. He shuddered. "Jesus, it's cold in here."

"How you doing, Bart?"

"Okay, sir. I did the math you wanted. On fuel."

"Yeah, we got to talk about that. Drills going okay?"

"DCA's running them. Concentrating on fire and flooding."

"We still seeing water in the CRP system?"

"No more than usual."

"Engine control consoles? Any more groundings?"

"Not so far." The CHENG laid out xeroxes of their fuel-consumption curves and positioned a calculator. "We refueled to 100 percent two days ago. Fast transit to patrol area, so we're down to 95 as of today. Our bottom's clean so I'm going to use the class manual for consumption curves. Here's our options. Our quietest patrol speed is thirteen knots."

Dan lifted his eyebrows. "That high?"

"Yeah, not what you'd expect, but we're actually quietest with both shafts powered and both props at 100 percent pitch. Got to re-align the masking system, but that's the way we put the least noise in the water. See, below 100 percent, your props cavitate. Slowest we can go at full pitch on both shafts is about 12.8 knots."

"That's going to cut way down on our on-station time."

"I get six days to 50 percent. Factoring in electrical load, with the radar going full power."

"Damn it, Bart. I just don't know if they'll be willing to break me out a tanker six or seven days from now. Anything could be happening by then." At 50 percent fuel he had to holler for help. At 30 he had to leave station, unless ordered to remain. He grimaced, remembering the weather report; heavier seas would increase fuel consumption too. Jamming him tighter and tighter into a very narrow corner. He sighed. "You said there's another option?"

"Kind of out there, but I can shift to a one-shaft, nonstandard-configuration low-speed mode. That gets me down to six knots. Not as quiet, but close."

"How many days does that buy us?"

"Eight days to 50 percent, ten days to 30."

"Not great, but better. What's the downside? Of this nonstandard configuration?"

"Got to run everything from Main Control. Not the bridge. So if you suddenly need to crank on the knots, it'll take longer."

"How much longer?"

"Depends on how much faster you want to go, but it won't be *that* long. Maybe five, ten minutes."

Dan blew out and scratched his head. "I don't like it. But I guess we have to. At least until we get some clue how long we'll be out here. —Cheryl, d'you hear that? We're going down to six knots, but—"

"I have it, sir." Staurulakis rattled her keyboard.

Danenhower didn't linger once a discussion was over; he nodded and left, taking the calculator and graphs but leaving a one-page summary. Dan folded it into a pocket. "Shit," he muttered. Then went back to the message he was writing. He read the last paragraphs on the screen once more.

4. (S) IN VIEW OF THE FOLLOWING:

    A) INADEQUATE TBMD LOADOUT (ONLY 4 SM-2 BLOCK 4A WEAPONS)
    B) MARGINAL CREW TRAINING AS EVALUATED BY BOTH JOHNS HOPKINS CONTRACTOR RIDER AND OWN SHIP TEAM
    C) AEGIS REDUCED REDUNDANCY FROM SPY-1 DRIVER-PREDRIVER FIRE (CASREP REF C)
    D) POSSIBLE MUTUAL INTERFERENCE WITH ISRAELI PATRIOT AND ARROW
    E) SEVERELY LIMITED SELF-DEFENSE CAPABILITY IN ABM MODE

CO CONCLUDES SAVO ISLAND'S MISSION CAPABILITY FALLS
BELOW ACCEPTABLE READINESS.

5. (S) IN VIEW OF POSSIBLE GEOPOLITICAL CONSEQUENCES
OF A FAILED INTERCEPT ATTEMPT, IT MAY BE PREFERABLE
TO RETRACT WHATEVER COMMITMENTS HAVE BEEN MADE,
AND RETURN SAVO ISLAND TO TASK GROUP DEFENSE OR TOM-
AHAWK STRIKE ROLE RATHER THAN CONTINUE AS INDEPEN-
DENT TBMD GUARD.

6. (S) IF MISSION JUDGED POLITICALLY NECESSARY, REQUEST
ADDITIONAL SURFACE ESCORT FOR ASCM OWN SHIP DEFENSE.

BT

He stopped typing, hunched over the screen. As if, he realized, trying to shield what he was writing from everyone around him. Up on the readouts, the ship's speed was already dropping.

He wasn't just saying *I don't think we can do the mission,* but also *Should we even have been committed?* If he'd sent it the day he took command, it would've looked bad enough. To send it now, when he was actually on station, would make him look . . . negative. Even craven.

No, they probably wouldn't think that. Not with his record.

And it was the truth. If anything, he was overestimating their capabilities.

But it wasn't the kind of message any commanding officer wanted his name on. His cursor hovered over the Send button. Then dropped to Save As and filed it as a draft once again.

Beside him Cheryl murmured, "Sir, sending the revisions to the steaming orders you asked for. Incorporating the lowered patrol speed discussed with the chief engineer. Warning and exclusion zone. No approach within two miles. Random course changes at least every twelve minutes. Doubled lookouts, with focus on threat bearings to landward. Anything more?"

"Sounds good." It was sobering that their first warning of a sea-skimming cruise missile might be a distant glint between the waves, observed by a sharp-eyed seaman with binoculars. But antiship missiles were designed for minuscule radar signatures. The types they were facing out here—the C-802s, the Bastions and Onyxes the Russians had supplied their Syrian client state, the sea-launched Styxes Syrian Komar boats carried—could target them from over the horizon, if their quarry had its radars on.

Which *Savo* definitely did. Electronically, they were standing out like a lighthouse, with the huge pulses of power they were putting out. And now, of course, they'd be poking along, with five to ten minutes' lag before they could come back up to full speed. "Which reminds me. Phalanx is in automatic?"

"Sea Whiz has been in auto mode since we arrived on station, Captain. I briefed you that yesterday. Like our chaff system and the rubber duckies. I'd like to do a program reload soon, though. We're overdue on that."

"Yeah, yeah, I remember now. Not just yet. Unless you think there's some kind of software corruption going on . . . No, wait a minute . . . it might be better to do it now rather than later. Yeah." He was starting to babble. Was she looking at him differently than usual? Was that a suspicious squint? He should just buckle the fuck down, and stop obsessing. Okay, slow deep breath. Another. On the display the spokes glittered. Faces hovered green-lit above screens.

Waiting.

Which was all he, too, could do now.

AT a little after 0900 Sonar came up on the 21MC. It was Rit Carpenter. *"Hey, Dan, you there?"* Staurulakis frowned. Dan had to remind himself the old submariner was a civilian now. He thumbed the worn Transmit lever. "Here, Rit. Whatcha got?"

"Voice call from Pittsburgh. *Reporting in. She holds us one-zero-zero at about six thousand yards. Want me to answer up?"*

"Got her on sonar?"

"Yeah, now. But we didn't, coming in. Our fucking tail is on the rag down here, and we're getting more self-noise since we slowed down."

Not good, that a nuke boat could get that close without being detected. But maybe it also meant its submariners were sharp enough to protect *Savo* from any undersea enemy. At the moment, though, he was more worried about air and missile attack. Which even the most modern sub was impotent against, save for its own invulnerability beneath the waves. "Yeah, Rit, roger her back. Ask if there's a chance the CO can crossdeck for a gam."

Carpenter clicked off. Staurulakis murmured, "You want him to come aboard? Is that really necessary?"

"Sometimes it's good to make personal contact."

"There's always a risk involved in boat ops. Especially in winter."

Dan regarded her. Quiet, short blond hair, always kempt, always competent. Her great-great-grandfather had served aboard a monitor during the Civil War. He'd never asked a question she hadn't had the answer to, usually to a depth well beyond what she needed to know as a department head. "Cheryl, I imagine you'll be a CO someday. So you have to learn you can't run a ship by this 'accept no unnecessary risk' doctrine. That mind-set comes out of DoD. Mainly, I guess, to cover their ass in case we screw up. I agree with part of it—think ahead, assess the hazards, plan to meet them, commit the resources, communicate. No-brainers, every good skipper does that. But just going to sea puts us at risk, and we're out here to fight. You can't be guided by fear."

She cocked her head. "I guess it's a balancing process."

"Balancing what you gain against what you put on the table. Sure. And in this case, doing boat ops—that's something I expect my crew to take in stride." He waited, but she didn't seem to have anything to add.

"*CO, Sonar.*" The 21MC again.

"Go, Rit."

"*Got* Pittsburgh *actual on the line. He says okay to a boat transfer, but he wants to stay at least a mile away. Oh, and he says he's picking up a set of high-speed screws out to the east of us we might want to keep an eye on.*"

Dan shook his head, recalling from the SATYRE exercises he'd conducted how terrified nuke skippers were of getting anywhere near what they called "skimmers." As if everyone on a gray ship's bridge was incompetent. "Tell him that's too far to send a boat in these conditions. I'll put my RHIB in the water and head west. He can move in from the east as we clear the area, and the boat will essentially stay in the middle. Clear that with him."

Carpenter rogered, and Dan called the bridge to get them ready.

PITTSBURGH surfaced well over a mile distant. Through his binoculars, he watched the black sail cut the slate sea like a hammerhead's fin, throwing white water to both sides. She was making about fifteen knots, ballasted down to minimize rolling in the five-foot swells. From atop the black blunt tower tiny figures studied him back.

It had rained during the night and the wing was still filmed with a sheen of dampness, and bright water slid back and forth beneath the gratings. Clanking and shouting from below; he swiveled in his chair to monitor the RHIB crew swinging out their gray burden. He could wish for calmer seas, but he'd told Cheryl the truth. Any destroyer crew worth its salt had to be ready to do small-boat ops, in case of a man overboard, a helo crash, or own-force protection in port.

The silvery swollen bulk of the rigid inflatable swayed as the ship rolled. Red-helmeted seamen staggered at the ends of steadying lines like handlers trying to manage an unruly elephant. A surge broke along the side and spray blasted up the hull-sheer and drenched them like rain. The rest of the crew mustered aft, at a Jacob's ladder. Dan set his glasses on each man, making sure his life preserver was properly fastened and secured to his safety line.

Amid hollering and gesticulating, the engines snarled and the boat dipped, yawed to a wild wave, slammed its stern into *Savo*'s steel, and sheered aft. Another shout, and the crew scrambled down. It curved away, gaining speed and jumping crests awkwardly like a baby dolphin as the crew crouched. Only the coxswain stood erect, boots rooted wide, leather gloves steady on the chromed wheel. The OOD put on hard left rudder and the cruiser's massive bow came around deliberately, pushed by the single screw on the line now, and accelerated away from the glow of the hidden sun.

Dan's Hydra beeped. "CO," he muttered.

Staurulakis. *"TAO here, sir. Got an E-band air search radar active on zero nine five. Out where you told us the sub reported high-speed screws. Okay to notify?"*

Dan rubbed a bristly chin. That was a military radar. So anything carrying it was *prima facie* a threat. Notify, query, and warn were the ascending levels of communication with an unknown. After that came defensive action, if the contact continued to close or demonstrated hostile intent. "Range?"

"He's out of the beam for the Aegis. I can get you a range, but we might have to put the gun radar on him."

"What's wrong with the surface search?"

"Offline for maintenance."

"I should've been told."

"Sorry, Captain. Was about to."

"Don't use the gun radar. Notify on Channel 16."

"On it, Captain. TAO out."

The RHIB shrank behind them. Dan watched it bob and reappear between corroded-looking waves. The black tower in the sea had altered course toward it. Gulls skimmed the wavetops, vanishing between the swells, then reappearing. Like sea-skimming missiles . . . What was Ammermann doing? He really ought to stop by and see the staffer. At least tell him there wasn't any answer yet to the offload request. It didn't cost anything to extend due courtesy.

Minutes later the OOD came out, clutching his cap against the cold gusts. "Skipper, contact at zero nine five, twenty thousand and closing . Designated Skunk Kilo. Looks like a constant bearing."

"EW has him too. He's still on a closing course?"

"According to the surface search, Captain."

"It's back up again?"

"Yes sir."

He hit the Hydra again. "Cheryl, CO. Did your E-band answer up to the notification?"

"Stand by . . . Sir, our surface search is back up. Also, yes, they replied. INS Lahav requests permission to close."

He dropped his bootsoles to the wet gratings with a thud. *Lahav* . . . memory supplied a Sa'ar-class corvette. U.S.-built, but Israeli flagged. Smaller than *Savo* but heavily armed, with guns and Harpoon. Actually, he remembered seeing them being built down in Pascagoula, their superstructures slab-angled to reduce radar signature. That might explain why she'd not popped up earlier; at twenty thousand yards she was already inside missile range. They'd actually detected her, or at least the sub had, farther away by sonar than by radar.

Which raised another question. Any ship with an electronic-warfare stack could detect the side-lobes of the invisible yet massive beam of microwave radiation those big octagonal panels above him were projecting over the horizon. Why had the other skipper approached on a bearing he had to know, or at least suspect, he wouldn't be readily detected on? Was that some sort of message? Or even, threat? Aloud Dan asked, "Permission to close us? Why?"

"No reason given."

"Says he's Israeli?"

"Consistent with the EW. Checks out against GCCS."

Dan rubbed his chin. The Israelis were normally happy to see a U.S. ship. They only shadowed what they weren't sure of. Something wasn't kosher. So to speak. "We should have known about this dude as soon as he cleared port."

"Yessir. Backchecking on that. Do we want to hold him outside five miles?"

He paused in the pilothouse, catching the Troll's eye again as he keyed the Hydra to answer. "Tell him . . . no, *request* him to halt at five miles. Make sure he's clear on who we are. Again: don't illuminate him. I'm on my way down." He didn't want to give offense, and so close to Israeli territorial waters, no wonder they were being checked out. But he didn't want to take any chances. *Unnecessary* chances, he reminded himself ironically.

The officer of the deck. "Captain, RHIB's picked up *Pittsburgh*'s CO. Sub is retiring; permission to reverse course."

"Affirmative. Go in and get 'em." He looked past the helmsman at the choppy sea, reflecting on how their course reversal would affect the five-mile radius he'd asked the corvette to stay outside. And what if he didn't respect the request? "Make it fast. I want that boat back aboard, and us to be ready to maneuver."

THE submarine commander more than filled the chair in Dan's in-port cabin. He looked Hispanic, or perhaps Indian; his name was

Youngblood, not noticeably non-Anglo, but not giving any clues to his ancestry. Dan checked the other man's left hand. No Academy ring. The large bruise beginning to darken the side of his face didn't seem to dampen Youngblood's spirits; he was practically bouncing in the chair. "That? Got it during the boat transfer. Slipped on the curve of the hull."

"Been there, done that," Dan said, remembering boarding another sub in the Korea Strait. The only time, actually, he'd sailed under a flag of truce. "Glad you weren't badly hurt, Jack. We could get some ice for that—"

Youngblood grinned and waved the offer away. "Picked up a hard roll, that's all. Hey, I think we got a friend in common. Andy Mangum? Had *San Francisco*, out in Westpac, couple years back?"

"Yeah. Yeah, I know Andy. What's he doing now?"

"He had DevRon Five, after *San Fran;* now he's the chief of staff at ComSubPac. Ran into him at a technology conference in Bangor. He told me some . . . sea stories. About you and the North Koreans." Youngblood winked broadly, then chuckled, as if he knew Dan couldn't comment. "Course, I didn't believe a word. Anyway, this is my formal inchop, right? Or do I need a message, too?"

"No message necessary. I'll just include that you checked in, in my daily report."

A tap at the door. "Come in," Dan called.

Ammermann was in khaki slacks, running shoes, and a dark green silk polo. He blinked and gave Dan a tentative half-salute. Dan cleared his throat. "Jack, this is Adam Ammermann. We're not really sure how long he'll be staying, but he's a sort of public affairs staffer out of the West Wing. Adam, Jack Youngblood, USS *Pittsburgh*. Uh, a nuclear submarine. She'll be in company with us over the next few days. I thought we'd have lunch, the three of us, and get acquainted."

The big submariner and Ammermann shook hands, and they moved to the large table, which Longley had set for three. Not with the formal silver service, which was reserved for VIP or diplomatic guests, but regular wardroom china. It was Chinese day, with pork lo mein, somewhat crooked spring rolls, and steamed rice. Dan glanced again at the other CO's profile, hoping he wouldn't take the menu as some kind of insult . . . no, shit, he was getting paranoid again. "So . . . looks like we're going to have a war on our hands in the next couple of days."

"Never good." Youngblood shook his head. "I think we're ready. But let's hope they can find some other way."

"The president gave them forty-eight hours to leave," Ammermann said. "Him and his sons."

Youngblood frowned. "And why exactly are we doing this now?"

Ammermann smiled, laying a finger on the submariner's arm; Youngblood stiffened. "We have absolute proof they have chemical and biological weapons, maybe even a nuclear device. You don't wait around to be attacked. That was our mistake on 9/11. They've lied and threatened us long enough. We can bring democracy to Iraq, same as we brought it to Germany and Italy and Japan and Russia."

Dan applied himself to the lo mein while it was still hot and let them argue, but he couldn't help remembering what Freya Stark had written about Rome wanting only weak states on her periphery. The Romans had followed a policy of crushing any bordering state that seemed likely to become powerful. But when she'd destroyed these prospective buffers, far more dangerous barbarians, pushing through the chaos and debris, had eventually brought down the empire.

When Ammermann ran out of steam Dan put in, "Not to change the subject, but—Jack; that Israeli corvette, to the east. He's parked five miles out, where we asked him to respect our safety zone. Any idea what's on his mind?"

Youngblood chewed for a moment. The broad head cocked. "Maybe he's wondering the same about us."

"Adam, what do you think? The Israelis must know what we're doing here. Wouldn't somebody from the West Wing, or State, have notified them? Officially, or . . . ?"

"I can make a call and find out. If you'll give me a secure hookup."

"That'd be awkward. I've put my entire crew, and myself, on personal comm restrictions." That wasn't why he didn't want this guy on the horn, but he wasn't about to say, "I don't want you reporting back on me."

"He actually might be here to protect you," said the submariner.

"Yeah, I wondered about that." *Lahav* might be his missing "shotgun" . . . his escort when *Savo Island* was so focused on her mission she couldn't defend herself. It might make sense. The administration was wooing Arab states to join the Coalition of the Willing. Few had, but at least they weren't joining the other side. In that case, keeping any U.S.-Israeli military cooperation covert would be smart. "But I can't even talk to their ABM side, to deconflict. That doesn't sound like cooperation."

A beep. Dan said, "Excuse me," and unholstered his Hydra. Turned away from the table. "Captain."

"Cheryl here, sir. INS Lahav is calling CO-to-CO on uncovered voice."

He swallowed one more forkful of lo mein and wiped his lips with a napkin. "Gotta take this. It's from *Lahav.*" To Staurulakis he said, "Be right there. No—on second thought, I'll take it on the bridge. But stay on the circuit taking notes. And see if you can get Radio to record it. Just in case."

THE voice was clear, hard, accented but perfectly enunciated. *"Good afternoon, Captain. This is Captain Gabi Marom of INS* Lahav. *I am recording this conversation. Over."*

Dan peered out. The corvette was barely visible, a dark speck on a ragged horizon shrouded in overcast. A plume of white spray leaped up as *Savo*'s bullnose burrowed into a steely sea. It wavered across the forecastle and forward gun, and clattered down against the window. Damn, blowing harder already, and they were picking up a nasty roll. "Good afternoon. Dan Lenson, CO, USS *Savo Island.* We're taping on this end too. What can I do for you this fine day at sea, Captain?"

"This is Lahav. *I am respecting your eight-kilometer safety zone. At the same time, you are within the hundred-kilometer exclusion zone my country has declared. I must ask you to declare your intentions and how soon you intend to return to international waters. Over."*

Dan trapped the handset between shoulder and chin as he hunted around on the nav console to zoom out. "Captain, I hold us well outside your country's twenty-mile Maritime Exclusion Zone. And also outside your twelve-nautical-mile coastal zone. Therefore, we are both in international waters. Suggest you check your navigation. Over."

"Captain, you are speaking of the standard MEZ. I am referring to the special security zone Israel announced one week ago. Over."

Okay, great . . . He made sure his finger was off the Transmit button and keyed the Hydra with his free hand as *Savo* reeled. He twisted to wedge himself in next to the nav console. This put his thigh against the bridge's heater element, but it wasn't quite hot enough, through the fabric of his coveralls, to burn. "Cheryl, any input?"

"The official position: We don't recognize any claim to limit innocent passage beyond twelve miles. Including unilaterally declared exclusion zones, like Libya and China keep trying to impose."

"So the question is, are we on innocent passage?"

"No sir. The question actually is whether you're going to let him bluff us out of where our orders clearly place us."

Well, that was pretty clear-cut. He double-clicked her off and told the Israeli, *"Lahav*, this is *Savo Island.* I say again, we are in international waters and exercising right of innocent passage. Please respect our safety zone while conducting military operations. Out."

"This is Lahav. *Interrogative: What type of military operations are you conducting? And what is their termination date? Over."*

Dan frowned. He couldn't blame them for being hinky about foreign ships off their coast. But had no one told the Israelis he was shielding them from hostile missiles? Or was that information stovepiped somewhere in the political-military bureaucracy, and just hadn't trickled down to their navy yet? He started to answer, then socketed the phone. Let the other guy buck his beef up his own chain of command, until it hit the bona fide skinny coming down.

At the same time, he couldn't just pretend a missile-armed warship with an inquisitive—no, actually somewhat hostile-sounding—commanding officer wasn't within striking range. Off the Sinai, inside a declared security zone during the Six-Day War, USS *Liberty* had been attacked and badly damaged by Israeli jets and torpedo boats. If the State of Israel felt threatened, *Savo* had better look to her defenses. He lifted the portable radio again, then changed his mind and used the 21MC. He wasn't sure how far outside the skin of the ship someone could eavesdrop on Hydra transmissions. "TAO, CO: Fifteen seconds' illumination of INS *Lahav* with SPQ-9."

"Shine her with the gun radar?"

"Affirmative."

A minute later she was back on the intercom. *"Bridge, TAO: Incoming threat emitter, I-band radar, bearing one one five."*

He squinted along the gyrocompass repeater, just to confirm it was *Lahav*, beaming back the same challenge he'd just aimed at her. The corvette lay under a gray storm-cloud, menacing, holding her distance, neither closing nor opening. "*Threat emitter ceased, time five one,*" Staurulakis added.

He checked his watch. "Very well. I'm going to need a message—"

"*Already up on high-side chat with CTF 61 TAO. Keeping them informed in real time, sir.*"

"Good. Real good, Cheryl. Let's double up on our EW watch, one on three sixty, one on this guy—"

"*Manning up Console Two now.*"

"Okay, Cher. Good work." He signed off, almost resenting the calm rational voice that was always a step ahead. Looked out to the distant speck once more. Beyond it lay a land embattled, and beyond that, one about to be invaded. Somehow he had to share intel with the Israelis. Or at least get their watchdog off his back. But how? If only he had a genie aboard. He'd wish *Savo Island* and her crew far from here. No, he'd wish war itself and the eternal suspicion between nations, classes, and those of different hues of skin, over and done, existing only in a past of myth and legend. Something you read about in the history books, like the centuries-long duel between the Romans and the Parthians . . .

"Captain?" Almarshadi's thin, nervous features were shadowed like a foretaste of dusk. "Boat crew's wondering, it's really looking like it's going to kick up, they're not sure they can stay out much longer. Got a call from the XO on *Pittsburgh*, too. What's the plan? When's Captain Youngblood heading back?"

"Call the whaleboat in, Fahad. We'll call him away before it blows any harder. I'll come down to see him off." He turned away, gripping the overhead cable as *Savo* leaned into a roll that seemed to have no end.

But war wasn't going to end. Not as long as men were men, and contended each against the other on a steadily eroding sphere compounded of the dust of the dead. Wish all he liked. There'd still be violence. Still be war. Most relentless of the Four Horsemen. And doubly bitter because Man, along with the ants, was a species that inflicted its greatest plague on itself.

11

THE rest of the day passed swiftly. He checked in again with Staurulakis, asking how she'd set up the watch rotation. The forty-eight-hour deadline would expire tomorrow; he wanted them ready for whatever happened. The senior watch officer said she was running an overlapping rotation. It was tight; the admiral's mast, on top of *Savo*'s already reduced manning, had cut deep into their bench. She and Mills would be standing five hours on, five hours off. Either Dan or Almarshadi would be on call, again five and five, though they wouldn't actually have to be in their seat in CIC. They had a bit more slack on the bridge, with three qualified officers of the deck: Pardee, Garfinkle-Henriques, and the comm officer, Dave Branscombe. She said Gene Mytsalo was doing well as JOOD and might be able to step up to OOD soon. "But I think we can keep them going up there for quite a while, four on and eight off."

Next he went down to the engine spaces, undogging and then re-dogging each door and hatch as he passed through, observing the damage-control drills.

Almarshadi secured everyone from general quarters at 1400. The wind had increased to twenty knots, twenty-five in gusts. It stayed dark as hell all afternoon. *Savo* rolled, top-heavy like her sisters, but she could take six- to seven-foot waves forever. He ate evening meal in the wardroom, not contributing much to the conversation. He could feel himself starting to sag. Better sleep while he could.

Instead, he went back up to the bridge and stared at the running lights of the Israeli corvette, still soldered to the northeastern horizon. He contemplated the radio handset. Perhaps he should call Marom, ask him to increase the standoff distance, at least during the hours of darkness. Finally he decided, to hell with him. As night fell he went back down to his at-sea cabin. He stripped off sweat-smelling coveralls and stuffed them into his laundry bag. He picked up Freya Stark; read a page or two about Diocletian's increasing recruitment of mercenaries for the defensive armies, rather than Roman citizens; and turned off the light. Sleep? Yeah, maybe . . .

THE fucking buzzer. No, the call note on his Hydra. He fumbled getting it out of the recharging base and it hit the deck. The leather case must have damped the impact, because it was still working when he hit the Reply button. "C'm," he grunted. Then cleared his throat and said again, louder, "Captain!"

"Sir, maybe you better get up here." Mytsalo, voice high and young, frightened as a child's.

Dan dropped the radio, found his shoes, and sprinted out the door. But the left turn, or rather, the roll *Savo* had just plunged into, betrayed him, and he caromed full tilt off the opposite bulkhead. He groped for the ladder up in the dim red light, shoulder aching, cursing.

Utter darkness, pierced by the whine of the wind. He blundered into a soft short shape and heard a sharp intake of breath, a gasped-out, "Captain's on the bridge."

"Where's the OOD? What's the problem?"

Another shadow, and Garfinkle-Henriques's voice. "Off to starboard, Captain. Constant bearing, decreasing range. I reported it to Combat—"

He couldn't help a sharp intake of breath, at the icy wind on his underwear-clad skin, but much more at the closeness of the green and white and red lights. The other ship was nearly bow on. He couldn't say how far because he didn't know how large it was. But far *too* fucking close. He caught the distant wink of the corvette's stern light. If that was five miles, this ship was only a few hundred yards off. Hell, he could *hear* it; the steady whoosh of machinery and ventilators even through the whine of the wind. What *was* this thing? It was *enormous*.

The supply officer, beside him. He could just make her out, binoculars clutched to her chest. "We're stand-on vessel. I notified the XO, sir. He said maintain course, he'd warn it off on VHF—"

"Did they answer? You've got Channel 16 up here, right?"

"I didn't hear an answer. No sir."

"Where's your rudder? Never mind. Right hard, *right hard*. All back full!" He gripped the pelorus, staring over it at approaching disaster. On second glance, it was much bigger than *Savo*. Which might not be bad; it might be slightly farther away than he'd thought. But it was hard to be certain. Spray or rain laced the night, making the port running light a carmine smear, the starboard a turquoise glow. The centerline white lights were blurry opals in a deep black velvet night. Was the uppermost very slightly to the right of the lower? A port bow aspect? It all felt so much like his nightmares he had to reach out and grind his knuckles into the gritty steel of the bulwark. No, fuck, it was real. Were the lights sliding left? Or was that the effect of their own rudder, hard over to the right? He couldn't tell, but couldn't wait to see. He turned back into the pilothouse and yelled, "Sound the collision alarm."

"Lee helm control's not responding."

Oh, Christ. "You don't have engine control up here! Remember? Call Main Control. All back full! All back emergency!"

Dit dit dit. Dit dit dit. The triple blips of the collision alarm stuttered over the 1MC. He glanced left, then ran back out onto the bridge.

To his astonished relief, the gap between the white lights had widened. The green starboard light was occulted; the port one shone out clear. But the ship was so close that even in the dark he could make out its silhouette, black against blacker black, in the same way the unlit circle of a new moon was visible against night sky. Pearly aureoles around sulfur-orange lights tapered back in a long line, fading along its . . . upper deck? In the dark, the obscuring mist, it was hard to tell exactly what he was looking at. Some sort of tanker, oil or natural gas. Or maybe a really huge bulk carrier.

"Main Control responds, all back emergency," the OOD said,

edging onto the wing with him. Still gripping her glasses. "They never answered on VHF."

He took a deep breath to keep his voice from shaking. "All right, rudder amidships. Secure from collision alert. —You should have called me before this, Hermelinda."

"I notified the XO. He said you were asleep. That he had the duty."

She was right; in Condition III, whoever was in the CO's seat in Combat was the go-to guy. But what had happened, that Fahad would let a contact get in this close? "O . . . kay. I'll take it up with him, then."

"Do you want me to ask for a relief, sir?"

"No. You have the deck. You never turned it over, I never assumed it." He stared out the forward windows at the lights, already shrinking into the distance, and shivered; it had been all too fucking much like the last seconds of the doomed *Reynolds Ryan*. He wrapped his arms around himself, tightening his jaw to keep his teeth from chattering. No wonder, he was still in shorts and undershirt. "Wait till he's clear, then resume course. I'm going down to Combat."

HE stopped for his coveralls, steadily growing angrier. That ship should never have gotten within miles. If she didn't respond to a verbal warning, there were other ways of getting her attention. If all else failed, *Savo* should have turned away, long before the situation became dangerous, and opened the range herself.

Maybe there was a reason Imerson had kept Almarshadi off the bridge.

When he got to CIC the exec was sitting at the command desk, fingers laced over his face, thin shoulders hunched. Matt Mills glanced up from the TAO chair; Singhe watched from where she stood behind the Aegis watchstanders, dark eyes hooded. The compartment was crowded with men and women at consoles, but no one said a word. Dan slowed himself down by checking the screens. Only an occasional contact incandesced here and there, sparse stars where typically constellations boiled around the ports of the Levant. The contact they'd just missed was outbound, headed west. He took another deep breath, cleared his throat, and said to the hunched shoulders, "XO? Can you step out in the passageway for a minute?"

Almarshadi stood without a word, and followed Dan past the silent watchstanders.

Out into the passageway. Dimly lit. Not with red, because it didn't open directly to the weather decks, but with half the fluorescents off. The ship creaked around them, and Dan braced an arm to an equipment enclosure as she rolled. When the door thunked shut he said, restraining himself with an effort, "What just happened, Fahad? Because what it looked like to me is, my XO's a point of failure. And right now, I can't afford any points of failure."

"I guess I . . . I misread where he was going." The XO wouldn't meet his gaze.

"What was initial detection range?"

"We've only got the surface search radar. It came up at fifteen thousand yards." Almarshadi hesitated. "Actually a little before that . . . an intermittent contact . . . but we thought it was sea state. Peaking waves."

"Sea state? That thing was enormous. Forty, fifty thousand tons. And you'd pick up its radar on EW—"

"There was no EW detection," the XO stated. His voice got a bit stronger. "His radar was off. Or broken. Anyway, he wasn't radiating. And, Captain—he changed course on us."

"Meaning?"

Still not meeting his eyes, the slight officer explained that although the other ship hadn't answered their radioed warning, it *had* come right slightly. "It stayed on that course for about three minutes. That started to open the CPA on the VMS, so we thought it'd pass clear. The CIC officer thought so. And I concurred. But then it—it swung back. By the time we noticed it was closing again, it was inside two miles."

Dan rubbed his forehead. The Vessel Management System was the digital replacement for the old grease-pencil-on-the-radar-screen method for figuring out if an approaching ship was dangerous. It computed closest points of approach, course, and speed, and displayed ships' predicted tracks. It also recorded video, so it would be easy to go back and replay the near collision.

But he didn't feel like doing that. He doubted Almarshadi was lying. It was something even more dangerous. "Okay, but when it was inside those two miles, why didn't you call me? The first I heard was when the OOD buzzed me. By the time I got to the bridge, we were *in extremis*. We're talking lives, Fahad. If that thing had hit us, we might well have gone down."

"I was about to go up, Captain, and take the conn. I was on the ladder when I saw you bolt out of your stateroom. So I came back down."

Dan looked away. He wanted to have confidence in people, but when it came to keeping the ship safe . . . tolerate substandard performance, and it would become the new standard.

On the other hand, he couldn't be awake and alert twenty-four hours a day. And Almarshadi had done fine coming through the crowded, chaotic Strait of Messina, in Dan's experience one of the tensest passages on the planet.

He blew out. "I'm honestly not sure what to do about this, Fahad. Is something like this why Captain Imerson didn't allow you on his bridge?"

"No sir."

He waited, but the guy didn't elaborate. "Right now, I'm pretty angry. Right this second, I'd rather have Cheryl Staurulakis as my stand-in than you."

Almarshadi nodded but, again, said nothing, his gaze aimed somewhere in the area of Dan's belt buckle. Despite himself, he glanced down to see if his fly was open. It wasn't.

Savo rolled and plunged around them. Metal protested, yielding and rebounding against the strain. In the closed space, the dim light, Dan felt nauseated. He took a deep breath. "But I need you. I need every man, and woman, right now. Mission accomplishment, Fahad. 'Hard blows.' I'm going to give you one more chance. But also, a warning. If this happens again, you won't be standing any more watches aboard *Savo*. And I'll put you ashore at the first opportunity."

". . . happen again," Almarshadi murmured.

"What's that?"

"It won't."

"Once again. So I can hear you."

"I said, *it won't happen again!*" the man blazed out suddenly.

His head snapped up, and his cheeks flushed. His fists rose too. Dan would have stepped back, but there wasn't any room in a passageway so crammed with equipment enclosures that two men going in different directions would've had to slide past each other sideways.

But there it was, a reaction, at last. Did you have to insult him, to rouse his pride? It wasn't how Dan liked to operate, but if that was the only way to get the son of a bitch on the stick, fine. He'd press any buttons he had to, to get his XO up on step. But it was time to back it off a notch. He gripped the smaller man's arm, extended a hand. "Fahad . . . I can't do this alone. The consequences . . . I've seen what happens at sea when somebody looks the other way. That's not going to happen on my watch."

The thin shoulders straightened; the chin came up. Deep brown eyes met his at last, and Almarshadi returned the handshake. "I understand, Skipper."

"Okay then. Review those new ROEs. Let me know how they bounce against the theater Conops in the morning."

"Aye aye, sir."

Dan eyed him a moment longer, then nodded curtly and turned away toward the ladder.

Climbing it, he hoped he wasn't making a mistake. If his exec was a failure node, they were in trouble. But a Zero Defects Navy wasn't his Navy. Daniel V. Lenson had looked less than stellar now and then himself.

He did need to control his temper, though. Did he really have what it took to be a good CO? He'd thought so, once. Now he wasn't sure.

Not for the first time, he closed his eyes and silently asked for help.

BACK in his cabin, he couldn't get back to sleep. But he didn't want to go down to CIC, or up to the bridge. That would signal distrust. Plus, he was probably getting some rest just lying here, even though his brain seemed to be on some kind of naturally secreted speed. He kept replaying those looming lights like a preview of coming attractions.

If he did fall asleep, he knew exactly what he'd dream, and what he'd hear. The screaming in the dark, from when the first ship he'd ever served on had gone down in the Irish Sea.

He picked up the Freya Stark book again, found where he'd bent down a page, and read a few more paragraphs. About the Parthian Empire. How Rome had tried again and again to outflank and break it, and finally succeeded. But the ship rolled again, and he clutched the bunk frame until his fingers cramped. This high in the super-structure, you really felt the motion.

Enough. He got up and shaved, wedged into the narrow space in front of the sink, shoulders braced. Rinsed his mouth, shook out a fresh set of coveralls, and pinned on the eagles and rather tarnished surface line insignia and name tag. And last, the circled dull-gold star of command at sea. He pressed it gently into the blue cloth, feeling like the Cowardly Lion again.

He peered into the mirror once more. Not looking so alert your-self there, Lenson. Red-rimmed eyes. Those crow's-feet were getting deeper. And was that more gray on the sides?

He remembered what he'd called his skippers. Not to their faces, but what everyone else had called them too.

Now he was the Old Man.

THE mess decks were bustling. He slid his tray along the stainless rails, grabbed French toast with greasy aluminum tongs and added a sloppy spoonful of eggs. When he zigzagged out into the dining area DC3 Benyamin stood. He pointed to his table and Dan wobbled over. "Gonna get rougher, I hear, Skipper," he said as Dan climbed into the bench seat. The other men and women shoved over, making room.

"Yeah, we could be in for a blow." Dan blinked at the damage con-trolman's scarred pale arms. Wondering what his tattoos had been, and why he'd had them lasered out.

"Sir, hear anything back yet about Smack? What happened to him?"

"I'm sorry—Smack?"

A silence, broken only by the roar of engines from the big screen up front. Dan glanced that way; Pierce Brosnan was piloting a hovercraft in a chase scene. The men at the front tables stared at the screen, hardly eating. "That was Seaman Goodroe, sir," another man supplied. "You know, the guy who—"

"Right, right. Sorry, the chief corpsman wasn't able to make a determination. As to cause of death. And we haven't heard anything back yet from Bethesda."

An acned young woman said softly, "Somebody said it might be those anthrax shots they gave us."

"I don't think so, but I haven't totally ruled it out as a possibility."

"You'd let us know if there was ... like ... a plague aboard," a palely mustached young sailor said hesitantly.

"You've been watching too many movies," Dan told him, trying to sound kind but firm. "But for the record, yeah, I *would* tell you. But there's no plague. No curse, either." He grinned, sorry he'd even repeated the words. "Look, we've been pushing you guys pretty hard. But you know why now. Right?"

They nodded, more or less together. "So you realize, we could very well take a hit out here? Our radar's focused inland. Somebody could kick us in the ass and we wouldn't see him coming. So we need to be ready to fight fires and flooding. That's why Mr. Danenhower and the DCA, Mr. Jiminiz, and Chief McMottie are working your tails to the bone right now. Is that the word you're getting? I want to make sure everybody knows *why* we've got our balls ... our hair on fire about this."

On the screen Halle Berry undulated out of the ocean in an orange-and-white bikini. The sailors hooted and hammered the deck with their boots.

"I think we get the picture, sir," Benyamin said. "You're takin' us into harm's way, like they say in *The Bluejacket's Manual*. And we gotta be ready to take a licking and keep on ticking."

Dan looked at the sobered young faces, most sleep-deprived, bleary-eyed. Some still acned with youth. Some with hair too long, or buzz-cut violently short. Black and white and brown and Asian. "I know it's a lot of work, a lot of stress, but this is what we're out here for," he told them. "What the country expects of us. And any problems your chief or div-O can't help you with, my door's open. I mean . . . right now, I couldn't give you an uninterrupted hour, but I'm there if you need me. Okay?"

"Hoo-ah, Skipper."

"Yes sir."

When he turned his tray in the same kid took it who'd been there the first time. "What, you got permanent crank duty?" Dan asked him. But the kid just squinted at him, scraping the remains off into a garbage pail, as if he had no idea who Dan was.

THEY patrolled through seven- to eight-foot seas black as gangrened flesh. Long, deep seas, along the troughs of which he could look for hundreds of yards. Squalls spattered on the windscreen. The wipers whipped the raindrops away. Everyone on the bridge was in heavy sweaters or bulky green foul-weather jackets. Around noon the lead helo pilot, "Strafer" Wilker, came up to give him his cap, which Dan had apparently left on the mess decks, and to brief him on whether they were going to be able to operate. Dan watched him sway to the roll in his flight suit, palms clamped over elbows, and wondered why pilots were so different from surface officers. Perhaps their DNA was the same, but that was about all. "So, why 'Strafer'?" Dan couldn't help asking.

"Oh, I happened to come in a little too low once, on a pass over a reviewing stand."

Dan raised an eyebrow. "I see. Well, we might need you in an anti-ship role."

Wilker looked out toward the corvette. *Savo* was plodding south, so the distant dot winked on and off out on their port beam. "We got Hellfires. Like, you mean, this guy? Or is he a friendly?"

"Him? I think he's more of a . . . well, I don't really know yet." Dan explained his argument with the Israeli. "My impression is, he's waiting for orders. The main threat I'm looking at is antiship missiles from shore. But we might see small boats, a leaker." He massaged his eyes. "Even a Syrian patrol boat."

"Coffee, Captain?" The boatswain, Nuckols, stone-faced, with the stainless-steel ovoid of the bridge pot.

"Yeah, top me up. —Main thing that worries me is a trawler. Like what happened to *Horn*."

"Not sure I recall that, sir. Heard something about it, but—"

"A dirty bomb in a trawler. It looked like a plain old fishing boat.

But it wasn't." He blinked and swallowed, looking out to sea. Hell, was that a swirl of snow? No, just spray. The bridge heaters clanked and popped, but he still shivered. Having a helo patrolling out there with infrared vision, a laser designator, .50 cals and five-mile-standoff missiles, even if the warheads weren't quite big enough to take out a ship, would definitely make him sleep better. "How close are we getting to your wind limits?"

Strafer broke out a blue plastic-backed NATOPs manual from a cargo pocket and went over the diagrams. The limiting factor was pitch and roll. *Savo* had the RAST sled, a car that ran on rails on the flight deck. It was designed to winch the helo down out of the sky if they had to land in heavy seas. Dan had seen it get very white-knuckled at times. "I know this isn't the best weather we could have. But I've got to launch you," he told the pilot.

Strafer shrugged. "I'll tell you if I think it's not safe. But you're the guy who bottom line says go or no go. If it's an operational necessity."

"Well, I definitely want your input on that. Ideally, I'd like two missions per twenty-four-hour cycle. One starting an hour before dawn. The other, at dusk. That's when we'll be most vulnerable. Fly a circle, but with the wider radius to shoreward. The rest of the time, maintain as close to a five-minute standby as you can get."

"When we launch. Armed? Hellfire?"

"Absolutely. Hellfire, EW, and FLIR. But stay data-linked. And I retain positive control. Weapons are tight unless specifically released. Unless you're attacked, of course—that's in your rules of engagement."

"How long? Our endurance is four hours."

"If you can do two four-hour patrols a day, that'd be great. But I won't hold you to that. Two hours at dawn, two at dusk would make me happy. Don't push so hard you degrade. Clear?"

Wilker nodded and left. Dan mused for a while, then crooked a finger at the OOD. "Hermelinda?"

"Yes sir." She came over, still clutching her binoculars to her chest.

"I was down on the mess decks this morning, and I saw the same kid scraping trays in the scullery as last time I was there. That duty gets rotated, right?"

"I'm not sure who you mean, sir."

"I mean, make sure your crank duty gets rotated, okay? Don't let the divisions send you the same bodies over and over. Some of 'em'll do that if you don't stir the pot."

He settled back into the padded seat, and the next thing he knew, he didn't know anything at all.

HE woke with a snort and a flinch, realizing he'd been snoring. He cleared his throat and swung down, catching sidelong glances from the bridge team. Not sharp, Dan. A skipper was human, he needed to sleep, but it didn't help to do it in front of the crew. "Captain's off the bridge," he heard as the door closed, and waited, listening for chuckles, or any comment loud enough to hear.

But neither came, and he stopped at his cabin and shaved, then nosed himself and decided he could use a quick washup, too. A Navy shower: a quart to wet down, the shower turned off; lather up thoroughly; one last quart to rinse off. He threw his coveralls back on and rattled down the ladder to Combat. He was pulling up the SH-60B Tactical Manual on the LAN for a quick review when his Hydra beeped. He snatched it, heart instantly accelerating. "Skipper." Beside him Mills glanced over from the TAO position.

"Sir, this is Sid Tausengelt. Where are you right now?"

"In CIC."

"Be there in five."

"What've you got, Master Chief?"

"Better in person, Captain."

What fresh hell? He checked the vertical displays. Air and surface traffic had vanished east of Cyprus. Even the regularly scheduled commercial airlines had cancelled or diverted. The shadow of war lay across the Mideast. He checked the stats on Aegis. The system was at 87 percent. Not great, but not quite mission-compromising, either.

Tausengelt's seamed visage appeared, lit from below, back by Sonar. He peered around the darkened space uncertainly, then felt his way forward. Dan wondered if the older man was losing dark adaptation. Then he oriented, homed in, lifted his chin, and Dan saw that Chief Van Gogh was behind him. Zotcher as well. The sonar chief was in an ivory plastic neck brace. He glowered at Dan.

"Captain," the command master chief muttered, "you real busy?"

Dan wanted nothing less than to go into this, but nodded and got up. But Tausengelt motioned him back down and sidled past. He said a few words to Amy Singhe, who was perched on a stool in the Aegis area. Dark eyebrows knitted; she looked past him at Dan; her face darkened. She nodded abruptly, and stood.

"What is all this, Master Chief?"

The ship's senior enlisted said, "Can we talk out in the passageway, sir? And I wanted the lieutenant there too. 'Cause, basically, it's mostly about her."

"Have you taken this up with Commander Staurulakis, Master Chief? She's the department head. And the XO?"

"Sir, with all due respect, I think this is becoming a CO-level matter," Tausengelt said with great dignity. The others, behind him, nodded.

DAN told Mills where he'd be, and followed the command master chief and the others to an equipment room. A petty officer was hunched over a pulled-out rack with a tester. Tausengelt asked him gravely if he'd give them a few minutes. Wide-eyed, he slotted the computer blade back into place and left. Singhe stood with arms folded, glaring with such dark intensity that she seemed to be radiating in the far infrared. The three chiefs ranged themselves opposite her. "What's this little kangaroo court?" she said harshly, before anyone else could speak. "Should I have representation?"

"I'm not sure, Lieutenant. Master Chief, what's this about?"

"You said your door's open, Captain. Basically we—that is, some of the chiefs—have a grievance. I'm hoping we can defuse it before it escalates to the official level." Tausengelt eyed Singhe. "Which would not look good for any of us. As I'm sure the lieutenant will agree, if she takes a moment to think it over."

She started to speak; Dan held up a hand to silence her. "Let's hear what the senior enlisted have to say first, Lieutenant. You'll get to respond."

Tausengelt said, "Well, basically, sir, we've all been excluded from the discussion groups the lieutenant here's been running. The chat rooms. I believe I informed you about that."

"You did. Yes."

"And you said we should run with it and see where it went. But today Chief Van Gogh here logged on under the name of one of his petty officers."

"He lied to get into the chat room?" Singhe said, voluptuous upper lip curling.

"The petty officer gave me his password voluntarily," Van Gogh said, his anger just as apparent. "He wasn't comfortable with what was being said on there. And when I saw it, I wasn't very fucking comfortable either."

"What exactly was being said?" Dan asked.

Zotcher held out a printout. Dan ran his gaze down it, noting the exchanges highlighted in yellow. He pursed his lips. The foregrounded quotes seemed to be pretty much the kinds of summary and largely unfavorable judgments sailors had probably always made to each other around the scuttlebutt about their immediate bosses. Anatomically questionable references were made to the location of their heads vis-à-vis their anal canals, for example. But it did feel different seeing it in print. In particular, Zotcher and Van Gogh were coming in for a lot of criticism. At one point, where Singhe, leading a discussion on management styles, had asked the crew members to rate the chiefs in order of effectiveness, they'd tied for last place.

He cleared his throat. "Uh—interesting. All right . . . Lieutenant? Your response?"

Singhe cupped her elbows in both hands. "My response? The military's got to follow the path private businesses are blazing, as computerization and the importance of human capital increase. That means a less hierarchical, more direct interchange between the deckplates and upper management. I'm acting to facilitate the transition. You read my article, Captain! Our command structures are too slow, too cumbersome, and they stop us from adapting. Open and uninhibited discussion is essential to that process." She scowled at the chiefs. "Which is exactly why I excluded these men. Having them in the loop would make frank interchange impossible. As you can see."

Tausengelt shook his head. "Basically, nobody wants to escalate this. Like I said. But I'm sort of coming in on the middle. I understand the previous CO more or less tolerated this sort of thing. The lieutenant's . . . hobby." Singhe bristled and he amended, "I mean, *research*. But Captain Lenson may have a different point of view."

At that moment a sharp, loud crack reverberated through the metal around them. Dan flinched. He couldn't pin the sound down, but it hadn't been a noise he liked to hear a ship make in a seaway. He lifted a palm and they all fell silent, but it didn't come again. He thumbed his Hydra. "DC Central, skipper here. I just heard a cracking noise, below and just aft of CIC. . . . Uh-huh . . . Yeah, pretty loud . . . Right. Let me know what you find out."

He holstered the radio, both wondering what it had been and grateful for the moment it had given him. "Well, to get back to what we were discussing. My 'point of view' isn't really what's relevant here."

Singhe's angry frown was focused on him now. He chose his words carefully. "I think both sides have valid points. But what really matters here is what Navy regs say. Encouraging discussion— that's a good thing. But, Lieutenant, I do think—and I know this wasn't your intent—but encouraging this kind of speech, especially the personal remarks, can be prejudicial to good order and discipline. A lot of it reads like the loudmouths you get on every ship, blowing off steam just because you've given them a forum. Isn't it possible to let the chiefs monitor the discussions? Or even participate? You'd get more informed opinions then."

Singhe planted her boots farther apart. They all swayed together, as the passageway funhouse-leaned around them. "Then what's the point, sir? The whole idea's to surface issues that aren't being discussed, or *can't* be discussed, in the current forums. We have one group just for female crew. You might be interested, Captain, in what goes on. What they have to put up with, when the khaki's not around."

Dan couldn't help his eyebrows lifting. "Are you telling me there's—what? If there's any harassment, hazing, criminal activity, I want that reported immediately. Not walled off in some special chat room."

"Criminal activity? Maybe. Maybe not," Singhe flashed back, as much to the chiefs as to him. "But let's get this straight. You're backing them? Instead of me?"

"Let's not make this a personal issue, Lieutenant. It's a question of command philosophy and discipline. We all have to work together, officers, chiefs, and enlisted. Not create splits in the crew."

Singhe's face had gone mottled, blood suffusing her smooth cheeks. "*Personal?* Who's getting personal here, Captain? Maybe you should be asking them who Molly is. Instead of accusing *me* of undermining discipline." She said the last word as if it left a poisonous taste.

Dan looked from her to Van Gogh, who'd paled. "Molly?" Dan asked. "Who *is* that? Chief?"

"Nobody."

"Molly's nobody?"

"Right. There isn't any such person."

Singhe shook her head sadly. "Isn't that the point?"

Dan looked from face to face. Then, abruptly, lost his patience. "Okay, what kind of game is this? We're on TBMD station. A war's about to start. Who the fuck's Molly, and what's Lieutenant Singhe hinting around about?"

"Yeah," said Tausengelt, and the steel in his voice this time was for his fellow chiefs. "Who is it? Come on. Give."

Zotcher and Van Gogh glanced at each other, deflating inside their coveralls. The sonar chief jangled keys in his pocket, avoiding Dan's eyes. Van Gogh was examining the overhead as if inspecting a diamond for inclusions.

"I get a straight answer, right now," Dan said, and despite his resolve to stay cool he couldn't keep his volume down. "Or everybody here's going to regret it."

Zotcher looked at his boots, or tried to; the neck brace brought him up short. Despite the seriousness of the situation, and what looked like embarrassment, he also seemed to be stifling a laugh.

"All right," he said. "I'll take you down to meet her."

DAN called Almarshadi and asked him to take the chair in CIC, then followed the party down and aft. Aft and forward, then down again, until they were far below the main deck level and had to wriggle

through scuttles feetfirst. Finally he pushed open a door inscribed
SONARMEN DO IT AURALLY. The space was so far forward in the stem
that its bulkheads slanted inward. He'd poked his head in here during his initial inspection, but now faces turned, more men than one
would expect in such a remote space. Guilty, startled faces. And all
male.

Rit Carpenter rolled his chair forward and reached for a computer keyboard. Dan's hand intercepted his wrist. "Rit. I should've
guessed."

"Guessed what? Hey, Dan. Good to see you down here with us
peons. And who's this? The beauteous Lieutenant Singhe? Oh, *yeah*."
The retired submariner had established his own nook, with a black-
and-white photo of his beloved *Cavalla* taped above it and his copies
of *Hustler* and a shot of him with a fourteen-year-old Korean girl,
both players naked from the waist up. Dan remembered that girl, and
her little friend Carpenter had sicced on him, and how narrowly all
of them had evaded a military prison.

And again: Carpenter nearly getting them whacked after a sharia
court in the Philippines, when he'd gotten caught banging the wife
of one of the imam's best friends.

Same old Rit. Never overly concerned with political correctness,
or even halfway decent taste. Pretty much a caricature of what the
typical U.S. Navy sailor had once been stereotyped as, but which,
since Tailhook at least, was supposed to no longer exist. Dan had
thought it would be safe having him aboard, to help with the manning shortfall. But apparently Carpenter had managed to get on
Singhe's bad side. Dan gripped the expostulating sonarman's hand
and examined the screen. At the ladder, a seaman tried to maneuver
past a glowering Amarpeet Singhe. Her raised arm blocked the exit,
and he shrank back.

"So, boss, come down about that self-noise figure? We got the
whole stack dried out. Purged it with nitrogen and a hot plate. Learned
that trick on *Skate*. I got the numbers here someplace—"

"Who's Molly, Rit? Are you screwing around with one of the female enlisted? I'm only gonna ask once. So how about a straight
answer?".

"Molly?" Carpenter reared back in the chair, which protested alarmingly. "What, you wanna meet her? Can do, amigo." He turned the monitor toward Dan, chuckling.

"Fuck," Dan breathed. He touched the keyboard gingerly. It felt sticky. He hoped it was from the empty Pepsi cans heaped in the wastebasket. "What . . . where the hell did this come from?"

Carpenter shrugged. "Brought it along for shits 'n' grins. The boys need a little R&R, and they ain't getting any shore time."

The game was called Gang Bang Molly. Cycling through three scenes told him all he needed to know. Dead silence reigned in the confined space, except for the whoosh of passing seas and the never-ending, very loud creaking of the sonar, like an iron wheel slowly revolving inside a too-tight, never-oiled socket.

"Just harmless fun," Carpenter suggested, but sweat glistened at his hairline.

Dan took a deep breath. "This is about the most unprofessional thing I've ever seen. I know you're retired, Rit. But we have standards of conduct. Which you must have at least heard about."

Carpenter grinned, lopsided, the same little-boy-caught-and-unjustly-persecuted half-smile he'd offered before. "Hey—boss man—tell me you ain't taking this seriously."

"I take anything that contributes to poor crew morale and a hostile command climate seriously." He snapped his fingers. "The disk."

"The what?"

"The disk. The game disk."

"Hey, there's no *disk*. This puppy's on the LAN. Brought it aboard on a thumb drive. You can have that if you want, but—" Carpenter began making a show of slapping his pockets, looking around his pookah.

An audible intake of breath from Singhe. Dan closed his eyes. On the LAN? Being played all over the ship? He asked Tausengelt, "You knew about this, Master Chief?"

"No sir. I didn't." The leading enlisted looked as angry as Dan felt. "Well—I *did* hear a rumor. But I had no idea it was—basically, I agree, this is beyond the—this is not what people should be putting on the ship's network."

"Track it down. Pull it. And I want a list of everyone who's downloaded it." He snapped his fingers again and Carpenter reluctantly yielded up a small black memory stick. Dan buttoned it into a pocket.

"I'm confiscating this. Delete it from the LAN. And get me that list of names," he repeated, and headed for the ladder up.

TOPSIDE, main deck. With Singhe standing silent beside him, he held the drive out between thumb and forefinger over the braided sea. A cloud trailed silver skirts miles off, but for the moment, though the decks glistened with rolling laminations of condensed spray, it wasn't raining. "Thanks for bringing this to my attention," he told her. "How long did you know?"

"One of the girls e-mailed me this morning." She stood erect by the lifeline, hands locked behind her in a textbook parade rest, looking out to where a distant silhouette melted into the squall. When she turned her head, those remorseless dark eyes set in that goddesslike face met his. "Are you saying you didn't know? Sir?"

"Of course not! No."

"Carpenter's one of yours. You brought him aboard. You didn't know he'd do something like this?"

Dan had to look away. Because the uncomfortable truth was, the guy *did* have a history. He'd never expected this . . . but on the other hand, he wasn't exactly surprised, either.

She added, "The truth is, sir, the chiefs on this ship—okay, some, not all—but the majority are more of a barrier between the enlisted and the officers than a link. They don't want change. They obstruct and stonewall organizational innovation. That's the kind of middle management an effective CEO gets rid of. Or at the very least, isolates and bypasses until he can downsize them."

"Uh, that's a pretty damn harsh indictment, Amy," Dan said. "I'm not sure I can totally buy into that. It takes a little while for everyone to get with any new program, and the Navy's not exactly out front in managerial reform. I'm sure most of the chiefs are doing the best they can."

"Really." She put her hand on his sleeve. "Then how do you explain obscene games like that? And not even played privately, but on the ship's network? I'm glad you saw it. Now you know what they've been trying to do to me. And to the other women aboard. They failed with the board of inquiry. But they haven't quit."

To her? To the other women? The grounding board? Somehow

she thought this was all aimed at her. Dan looked down at her hand, the tapered graceful fingers, and suddenly felt like shaking them off, as he would some poisonous centipede. The brown eyes burned into his, trusting, demanding, but with something else behind them.

He wasn't attracted. Quite the opposite. But some instinct warned him not to reveal that. So he smiled back, held the little plastic device out farther, and let it drop. The wind caught the drive as it fell, curving its path. Then it vanished into the heaving sea, leaving a widening ripple that only slowly moved aft, visible for a long time, before *Savo* finally left it behind.

12

War Day

DAN was napping in his chair in Combat when the message came in. He woke to Cher Staurulakis shaking his arm. "Captain. Captain!"

"Yeah!"

"The Air Force is hitting downtown Baghdad."

His first instinct was to check his watch. 0440 local, Bravo time, one hour earlier than it was over what was now, officially, an enemy capital.

The warning order had come down several hours before. They'd gone to darken ship and full battle readiness. Everyone on the bridge was in flash gear, with goggles handy. Here in CIC, gas masks, life preservers, and helmets were stacked in neat piles or slung from consoles. He ran his eye over displays and status readouts. The starboard bow array wasn't operating as well as it should. The chillwater flow was still a problem.

Other than that, and the slow engine response due to their artificially low patrolling speed, *Savo* was as ready as he could make her. Right now they were on a southeasterly course, which pointed the port quarter array out along the main threat bearing, but they were nearing the southern limits of their area. He'd have to turn north again in another hour or so, or lose geometry on the acquisition basket.

He'd come to visualize this as a circle hovering sixty miles above and slightly north of Amman. *Ezekiel saw that wheel, way up in the middle of the air.* . . . Donnie and Mills were down trying to improve the numbers on the other array. If they couldn't get it above 80 percent, he'd have to head west rather than north. Which would gradually open the range, and thus reduce their probability of kill.

Stuck to them like a tick, the bright pip of *Lahav* rode five miles off. During the night the Israeli corvette had repositioned to the north. Staurulakis had interpreted that positively. "He's clearing our downrange bearing. Letting us do what we're here for," she'd murmured, typing rapidly. She was monitoring the chat from the U.S. and British ships that had slammed open the doors of Iraq's defenses with salvos of Tomahawks from the Gulf and the Red Sea. "There won't be a long air campaign before the land assault this time. The Army and Marines are already crossing the Kuwaiti border."

"They'll burn the oil fields again," Dan said. Remembering the stench of burning hydrocarbons that had hung over that land, like smoke over Mordor, during the last war.

"Maybe not, if we can take them down fast enough. SpecOps are mounting an amphibious assault on Basra. It's going to hang on what happens when the Army hits the Republican Guard."

"Good luck to 'em," Dan said. When it came to war, the football-field enmity, always half a joke anyway, vanished, and the services rolled as one.

Terranova came out of the darkness holding a thermos and a plate. "Coffee, Captain? And they sent us up some cinnamon buns. Special, for the tracking team."

"Nice. Thanks, Beth." He took two; his mirror had been telling him he could afford some empty calories. He winced as the fresh charge of java burned his tongue. The buns were drizzled with crystallizing frosting; he wolfed one and half the second. Sucking the sticky sweetness off his fingers, he repositioned his keyboard and switched from one camera to the next. Damn, it was dark out there. Even in the infrared. He cranked up the magnification and searched the horizon, then guiltily switched it off. The gunners on the ROC consoles on the bridge were scanning, backed up by the CIWS watch team. He needed to stay up at angels one hundred. Keep his mind clear, his head on the main mission.

ALIS—the acronym dated from the LEAP Intercept program, but specifically, now, meant only the software patch in Aegis that drove the TBMD programming—was up. On the right-hand display, the spokes clicked back and forth with metronomic regularity. They'd turned off everything from 0 to 0.5 degrees elevation and put all the system resources into above-horizon search. He stretched his arms until tendons cracked. "Okay, where are we, Cher?"

"A reminder on the high side to watch for indications of missiles being fueled. Any intel will be forwarded to us Flash precedence, but we'll probably hear it over chat first. Increased threats from enemy leadership—"

"Double-check on that." So if the satellite chat went down, they'd lose time on getting the warning order. He had to talk to Branscombe, make sure their cybersecurity was up and they had backup receivers standing by on the satellite downlink. If they couldn't get alerts fast, *Savo* was nothing but a fat target out here.

"Correct. Weapons posture to TBMD—check." She tapped the keyboard, and dawn came up on the middle screen. Seen through the camera from the port 25mm, the horizon seesawed, rising and falling, since the gun's gyros were in standby. A gradually brightening patch, far off, a cast-iron sky over a sooty sea.

Dan squinted. Leaned into it. "What's that?" Tiny specks dotted on the screen, seemingly on the lens itself.

Staurulakis murmured, "Snow."

"Crap," he muttered. They really didn't need the blizzard that Fleet Weather had said for days was coming down from Europe. He didn't mind degraded visibility. If a small boat or an explosive-laden trawler was out here trying to find them, reduced viz would be a plus. But heavy snow could degrade the tightly focused SPY-1 beam, searching like the flaming Eye of Sauron far out over Palestine and Jordan and the Iraqi desert. Searching for that ascending spark that meant missile.

From that first instant, assuming they picked it up as it cleared the radar horizon, he'd have roughly fourteen seconds to lock, track, evaluate, and launch. They might get a few seconds more if the Obsidian Glint, far overhead, caught the heat plume from the booster. But he wasn't confident about the handoff from the Defense Support Program satellites. No one had tested the cuing procedure, and he wasn't getting actual video, just text from the ground station. The

Army had space-based imagery in real time, but the Space and Missile Defense Command Operations Center hadn't responded to Dan's request that *Savo* be placed on distribution too. Not that he had the intel capability to interpret photos, but access would be nice. AWACS, orbiting over Saudi Arabia, might also pick up the ascending weapon.

But all in all, his response time was disappearingly meager.

A cough, a sniffle from over by the Aegis area. When he looked that way Noblos was wiping his prominent schnoz, bent over, staring blearily at the screen. "Doctor." Dan raised his voice. "Bill!"

Noblos looked his way. "How you feeling?" Dan called.

"Recovering. I believe."

"Good."

"I wish I could say the same for your system."

Dan motioned to a seat. Noblos pulled it out and settled. He coughed and muttered, "I was out, but not idle. I read up on what type of warheads we might be intercepting."

"Scud-type missiles. Right?"

"Those would be our most likely targets. True. But did you read the DIA report?"

"Which one? I read one that said they believed Saddam had both bulk chemical and biological weapons." What he didn't add was that the report had referenced the report of the Signal Mirror team—which, by the way, he'd written—to indicate the possibility of weaponized biological submunitions. Lower on the list, but not ruled out, was the possibility of what the report called a "baseline fission weapon," defined as a fifteen-kiloton, single-warhead design.

Blinking at the GCCS screen, Noblos muttered, "Here's what I wonder. Why make Tel Aviv the target? They only have a few missiles. We're scouring the desert, blowing away any we find. But why not use them against the Coalition forces? The amphib landings at Basra? That'd be a more rewarding target set."

"The Army will be shielding those," Dan said. "They've got THAAD and Patriot. We're holding the back door while the Army and Marines are going in the front."

"The point I'm making is, we keep assuming they're using countervalue targeting. What if they start with counterforce?"

"Countervalue" was strategic shorthand for striking enemy population centers and political targets. "Counterforce" meant targeting the enemy's armed forces, particularly his strategic missiles, command, control, and air defenses. Dan frowned. "You mean—what? The task force? They're out of range of a Scud. Even with that uprated booster they're supposed to have developed. The, uh, the Al-Husayn."

"Right." Noblos coughed, covering his mouth. "But *we're* not."

Dan leaned back, nodding as he tumbled to where the scientist was going. "You're saying, the first couple could be aimed at us? Well . . . maybe. But nothing I've seen argues they've achieved that level of accuracy. We're a damn small bull's-eye. And we're not moving that fast, but we *are* moving."

"We can be tracked from shore," Noblos pointed out. "In fact, the EW chief told me we *are* being tracked—by that coastal radar in Tartus."

Dan massaged his throat. He'd expected radar surveillance from Syria. After all, they were only about thirty miles off the coast at the north end of their patrol area. But what Noblos was suggesting was more ominous. "You're saying they might pass cuing to Iraq."

"Exactly. We share data with our Coalition allies. Why can't Syria share with Iraq? They have landline connections. They're both Ba'athist regimes. All they'd need is GPS coordinates and some kind of terminal homing on the missile. If they can take us out, along with Israel's own BMD capability, Tel Aviv's defenseless. At that point Saddam says, Yeah, I'm dirty, I *do* have WMDs—and I've got seven million Israelis as hostages."

Dan slumped in his seat as he thought it through. The Syrians were supposed to hate Saddam. But did they hate him more than they loathed Americans and Israelis? Probably not. The modified Scud-Bs the Iraqis had employed in the Gulf War had been notoriously inaccurate. But since then, according to the informed speculation he was reading, both range and throw weight had been upgraded. Why not accuracy?

He shivered in his chair, but it had nothing to do with the airconditioning. Actually, they didn't even need terrific accuracy, in the old sense that the ballistic missileers had inherited from the artillery community. All they'd have to do was bolt on a radar-homing antiaircraft missile—like the ones the French and Soviets had sold them—as the upper stage. Dial in *Savo*'s track, relayed from the Syrian coastal radar—and fire. *Savo Island* would light up the path for her own attacker; Aegis was putting out so much energy, a homing warhead could fly right down the beam.

Unfortunately, there was no way to tell, until it was well into endoatmospheric phase, where a ballistic missile was aimed. And with the malfunctioning of her space tracking system, to calibrate against satellites of known altitude and speed, *Savo*'s track precision was itself in question.

"Doc, what about SCUS? It's still degraded. The Block 4 warhead guides itself in terminal phase. But to predict point of impact, we've got to have track precision."

"Correct. You can't predict POI without SCUS."

Noblos sounded so unconcerned, so lofty, Dan had to turn away and run his hands through his hair. He made himself turn back. "Well, maybe it's better if we *are* the target. At least we'll be decoying the missile away from population centers."

Noblos shrugged. Looked over Dan's head. Sniffled, and wiped his nose again. "Was there anything else?"

Dan sighed. "Guess not." He shook his head at the scientist's ramrod posture as he stalked away. Fucking . . . *great*. He just hoped they had some warning before the first missile lifted off its portable erector-launcher. And that their hastily upgraded Standards worked. A warhead coming in at them, at the velocities they were talking about, would be well beyond the intercept capabilities of anything else the Navy carried.

Someone cleared his throat behind him. The corpsman, Grissett, was holding a clipboard. "Yeah, Chief?"

"Sir, you asked me to let you know if we saw any more respiratory illness. I've got a sick-call case with mild fever and a good deal of congestion. One of the helo crew."

Not without an effort, Dan extracted his head from ballistics and radar. "Uh, right. We're seeing a lot of that, seems like. Flu? Like what Doc Noblos had?"

"No sir. This looks like just a bad cold. He says he probably picked it up on the carrier. That makes sense. On a long deployment, whenever you have liberty the troops tend to bring back these minor upper-respiratory infections. On a small ship, they burn out quick.

On something the size of a carrier, they can pass it around for quite a while. I'm keeping an eye on him."

"Actually . . . is there any way we can isolate him until he's not infectious? We're so shorthanded up here, even passing a cold around could degrade readiness."

The corpsman shrugged and said he could check him into sick bay, but it was probably already too late; the mechanic had been walking the passageways for two days now. "But you asked me to report."

"Right, I did. Thanks, Doc." Dan checked his watch, suddenly conscious the cinnamon buns had worn off. 0700. "Cher, I'm going down to breakfast. I'll leave my Hydra on."

SAVO plowed on through the morning, bucking seven-foot seas and the occasional snow flurry. Dan told Almarshadi to scrub all training and relax berthing restrictions. If people weren't on watch, he wanted them to catch up on sleep or maintenance. He'd love to get his own head down, but that didn't seem to be in the cards. Highside chat said both Lebanon and Syria had filed protests about *Savo Island*'s presence so close to their coasts. Dan filed that for reference, but not without wondering why Lebanon was even bothering to get its stick in.

At 1000 Branscombe called to ask if he wanted a CNN feed to the mess decks. After a few seconds' consideration, Dan said no, at least not for the moment. He wanted everyone's head on his or her own job, not on what was going on to the east. There, the Army was punching hard into southern Iraq. The Air Force was laying down ordnance across the country, hitting command and control, trying to decapitate the regime.

How would "decapitation," if they could pull it off, affect his mission? If the Iraqi command structure got turned into shredded meat in a bunker, what were the enemy's rocket forces' standing orders? Stand down? Acquiesce in occupation? Or unleash a last spasm of destruction? The last sounded a lot more likely.

He'd just socketed the J-phone when Almarshadi undogged the bridge door, shaking snow off his foul-weather jacket. A few flakes blew in with him. Dan returned his salute gravely. The XO sighed, glanced at the OOD, and sidled close. At some unseen signal the rest of the bridge team drifted to the starboard side, giving them privacy, as long as they kept their voices low.

Which his second in command did. "Sir, we've scrubbed down the LAN. That . . . program . . . is no longer available on it. And we made sure there's no backup. At least on the ship's network."

"There's no backup on the LAN? What if the downlink goes . . . wait a minute. You're talking about that fucking rape game."

"Yessir. Sorry, I wasn't clear."

"My bad, my head was on something else I have to talk to Dave B. about. If you see him, send him up. So, you don't think I was overreacting? There seemed to be a lot of resentment among the female crew."

"No sir, that was probably the right call. Considering . . . I guess, considering how ready everybody seems to be to jump on anything like that these days." He pulled paper from inside his jacket. "Here's the list you wanted. Everyone who accessed or downloaded it. The game kept a players list, so you could see how your, um . . . scores . . . compared with the others. That's the number to the right of the name. Where it says 'player,' 'thug,' 'hustla,' 'gangsta,' 'baller,' that's your ranking."

Dan didn't want to know how you got points in a game called Gang Bang Molly. He almost said just shred it, but at last accepted it. The list wasn't as long as he'd feared. Maybe a dozen names, and all junior enlisted. No chiefs. One first-class petty officer. Carpenter, of course, was the high scorer. Benyamin was number two. He grunted. "Okay. What do we do with this?"

"Do you want to take disciplinary action, sir?"

"Of course we do, XO. I don't give a shit about swimsuit posters in the work spaces, the women can put up beefcake too. But a rape game's over the line. Tell me if you disagree."

"No sir, I think you're right."

"At the same time, I don't want it to be a career breaker. I know things have changed since I had *Horn*—"

"Yes sir. They have. The guys call a captain's mast a 'delayed admin discharge.' One conviction at mast, they can deny your reenlistment."

"Well, I don't want that. Can you do XO's mast? What exactly are the regs now?"

"I can do XOI, yessir. The maximum award is twenty hours of extra military instruction."

The newest euphemism for punishment detail. "What kind of EMI?"

"Typically mess duty, or extra cleaning."

Dan said, "I don't want to be too much of a stickler here, Fahad, but I'm recalling extra military instruction can't be punitive, it has to be actual training."

"Yessir. That's OPNAV Instruction 3120. It has to be bona fide training to improve unit efficiency, not a substitute for punitive action under the UCMJ."

No question, the days when a captain could lash a recalcitrant to a grating and let the cat out of the bag were long gone. "So we can't punish them without mast, but if we do take them to mast, they won't be able to reenlist?"

"About the size of it, Captain."

They went back and forth about this for a while, Dan actually enjoying the angels-on-the-head-of-a-pin debate on Navy regs and how to best skate around or in between them. It was more pleasant than thinking about what occupied most of his plate. Finally they got it boiled down to an agreement. Almarshadi made a note, then glanced around, as if making sure the others on the bridge were still out of earshot. "However, this brings up another issue. A personal one, sir."

"Go ahead."

"I would like to be relieved."

Dan tried to mask his surprise with a squint out the window. Through a gauze of snow the Israeli corvette seemed, through some queer fluke of the waning light, closer than ever. In the U.S. Navy, officers didn't ask to be relieved. It was theoretically possible, but he couldn't remember ever hearing of such a thing. "Uh, Fahad, what exactly are you telling me here? Relieved as what?"

"As exec. I do not feel, any longer, I am performing to your satisfaction." When the Arab inclined his head with a dignified courtesy Dan caught the beginnings of a bald patch under a careful comb-over.

"You said I am the . . . point of failure in our system. I don't want that responsibility. Therefore, I would like to be released . . . I mean, relieved."

"This is a surprise. I don't really know how to respond."

"I am being accurate? That I am not fulfilling your expectations?"

"Hey now. I admit I was ticked off the other night. About the near miss. And I chewed your butt. But that doesn't mean I wanted to fire you. Believe me, if I did, you'd have been on that helo to the task force, the one we sent back with Goodroe." He glanced away, then back, trying to read the closed stubborn face. Remembering the anger and pride he'd seen a flash of, there in the passageway, when he'd used that phrase. *Point of failure.* Obviously it had sunk deep into this man's soul.

He had to try harder to remember how powerful a CO's words could be. But couldn't the guy take a reaming and keep on steaming? Any XO, by design, had a stressful job: to demand more than anyone could offer, and keep the standards of performance, cleanliness, and professionalism in the stratosphere.

In other words, he was almost guaranteed to be unanimously hated by everyone beneath him. Dan smiled as he recalled the joke about it, about why the insignia for lieutenant commanders and commanders was an oak leaf. The punch line was "So the pope gave the order to cover all the pricks with leaves." Dan had been there, executive officer aboard USS *Turner Van Zandt*, in the Gulf, under Benjamin Shaker, for Operation Earnest Will. It was a hard role. Was Fahad Almarshadi just not going to fill the bill?

"Fahad—surely you've gotten chewed out before. The idea's to take direction, reorient, and keep charging." The head remained stubbornly lowered; the dark gaze didn't rise. Past him the helmsman and JOOD were watching curiously. They looked away quickly.

Or was something else going on here? "Wait a minute. This wouldn't be about Iraq, would it?"

That called forth a furrow down Almarshadi's brow. "Iraq?"

"It's not that, then. For a minute, I wondered—never mind."

"You wondered that since I was Arab, I would be on their side?"

"I didn't say that, Fahad."

"Now you insult me. First I am a point of failure. You would rather have Cheryl as your XO. Now I am disloyal, not to be trusted."

Jesus. The guy had remembered every word he'd said, then made up some he hadn't. "Cool the fuck down, XO. And lower your voice." Dan swung out of his chair. "We'd better take this to my cabin."

"No sir. I think we have said what we both needed to say."

Almarshadi started to turn away, but Dan caught his shoulder and none too gently jibed him back around. "I'm not done talking, XO. You'll stand there and listen. And look me in the eye when I'm speaking to you."

"Yes sir." The murmur was submissive, but the dark eyes were blazing now, as they had been once before.

"You need to start paying less attention to what I say to you, especially when I'm not getting enough sleep, and more attention to your job. The only thing I see wrong here is that you lack self-confidence. But do you think you're the only one who feels that way?" No answer. "Do you?"

"I do not know."

His gaze had dropped again, but Dan saw he'd hit some kind of nucleus. Maybe not hard enough for fission, but the angry flame seemed to be turning down to simmer. He started to lower his voice, then looked past the small man and instead raised it, so the others in the pilothouse could hear. "XO, sorry for losing my temper last night. Hear me?"

"I hear you, sir."

"I have every confidence in you. Do you hear me?"

"Yes sir. I hear you."

He lowered his voice again. "And something else. If you don't think you're up to the job? Neither do I."

"Yes, you made that very—"

"No. I mean I don't feel, deep inside, that I'm up to mine either."

Almarshadi's eyes widened. They came up and locked with his.

"That's right," Dan said, still keeping it low, between them, his grip on the guy's shoulder digging to thin bone beneath the slight musculature. "I feel like I'm going to fail and give way. Like I'm making it up as I go along. And I'm never sure I'm doing the right thing."

"But . . . you are the captain," the little man whispered. "You have the . . . you have the Medal of Honor. You mean you do not . . ."

"No," Dan said. They stood there face-to-face for a second, then another. Then he added, turning on just a little anger again, "So get used to it, and grow the hell up. We're at war. Do your duty. Get us ready to fight. Press on. Then you'll do everything I expect of you, and you'll be a leader, Fahad."

He opened his hand, releasing his grip. The little man held his gaze, still looking as if he did not quite believe, but in that moment unguarded as Dan had not seen him before. He nodded, once, then again. Stepped back, and turned away, catching himself with an outstretched arm as *Savo* rolled.

He vanished down the ladderway, leaving Dan, soaked with sweat and feeling as if he'd run many miles, listening to the hissing whisper of the snow.

HE was back in Combat when GCCS and high-side chat came up more or less at the same time. He narrowed his eyes at the screens, then called up the DIA classified site and looked up the ship.

A premonitory—no, a *remembered*—chill trailed cold fingers up his spine.

A Vosper Mark V frigate. Fourteen hundred tons. And heavily armed, including Chinese-supplied antiship missiles.

He knew this ship. Had sweated under its prosecution before, scraping the keel of a stolen submarine across the shallow sands of the eastern Gulf. Had fired his last and only weapon at its consort as it charged in to destroy him. It had connected, but the sister frigate, this one, had swung in next. Only an unexpected intervention had saved him.

Now INS *Alborz* was exiting As-Suwys—the mouth of the Suez Canal—accompanied by a second combatant and a supply ship. A small Iranian task force, according to the intel summary. Heading in his direction?

"A hundred and forty miles," Matt Mills murmured from the TAO chair. Damn, Dan thought, am I getting that transparent? Or was it good that he and his TAOs were thinking along parallel lines? He sucked the inside of a cheek, replaying bad memories about that area of the Egyptian coast. That was where he'd patrolled with *Moosbrugger* and *Horn*, and intercepted the battered trawler that had turned out to be carrying something the West had dreaded for years.

He sighed, and reached for the phone.

Ammermann answered on the first ring. Dan asked him if he could come to CIC. While he was waiting, he researched the rest of the task force. The second combatant was a Sina-class missile boat, built to a French design in Iran. It too carried antiship missiles. The third must have been a support or logistics ship, or even civilian general cargo. His references didn't list it, though the intel report gave a name. "Make sure the EW team has the specs on their emitters," he told Mills.

The West Wing staffer looked around, as if impressed, when he let himself in. But the guy surely was used to large-screen displays if he'd ever been in the Situation Room. Dan motioned him over. "Matt, give Adam your seat for a little while. Take a pee break, or whatever. I'll watch your screen."

"Yes sir. Remember, Weps is starting morning systems-operability tests. You might see the 'missile ready' numbers going up and down as they take them off the line."

"Okay, thanks. —Adam, sorry, we've sort of neglected you."

"That's perfectly okay, Dan. I know things must be getting tense for you."

Was that a dig? He couldn't read this guy. He acted sincere, open, but what political animal, from either party, didn't have layer beneath layer, motivation beneath motivation? Maybe this one just had a better poker face, but his smooth, wide, roughly shaven visage looked guileless and eager to please. Dan noted a simple yellow-gold ring with a deeply embossed crest he couldn't see well enough in the subdued light to identify. He tapped it. "Harvard?"

"Yale."

"Like the president."

Ammermann looked humble. "Oh, sure. But years later, of course."

"You know, Adam, I keep feeling like I should recognize your name. Why is that?"

"The heavy-equipment manufacturers. My family."

"Oh yeah, sure. Close to the administration?"

"We've been supporters, over the years. What did you need me for, Captain? Some way I can help?"

Dan explained the tight quarters of the launch box; the window they had to hit; the Israeli, still guard-dogging them to the northeast. "He's staying clear of our firing bearing, which is good. But I'm not entirely sure what he's doing out here."

"I could try to find out," Ammermann said earnestly. "Go right from our office to the ambassador. I believe that's possible."

Dan thought it over. He had his own contact with the Israelis, although he wasn't sure of the man's name: the smooth little diplomat, or spy, who'd surreptitiously slipped him the Israeli Medal of Courage at a party at the vice president's house. Back when he'd worked in the West Wing himself.

How ironic that he was now trying to safeguard the same city for the second time. "Well, that's not actually what's bothering me at the moment."

"What's eating you, Dan? Fuel consumption?"

A flicker on the status board caught his eye; a missile had gone offline. Daily testing, right. Where had Ammermann heard about their fuel state? "Yeah, that, and other things, but what I'm wondering about is this Iranian, uh, task force, I guess, that's entering the Med. They've never done that before, operated up here, and I'm not clear on what might be the motivation. We're taking on Iraq—their enemy—the Iranians, I mean. Sort of like the Romans took out the . . . well, never mind that. Any ideas on what they might have in mind?"

Ammermann made a strange side-to-side motion of the head, almost, Dan thought, a gesture he'd seen Indians make. A snakelike weave that conveyed something, but he wasn't sure what. "You think they've got their eye on *Savo*? Or on you?"

"Call me paranoid. We'll know more in a few hours, when we get a reading on their track. But it isn't that far from Suez to here."

"I could speculate, but it wouldn't be more than that."

"Okay. What would you speculate?"

The younger man shrugged. "Even if we're taking on one of their enemies, we're still an enemy too. Probably a more hated one, given the history—our support of the shah, the hostage drama, et cetera, et cetera. So if we've made a commitment to defend one of our allies—Israel—and we can't follow through for some reason, we take a pie in the face. How they could do that, how they might interfere—that's more in your area of expertise, Captain. The alternative might be, they're just showing the flag. They do seem eager to assert themselves, since Zhang's been backing them. Especially anywhere we show up first."

Dan tapped his teeth with a thumbnail. Just the mention of Zhang Zurong brought back bad memories. When they'd first met, at a restaurant near the Gallery Place Metro stop, "Uncle Xinhu" had been a colonel. Ostensibly a defense attaché, he'd actually been a member of the Second Department of the People's Liberation Army, supervising a massive program of technology theft. Dan remembered him as a middle-aged businessman in a dark suit, wearing metal-on-plastic Yuri Andropov glasses. Many years later, he'd suddenly emerged from the deliberate obscurity of the Chinese Politburo as minister of state security. And now, years after that, as the premier, with a new policy: testing and, when possible, displacing U.S. power.

To some extent, it was inevitable; as the U.S. fleet drew down, as the American presence became less imposing, rising powers would be tempted to help push them out. Maybe the Iranians *were* just showing the flag. But as CO of a task force himself, even if only of *Savo Island* and *Pittsburgh*, he was bound to put the most threatening construction on any new player in the east Med.

He glanced up as Ammermann was lighting a cigarette. Dan plucked it from his fingers before the flame from the Zippo could touch its tip. "Not in CIC."

"Sorry . . . wasn't thinking. What d'you want me to do?"

Past him Mills was balancing a fresh cup of coffee, listening. Dan nodded to him. "Matt, anything to add?"

"If Mr. Ammermann can find out what's behind this, it could help."

"Okay, Adam, I'm going to give you a covered line. Work your magic."

"I can't promise anything, Captain."

"Just do what you can. If there's any way we can persuade these guys to turn around and go home, or even just tie up someplace until this thing's over, it could deconflict the situation. Especially with Captain Marom on a hair trigger over there."

"Captain who?" Ammermann asked.

"Skipper of that Israeli corvette. That complicates it too—my chain of command."

"Sorry, I don't understand."

"I mean, Iraq's a CentCom responsibility, but Israel's always been a EuCom country. And my opcon, and tacom, as CTG 161 is to Sixth Fleet, which is under EuCom. But I'm supporting a CentCom mission—Infinite Freedom."

The staffer frowned. Dan got up and stretched. Something cracked in his neck, like a pretzel stick breaking, and he flinched. "Like I said—it's complicated. But don't worry about that." Ammermann rose too, and extended a hand. Dan shook it. "I'll have Dave Branscombe get in touch. He's the comm officer. He'll set you up. It'll be a secure circuit, but I don't have to warn you not to pass anything classified you don't absolutely have to."

"Do you still want me recalled? Sent back?"

"Well . . . I just don't think this is a good use of your expertise and influence, Adam."

Ammermann grinned, as if recognizing a clumsy attempt at disguising rejection. "I see why they still tell stories about you in the West Wing, Captain. You're not going to make it in politics."

"I'll take that as a compliment."

"Though I understand your wife's thinking about a run. She's a brave gal. After all that. The injuries. Don't quote me on this, but good luck to her . . . even if she's on the wrong side."

Dan shrugged. He didn't want to talk about Blair with this guy. For a second he missed her, terribly. He had to look away and take a deep breath. Even just talking to her would help. But he couldn't cut off phone comms for the crew, then make personal calls himself. He was starting to say thanks, already tapping the keyboard to go back to the high-side chat, when the 1MC chanted, *"Fire, fire, fire. Class Charlie fire in Aft VLS. Repair Five provide. I say again—"*

Not *again* was his first conscious thought. Not *now*. He was on his way out, headed for the bridge, before the word came over again,

but doubled back in the doorway, almost knocking down a petty officer. The man backed into the bulkhead, looking alarmed. Dan
crossed CIC at a run, barking his shin on the corner of a terminal,
and went out the other way, grabbing his Hydra, which he'd socketed into a recharge holder, en route.

13

T HE CCS space, which used to be called Damage Control Central and often still was, lay one deck below the mess area. It was already standing room only when he got there. Bart Danenhower was there, along with the top snipe, Chief McMottie, and the damage-control officer, Jiminiz. They and the damage-control technicians were so preoccupied they almost didn't make way for him. But he had no problem with that. They were the ones who were going to have to fight this thing.

A fire in the vertical launching system was a whole other beast than one in the Aegis power supply room. The difference was many tons of high-energy solid fuel and explosive warheads. The aft system held sixty-one missiles, each with its booster, standing vertically in a sealed canister, eight missiles grouped four in a row in a module. The modules were two decks high, separated by shoulder-width metal catwalks.

Standing there, Dan tried to organize his thoughts, but it all felt increasingly fuzzy. Too much. Too fast. The module was normally unmanned. "There's no one in there?" he said, just to get that clear.

Jiminiz shook his head without looking around. "No sir. We've cleared everyone out aft of here. Except for the damage-control teams."

"No possibility these missiles are going to launch?"

Danenhower said, "No sir. Combat shut down launch control. Those orders come in via a remote enable panel and a status panel."

Dan was clear on that. Once the fire order came through, the LCUs selected a ready bird and began the prelaunch commands. Part of that algorithm was opening the deck hatch assembly at the top of the selected cells, out on *Savo*'s main deck. This not only let the missile emerge, but exhausted combustion gases through a separate plenum that vented vertically through one uptake hatch for each cell. "Okay, but I read a class advisory on magazine authorization. It said something about being able to remove mag launch authorization, but the launcher still being able to fire."

"You'd have to ask the missile supervisor that. Sorry."

A picture came up on one of the monitors: the passageway outside the module. The heavy steel red-and-white entrance door was clearly visible. As was the damage-control party, in coveralls, hoods, helmets, boots, and gloves; masked, OBA-rigged, dragging extinguishers, hoses, and axes, manipulating stingers into position. Giving the impression of milling around, but actually, Dan could see, getting ready to unseal that door and go in.

The easiest and safest way to deal with an electrical fire was to get in quick, before it spread, and douse it with CO_2 or a low-velocity spray, so it didn't electrocute someone. Though the power supplies in the modules weren't high voltage, as far as he was aware. He didn't envy those masked crewmen their mission one bit, and they'd have to do it fast, before whatever was going on in there lit off one of those closely packed solid-fuel rocket engines. "Is this on the video recorder?"

The chief engineer said, "Bringing it up now, Captain."

"Have we got a camera inside the module, Bart?"

"Actually, we do, sir, but we couldn't see anything."

"Put it up."

Danenhower was right; the interior camera, aimed down the centerline passageway, showed only gratings and the white-painted, black-stenciled vertical walls on either side of the square-canistered missiles. There *might* be a trace of smoke-haze in the upper field of view. It was hard to be sure.

He crossed to the J-phone and, after some seconds, managed to get the missile system supervisor on the line. The petty officer said yeah, he knew about that advisory, but it didn't apply to *Savo*.

"Why not?"

"We got that change in version 2.3, Captain. I tested it and the cue lamp for the VAB blinks right."

"Does that mean it can't fire?"

"Correct. But that's not exactly the problem occupying us at the moment, Captain," the petty officer explained patiently.

"So what *is* the problem? Other than that something's on fire in there?"

"We can't open the hatch."

"Oh, fuck me. Why not?"

"Well, that's the biggest problem with the VLS, sir. The hatches. They get old, the seals fail, or they stick when you try to open them."

"Wait a minute. We can't open *any* of the hatches?"

"No sir, that's not what I said."

"What exactly are you saying, Petty Officer?"

"Sir, we can't open *that* hatch."

Dan told him to keep trying, but the tech said there was no power any longer to the module, so it was no use. So actually, Dan thought, they really couldn't open any of the hatches. Which meant that if a missile caught fire and ignited, he had no way to get rid of it.

Launchers in older cruisers had included provisions for ejecting duds or hot runs, physically booting the round overboard with a big hydraulic ram. But the VLS had no "launcher" as such and no provision for ejecting a contrary missile. He was stuck with it; they had to deal with the thing where it was. He hung up, whispering, "Shit. — Where exactly is the fire?" Danenhower, who was standing in front of the alarm panel, that silly engineer's cap hanging off his temple, didn't answer. Dan jabbed him in the ribs and asked again, louder.

The engineer flinched and pointed to a red indicator. "Module two. The GMMs are saying SCMM."

"Power's secured?"

"Yes sir. All power aft secured."

"I guess that's good, except it means we can't open the hatch now."

"Oh, no sir. We can open them from here," a petty officer said. "That's hydraulics. As long as we got hydraulic pressure—"

"What's the temperature in there now?" Dan interrupted, getting more anxious by the second.

A console operator said, "Aft module, air temperature ninety-nine, cell two readout, six hundred. And going up."

On the screen a damage controlman—was that Benyamin under the mask and hood?—pulled off a glove and laid his palm against the heavy steel door. He left it there for only a moment, then jerked it back. His mask turned back and forth; he was shaking his head.

Dan said, "There's obviously a fire. What happens when your team opens that door? Especially if we can't get the deck hatches open?"

"They go in and fight it."

"Right, but I mean, what happens in the p-way? If that's one of the boosters burning, we're gonna have massive toxic release. All through the ship."

Danenhower blinked. "The module's sealed, sir."

"Against blast? From a Standard warhead?"

The engineer grimaced. "We've got Zebra set, but that's a good point—any penetration and we'd get contamination all through the aft end." He snapped to McMottie, "Chief, tell the team leader to hold up opening that hatch. Have the backup team rig blowers and put positive atmospheric pressure in the firefighting area."

Dan nodded. "That's good, Bart. Now. We can flood—right?"

"I'd rather not."

"Me neither. But how many missiles do we lose if we do?"

"Each canister has its own deluge system. We can flood the whole launcher, too."

"We can't flood by modules? It's either one missile or everything?"

"Correct."

"Flood that canister," Dan told him. "Right now. I know, you're not sure. And I know water alone's not going to put it out if one of those boosters ignites. But I don't want guys walking in there if—you know what I'm saying. And crank open all the hatches—both exit and exhaust. If one of those engines lights off, at least it'll reduce the pressure."

He wasn't sure this was the best course, and every canister he flooded cost at least a million dollars. But right now, they had to get a handle on that short circuit, or whatever it was, before it cascaded. The module held more than enough explosive and high-energy propellant to tear the ship in two and kill everyone aft of the stacks. And in this cold water and heavy sea, even those left alive would probably die before *Lahav* and *Pittsburgh* could get there to help.

Danenhower seemed about to object, but instead rasped to a petty officer on one of the consoles, "Flood it."

Dan got his Hydra out, gaze still locked on the red-and-white door, the damage-control team, fidgeting as they waited. "Bridge, CO."

"*Bridge, aye.*" Singhe's silky voice.

"To both *Lahav* and *Pittsburgh*: high-temperature alarm, fire in my aft missile compartment. Stand by in case I require emergency assistance."

"*Bridge, aye. Do you want them to close?*"

He gave that a half second's consideration. "Yeah. But no closer than a mile."

"*Good luck, sir. Bridge out.*"

McMottie said, "Flooding complete."

"Temperature?"

"Six hundred and eighty. Six hundred and seventy . . . six hundred and seventy."

They waited. It seemed to be getting hotter in CCS, but Dan wasn't sure that wasn't his imagination. He blotted his forehead surreptitiously with the back of one hand. ". . . six hundred and eighty. Six hundred and ninety. Seven hundred. Seven hundred and ten."

"It's not in the canister. Or it didn't fully flood."

"Fuck. *Fuck*," Danenhower whispered.

"I put full firemain on it, sir," the petty officer on the console said. "And I'm showing pressure drop, so we got flow in there."

Dan nodded. They were running out of options. "Send them in," he said, and some inner self marveled at how he could sound as if he weren't sending men to their deaths. "—Wait. No! Wait."

Heads turned. McMottie said, "Hold on—Captain says stand by. Yes sir?"

"The missiles around it," Dan said. "Flood them, too. Before you send the team in."

The chief said, "We're not seeing much of a heat increase there, sir. And you're gonna lose all that ordnance—"

"You heard me. Flood. All eight. Every canister that—that touches the one we're seeing the heat in, that's contiguous to it. Flood it. *Now*."

The petty officer, looking scared, keyboarded seven million dollars more away. Dan couldn't watch. He located the temperature readout—the simulacrum of a thermometer, on one of the screens—

and walked over to monitor it. It seemed to vibrate, to tremble. For a few seconds no one spoke.

Into that silence penetrated a distant roar, like a waterfall miles away. Shoulders hunched. Hands reached out as if to brace against a roll. A few sailors left, drifting out unobtrusively. No doubt, to run forward, away from the unleashing hell back aft. The roar drew nearer, and began to shake the overhead. But no one at a console moved. "Ignition!" someone yelled over the rising din.

He lifted his chin, trying to look calm. As if they might not all be random atoms in the next moment. Battleships had disintegrated in World War I, in World War II, when their magazines had exploded. Torn apart from inside in a fraction of a second, consigning those not killed instantly by fire and blast to the sea.

The roar swelled, rose. The steel around them began to hum and shake. Something fell out of the overhead and bounced off a console. Everyone flinched away. The thing rolled this way and that on the deck, clinking. It came to his boots like an eager pet. He lifted his foot and stopped it. It was a butane can, the kind you refill cigarette lighters with.

McMottie had found an exterior camera. When the screen came up heads lifted. Someone whispered, "My God."

A stream of mingled flame and steam was vomiting up out of *Savo*'s deck, like an erupting fumarole. The plume trembled and wavered, but jetted on, sun-white at its center, the edges shading to marigold yellow, then sunset orange. Ash . . . no, *snowflakes* drifted past the lens as the ship rolled. Past that the sea was a forged-iron gray as the camera compensated for the brightness of the flare. The very tip of the flame, fifty feet up, vanished into a complexly folding shroud of white steam and chalky smoke, billowing endlessly as hot gases rushed up.

He leaned forward, squinting. The cell in question was at the aft edge of the module, not far from the turn of the deck. The five-inch gun mount was just visible behind it. Past the mount huddled a small dark bundle: the aft lookout, pressed against the life rail, arms clamped over his head. The hatch of the defective cell was still closed. Jammed, probably. But those around it stood open like the popped lids of tumblebug burrows. It was from those hatches, and from the exhaust plenum between them, that the flame and steam and what looked like sprays of water were jetting, like superpowered geysers.

He hoped the water and steam were absorbing the heat load, because somewhere down in that burning hell, perched right above the burning booster, was a missile warhead. If it caught fire, it was supposed to burn rather than detonate. But a high explosive didn't care how you hoped it would behave.

The chief tapped the keyboard, and the screen changed: to the module interior again, the central corridor, the upper deck. Unfortunately, each time white smoke blanked the screen. Only one distant flash of orange flickered through the murk, then disappeared. The camera switched back to the exterior view. It retreated, zoomed out; now the smoke plume was tending away, dropping lower over the waves, then seeming to sink into them. At least they weren't sucking it back into their own ventilation.

The roaring went on, but maybe not quite as loud. Then it began to lessen. Yes, the sound was diminishing. The shuddering was easing off.

"Get 'em in now, sir?" The petty officer, head lifted.

He nodded. "Send 'em in."

More minutes dragged by. The plume continued to shrink, but hot gas still jetted up, now and again blasting out bursts of spray and steam.

"Fire team leader reports: Reached the fire. Commencing cooling surrounding canisters."

They weren't out of the woods. Dan couldn't help pacing, glancing at the screens and gauges each time he turned. The name of the game now was to surround the fire, isolate it, cool it down. Wall it off until it ran out of fuel, or the continuing firemain flood dropped the temperature enough that it doused itself. He suspected, though, that rocket fuel, carrying its own oxidizer locked into the grain, would burn until it was all gone.

Meanwhile the team inside were running a terrible risk. Trying to cool the surrounding canisters and keep their boosters from cooking off too. Trying to keep accident from escalating into disaster. A glimpse now and then through the smoke by the passageway camera showed them struggling with cumbersome, turgid pythons of firehoses. Maybe that had been the right thing to do, sacrifice the contiguous cells. Dan prayed that, please, it could be so. He tore his gaze away to key his Hydra. "CIC, CO: How's it going up there?"

"Sir, Cheryl here. Lahav's closing in. Distance four thousand yards. Captain Youngblood wants to know if they should surface and stand by us."

"Not yet. Not yet. It's too rough. Unless he hears an explosion . . . How far away are they?"

"A mile. On the other side of us from Lahav."

"Good. That's good. Fahad up there?"

A short pause. *"No sir. XO's not here. Isn't he down there with you?"*

What the hell? He let up on the key, then forgot about it as a figure stumbled out of the smoke and lurched across the camera's field, clutching its mask. "Is he all right?" Dan asked the petty officer who had the direct line to the team leader.

"One man fallen out with smoke inhalation, sir. But they say they're getting water in all around that one missile. It's . . . says it's boiling off, but not as hard now."

Dan crossed again to the temperature readout. The affected cell read zero. He frowned. McMottie explained it had probably melted or shorted. "But the temps in the cells around it are starting to fall."

"How high did they go?"

"Around five hundred. Hit that, then steadied out." He touched the display. "Right now: only three fifty, and falling."

"Keep that firemain flood going," Danenhower growled.

Dan said, "How about the cells across the catwalk? What's the temperature on those?"

"High, but within normal limits."

"Good. Okay, who's in charge of the Mark 41? The VLS?"

A mustached chief pushed forward. His name tag read Quincoches. Dan gripped his shoulder. "Chief, the firefighters might have it under control. Once we're sure, you can go in. We've got to get as many missiles back to operational status as we can, just as soon as possible. What's first? Dewater?"

Danenhower said, "Already dewatering, Captain. Or we'd have flooded the module."

"Good. Chief, I need you in there just as soon as the fire's under control."

Quincoches drew a deep breath. "There's a mandatory thirty-minute wait time."

"We don't have half an hour to sit around with our thumbs up our ass, Chief. Maybe in peacetime. Not now."

Quincoches paled. "Uh, right, sir. In that case I'll go in first. Alone. With a screamer on my belt. I'll manually safe the missiles we flooded. Isolate that cell, then restore module power. Then we can get the guys in and desmoke. First thing, we're going to have to pull and dry out all the cables. The cells are supposed to be waterproof, but not the connections. Got to see if the heat warped any of the connectors, the hatches . . . then run a DSOT and see who answers up."

"Good," Dan said. "Do it."

The chief started to leave, then seemed to recollect something. Dan said, "Yeah?"

"I'll go in there, check it out, Captain."

"Yeah?"

"Because that's what we do. That strike officer, she ain't down here. Us chiefs, we are. Us *middle management.* I don't want to make a big deal out of this, but—"

He nodded. Grinned tightly. "Point taken, Chief. And I'll be sure and pass it along."

Bit by bit, as the temperature dropped, everyone in CCS began to murmur, then talk aloud. Dan blew out, and massaged his eyeballs, then stopped; it would make him look tired. The camera focused down the centerline passageway of the module gradually showed a clearer picture. On the exterior camera, the pillar of flame had waned to a jet of brownish smoke, which was lessening as the flooding went on. He breathed deep. Then again, flushing out the tension. "That might've been bad," he said to Danenhower.

"Damn close." The engineer nodded soberly. "How many birds you figure we lost?"

For a horrible second Dan wondered if they'd just toasted all the modified SM-2s. If so, their mission was over before it had really begun. Then remembered: two were up forward; only two were aft. The aft module held mostly land-attack Tomahawks, standard Standards, and most of their vertical launch Asroc. But that was why they were mixed loads, so a casualty to one magazine would still leave both offensive and defensive capabilities. "What was in those cells we flooded? Anybody know?"

He looked around for Quincoches, but the chief was already gone. "I'll find out," said Danenhower, and went after him.

Dan found an empty chair and sagged into it. Should he go out and observe as the gunner's mates, missile, went in? No. He'd just be in the way. Where was Almarshadi, though? He called CIC again, then the bridge, but the exec was at neither, and didn't answer on his Hydra. "What the hell," Dan muttered.

He got up, and raised his voice so everyone in CCS could hear. "Good job, everybody—plus we got lucky. Bart, I want you and Matt to head up an investigation team. Find out how that fire started and what we can recommend as a class change, so it doesn't happen again." He paused, wondering if there was anything he should add. If so, it wasn't occurring to him. His head felt like cast lead. "Okay, well, I'm headed back up to the bridge." He slapped McMottie's shoulder, gave a thumbs-up to everyone else, and stepped through a door someone jerked open for him.

BY the time he got back to Combat the reaction, whatever it was, was slowing him down. His throat seemed to be closing up. It was harder than usual to catch his breath after climbing four sets of ladders. He leaned on the back of his chair and took slow deep breaths, contemplating the large-screen displays. *Lahav* had closed; their two pips were nearly merged. The group out of As-Suways, the Iranians, were tracking northeast at twelve knots. Aside from that, the east Med was empty. He started to tell Mills what was going on, but the combat systems officer said quietly he'd already put the word about the fire out over chat. Task Force staff wanted a status as soon as he could get it but were glad it was under control. And the leading chief aft, Quincoches, was in the module now inspecting damage. He'd make a report as soon as possible on how the fire had initiated.

Dan nodded. "Good. I'm gonna depend on you to write that up, Matt. Then get with Quincoches and Amy and Hermelinda about what we need for repairs. Maybe they can helo-lift us some spare cables or whatever from *Cape St. George* or *San Jacinto* when this fucking snow lets up."

He ran a hand back over his hair, which felt greasy and sweaty. Unfortunately, he could forget about fresh missiles to replace the burned-out and flooded ones. VLS-equipped ships had such a large capacity to start with that the Navy had pretty much dismissed any provision for underway replenishment. He checked the status board; not surprisingly, the MISSILE READY number had dropped by half. He caught Donnie Wenck's eye on the far side of the compartment and went over. Christ, I'm juiced, he thought. He lifted his hand and watched it shake, as if it were someone else's. As he reached the Aegis consoles the door to CIC creaked and a slim figure slipped through. Singhe nodded, and he remembered Quincoches's dig. *"She ain't down here."*

"Afternoon, sir," she said. He nodded back coolly.

Wenck said, "Damn, sir, glad we got that sucker put to bed."

"You and me both, Donnie. But now we're down to two Block 4s. How's ALIS doing?"

"She's hanging in there," said Terranova from her console. "Actually, we got a little good news, sir. The space track system's back up."

"You're kidding. How'd you get that fixed?"

Wenck got that distant look. "Well, glitch was, when we downloaded the TLE data file, the Space Five wouldn't display any satellites. Like they wasn't there at all. So we're like, what the fuck, over? It was like, the system just wouldn't display any acquisition requests. Right?"

"Yeah, uh, I guess—"

Singhe said, "I can background you on that, sir. If you'd like it."

"All right. Sure."

She said, "When we're in tactical mode, SCUS develops the SAR messages based on satellite orbital data, own ship position, and common Aegis time-slash-date. This queues the array to search a given volume of space for something that meets the acquisition parameters. Turns out one of Petty Officer Terranova's team made a slight mistake. Eastwood downloaded the wrong bulk two-line element catalog data from a training-mode file. Not hard to do, by the way—"

"Just a second." Dan keyed the Hydra and checked in with CCS.

Temperatures were still falling in the affected cells. They'd gotten the hatch in 16 pried open, and dewatering was under way. "Sorry, go ahead. You were saying—"

"Sayin', they oughta have some kind of warning flag when you're accessing training-mode stuff," Wenck said.

Mills nodded. "I'll put it in my recommendations. But when the system bumps that against its own source selects for current ops, it deletes them all, because the satellite header data doesn't match. And you go blank screen."

The chief said, "Once we got that figured out we redownloaded from the right catalog and suddenly everything lines up cherries and bells ring and quarters start coming out."

Dan had more or less followed this explanation. "And who actually *did* figure that out? Just for my own information?"

Singhe pointed to Terranova. So did Wenck. "Okay, really good," Dan said. "Well done, Petty Officer. But I'm surprised Dr. Noblos didn't catch it. He's the one who's been telling us we're not up to expectations."

Wenck lowered his voice. "I'm not sure he's as much of an operator as he's, like, more of a high-level guy, Dan. I mean, *Captain*. He's got the math at his fingertips, sure. But when it's a question of which line of code you go to to pick up satellite ephemeridae, he's like a deer in the headlights."

Dan blinked, trying not to look like a deer. "Uh-huh. Well, good. So all your troops are straight on this now, Terror? I mean, Petty Officer Terranova? Eastwood's not gonna do that again?"

"Yessir, all my guys are on step. Got a checklist to run through when we download the data set."

"And how often do we do that?"

"Every twelve hours."

"We miss an update, what happens?"

"The solutions degrade," Wenck said. "But gracefully. We can miss one update and it's not a big deal. Miss two or three, the track starts to wander off. You don't know if you're looking at your own system degradation, or increasing uncertainty exactly where that piece of space junk you're tracking really is." Singhe nodded.

Dan nodded too. He started to turn away, then remembered. "Hey, any of you seen the XO?"

"They were looking for him a while ago." Wenck shrugged. "Wasn't here, or in Strike."

"He hasn't been on the bridge since before the fire." Singhe looked concerned. "We called his stateroom several times."

"Anybody go down and knock?"

"I'm not sure, Captain."

Dan clicked on his Hydra, but got a blinking low-battery alarm. He swapped it for a recharged battery and called the bridge. "CO here. Anybody seen the XO yet?"

Pardees's languid voice murmured that they hadn't. Dan told him to send the boatswain's mate down to check Almarshadi's stateroom. "Tell him we need him online right away, and where's he been—he was supposed to—no, never mind. Just tell him to contact me right away in CIC."

Singhe frowned. "Should we put out a man overboard, sir?"

"That's the next step, but let's see if he's just crashed so hard he's not answering his phone." Actually he didn't want to think about a man overboard. Not when he remembered how depressed and upset Almarshadi had been at their last meeting. If he'd thrown a leg over the lifelines, they'd never find him in these seas. He pushed that vision away. "Okay, we're still up on ALIS, our SCUS is back online, and we've got two Block 4s live. Eric, let *Lahav* know our fire's out and we no longer need his presence close aboard. So thanks and he can resume his . . . uh, his station on us. Or no—just thank him. Say we've got everything under control. Same to *Pittsburgh*. Okay, any updates from the war zone?"

Mills said nothing much new had come through from Iraq or the task force. The Coalition land forces seemed to be punching through the initial defenses. "They're saying this might not be a very long war."

"That'd be good." He slicked back his hair again. Why was he still perspiring? Maybe because if his defenses were crumbling, the dictator might not wait to wind up his Sunday punch. *Savo* might be the only shield between helpless people and that roundhouse, whatever shape it came in.

A stir at the door from aft. He lifted his gaze to Almarshadi, in darker than usual blue coveralls. The little man's onyx eyes slid aside, wandered back. The XO nodded to Mills, who pointed to Dan.

As he reached them Dan saw the darker tone was dampness; Almar-shadi's coveralls were wet through.

"Skipper? Looking for me?"

Dan kept his voice down, but with an effort. "Where *were* you, Fahad? We had a fire aft. I needed you on the bridge. We've been looking all over."

Almarshadi glanced at Singhe, Wenck, Terranova. "Where was I? Down in the breaker. Having a smoke."

"A *smoke*? We just had a magazine fire. For Christ's sake . . ." Dan got a deep breath, let it out. Not now. Not in front of their juniors. "Let's go over there and—"

Mills called, "Captain? McMottie on the line. Wants to ask about debris disposal?"

"Over the side."

"Got it, sir."

At the far end of Combat, by the darkened nav table, they were finally out of earshot of everybody but the Phalanx operator. Dan put his back to the console and muttered, "Damn it, Fahad. We had a burning booster in the VLS. You weren't on the bridge. Weren't in your rack. I was about to call away a man overboard! And you're down smoking in the breaker? This is totally unsat. I mean, there's got to be two of you aboard. Just one guy couldn't mess up this bad."

"I apologize if I don't meet your standards."

Dan slammed a fist at an equipment frame, pulling the punch at the last microsecond, so he didn't break his knuckles. "They're not *my* goddamn standards, Commander! We're in Condition Three ABM. We can get a missile down our throats on fifteen seconds' notice. I needed you to spell me in the command seat. Can I depend on you to be there?"

The liquid eyes slid aside. The exec was at parade rest, hands locked behind him. The ship leaned, creaking around them. A metal-lic snap somewhere aft. The superstructure again? Dan almost missed the softly spoken reply. "I'm not sure you can, sir."

He cleared his throat, suddenly at sea in more ways than one. What was going on here? He'd had difficult subordinates before. Been a headache to his own seniors more than once. But he'd never come across someone like this. How had this guy made com-mander? How had he made *jaygee*? "I'm sort of at a loss here, Fahad.

You're saying . . . I can't count on you? Or I'd better not? Or what? Exactly?"

"No sir. It was you who said that."

"So what's your take on it?"

"I was in the breaker."

"Why are you all wet?"

"There's spray coming over the bow. It's getting rougher out there." The little man tilted a wrist to check his watch. His voice quavered, but he appeared to be growing more resolute, not less. Dan was fitting together words, exploring how to ask whether he'd been down there contemplating doing away with himself, when his second in command murmured, "I don't believe this was my scheduled time in CIC anyway. Not according to the rotation."

"True, but I needed you." He remembered the Motorola, and glanced at Almarshadi's belt line. The XO wasn't wearing it. "Where's your Hydra? We've been calling you on that just about nonstop."

"It's back in my stateroom. Recharging." Almarshadi frowned, as if taking back the initiative. "Captain, I have to protest. I was off duty. I went to my stateroom, put my battery on charge, then went down to the breaker for a smoke. Yes, I heard something aft. I didn't know what it was. But the next thing I know, when I come in, you're about to call away a man-overboard muster for me. And then you're insulting me in front of the junior officers. Even the enlisted.

"To be frank, this is unjust. I know your wife was injured in the attack on the World Trade Center. I know you were hurt at the Pentagon. And yes, I am an Arab. I may have my shortcomings as an exec. If I'm not performing to your expectations, relieve me. But I'm not your enemy, Daniel."

Dan splayed his fingertips to his temples. What was this asshole saying? That this whole fuckup was *his* fault? He said thickly, "This discussion's over. Go to your stateroom. Don't leave it again. Until I get . . . until I decide what to do about you."

"Aye aye, sir." Fahad nodded, about-faced crisply, and faded like a specter down the row of antisubmarine consoles, past the curtains of Sonar, passing from sight.

Dan lowered his hands, shaking. He'd pressed them to his temples so he couldn't wrap them around Almarshadi's throat. "Son of a *bitch*," he whispered. Every time he faced off with the guy, he understood him less. He was sinking away, losing contact. Only who was actually receding? The other, or himself?

Mills, voice lifted to reach the far end of the space. "Captain? Prelim bitchback from Chief Quincoches. On the 21MC."

"I'll be right there." He cleared his throat, which seemed to be closing up again. Then with swift, tired strides, headed back for his post.

14

Oparea Adamantine

H E shifted in his chair as the night came for him out of the east. Out of a graphite, darkening sky, out of the blasts of snow.

The bridge was in full darken ship, every pilot lamp and screen turned to its night setting. The bridge team spoke in murmurs, near whispers. Dan kneaded his cheeks. So fucking tired. . . .

He'd watched as Quincoches and the other gunner's mates had very gingerly boat-hooked the charred remains of a Sparrow II RIM-7P frag-and-blast warhead up out of the pried-open hatch. They'd set it on a cargo net. Ollie Uskavitch had pointed out the fuze booster to Dan, the weapons officer explaining how it had been designed to melt instead of detonating the main charge. It was melted, all right: a shapeless blob of blackened material that didn't look like much of anything now. The main charge had burned entirely, leaving only a cagelike structure of charred, warped steel. Dan couldn't stop a shiver ratcheting his spine as Grissett, who seemed to be the ship's photographer as well as the chief corpsman, bent close, snapping off shot after shot. Turning the thing over, snapping off more. The lightning flicker of the strobe illuminated only a tiny circle of the deck.

When the postmortem ended, they'd regathered. Lifted the charred warhead, like firemen around an old-fashioned life net, and walked it toward the side. The boatswains had unreeved the deck-edge nets. The tumble home at that point bulged out slightly, so it wasn't a straight drop. With cautious unanimity, they'd swung the net, *and-a one, and-a two.* At a muttered "three" they'd given it a last heave, and let go. Net and contents had vanished into the gathering dark with a muffled splash. As the disturbed patch eased aft, everyone concerned had straightened, sighing.

None more deeply than Dan. He'd given them all high fives, then gone below for a walk-through of the VLS interior.

The blowers had been howling, and the smells of burnt insulation and seawater were choking, but the metal trusswork bracing and the unaffected cells stood undamaged, though their corrugated white-painted exteriors were smoke-stained. Techs were disconnecting cables, running continuity checks with portable testers. They'd showed him a stub of connector. Quincoches and the chief electrician's mate agreed it was the most likely place for the fire to have started. Most of it was burned away, though, so they couldn't be sure.

Dan had walked the module from end to end and port to starboard. Then started to tell them they needed everything back up as soon as possible. But instead, bitten his tongue. They knew. Having the skipper say it again wasn't going to get ordnance back on the status board any faster.

Now he stared out into the dark as *Savo* staggered and corkscrewed. She was on a southerly leg, the seas slamming into her quarter. The invisible beam lanced out from their port aft panel. He imagined it boring a hole through the overcast. They said the SPY-1, at full power, radiated enough microwave energy—four million watts, enough to power a good-sized town—to melt snowflakes. Fry seagulls in midflight. He hadn't seen it do anything like that yet. Maybe in the morning, if it was still snowing, he'd go out and take a look.

"Captain?"

A vanishing shadow he identified only by voice. "Yeah, Cher?"

"You wanted to talk about rejuggling the watch bill. I made up a draft, taking the XO out of the rotation. For now."

"Right. For now."

"Who do you want to replace him with?"

"Put your name in there, Cheryl."

She hesitated, then must have nodded; a faint red light illuminated a clipboard. "That makes you and me in the command seat. Lieutenant Mills as port section TAO. For starboard section, I recommend Mr. Branscombe."

"I wish Noah had gotten to school."

"I agree, sir. Mr. Pardees strikes me as levelheaded. But he hasn't had the training—as you said. Nor has Lt. Singhe. The only other alternative is Chief Slaughenhaupt. Our leading fire controlman. But we need him as combat systems officer of the watch."

"Okay, you're right—make it Branscombe. How about our OODs?"

Staurulakis proposed moving Mytsalo up to officer of the deck. Dan kept his voice low, in case the ensign was on the bridge with them. "Who else've we got? An ensign—I don't know. Who're our other JOODs?"

"Sir, the officer of the deck under way doesn't have the responsibilities he used to. A lot of that's been absorbed by the TAO."

"I know that, yeah. But still—"

"The only other possibility's the chief quartermaster."

"Van Gogh?" Dan ping-ponged that around in his skull. It'd mollify the goat locker, seeing one of their own fleeted up. "I don't have any problem with a chief standing OOD. Not the navigator, anyway. He'd certainly be on the stick as far as where we are relative to the basket. . . . Okay. Make it Van Gogh. But give him Mytsalo as JOOD, and tell Gene he's gonna be next in line, soon's he gets a little more seasoning."

"Good thinking, sir." The clipboard light winked out.

"What about this freakin' snowfall, Cher? Will this degrade our beam numbers?"

She explained the main problem was side-lobe visibility. "The snow adds more background clutter. We have better discrimination with the D, but especially in the high-clutter near-shore environment, along with all this sea return this wind's kicking up . . . yeah, the snow can degrade us . . . especially for something like a low-flying C-802. But Chief Wenck thinks he can combine pulses to build what he calls a 'synthetic wideband image' out of one of the side lobes."

"You lost me, Cher."

"I mean, along with the main beam, you get side lobes—"

"I know that. Any beam has side lobes. Like harmonics."

"Well, normally that's wasted power. But he's trying to tinker with the signal processing to turn that into an extra radar. To give us a better look along the coastline, to alert us to any cruise missile launch."

"That's great, but I don't want it tuned in such a way it degrades our ABM search function."

"Noted, sir."

"Have Donnie give me a call. I really don't want to trade main mission for self-protection."

"Aye aye, sir."

"Will the cloud cover degrade satellite cuing?"

"Obsidian's more of a sideways-looker. And it's an infrared sensor. I'm not sure how much snow or cloud would degrade that."

The STU-3 beeped. Dan flinched. The scarlet light above it was flashing so brightly it lit up this whole end of the pilothouse. The boatswain hurried over with masking tape. "Stand by, please, Ops," Dan said, and got the phone to his ear. "*Savo Island* actual here."

"*This is Jen Roald. Over.*"

"Commodore. Lenson here. Over."

"*Dan. I just got this. You had* another *fire?*"

"More serious this time. In the aft VLS. Lost eight missiles to fire and flooding." Staurulakis put her hand on the remote box; he nodded; she turned the speaker on.

"*That's not good. But it wasn't the Block 4s? Are the rest of your cells back up? Over.*"

"We're running operability tests now. I'm hoping to get them back up shortly."

"*Message on the way. Things are moving faster than anyone expected. The Army's crashing through the border defenses. Also, and this may be of interest to you, there are mutterings of support from Iran.*"

"Meaning, their task group? Over."

"*They've announced their first port call. Syria.*"

Dan shook his head. "Taken on board."

"*Good. We also have a warning order from EuCom. We want your total attention focused on the western part of Al-Anbar Province. CentCom's trying to interdict the launchers with air and ground teams, but you're the backstop.*"

"Copy, over," Dan said into the phone. "Map of Iraq," he asided. The clipboard riffled. A moment later it was in his lap, with Staurulakis's red penlight illuminating the area just east of the Jordanian border. From the topo, it looked like desert. Nearly unpopulated,

DAVID POYER

and unroaded, too, from the absence of town or road symbology. He'd seen Saddam's hulking Russian-supplied TELs—transporter, erector, launchers—with his own eyes, in a secret installation beneath Baghdad, during Signal Mirror. Obviously they weren't in the capital anymore, and their eight all-terrain wheels, much taller than a man, meant they could go cross-country, hide in wadis or under overpasses. The intel said it took half an hour from parking to launch.

"Commodore, that's where we've been looking. But can anyone neck it down a little more? The more localization we have, the narrower we can set the gate functions, and the more confident I'd feel about early detection. Over."

"*Stand by.*"

A short pause, during which Dan shifted in his chair. When she came back on, Roald read off six-figure geocoordinates. Dan jotted them on the map's margin, glanced at Staurulakis; she nodded. He read them back, slowly, enunciating in the exaggerated radio speech learned so many years before. "Thuh-ree. Zee-ro. Nine-er."

"*That's correct. Not to limit your search to that area, but that's what they've given us as what they're calling the Western Complex. They operated from there during the Gulf War, too, and we had a hard time locating them then.*

"*What's it like weather-wise on your end? I'm seeing this cold-air surge hitting you soon.*"

He looked out the window but couldn't see much in the darkness. "Correct, the front's hitting now. We're getting snow and six-foot seas."

"*What's your Israeli friend doing?*"

Dan craned down for the repeater but couldn't quite reach it. The OOD came in from the darkness. He muttered, "Still out there, sir. Ten thousand one hundred yards."

"Any other surface contacts?"

"No sir. Not for this whole watch."

"He's still with us, Jen. Like a bur. Any progress on that link to the Patriot battery at Ben Gurion? It would really help."

"*I knew there was something else. I think we've got you up at least on voice. I'll get the freq to you. Watch your TAO chat.*"

Roald signed off. As Dan socketed the handset he was suddenly racked with nausea. Up here, in the dark, the motion seemed to be getting worse. He envisioned his bunk with the hopeless yearning of unrequited love. Deep . . . slow . . . breaths. The sickness backed off and he fumbled for the reclining knob on the seat. Dropped it as far as it would go, and leaned back with a sigh. Closed his eyes, and listened to the regular *whip-whip* of the wipers. *Whip-whip. Whip-whip. . . .*

"CAPTAIN? You awake?"

"Uh . . . yeah."

The dream had been so real, so detailed, waking was like coming back from another life.

He'd been much older. Gray. Bent. And, weirdly, he'd been some kind of pastor—Lutheran? It hadn't been exactly clear. He'd been in a concentration camp, with barbed wire around it. Just before he'd been awakened, the guards had been herding a group of prisoners past. They were ragged, starved, in much worse shape than he. Though he was also an inmate, there was some deep difference between them. Some profound foreignness about their features, and the language they gabbled as their captors harried them along with bayoneted rifles.

He'd stood at the gate, watching the others being shoved and cursed past to another part of the camp. He didn't know why, but something irrevocable would happen to them there. And for some reason, though he too was a captive, he felt intensely guilty. He'd reached out to one woman. "I'm sorry," he told her. Raised his arms, as if to bless them, and called, "And may God keep you all." Dark eyes rose, but no one spoke. The guard growled some harsh phrase he did not understand, and someone's hand gripped his arm—

"Who's that?" he muttered, trying to retrieve who and where he really was.

"Chief Grissett, sir. This a bad time?"

"I don't know. What time is it?"

"Local 2310, sir."

He cleared his throat. He was on the the bridge. USS *Savo Island*. Still dark. Still snowing. And in fifty minutes, he'd have to relieve Cheryl Staurulakis in CIC. "What've you got, Doc?"

"Sir, if you're trying to sleep—"

He snapped, "You woke me up. Now what the fuck d'you want?" Then winced. "Sorry. Didn't mean that. Just tell me it's not another death at least."

"That's all right, sir. No, not another. I'll come back—"

"What is it?" he said, trying not to put *I am being so immensely patient* into his tone.

"Sir, it's the XO."

He hitched upright. "The exec? What about him?"

"I looked in on him. In his stateroom."

"You . . . why?"

"Well, that's sort of my job, sir."

"And?"

"Well, he seems depressed."

The ship leaned. Something rattled and clattered on the darkened bridge. He wanted to say, "And this is my problem because . . . ?" But didn't. "He's in his stateroom because I put him there. Occasionally, Chief, we still have to discipline people in this organization. That goes for O-5s, too. Not just E-2s."

"Yessir. I grok that. But he's not responding to conversation."

Dan frowned. "What d'you mean?"

"Monosyllabic replies. Not making eye contact."

Dan remembered the wet uniform. Almarshadi's repeated statement he'd been in the breaker. Of course, the guy usually *didn't* meet your eye. That was normal—for him. But what *had* he been doing in the breaker? Just smoking and looking idly down into the passing sea?

Or wondering if he should sling a leg over the lifeline, and let it all go?

"Okay, Chief. Thanks for bringing me this. You think he could be suicidal?"

"Not crossing that off the list, sir."

Dan hitched himself erect again. "Is he alone down there?"

"I have the duty corpsman posted in the passageway outside his room."

"Think it's that serious?"

"I don't know, sir."

"Right. Well, do you think he should be medicated?"

Grissett cleared his throat. "Well, sir, I'm not qualified to dispense psychoactive medication. I've got it, but there are a couple of complications. Sometimes it actually makes people more prone to . . . offing themselves. According to the literature. And another thing. If I dispense, I have to certify the member as unfit for duty. It's a disqualifying condition. That should be certified by a qualified medical representative. If there isn't an MD around to do that, in an emergency, I can dispense it. But I have to report it to the CO. And put it in the member's record. There's a waiver process, but . . . it's complicated."

"I'll bet. You're saying, if he goes on these meds, he's unfit for duty?"

"Yessir."

"And that's it for his career."

"That toy's out of my playpen, sir."

"Uh-huh. Do you think he needs it? Medication, I mean?"

"Right now, it'd be even money, in my humble opinion."

Dan kicked back in the chair again. "Unfortunately, we just rebuggered the watch bill . . . put Chief Van Gogh on as OOD. . . . Okay, you brought me the issue, now give me a recommendation."

"I'd say put him back on duty. Unless you're absolutely convinced he's, I don't know, totally incompetent," Grissett said. "But is that the case, sir? I see a lot of him for medical stuff and XO's masts and so on. I guess what I'm asking, is he really that bad? If he isn't, lighten his load. Don't wall him up. Maybe I didn't get the whole story, but the word going around is, he took a smoke break, and now he's being hammered for it."

Dan frowned. "Is that really what's going around?"

"It's the scuttlebutt. But like I say, you're the CO."

"Thanks for the reminder." He sighed and dug at his eyes again. "Bo's'un? Any hot coffee in the neighborhood?"

"Just came up, sir. Stand by one."

"You say he's awake now?"

Grissett said he believed so. Dan sighed again and selected the CO/XO channel on the Hydra. "XO, CO here. . . . Fahad? . . . —No answer."

"Want me to go down, sir? Knock on the door, tell him you want him?"

Dan kneaded his forehead. He'd already given the guy a second chance. But if the chief corpsman was right . . . Almarshadi was emotionally labile, that much was true. But maybe this wasn't the best time to take him out of the loop.

The Hydra beeped and he rapped out, "Skipper."

"Wanted me, sir?"

It was him. Dan leaned over to check the radar repeater. Aside from *Lahav*, screwed into position like a rusted-in bolt, it was empty of surface contacts. "Yeah. Look, I need some relief up here. I'm gonna try Cher and me on and off in CIC. I need you to take over on the bridge. Pretty much full-time, I'm afraid, until we get out of Condition Three. Could you handle that for me?"

A short hesitation. Then *"I can do that, sir."* But the voice was flat; Dan couldn't read any emotion at all into it, either resentment or pleasure.

"Can you get up here like at midnight?"

"I'll shower and be right up."

"CO out." He made sure it was off and muttered, "Okay, he's gonna come, but he doesn't sound happy about it."

"I think that's the right decision, though, sir."

"How's everything else going? How about that guy with the cough?"

"He's doing okay, sir. Temp's up slightly, but he's resting. The question is, how are you doing?"

"Me?"

"Yessir, you. You're not getting much sleep. Napping in a bridge chair—"

"Don't worry about me." Dan scowled. "I'm all right."

"You need sleep, sir. Or a go-pill. Whenever you think you need one—"

"I *don't* need a go-pill," he gritted out. "Just don't wake me up again to tell me I need sleep! All right?" He put his head back again and closed his eyes.

The boatswain brought the coffee over and stood for a moment, listening to his captain snore. Then, balancing the mug against a heavy roll, he felt his way across the bridge and poured it back into the carafe.

MIDNIGHT on the Sea of Good and Evil. Combat was icy cold. Nothing wrong with the AC anyway. Dan swirled another cup of joe.

It tasted horrible, but that wasn't the brew's fault. He was just drinking too much, past the point where it seemed to have any effect. Grissett wanted him to think about a stimulant. Later, maybe—he wasn't totally ruling it out—but not just yet.

He scrubbed his face with his palms, dug grit out of his eyes, tried to refocus. *Savo* and *Lahav* floated in an existential void. Far to the south, the GCCS showed the three pips of the *Alborz* group—the Iranian surface force—creeping northward. He should get *Pittsburgh* down there, to pick up trail and surveillance.

He blinked and squinted again. To the northwest, off Cyprus, a red callout had suddenly popped. As he stretched for the keyboard, data bloomed. Dave Branscombe, the comm officer, newly installed in the TAO chair, had leaned forward to bring it up.

"Distress alert, Captain."

"I see it." He squinted harder, shading his eyes; damn, were they going fuzzy too? The comm officer's keyboard rattled. The display zoomed in; the coast of Cyprus enlarged.

"Source of data's GMDSS," the lieutenant murmured. The global maritime distress and safety system, a satellite-based international network. "Automatic alert. SS *Agia Paraskevi*. Cruise ferry. Greek flag. Sixteen thousand tons. Capacity six hundred passengers." More keys clicked, and an image came up: white hull, swept-back, winged funnel with a smoke deflector. Row after row of portholes, tiered decks, lidos . . . "Thirty miles off Cape Gata, reporting loss of power and flooding."

"What the hell's a cruise ship doing out in March?"

"A cruise *ferry*. Guess they still run during the winter. I'll try them on HF distress."

"Hold on a second, Dave. Exactly how far away are they?"

"Wait one . . . about a hundred and twenty miles. Course to intercept, 340."

"Concur," said a petty officer behind the TAO.

Dan stared at the image. They could be there in four hours at flank speed. No, four and a half, considering the sea state. But he was pinned to his station.

Against that, every tradition of the sea dictated that any ship within radio range had to respond to a bona fide distress call.

"Think it's for real?"

Dan twisted, to find Ammermann behind him. The civilian staffer had borrowed a foul-weather jacket somewhere. It had the *Savo* patch on the breast. He'd gotten himself a ship's ball cap, too. The overall impression was the opposite of what he intended, if he was trying to fit in. "I don't think they'd put out a false SOS," Dan told him. "That's not looked on with amusement. In fact, it's a criminal offense."

"GMDSS has experienced a lot of inadvertent Maydays," the comm officer observed. "It's a new system. The maintenance is complicated."

Dan said, "We're up on International Distress, right, Dave?"

"Always, sir."

"Jack up whoever's monitoring. See if they've heard anything."

"You're not thinking of leaving station, are you, Captain?"

"I'm not thinking of anything right now, Adam. Just trying to stay current on what's going on around us."

"We don't want to get diverted from—"

"Absolutely not."

The 21MC. *"CIC, Radio: Faint distress call on 2182 kiloherz, international marine distress channel. Weak and garbled, but it seems to be from USS* Paraskee. *We're in EMCON. Permission to reply?"*

Dan blew out. "USS *Paraskee*" was a reasonable mistake for SS *Paraskevi*, given a Greek accent and a weak single-sideband transmission. Emission control on the radio circuits was pretty much pro forma, considering *Savo* was putting out five megawatts of microwaves. So he didn't have much misgiving about answering the call.

On the other hand, once he *did* respond, he was legally obligated to render assistance. Of course, it wasn't that clear-cut. But if it came to an investigation, it would definitely weaken his defense. He grimaced, not liking thinking in those terms, and leaned to the bitch box. "Radio, CO: Anybody else answering up on 2182?"

"No one, sir."

"Not *Lahav*?" If *Savo* was in range, the Israeli frigate should be too.

"No sir."

He swept the surface display again. Usually hundreds of contacts would be swarming the screen at this zoom level. But the east Med had really emptied out.

Ammermann found a folding chair somewhere and scraped it up beside him. "Could be just to pull you off station."

"I don't think so, Adam. And it's not an inadvertent actuation, like Dave suggested. Not if they're following it up with a voice call." Command decision time. But even as he thought it, he'd already decided. "Give me International Distress," he told Branscombe. The lieutenant reached across his lap and snapped the selector on Dan's remote to 4.

Right, he knew that. God, he was getting stuporous. . . . He cleared his throat and unsocketed the worn gray handset. "SS *Paraskevi*, this is U.S. Navy warship *Savo Island*. Over." Too late, he remembered he wasn't supposed to use their real name in the clear. Oh well.

"Want me to do that, sir?" said Branscombe.

"Thanks, I got it. —*Paraskevi*, *Paraskevi*, this is *Savo Island*, *Savo Island*. Over."

Branscombe laid a publication in front of him, open to a page that showed a military joint rescue coordination center in Cyprus and a naval base at Zygi. "They're a lot closer than we are," he murmured.

"Are they responding to the call, Dave?"

"I'll get Radio on their coordination band and see."

"If they're not, we can pass data," he said. Everyone in Radio and Branscombe too already knew that, but he had to say it. Actually, since the distress call was up on GMDSS, they had to have the basic data—lat, long, type of emergency—already on their screens. It took getting used to, this idea of information existing everywhere simultaneously.

"We can't lose focus on our mission," Ammermann murmured beside him.

"Goddamn it, we're focused! I've got four people over there full-time! I don't need you at my elbow telling me what to concentrate on."

Startled faces turned. "Hey. Hey." The staffer lifted his hands, palms out. "Take it easy! Didn't mean to—"

Dan gripped the handrests of his chair. "Keep your advice to yourself until I ask you for it. Otherwise, you're going to have to stay in your stateroom. All right?"

"You got it, Captain," the staffer said. But added in a murmur, leaning in, "But I hope you don't mind my saying, a lot of folks seem to be getting confined to their staterooms aboard this ship. Is this how the Navy does business? Anybody who has a different point of view gets put in the corner for a time-out?"

Dan took a deep breath, close to exploding. "If you mean Fahad Almarshadi, he's on the bridge right now. Come to see me before you believe the scuttlebutt—what gets passed around word of mouth."

"I know what scuttlebutt is, Captain. But you can't both tell me to come to you, and restrict me to my cabin. I came out here to help. Offer access. But you're not making it easy." The staffer pushed dark hair off his forehead, looking both put-upon and satisfied. His round cheeks glowed. He waited, obviously expecting an apology.

Too bad. Dan lifted the handset and tried to reach the ferry again, but no answer came back. He resocketed it and turned back to the screen as a piercing buzzer racketed from the EW console. The speaker between the CO's station and the TAO's announced tersely, "Radar jamming from bearing zero seven zero. Correlates with Heart Ache. Designate Music One."

The Heart Ache was a Russian high-power noise jammer, truck-mounted, that was supposed to counter surveillance and observation radars—such as the SPY-1—and jam airborne and nap-of-the-earth flight-control radars, among others. It was fairly effective in beam mode at short distances. But the fact that someone was trying to jam *Savo* was significant. They were dueling with microwaves, high over Israel and Jordan. A hum of voices from the consoles rose above the eternal rush of the air-conditioning, and the cicada chatter of keyboards sped up too.

Dan twisted in his chair, to see Amy Singhe's hawk-nosed profile bent over, green-lit, peering past Terranova's rounded babyish features. Beside him Branscombe was on the SPY-1 coordination circuit. "Is that giving her any problems, Amy? . . . Good . . . good." The TAO signed off. "We're shifting to an anti-jam waveform, and freq-hopping. The jammer's trying to follow, but its response time's lagging our shifts. Probably older-model equipment."

"I know the brand. Syrian, you think?"

"The bearing would say so."

The speaker said, "Second jamming emitter. Bearing zero six eight. Designate Music Two."

Dan slapped his cheeks to wake up. *Two* jammers? This was getting serious. "Tell Bart we need both shafts and all engines back on the line for battle maneuvering. Check your illuminator coverage. Check all doctrine statements."

Branscombe was acknowledging when the EW warning speaker stated, "*Third* emitter. Bearing zero six nine. Designate Music Three."

"Something in the works?" said Ammermann, getting up from the chair and questing back and forth like an alerted bird dog. God, the guy was annoying. Dan made a pushing-off gesture. He concentrated on the rightmost screen, where a launch would show up. Mobile jammers were, of course, mobile. But still, they were fat targets for U.S. antiradiation missiles. So they usually didn't start transmitting unless there was a good reason.

And he could think of only two reasons for a coordinated jamming attack on *Savo Island*'s main radar.

One: An enemy missile was about to launch.

Two: An attack was imminent on *Savo* herself.

Regardless, the duel was on. His own beam was more powerful, and far swifter, a rapier to the daggers of the truck-mounted shoreside jammers. But many daggers could defeat one rapier.

Again: It was a duel of light sabers. At each point the beams clashed, the SPY-1's radar picture was distorted, even obliterated. If the threat originated within those jammed regions, she couldn't see it. No matter how powerfully her own beam burned.

The 21MC. "*CIC, Radio: Voice transmission from Cypriote joint rescue coordination center at Zygi. They don't have a ship available to render assistance. M/V* Paraskevi *is foundering. Four hundred and eighteen souls. Lifeboats available, but seas are heavy. They request we render assistance, at the following position. Latitude thirty-four degrees, twelve minutes north. Longitude, thirty-two degrees, fifty-nine east . . .*"

The voices faded. Heads lifted across the compartment, swung in his direction.

Data existed everywhere. Simultaneously. But decision, power . . . was that what he had? It didn't feel like it. It felt as if he had no choice.

The hoary sea, cold and remorseless. The vessel you'd trusted to keep you safe, slipping beneath the waves. Leaving you alone, help-less . . . Instead of power he felt impotence. Instead of choice he felt locked in. His trachea seemed to be closing again. He kneaded his neck, tried to slow his breathing from a pant.

He could not leave his post to help them. It was as simple as that.

He depressed the metal lever on the bitch box. "Radio, captain here. Tell Zygi: Regret unable to leave station. Urgent operational commitment."

"Unable to respond, sir?" said the TAO petty officer behind them. "But . . . that's a Mayday. And if it's coming from the coordination center—"

"I agree, it's probably a valid SOS," Branscombe said quietly. "But it's up to the CO to make the call."

"You all heard the skipper," Ammermann said. "That's the right decision, Dan."

"Adam, I don't need your backup. I told you, keep quiet or get out."

The 21MC said, in a different voice, *"This is the chief of the watch. Captain, confirm what the petty officer just told me? That we're not going to respond? I have to log our answer."*

Dan pressed the lever again. Said, as evenly as he could, "That's correct, Chief. *Savo Island* heard the request for assistance, but cannot leave station. Log that the commanding officer made that decision personally. I'm sorry . . . and may God keep them all."

There. The decision was made. And now that it was, he had to pretend it was right. That was what a leader did. No matter what guilt, or regret, gnawed at his throat.

He frowned, worrying at some tenuous wisp of memory. It strug-gled to escape even as he seemed to grasp it. . . .

Then he remembered. His dream. The words he'd said to the ragged men and women as they passed through the gate, never to return.

And may God keep you all.

What he'd just said, leaving four hundred helpless passengers to the mercy of a winter sea.

"CIC, EW: Radar illumination from shore. X-band radar. Con-sistent with illumination from missile-tracking radar."

His gaze went to the clock above the vertical displays. 0211 local.

He bent forward, clutching his stomach, gagging on coffee-flavored acid as he tried again and again to pull air through a narrowing windpipe.

The battle had begun. And already, the casualties were starting to mount.

15

THREE Musics, jamming from Syrian soil. Lagging *Savo*'s frequency-hopping but still, inevitably, degrading the ship's already constricted coverage. And an X-band illuminator from not far away. Aircraft? Patrol boat? Shore battery of Chinese-made C-802s? Hunched over the command table, Dan wiped his mouth, squinting through aching eyes at the rightmost display. The beam clicked back and forth, sous-chef-dicing mountains and desert into tiny digital wedges. *Savo Island* groaned as she leaned. In the darkness outside, the sea raged, and in the infrared images transmitted from the gun cameras snow streamed across the screen.

"Sir, I'd like to get Strafer in the air." Branscombe looked pale, but his voice was firm. "Get Red Hawk out there. I know he's probably in the sack, but if the balloon's going up, we need his sensor package active."

"It's awful rough . . . but, yeah, you're right. But have him call me before he launches." Dan searched the slanting space, for what, he wasn't sure. "Also, call *Lahav*. Inform Captain Marom we're being illuminated and jammed. He probably already knows, but pass the heads-up anyway. He's next to us on the bull's-eye."

"Put Sea Whiz in auto, Captain?" called Slaughenhaupt.

"Not just yet, Chief. Make sure you got a doctrinal cutout in there so we don't fire at *Lahav*, or our own fucking helo. Okay?—Petty Officer Terranova. What kind of gates you got set? If they're going to launch, it's probably going to be now, while the Syrians are jamming us."

Her voice rose high, clear, soft as a child's. "Sir, got a user-defined script running, approved by Chief Wenck. Acoustic alert for anything over a thousand knots between angels five to angels ninety. That automatically trips as a space track and gets designated hostile."

"Very well." He rose slightly to squint across at her saffron-lit, almost Madonna-like countenance. She was twenty-three. Not just his fate but that of thousands of others might shortly ride on her competence. But she'd been cool under criticism. Maybe she was just ice under pressure—even if she looked like she belonged in the Toms River High Marching Band. Wenck stood behind her, hair sticking straight up; and at her other shoulder hovered Amy Singhe, like Kali the Dark Mother come to earth for battle. And back in the abyssal shadows of the darkened space, Dr. Noblos. Miniature screens glowed, reflected in his glasses.

They watched, but ALIS would act. Human beings could not react quickly enough. The software would evaluate the threat parameters through to engagement orders. Yet still, with human eyes and brains tracking the process. "I retain release authority," he told the space at large. "If I'm disabled, authority passes to the TAO." He nodded at Branscombe.

He checked the boards above the displays once more: in the green, except the aft VLS was still down. Their effective-weapons count was half of what it had been before the fire. He reached for the Hydra, then instead leaned past Branscombe along the command table. "Chief?" Slaughenhaupt lifted shaggy eyebrows. "Can you get on the horn, see if Quincoches is making any progress aft? This'd be a good time to get that ordnance back on the ready board."

"Will do, Captain."

Okay, time to shift focus. Dan cleared his throat and picked up the Navy Red phone. In four crisp sentences, he brought the duty officer at CTF 60 up-to-date. The foundering liner. The jamming. And now, radar illumination. He requested air support, if available. Then signed off. Branscombe's keyboard was machine-gunning; the same update was going out over the high-side chat. Putting it out to the world, or at least, the whole U.S. Navy.

When he resocketed the handset the space was quiet for a second. Then another. The AC hissed on endlessly. A shiver harrowed his spine. Either the temperature in here had dropped ten degrees, or he was getting chills. He scratched a flake of gray paint off the circular worn spot around the black rubber trackball inset in front of him.

A trill: his Hydra. The helo detachment commander, Wilker. "Strafer, can you get the bird in the air in these conditions?" Dan asked.

"The guys are still overhauling from the evening patrol. But I can tell them to button up. That what you want, Skipper?"

"This wind's not too strong? Snow's not a problem?"

"We can eat the snow. We launch on instruments anyway, at night. It's deck motion that defines the launch limits."

"Eight degrees, right? We gotta be close to that. On this course anyway."

"Yeah, it's pretty fucking borderline, Skipper. You might have to back down to take us back aboard, if this wind blows any harder. But if you need us, we'll go."

Dan updated him on the jamming, the threat emitters. "I don't think you'll need weapons, so don't delay if they're not on the pylons. But load heavy with IR flares and decoys. I want you out there ASAP. Between us and the Syrian coast."

Wilker rogered and said he'd launch as soon as possible. Dan rogered back and clicked off. Too late, he wondered if Strafer had been joking about backing down. From the guy's tone, he couldn't tell.

What else? He couldn't think of anything.

He hated to sit and wait. Hardly anything was drilled into a naval officer more thoroughly from day one than a bias toward action, even if it was the *wrong* action; you never just steamed ahead on the same course, fat, dumb, and happy. That guaranteed the next enemy salvo would land on top of you. Unfortunately, with the SPY-1 in BMD mode, he kept having that tickle at the nape of his neck, the sense that someone was creeping around behind him. As if, sooner or later, some shadowy menace would wind up like a baseball batter and take off the back of his head.

Ammermann said, "Captain, I don't understand. What about this cruise missile that's threatening us? Can you take it out? Or get air from the carrier to do it?"

Dan took a deep breath, not looking at the civilian. *"Can* I? I could. We're in Tomahawk range. But Sixth Fleet rules of engagement are clear, Adam. We can't fire on a nonbelligerent. Not until he fires first. And an air strike on Syria would take presidential approval."

"I don't think we need to wait, necessarily." He lowered his voice. "I can assure you now, preempting the threat will not be looked at askance."

"Then that direction should have been in an addendum to my ROE," Dan said. "I don't have time now to discuss my chain of command. But I'm not going to short-circuit it. There's a reason it's there."

He spared one microsecond to reflect sourly on how Nick Niles would probably fall out of his chair laughing, to hear Dan Lenson say that. But he wasn't about to accept orders from Ammermann.

He snapped his attention back to the screens, tuning everything and everyone else out. From now on, each passing second would call for a decision, while he kept a hundred variables in mind. They were like a basketball team, following the ball around the court. Right now that basketball, called the initiative, was in the enemy's hands. But at some point he'd fumble, and whoever recovered it would win the battle that was nearly upon them.

At the same time, he, at the little end of the funnel for all this information, had to rise above it, stay both focused and open, both engaged and aloft at ten thousand feet, seeing the big picture.

His legs ached, as they usually did when he went without sleep too long. He wished he could unlace his boots and prop stockinged feet on the command table. In front of them all. He'd known captains who wouldn't have hesitated. Instead, he felt in his coverall pocket and located a lint-coated Aleve. Swallowed it with a gulp of tepid coffee.

Then leaned back, the chair creaking, and closed his eyes.

HE opened them some time later to the TAO tapping his arm. "Sir, we're getting intel feed," Branscombe said. "Coming in Zircon chat. Lat-long of a suspected launch site."

"Uh . . . put it on the screen." Dan shook his head and scooted himself up in the chair. He looked around for the coffee cup. Where the hell had it gone? "Amy, you getting this?"

"On it, sir. Coming up now."

On the center screen, the geo plot of Iraq and Jordan, two trape-zoids of the same shape, but different sizes—of course, the displays were at different scales—winked on. Their borders flashed alter-nately orange and bright blue, cycling five times a second. The effect was nauseating, but it popped. The boxes were ninety miles due east of the Jordanian border, deep in Al-Anbar Province. What intel had called the Western Missile Sites.

Dan massaged the orbits of his eyes with the heels of his palms, pressing so hard that black-and-white digital-looking patterns ras-tered his retinas. Then he went to his keyboard. He located the chat but couldn't make sense of the source code. A low-flying A-10, scout-ing for TELs. Or a Special Ops team, buried under some dune with infrared scopes, freq-hopping satellite uplinks. Brave men, deep in a hostile land. He flashed back on his own mission into Iraq. Stum-bling across the desert. Discovered, once, by a shepherd. A dirty-faced kid with a harelip, and something brown stuck between his teeth, and long dark lashes like a girl's. Dan could still recall his frightened, hopeless eyes.

"They've identified a mobile erector," Branscombe said, obviously ahead of him reading the brief, cryptic tweets that floated upward, one after the other, as new transmissions joined the queue. How strange war felt when you could follow it moment by moment, like a video game, as tankers, airmen, staffers, each added his or her own glimpse of unfolding reality. Of course this specific chat was the highest of high-side discussions, limited to the ballistic-missile hunt west of Baghdad. But he could skip from one room to the next and sample war as it fractaled like a nuclear reaction going supercritical.

"All right." Dan sensed a strange, mystical coldness descending like a liquid nitrogen–chilled Pyrex cylinder coming down between him and everything else. If it was time, it was time.

At that moment a digitally generated double chime sounded, one he'd never heard before, from the Aegis area. "Launch cuing incom-ing, Link 16," Wenck yelled.

Link 16 was the primary path for long-range cuing information, a digital 25-kilohertz military satellite channel. There were a number of possible inputs for detection information, but the most likely would be either AWACS, orbiting far to the east over the Gulf, or the down-looking sensors of the geostationary Obsidian Glint, twenty-five thousand miles up.

He pulled over his notebook and called up a little program he'd written. It modeled the engagement geometry in the form of an oblate spherical triangle, with the apexes at the LPE, the launch point, the DOA, the defended area, and their own ship position. It was a simplistic algorithm, but he felt better having an independent check on what ALIS was putting out. The firing point was from western Iraq. That was good; their angle on the incoming missile might be okay.

"We need LPE, IPP, AOU!" he yelled. "Call 'em out and put 'em on the screen."

"Coming through now."

"Put it up! Put it up!" Amy Singhe was yelling. The leftmost panel flickered, then came back. "It's up," she said, voice pitching high.

Dan sat hunched, staring up, fingers poised over the notebook's keyboard as the preformatted TADIL message displayed on the left-most screen. Of course ALIS had already ingested this data. It was developing a track, computing the intercept trajectory, and initializing the Standards. The human eyes and brains reading the formatted message were already seconds behind.

But there it was. Launch point, impact-point prediction, area of uncertainty. The second two numbers he could ignore for now. Even the satellite was only guessing until booster burnout and pitchover. He typed in bearing and launch point. They wouldn't get an intercept angle until they had the impact-point prediction, but he was hoping for no more than five to seven degrees. That would make the basket, that imaginary, suspended circle their interceptor had to go through, as wide as possible.

Above all, he had to keep his limited inventory in mind. Four rounds total, and at the moment, only two available Standard Block 4A theater missile defense missiles. Once he flipped that red Launch Enable switch inches from his right hand, the weapon would run through a built-in system test, match parameters, and fire itself.

To intercept, it had to clear the tube no later than eight minutes after its target had launched. Thirty seconds had already ticked away. . . .

The Aegis display jerked, then jumped forward, as if they were falling toward the desert at some unimaginable velocity straight down from space. The effect was sickening, but he kept his gaze nailed to it, gripping his armrests, as they hurtled down, down. . . .

Toward an infinitesimal white dot. The "gate," a rapidly throbbing bright green bracket, the automatic hook of the radar's acquisition function, curved in from the right. It overshot, corrected, locked on. It vibrated, but the white dot, growing inside the bracket, remained centered, as in a fighter plane's reflex gunsight, or as in some arcade game, where the meteor threatening your spaceship has to be blasted to bits with the photon torpedoes.

No photon torpedoes here. For all her technology, *Savo Island* wasn't the starship *Enterprise*. They might be at the cutting edge of technology, but it was a brittle, fragile blade.

Meanwhile the litany had gone on. When it paused he said more or less by rote, "Concur. Manually engage when track's established."

A stir beside him. Staurulakis slid into Branscombe's seat. She tilted her head, fitting the headset to her ears, and began speaking urgently, cluing the bridge into what was going on. At the same time her fingers blurred on the keys. The leftmost screen, the TADIL feed, toggled off. In place of western Iraq she brought up the GCCS plot, zoomed down to central Israel. The right screen was still raw video from ALIS. "We actually need four screens for the TBM mission," she murmured.

"Save that for the lessons learned," Dan told her. Adding, but not aloud: *If we're around to file one.*

Yeah, that was all they needed to hear from the CO.

The alert-script buzzer went off, a little bit behind the action. "Profile plot, Meteor Alfa," Terranova's soft voice announced. "Meteor" was the new proword for an incoming ballistic missile. "Elevation thirty thousand . . . forty thousand . . . fifty thousand. Very fast climb. Identified as hostile TBM. ID as hostile." She called out lat and long on the launch point. Dan jotted it into his notebook as it came in, and checked it against the LPE from the TADIL.

And . . . they didn't match. "What the *fuck*," he muttered.

He was about to ask for confirmation when the double note chimed again, and a foresense of doom oppressed him. "Second launch cuing," Wenck said, and the same dire note was in his voice too.

Two launches, within seconds. One detected by whoever was out

THE CRUISER   225

in the desert and relayed through the alert network; the second observed by the infrared plume generated by its booster, noted by the camera twenty-five thousand miles up.

Then the buzzer again, from the Terror's console. "Profile alert, Meteor Bravo . . ."

The soft chime again . . . then the buzzer. Yet a *third*. He didn't catch the source this time. Could the three reports be of the *same* launch, recorded by different sensors? No, then they'd have the same launch-point estimate. And the LPE was different for each. Only by a few miles—they were all coming from Al-Ansar—but with enough geoseparation, and different time markers, too. Clearly not the same event.

Three hostile missiles on the way. And just two antimissile rounds to take them on with.

"Meteor Charlie. System lock-on."

"Coordinated launches," Branscombe breathed. Dan didn't answer, or move; eyes narrowed, laptop forgotten, he was riveted on the rightmost screen.

Which jumped from one burning-white dot to the next in abrupt disorienting lurches. As Terranova, or maybe ALIS, switched attention from one contact to the next, the data beside each vibrating bracket laddered upward faster than the flickering numbers on a gas pump.

ALIS settled on the first missile. Its elevation callout, in angels, or thousands of feet, passed five hundred. That number kept climbing, but the white dot, gripped by the pulsating brackets, which up to now had seemed stationary relative to the ground return around it, began to drift. It oozed slowly, but with a steady increment of acceleration, to the left.

The display jerked, shifting to the second missile. Then the third.

A shuddering roar penetrated the armor around them. Dan tensed, then recognized it.

"Combat, Helo Control."

He pressed the lever on the 21MC. "Go, Control."

"Red Hawk wheels up. Request initial vector."

Had he given them a green deck? Maybe he had. "Between us and the coast. Execute skimmer barrier. Get vectors from your controller. We're busy here." He signed off, then hit the lever again and said rapidly, "Pass to Strafer, I want him to conserve fuel. I may not be able to come to a recovery course for a while."

They rogered and he exhaled. At least one minute gone of their allotted eight. Maybe more. But he didn't feel quite as blind with the helo between them and the shore. The SH-60's armament was useless against a sea-skimming C-802. But the onboard radar would give a heads-up, and the aircraft could provide decoy coverage. Actually, he had more confidence in the decoys than in anything else, though Sea Whiz, their last-ditch defense, was a robust system. The last barrier any missile had to make it through was its nearly solid storm of 20mm depleted-uranium slugs, fired so fast it sounded like a continuous note from a very loud bass viol.

But more important just now: the three ballistic missiles on the way, with only two rounds in his magazines. He pushed sweat off his forehead. His calf muscles were knotting painfully, and he stretched out a leg and flexed it.

Slaughenhaupt leaned across and said past Staurulakis, "Captain? *Lahav*'s changing station."

"What's that, Chief?"

"Dropping back. Still maintaining five miles, but looks like she's repositioning."

What the hell? "Which way?"

"South."

"Okay, keep me informed." Dan reared back, but couldn't see over the consoles between him and the electronic-warfare stacks. "And Cheryl, make sure we have the first team back there. This'd be a great time to clobber us from behind."

A stir in the rear of CIC; someone clunked the door shut and dogged it. At that moment Ammermann hitched his chair forward. "What's going on? Are you shooting them down?"

"Silence," Dan snapped, then realized the old powder-magazine command—to freeze in place and shut up—wouldn't carry much meaning for the civilian. "No time to explain. Keep quiet, or leave."

The right screen jumped second to second among the three rising missiles. The elevation numbers on the first, Alfa, were still ratcheting upward, but the rate of climb was slackening. At the same time, though, it was gathering velocity westward. Converting the awesome speed accumulated in ascent into horizontal swiftness. Bent, by gravity's rainbow—Pynchon's phrase—into a ballistic arc. The others, lagging by a few seconds, had not yet reached that phase of flight.

A cunning tactic. Multiple incomers would saturate any defense, not just his own, but Israel's. He remembered his computer, but didn't have time to type. He had to be the consciousness above the action, keeping it all in his head. *Savo* was nearing the south limit of her patrol box. He'd have to choose. Either turn back, risking the loss of his targets while reorienting the locked-on radars; or increase his launch angle, and reduce probability of kill. All the while keeping in mind the threat from shore; the souls in Red Hawk, hurtling through utter darkness, over rough seas, fighting gusts and snow; and the Israeli frigate close aboard, engaged in some puzzling maneuver of her own device.

He clicked the notebook closed and set it aside.

"Getting a better IPP on Alfa," Staurulakis murmured. Dan shifted his attention to the center screen, and caught his breath.

The predicted point of impact was still altering shape with successive recomputation. But with each recalculation, the oblate oval was contracting. He'd expected it to center on their defended area. But it wasn't even over land, much less over Tel Aviv.

The shrinking circle of the first predicted impact point was twenty miles out at sea.

Right over the blue plus-sign-in-a-circle that meant *own ship*.

16

Point Amphitrite

"COMING right down our throat," Wenck said. He'd come over to stand behind Dan.

"Uh-huh. Any last-minute ideas?"

"Just one, Captain. Remember, Block 4's a terminal-phase interceptor. We shoot too soon, the sustainer'll flame out before it gets there. Or lack the juice to maneuver?"

"You're saying, whites of their eyes."

Wenck looked puzzled, then nodded. "Yeah. Whites of their eyes."

Slaughenhaupt passed it on in a murmur over the voice circuit. Great, it'd be all over the ship in minutes. A few feet away Ammermann, looking scared, had taken out a BlackBerry and was busily clicking something into it.

Okay, it was as good a battle cry as any.

The screens kept changing. He wanted to tell Cher to slow down, but there were only three screens and she had to channel-surf to keep up. The ALIS feed kept flickering too, switching among the trio of incomers now entering exoatmospheric flight. Meteor Alfa was streaking westward now. The impact prediction twitched off *Savo Island*'s symbol, but then crept back. The oval kept shrinking, contracting, but stayed centered on them.

He murmured, "What's the plan, Cher?"

"Recommend we take out Alfa, sir. Two-round salvo."

"What about the other two?"

"Their IPP's not us." She toggled and he saw this was true. The second and third ovals were taking shape, vibrating like stranded jellyfish and sort of shaped like them too. The two follow-on warheads would impact well inland.

"They're targeted on our defended assets."

"Yessir. But self-defense comes first."

Something about "self-defense" reminded him they weren't alone out here. "Get that word to *Pittsburgh*. He'll probably be okay, but he doesn't want to be at 'scope depth right now."

"And *Lahav*?"

"I'll call him." He dialed to Channel 16, bridge to bridge. "*Lahav*, this is *Savo Island*."

The response took only seconds. "Lahav. *Over*."

"For your information, I am taking three incoming theater ballistic missiles under fire. Two are targeted on your capital city. The other's aimed at me. I'll be trying to shake it, but it's possible it may decoy onto you. So be warned, and please stand clear while I'm firing. Confirm. Over."

"*This is* Lahav. *I understand. Should I clear to the east? Over.*"

"This is *Savo*. Negative, that won't make much difference before it's here."

Another voice, stronger: Marom's. The Israeli skipper must have been on the bridge, or in the corvette's CIC. "*Copy your launch warning. Thank you for the heads-up. I will continue to guard you.*"

Dan exchanged an eyebrows-up with Staurulakis and Slaughenhaupt. "*Continue* to guard you." Would've been nice if he'd made his mission clear earlier. "Roger, out."

The hiss of ether, then Marom again. "Savo, *this is* Lahav. *Thank you for protecting our country. Out.*"

He socketed the phone, oppressed by the sense of time ticking away, of weapons that would in minutes drill down through the fringes of mesosphere sixty miles up. He reviewed the problem. He'd have to decide very soon now.

Boost phase was over. The lead missile was entering midphase, coasting in that great arc outside the atmosphere. Outside, so despite its terrific speed there was no friction heating. This was the hardest part of its flight during which to maintain track. It was nearly head-on, so not only was it infrared-dim, but its radar cross section was at a minimum.

Thus far, though, ALIS seemed to have a solid grip, to judge from the callouts, which were now registering a high but unvarying speed consistent with ballistic flight. That velocity would remain constant across the crest of the exoatmospheric arc, then build again as it plunged.

Entering the terminal phase, when the gravity-accelerated delivery vehicle hit those first air molecules. Along with a heat signature, the warhead would grow an ionization trail as its ablative sheathing charred away. The cross section didn't grow much, but the electrically charged ionization plume bounced a radar signal too—actually a bigger one than the warhead at its heart. As with the Scud attacks back during Desert Storm, the challenge then became to discriminate between the payload proper and any debris or decoys reentering along with it.

Since his Block 4s were terminal-phase homers, he had to engage then. At that point—ticking rapidly closer, as the delivery vehicle nosed over, ninety miles above Jordan—his decision time would shrink from minutes to seconds, and not many of those.

Along with that, he had to keep in mind the other systems presumably locked on the incomers as well. The battery at Ben Gurion, for one. Israel's other ABM defense, the Arrow, he knew very little about. A midphase interceptor, though. By the time he had to make his call, he shouldn't have to worry about it.

He'd have to watch for the Patriot launch, though. *Savo* and the Israeli army battery might be firing nearly simultaneously. That was another terminal homer, and it was closer to the enemy. *Savo* would be shooting over its shoulder.

Which would not be good for either's P-sub-K. He called, "EW: Sing out if you see a Ku-band homer from that Patriot site."

"Roger, sir."

A touch at his elbow. Ammermann, the broad earnest face sallow now. "Captain. Do I understand one of those missiles is aimed at us?"

"The first one. The intent being to take us out first. Then the Patriot battery, is my guess. The third, and the ones after that, can strike undefended targets."

"Can you take that missile out?"

Dan said, "The question is, do we want to."

"What do you mean? You have to!"

Terranova said, loudly but without any stress in that Joisey accent, "Meteor Alfa, apogee. Hundred and forty kilometers up. Fifteen thousand miles an hour. About to commence terminal phase. Lock-on is firm."

Wenck added, "Request permission to engage Track Alfa with SM-2."

Dan waved the staffer away. Said to the TAO, "Where are we in the launch basket, Cheryl?"

"Damn near at the hairy edge, Captain. But I don't think we want to initiate a turn right now. Two-round engagement?" She hesitated, carefully dressed nails poised over the keyboard. No color, as per regs, but they were neatly manicured and shiny with clear polish.

"Permission to engage?" Wenck asked again.

"Not yet," Dan said.

She turned, and those wide blue eyes searched his. "Two-round engagement," she repeated, this time without the question mark. "At least, can we roll the FIS to green?"

The firing integrity switch wasn't really used as a safety, but it ended up being used that way by default. He said slowly, "FIS to green. But negative on permission to engage."

Another tug on his arm. "That's against the *first* missile, right?"

"Mr. Ammermann, I've asked you before. Now I'm telling you. *Keep out of my way!* —Stand by, Cheryl. Donnie." He tore his gaze from her and nailed it onto the rightmost screen, where the quivering brackets held the center of the picture as the mountains and wadis across which the armies of Egypt and Babylon and Assyria, Rome and Britain, had marched, clicked past with each sweep-and-refresh of the beam.

The Eye of Sauron. If only he could reach out with that demonic entity's power to destroy. It seemed counterintuitive, that the assemblages of metal and solid fuel, electronics and explosives, sleeping umbilicaled in *Savo*'s deep-racked womb could in mere minutes be hurtling through space. To hit a bullet with a bullet . . . it seemed impossible.

And judging by the tests to date, the probabilities weren't all that high.

He rubbed his face, creepy with déjà vu, recognizing the nightmare scenario he'd dreaded. His magazines were almost empty. Should he take the most imminent incoming threat? Increase his probability of kill? And leave the pair following in its comet trail down through the troposphere to impact in their defended area?

Or: Fire one on the first incomer, and the second on the first Israel-targeted warhead?

If only he knew their payloads. Explosives? Nuclear? Chemical? Poisonous isotopes, with half-lives in the centuries?

Or worst of all, the secret horror he and the Signal Mirror team had discovered years before, in those silent tunnels beneath Baghdad. He shuddered, remembering blanket-wrapped bundles, infected technicians hidden away to die . . . shivering, feverish, unconscious, faces and hands scabbed with horrendous lesions. . . .

Dr. Fayzah al-Syori—"Doctor Death"—had started with the most deadly disease in history. Then engineered it to increase its virulence, enhance its lethality, and enable it to jump from host to host on the wings of touch, breath, even the wind.

Classic smallpox killed 40 percent of an unvaccinated population. The death rate from the hemorrhagic variant was double that. And, an Army doctor had told him then, it wouldn't stop at national boundaries.

He shook his head, finding it hard even to breathe. If what he feared was true, only his last and final alternative made sense. He should use both his weapons on the delivery vehicles targeted on the city.

But that would leave *Savo* naked to what had to be some kind of homing weapon, even now screaming down, less than a hundred miles away, closing at twenty thousand miles an hour. When his gaze sought the IPP oval again, it had shrunk to a pinpoint.

Meteor Alfa was still aimed right at them.

"Sir. You still haven't given permission to fire," said Staurulakis. Her lips stayed parted. Her pale thin face hung abeyant, staring at him. The CIC itself seemed to have grown larger, the steel around them thin as the shell of a blown egg. Dan was sweating. His mind was cold, the way it always, or almost always, got when things became really tense. But his body didn't agree. He pressed his palms down on the desk, so no one could see the CO's hands shaking.

"I know. Whites of their eyes, Cher," he said again, as calmly as he could manage.

"It's inside our outer engagement envelope."

"Captain, what's going on here? Aren't you going to fire?"

"Mr. Ammermann, one more word and I'll have you removed. —I know, Cher. But like Donnie says, the later we shoot, the more maneuverability the homer has. We've got another, what, fifty seconds? Just stand by. Just stand by."

"Very well, sir." She closed her mouth and turned back to the screen.

Suddenly, he made his decision. Though it really hadn't been a choice. Just remorseless logic. He reached for the 21MC. "Bridge, CO: Come left, steady on zero seven zero, bring her up to flank. Pass Circle William throughout the ship. Launch-warning bell forward." He clicked to Helo Control. "Pass to Red Hawk: Remain to our east and stand by to dispense flares." As *Savo* began to lean, he told Slaughenhaupt, "Deploy the rubber duckies. Stand by to launch chaff."

The orders clamored away, repeated down the line. Circle William shut down ventilation, sealing them off from outside air. Ticonderogas weren't designed to endure chemical- or biological-warfare conditions. They didn't have filtered air supplies or positive ventilation. But securing blowers and dogging every access topside would at least give them a few minutes' grace, during which, perhaps, they could steam out of a wind-carried contaminant plume. The "rubber duckies" were decoys. An array inside the inflatable tetrahedron simulated the cross section of a ship, presenting a radar-guided missile with a simulacrum of *Savo*. With any luck it would select the wrong one . . . that is, if the incoming homer *was* radar-guided.

"You're going to take it head-on?" Staurulakis murmured. "We sure about this, Captain?"

He wanted to say, *Duh . . . Hell no*, but muttered, "That's what we're here for, Cheryl. What do cruisers do? When they're in the screen, protecting the high-value unit."

"Exhaust our magazines. Then absorb the last salvo ourselves."

"Exactly. If we can sacrifice ourselves to shield the carrier, we damn sure can go down protecting a city."

"Wait a minute—Captain—"

Dan nodded to the chief master-at-arms, who with a grim-visaged Master Chief Tausengelt had been standing behind the White House staffer for the past few minutes. He didn't know who'd called them, but it was time. "Mr. Ammermann, I'll ask you to leave now. But stay inside the skin of the ship. And don't try to interfere again."

"You can't—you can't just . . . just *sacrifice* us. This is insane. You have to—"

"Take him out, Sid," Dan told Tausengelt. The old machinist's oversized hands closed on the staffer's shoulders. Ammermann's face went white, and he gave a grunting squeak.

The chiefs hauled him to his feet and led him away. Dan squinted after them, then back at Staurulakis. "Cher? I gave an order."

Her face seemed to waver, and finally, set. "Got it. —Shift fire gate selection. Launchers into operate mode. Set up to take Meteor Bravo, one-round salvo. Next salvo, Meteor Charlie, also one-round salvo. Salvo warning alarm forward. Deselect all safeties and interlocks. Stand by to fire. On CO's command."

Her fingers raced; he leaned in his seat, body-Englishing *Savo* into the turn as she heeled harder, bringing her bow on to the incoming payload. Making herself as small as possible, like a dueler turning sideways to his opponent's pistol.

Time slowed. He lifted his head, attention flicking from screen to screen, which seemed to strobe more and more slowly. A camera picture shutter-flicked past; the black sea, gleaming as it heaved; the drive of snow sideways like a white wall. Cold outside. Air-conditioned cold within.

And bearing down on them, burning down through the thickening air at a heat far beyond what even steel could stand, a weapon that would in seconds begin searching for its prey. If it got through, they could all die. If it hit the VLS. Or the gun magazines. They had a little steel and Kevlar around them, here in the command spaces. The magazines, a few inches of hardened armor plate. But neither would stop a projectile arriving at three miles a second. The thing wouldn't even need an explosive charge. Like an antitank round, its velocity alone would be enough to drill through whatever it hit. If it was a heavy pyrophoric, like depleted uranium, it would spread flame and toxic smoke wherever it penetrated.

Not looking at what his hand was doing, Dan flicked up the red metal cover over the Fire Auth switch. Deep in its silicon blades of reason and memory, ALIS was computing the parameters that en-sured the highest probability of kill. When he clicked the switch to Fire, the computers would fire at the instant P-sub-K peaked. At his elbow Staurulakis typed away, entering her own command in case the switch failed. A microsecond's hesitation; then she clicked again, and the rightmost screen switched.

"Duckies deployed," someone called behind him. "Standing by on chaff."

The launchers would mortar out a dozen rounds at once, spaced to burst to both sides of, ahead of, and behind the ship, littering the sky with millions of tiny radar dipoles. They also carried pyrotech-nics that burned fiercely in the same infrared spectra as the ship's exhausts. But they didn't burn long, and the dipoles needed time to bloom. They'd have to fire the chaff no more than twenty seconds before the enemy homer arrived.

Which meant . . . *now*. "Stand by on chaff. Pass that to Red Hawk, too, on chaff and flares. Stand by—"

"Terminal body separation," Terranova called.

Dan jerked his gaze up. Blinked at the screen, unable to make sense of the blurring, vibrating images. Instead of a single radar re-turn, grotesquely swollen with the ionization plume, the screen now showed two. As he blinked again the larger one subdivided. Now *three* blips pulsed, two brightening and dimming like pulsars, but unsynchronized; one strobed twice as fast as the other.

"Meteor Alfa's breaking up," Wenck called.

Dan pitched his voice across CIC. "Noblos! Is that a breakup, or just the warhead detaching from a second stage?"

The PhD's voice came hesitantly, then gathered force. "I don't read that as a warhead or a—or a decoy. See that brightening and dimming? That's something tumbling over and over. Varying the cross section from our viewing angle. There—see—it's disinte-grating."

"Ionization bloom," called Terranova.

The rightmost screen jerked and zoomed back as more and more numerous fragments, each surrounded by a comet-halo and streaking trail of radar-reflecting gas, drew apart from one an-other. Now five or six, seven, were pulsing, each at its own rate, tumbling over and over as they fragmented under the g-forces of hypersonic reentry.

Meteor Alfa was burning up. "Whatever they cobbled together, it didn't hold," Cheryl murmured beside him. "Came apart in reentry."

"Okay. A lucky break. Ready to kill Bravo now?"

The keyboard clicked; the brackets snapped into place around the second incomer. "Ready to fire on Meteor Bravo. One-round engagement. Followed by Meteor Charlie, also a one-round engagement."

"Kill them both," Dan said. He waited until he was sure the brackets changed color—he absolutely didn't want to fire on any of the still-incoming debris—and flicked up the switch cover.

A long, heart-stopping pause, during which the toxic vent dampers clunked shut. The recirc ventilation wound down, and the steady rush of cold air ceased.

He was just starting to think *Is it going to*—when the roar came through the deckplates, the stringers, the hull, and the falling snow glared bright white in the camera display.

"Bird one away . . . Bird two away."

On the center screen two small bright symbols left the own-ship circle-and-cross. They blinked into blue semicircles rapidly moving east. Dan eased a breath out, then pulled his mind back from the departing missiles and swept it out and around. "Cher, inform Higher we fired on two TBMs, launched from western Iraq with predicted points of impact within our defended area. That exhausts currently available inventory of Block 4s, but we're working to bring the second pair back online."

"The missile targeted on us? Mention that, too?"

"Sure. It's a new capability, but obviously not quite operational yet. Too bad we didn't get to see if the decoys worked on it." He caught her wide-eyed glance and grinned. Keeping his palms flat, so she couldn't see how shaky he was himself. "Just joking. Okay, let's get around headed north, get back into our area. Fuel state on Red Hawk?"

"Half hour to bingo fuel, Captain."

"EW: Any change on those threat emitters?"

"No change, Captain. . . . Stand by one. . . . Ku-band from Patriot. Patriot going active? . . . Lost track, freq shifting too fast to follow."

He keyed combat systems maintenance central, but got no joy from the report on the after VLS. *Savo* rolled through the night, powerless against another attack. Surely these weren't the only missiles the enemy had. But he too might be keeping something in reserve. A bargaining chip.

On the center screen the bright symbols of the outgoing missiles were still clicking east. The first was already almost to the red caret of the first reentering body. A chill trickled through him; the hairs erected at the back of his neck. But for that moment, in his mind, there existed only the digital world. Reflecting the universe not as it existed, nor as human beings knew it, but as machines alone perceived it: sheared of all meaning and all value. Only atoms, and the void.

"Stand by for intercept . . . stand by . . . *now*," called Singhe, from her hover behind Terranova.

The callouts merged. Then the red brackets jerked, slewing crazily off Meteor Bravo into space. They hunted back and forth for a second or two before finding it again and locking on once more.

Beyond that, nothing happened. The nimbus of ionized gas kept growing. The incoming warhead was plunging fast now, deep into the terminal phase. The blocks of a city stretched below it, dimly limned ghosts in Aegis's omniscient vision. That city lay helpless except for the twin beams, one *Savo*'s, the other the Patriot battery's, that tracked the weapons meant for it. Dan clutched the arms of his seat. Had they waited too long? Had the two radars, locked on the same object, spoofed each other? Or had the Block 4 homer simply malfunctioned? A near miss, a close pass, wouldn't be enough.

One side of the comet-nimbus began to swell. It grew, very slowly, while the other side shrank.

The whole glowing mass, reflecting Aegis's beamed power as if it were one huge solid object, began to pulse. Slowly at first, then to a steadily accelerating beat.

"Launch from Ben Gurion," Terranova called. The screen shifted, and the brackets searched before locking on to a new contact. Its callouts spun upward, the numbers blurring as it ascended at an incredible pace, far faster than either the Al-Husayns or *Savo*'s Standards. A Patriot, rocketing up in a last-ditch intercept. Dan opened his mouth to remind Terror to drop track, so as not to confuse their own missile, then remembered: The Standards were on their own; in the homing phase, they were full-active; their seekers could care less what their mother ship did, miles behind them.

The screen flickered again. When it steadied this time Bravo looked so different he had to check the callout to make sure of what he was looking at. With a huge silent burst of ionized gas, it had come apart into dozens of tumbling pieces, each surrounded by its own coruscating nimbus, each diverging from the original track. Like a fissioning nucleus, first wobbling as it went unstable, then splitting all at once into protons, neutrons, gamma particles, bursts of pure radiant energy.

The whoops and rebel yells from the consoles died away as the screen switched back and forth between Bravo, still disintegrating, to Meteor Charlie, a few seconds away from intercept. Dan leaned back and passed a shaky hand over his hair. Two down. One to go. Could it be possible, they might meet this challenge? Thrust into action too soon, with patched software, marginally trained operators, and too little ordnance, could they actually succeed? He glanced at Staurulakis; she was rapt over the keyboard, frowning at the screens; the manicured fingernails rested on the keys, motionless.

He zoomed his attention back so the big picture opened out again. *Lahav* was lagging to the south. Opening the bearing in case, Dan fired again, and getting a better angle if one of those threatening shore radar sites unleashed an 802. This would be the perfect time, with his attention welded to the incoming warheads. He hoped the Syrians and Hezbollah continued to opt for caution over solidarity. The surface search radar showed nothing else within forty miles. The air search, too, showed vacant space. "Time to bingo, Red Hawk?" he called. At all costs, he had to be able to come to a recovery course; the only alternative would be to divert them to some shore airfield. But that would not be good. Even money whether the diplomats would let *Savo's* SH-60 take off again.

"Twenty-five minutes to bingo fuel, sir."

Singhe's velvety voice came again, over the creak of steel in a seaway. "There's the Patriot, targeted on Meteor Charlie. Looks like intercept . . . *now.*"

CIC went silent again as the screen showed no change in the contact. None Dan saw anyway. Singhe said, after a pause, "Stand by for Block 4A intercept, Meteor Charlie . . . stand by. . . . Mark. Intercept."

"Shit," somebody murmured.

The rocketing comet, wrapped in its blurring shroud of ionized gas, just kept growing. It didn't wobble, or lurch, or split apart.

"I believe we have a miss," Noblos said, too loud.

"Petty Officer Terranova? Chief Wenck?"

"Don't see terminal effects, sir."

Dan sucked a deep breath. Nothing more he could do. "Patriot?"

"Ku-band still radiating."

"They're not refiring?"

The rightmost screen was suddenly empty. The last bracket winked out. The amber spokes clicked back and forth over an empty sky.

"Meteor Charlie off the radar," Terranova said, voice falling. Staurulakis shook herself and began typing again. Dan massaged his cheeks. The bristly stubble felt greasy. How long had he been here? It felt like days. And why was it getting warmer? Oh yeah—he'd secured the ventilation. He told the TAO, "Okay, Cher, get Red Hawk back aboard. Come to optimal recovery course, regardless of the array angle—nothing we can do now anyway. Tell *Lahav* firing is complete. Remain at Condition III, but we can relax Circle William now."

Her fingers lifted. "Aye, sir. What shall I report to CTF?"

"What happened. What else? One reentry body breakup in terminal phase, one successful intercept, one miss." He shoved himself to his feet. "Going to take a leak. Stay on it, we're not done with this yet."

But instead of making for the little head just outside CIC, he went up a deck and let himself into his sea cabin. Splashed water on his face, bent over the stainless sink. Considered vomiting into it, but didn't quite need to.

Eyes closed, he sagged into the bulkhead. Gripping an exposed pipe, he pounded his head lightly against it. The blows felt good. "Why couldn't we have hit them both?" he muttered. "Was that too much to ask?"

But a 50 percent kill rate was as much as they could have expected, given the Block 4's record. Even a bit better. If he'd been able to throw a four-missile salvo . . .

But excuses didn't matter. He should have gotten them all.

An hour later, he was still in CIC, drinking his millionth cup of Sonar coffee, when the news came in. A high-explosive warhead had hit a shelter in a suburb of Tel Aviv. They were still digging out bodies, but the first estimates were 190 dead.

17

UNDER gray but now snowless skies, *Savo* rolled south again. The seas surged in, crests breaking into white patches that heaved here and there across the empty sea.

Dan sprawled in his command chair, boots propped on a binocular box as a spatter of rain blew across the windows and was instantly smeared by the wipers. A clipboard lay checked off on his lap, but he hadn't handed it back yet to the messenger, who was chatting in a murmur with BM2 Nuckols. The bridge team seemed subdued this morning. Over two hundred dead was the latest report. Civilians. Women. Children. Blasted apart and suffocated in a bunker under Hayarkon Park, a suburb north of the city center.

Yeah, he knew . . . *he* hadn't killed them. Someone else had designed, and built, and launched the uprated Scud called the Al-Husayn. But *Savo* hadn't prevented it. You could give reasons why. But the ultimate responsibility was his.

And now and then he wondered, because he too had designed missiles, and tested them, and more than once launched them: Was this really how human beings were destined to live? What curse of Cain, what original sin, had been laid against them, to condemn them not just to kill each other, but to revel in doing so?

He knew by now there wasn't any answer. Through each century Mars still marched, wrecking economies, empires, and individual lives by the millions.

Rid yourself of all illusion. That's what one of his old teachers had said.

Men's hearts, it seemed, were not going to change.

"Done with that, sir?"

"Yeah." He waggled his head, sketched a routing on the topmost sheet, and scribbled his initials.

The message was from Commander, Sixth Fleet. At long last, U.S.-Israeli missile defense coordination at the tactical level had been authorized. It outlined protocol for direct communications with the Israeli Army unit responsible for the Patriot battery at Ben Gurion, with the two Air Defense Forces Arrow batteries to north and south, and with the IADF ballistic missile command and control center, code-named Citron Tree. An addendum laid out a schedule to work out procedures for deconflicting the two nations' missile-defense networks. Dan fanned himself with it, wondering why it always had to take a disaster to make things change. Then cleared his throat. "Get that to Lieutenant Branscombe. We need to set those voice channels up as soon as possible."

"Think the chief's already on it, Captain, but I'll make sure he gets that word."

Dan shifted in the chair. He'd gotten three hours' sleep that morning, but felt ragged and woozy. Plus, he still had that nagging cough. CIC remained in Condition III TBMD. The bodies in the seats had changed, but Aegis was still scanning the skies.

"Captain?" Quincoches, looking haggard. Dan returned his salute. The chief's coveralls were rumpled, as if slept in. But Quincoches didn't look as if he'd slept. "We're back up, aft."

"Aft VLS is up again? That's good news, Chief. But I gotta tell you, I'd have been a lot happier to get it last night."

"I know, sir. We had to splice cables, not enough spares—then test—and it turned out, we had to request wiring data from the contractor—"

"I know." Dan held up a palm. "I take it back. Your guys did everything they could. It was just shitty luck."

Quincoches looked out to the sea that slid by, uncaring, bleak, wintry. Reddened lids squeezed slowly closed. When he rubbed them his fingertips left sooty stains. "D'you think . . . we could've saved them? In the shelter. If we'd given you two more rounds when you needed them—"

"Chief. No." Dan gripped his elbow. "The other side killed them. Not us. And the Army and Marines are going to iron their laundry. If there's anyone at fault here, it's me." He rubbed his own eye sockets. "Should I come down and talk to your guys?"

"I don't think you've got to do that, sir. Not necessary. I'll tell them what you said."

"Okay then." He started to squeeze the FC chief's elbow again, then thought better of it. Nobody really liked a touchy-feely skipper. "That's good, that we have those last two Block 4s back. We may still need them."

Quincoches nodded. He inclined his head once more and left.

Dan pulled out his Hydra, noting *Lahav* on the horizon. The corvette had sidled gradually nearer after dawn, and rode now two miles off, paralleling *Savo*'s course, turning when she turned, but leaving the scanning and firing bearing clear to land. Should he call Marom? See if they needed to coordinate defenses? He couldn't think of anything they could be doing better. Leave well enough alone. But it was reassuring, knowing they were on the same side.

Especially since the *Alborz* task group—the Iranian surface force—was nearing their position. *Pittsburgh* was trailing, occasionally forwarding a report. He coughed into a fist, eyeing the radar. They weren't in range yet, but soon. Maybe that was something to discuss with Marom, since he had no idea what the Iranians intended. Their very presence had to be considered a threat. Maybe he should ask Ammermann about it. But he felt angry even thinking about talking to that guy. Fuck him. Let him stew.

He made a couple more Hydra calls. He and Danenhower discussed their fuel state. The engineer was pleased with their consumption rate at this reduced speed. He was using the down time on the other turbines to catch up on deferred maintenance.

Dan was about to sign off when the boatswain called, "XO's on the bridge."

Almarshadi was stone-faced. Dan returned his salute, still on the Hydra, and said to Danenhower, "Bart, XO just came on the bridge.

It's good you're getting ahead on maintenance, but I want to keep our damage-control teams at peak performance. Can you get with him, set up a drill for this afternoon?"

"Sure, Skipper. Anything special?"

He thought about the incoming surface group; of the Syrian batteries that still, on and off, were illuminating from the coast. "Drill missile hits forward, midships, and aft. I don't want anybody wondering what to do if we take a shot in the gut. —Fahad, I'm asking him to set up a drill—"

The XO nodded. "I heard, sir. I'll get with him and supervise."

"Well, I'd actually rather have you up here on the bridge. Have Mr. Jiminiz run the drills."

"Whatever you say. I'll pass that to the DCA."

Dan sighed and sat back. Now what? He was about to ask when the red phone interrupted them. He snatched it out of the cradle. Waited for the sync.

It was Commodore Jen Roald. She sounded rushed. *"You got the word about the bunker hit? Over."*

He swallowed. "Affirmative. Over."

"It doesn't make us look very effective, but on the other hand, their own defense systems missed it too. But be warned: there may be blowback."

"I'm not sure what you mean, Commodore. Over."

"You saw the message about coordination. Some will ask, why didn't we do that before?"

"Um, I was wondering that myself, Jen."

Her tone sharpened. *"Congress imposes restrictions on release of BMD technology. And I understand that. But then, they ding us when there are adverse consequences. Don't get me wrong. I know what you're laboring under. But some people want a magic shield. And some of those are the same people who defunded . . . well, never mind. New subject."*

"Go."

"Just got word from Strike Center. They're ginning up verbal authorization for you and Pittsburgh *to spin Tomahawks. A source on the ground has eyes on the hide sites for the rest of the Al-Husayns. Also, the green-door folks have something solid on*

the comm nodes. *They're going to the Sit Room to get authorization to clean that mess up. Copy so far?"*

"Copy all," Dan said. "Where do you want me?"

"Up in the east Med four whiskey grid. Pittsburgh is getting this from SUBOPAUTH as we speak. I'll shift tacon to you once you're both in your shooter box."

Dan covered the mouthpiece with his hand. "Fahad, tell Bart to get all engines back on the line. We're headed north to a Tomahawk MODLOC. Have Singhe and her strike team in Combat. I want to meet with them"—he checked his watch—"at noon." As the exec wheeled away and began giving orders he asked Roald, "How many more have they got? Missiles, I mean?"

"Those numbers have always been squishy, Dan. There's also the question of how many transporter-erectors they have left to fire them from. But here's something that just came through: The one you shot down had a concrete nose cone."

"Those are the chemical warheads."

"Correct, with sarin and possibly VX. So if we can destroy them on the ground . . . you're moving north to a launch basket in the vicinity of 35 east, 33-10 north. From what CAG and CVIC are telling me, you'll get an MDU for the target set right about the time you hit your box. Shoot as soon as the missions are validated. My strike chief's in with the APSDET helping them get everything expedited, so he'll be giving you a heads-up over chat."

So the data for their Tomahawk strike was on its way. Chief Van Gogh had come up silently to listen in. Dan showed him the launch box position, jotted on his palm with his Skilcraft. It was only about sixty miles away. Almarshadi had Main Control on the line and was passing the word to Danenhower. The OOD had them in a turn. Dan rubbed his face, heart rate accelerating again. "Roger. Coming north now. But . . . we could launch from here. Why are we . . . ?"

"Look at the map, Dan. And let them have it good. We stomp these snakes in the nest, maybe more civilians won't die."

"Aye aye, ma'am."

Roald signed off. Dan socketed the handset and swung down. The bridge was suddenly full of many more people, all busy. He debated staying, but his strike station was in Combat. Still, he stood over the chart for a moment, frowning. Then noticed the international bound-aries, and suddenly understood.

If they launched from the position Roald had just assigned him, the low-flying cruises could follow the Lebanese-Israeli border east, allowing both countries to deny they'd granted overflight rights. Past that it got more complicated, with Jordan and Syria still be-tween the sea and western Iraq. But Jordan generally cooperated with the U.S., and Syria might need the unmistakable threat a dozen missiles violating its airspace would provide.

All that was beyond his pay grade, though. The kinds of things he'd worried about when he was in the West Wing.

Past the bustle he caught a glimpse of Longley. His steward lifted a covered tray, eyebrows raised. Dan shook his head at him—*not now*—and brushed past.

HE was intercepted on the ladder down by the chief corpsman. Grissett was lugging a heavy black tome with a scarlet-and-gold-embossed cover. "Skipper, got a minute?"

"Not really, Doc. But if it's important—"

"It might be. Yeah. I think it could be."

"Quick download. We're getting ready to launch a Tomahawk strike."

"This won't take long. We got an autopsy and lab reports back on Goodroe."

Dan coughed into a fist, experiencing a bad second before he remembered who Goodroe was. Then it came back. A peaceful-looking, heavy-jawed face, nude chest. Dried foam at the corner of a livid mouth. A flaccid, purplish penis, and the thin tube of the catheter going in . . . And nobody seeming to have much idea why the sailor had died. It felt like it had happened months ago, but of course it had been only days since they'd helo'd the body out. Gris-sett said, "This is from Bethesda, but looks like they got Fort Det-rick in on it too."

Dan took a fast breath. Fort Detrick was Army, infectious dis-ease. And not only that, biological warfare. He'd spent time there himself. Locked in a negative-pressure Maximum Biocontainment Patient Care suite while they'd waited to see if he, and the rest of the Signal Mirror team, would sicken and die. "Give me the—no, just tell me. It wasn't drugs, was it?"

"No sir. No trace of any drugs."

"The anthrax shot?"

"Probably not, although they can't rule it out. They think it's fungal."

Dan turned at the landing and started down the next ladder, head turned to keep talking to Grissett, who followed. "Huh. Fungal? Not viral?"

"No sir. They list the organisms they suspect. Question is where he could've picked them up. Also, we got two more guys down."

He stopped in the passageway, staring at Grissett. "Two more *dead*?"

"No sir, no—I meant, two more on sick call. Cough, elevated temperature, torpor. I dose 'em with cipro, but I'm stumped as to what we're actually seeing." The corpsman opened the tome, a heavy medical reference. Started to hold it out, then closed it again as Dan waved it away. "Actually, the cipro may not even be helping. Which might explain why some of them don't seem to be getting better."

Dan lowered his voice, though they were alone in the echoing narrow ladderwell that slanted as *Savo* rolled. "Are you saying there's something infectious aboard? Something Goodroe died of?"

"That might be one conclusion."

"Can it be bacteriological? I mean—obviously it's bacteriological—I mean—"

"A deliberate attack?" Grissett looked grave. "If so, it's too late to fend it off. I'm seeing cases all over the ship. At first just one. Now I'm getting four, five at each sick call. Not all bad enough to sick-bay. But it's definitely building."

"Christ." He sucked a breath, then remembered where he'd been heading. "Give me the message. . . . Is it on the LAN? I'll read it right away and get back to you. Is there anything we can do?"

The 1MC came on, hissed, then said, *"Captain to CIC: Now set Condition Two, Strike. All strike personnel report to CIC."*

Grissett said, "Researching it, sir. Can I see you later with that?"

"Yeah, but if we need to take action, let's do it before more of our troops go down."

The corpsman nodded, and stood aside.

IN Combat, with the air-conditioning whooshing and the whole ship vibrating around them as they drove north at flank speed, Dan sighed. Someone brought him coffee. Without conscious thought he updated himself from the displays. The Iranian strike group was closer. *Pittsburgh* had left them behind, headed for the same MOD-LOC as *Savo*. The weapon-inventory summary, above the large-screen displays, showed his last two Block 4As operational again aft. The eight Tomahawks aft and eight forward, evenly divided among the C and D TLAM versions, indicated green mode, ready to launch.

Not the stuff of his nightmares, but rather, a ship ready to fight. He checked his watch: a few minutes before the strike team meeting at noon. Mills was in the TAO chair, talking urgently at the same time he typed. Apparently bringing *Lahav* up to speed, in both senses, on their sprint north. A glance at the surface picture told Dan the corvette was accompanying him.

The TAO saw him. "Captain's in CIC. —Sir, TSC just called and told us to power up eight C3s and stand by for tasking. This came in unexpectedly—"

"Yeah, I just got a heads-up from the commodore. They got eyes on target and intel they think's solid. We'll get a short-notice update and shoot as soon as the missions are validated."

Dan folded himself into his seat, reflecting on how much had changed since he'd coordinated the very first Tomahawk strike, for Operation Prime Needle. The "flying torpedo" had been an untested concept then. And a clumsy one, its targeting entailing hand-transporting bulky hard drives that contained the route points, and long hours spent hand-programming the seeker heads.

Now routes and targeting came down via satellite. The shift to GPS navigation meant he didn't have to sweat the problems they'd had with flat terrain. Tomahawk was the cornerstone of the fleet's ability to project power inland, either clearing the way for air strikes from the carriers or, the way they were going to use it now, to hit high-value command, control, and communications nodes, and possibly enemy missiles as well, before they rolled out on their transporter-erector-launchers and fanned out to fire.

He clicked from voice circuit to voice circuit, then spent a couple of minutes on high-side chat. Twisted in his chair to see who was at the Aegis console. He had to call three times before Wenck snapped out of his mesmerized fixation on the screen. The chief turned it over to Eastwood and ambled over, scratching until spiky blond hair stood straight up. "Sir?"

"Look like you need some sleep, Donnie."

"You too, Skipper. Why're we heading north? We're gonna constrain our geometry."

"We're already constrained. But they're pulling us north to spit some Tomahawks. See the message about high-level coordination with the Israelis?"

Wenck picked up Dan's cup and drank from it. Dan would've been taken aback, except by now he knew the guy was totally unconscious of doing it. Donnie didn't multitask, but his powers of concentration were terrifying. In the Gulf, he'd read binary code from the callout lights while it was loading into a Russian MVU-199 fire-control computer. "Yessir. We got a freq set up. But you know, it's uncovered."

"Uncovered? That's not so good."

"Better'n nothing. Actually it might be okay. At least for now. Long as we can say, 'You take the one on the right, we'll take the one on the left.' Or whatever." He looked at the cup. "Was this yours? Sorry."

"Take it, since you started it. How's that cooling-system problem? Did we get that taken care of?"

"Slaughenhaupt's guys replaced the flow rate sensor couple days ago. Part came in on the chopper. You didn't hear?"

"Probably somebody told me. But it's been . . . whatever."

"Yeah, I get you." Wenck glanced at the rightmost screen, and winced at something Dan couldn't even see. "Uh, I better get back. But you know, Dan—I mean, Captain—you got to sort of let go of some of this. Let us take care of business."

"I thought I was doing that, Donnie. You think I'm getting too micro?"

"It's not a criticism, sir. You saved all our fucking lives, there on *K-79*. At least here we got air to breathe."

"Yeah, there is that." Dan swallowed, remembering despite himself the terrifying hours beneath the surface in a sub they had to guess at how to run, unable even to read the labels on the gauges, with most of the Iranian navy trying to kill them.

Someone cleared her throat. He looked past Wenck to Lieutenant Singhe, who was tapping her foot. He glanced at his watch again. Five past twelve. "Okay, I'm gonna be with the strike team. Let me know if anything happens."

"Okay, sir, and remember—every mile we go north out of the basket, the dumber we're gonna look if Saddam launches again."

WITH a reminder he really didn't need ringing in his ears, Dan joined the team back by the nav table. Their Barcos, their consoles, were the entire center aisle; the little cleared area was a natural meeting place. Some perched in empty ASWS chairs. Others stood with arms folded. Singhe, shoulders sagging, braced herself against the nav table beside Dan. Matt Mills, the combat systems officer, grabbed a folding chair and dragged it over. He nodded to Dan, then gestured to the chair. Dan straightened, not pleased at the offer. He ran his gaze around the faces. Slaughenhaupt. Redmond. Crandall. He knew their names, but he didn't know this team nearly as well as he'd come to know the Aegis gang. The admiral's mast in Naples had hit the strike team hardest. Torn the guts out of it, in fact. Half the replacements were off Jen Roald's staff; the others, fleeted up from lower-ranking enlisted. Neither Noblos nor Wenck had given them high marks. He half turned, to see Almarshadi fitting himself into the end seat on one of the RGN-651 consoles. Then faced front again as Singhe cleared her throat.

"Captain, we just got verbal direction to spin eight TLAM 5. I acked the message. The DesRon strike chief told us over chat we're going to get some fast plan-and-shoot tasking."

Dan nodded. "I got a heads-up from the commodore."

Before she could answer, the red phone labeled TLAM C&R beeped and flashed. "Savo, Pittsburgh, *this is* Cutlass, *over*."

"This is *Savo*, roger, over," Singhe said. She had it on speaker, so they could all hear.

"This is DesRon Strike. Just wanted to pass on what you're about to get MDU'd. The targets are suspected hide sites and C4I nodes in what's being called the Western Complex, or Western Missile Sites. Where the launches last night came from. Strike will be coordinated with real-time intel. The idea's to target any TELs which sortie from their pookas and attempt to set up and fire before the strike arrival.

"Break. Savo, *how copy, over?"*

Singhe glanced up at him; he nodded. "This is *Savo,* copy all," she said. "Continue, over."

"This is Cutlass. *We'll finish validation on our end in five mike, and start the MDU then. I show both shooters active in MIRC, so I'll pass the MDU over EHF."*

"This is *Savo.* Works for us, over."

"Pittsburgh. *Good for EHF MDU here also, over."*

"Any problems, I'll be on Coordination. Also, we tasked extra Charlies. Keep them powered up. The admiral may or may not keep you in the shooter box. Lot of discussion here. Your Charlie Oscar may be getting some questions regarding time and distance. Stay in the loop. Cutlass, *out."*

Dan sat back, keeping tabs as Singhe finished the prelaunch brief. He felt uncomfortable with the way mission data was being passed on voice and over chat. This seemed to be a time-sensitive tasking, though, so he didn't object.

"All missiles mode seven," said one of the launch controllers.

Singhe said, "Copy mode seven." She picked up the red phone and gave the Line India report.

The leading FC, who was on chat, said, "MDU inbound."

"Get it down to TCR. Get it set up. —Captain, just got mission numbers and other data from *Cutlass.* Request permission to start planning."

"Permission granted, but don't execute until the strike controller tasks the missions."

Dan got up and strolled a slow circuit, looking at each screen. He was settling back into his chair when the 21MC in front of him clicked on. *"CO, OOD."*

"Go, Mr. Mytsalo."

"Sir, report arrival at MODLOC. Request course from here?"

Dan leaned on both elbows, studying the surface picture. Clear, except for the single pip of *Lahav* off to the southeast. Far to the right, faint indications that might or might not be the mountain peaks behind Beirut. On the rightmost screen the saffron spokes of the search beam clicked steadily back and forth, still scanning the Al-Anbar desert.

Once the Tomahawks crossed the beach headed inland, Syrian air defense would have to recognize where they were aimed. If they passed that word on, whoever controlled the Western Complex would know they were on their way.

Mills said in a low voice, "Our course doesn't much matter, sir. Whatever minimizes our roll, I'd say."

"Mr. Mytsalo: Choose a course and reciprocal to mimimize roll."

A pause, then a startled, *"Aye aye, Captain."* Dan grinned, remembering how seldom he'd gotten to make a decision as an ensign. Then sobered. "Matt, what am I overlooking? Anything else we should be doing? We don't have long until this launch window."

"Going through the checklist, Captain."

Dan reached under the desk, found the current NavSea manual for launch procedures, and ran down chapter 4. Amy would be backstopping her team, making sure they followed their own station checklists, but he couldn't help surreptitiously making sure no one made any stupid mistakes. He knew the procedures. Some of them he'd designed, back at the Cruise Missile Project Office. But he'd actually launched Tomahawks only once before, aboard *Horn*.

He sucked a breath as he remembered the last-minute glitch in the nav system of one of those missiles, a shorted relay or fried circuit board. The launch code back then had been extremely restrictive. Unless it knew exactly where it was going, the missile would refuse the launch order. And since the system fired weapons in serial then, a hitch in number one meant none of the others would fire either. He'd had to execute a series of S turns, and reposition the ship exactly where the first missile's gyro had frozen.

That had been three or four iterations ago. So that particular problem shouldn't recur. But any others that popped up . . . He hoped the team was on top of this.

"Captain, MDU complete."

"Very well, Lieutenant Singhe." He stretched to work out a cramp in his back, wishing NavSea would spend a few more of those defense dollars making the chairs a little more comfortable.

The red phone again. "Savo, Pittsburgh, *this is TSC. Verbal Indigo 001 Delta Tango Golf follows.* Savo: *Mission target 1A1, verification CODE 56342. Quantity, one Block three Charlie. Time on top: Shoot soonest.*

"Savo: *Mission target 1D1. Code 14353. Quantity, one Block three Charlie, time on top . . .*" The voice droned on; the team, heads down, were scrutinizing each target and code on the screens. *"Break; how copy, over?"*

Singhe repeated back, exactly, what the strike controller had just passed. Not a lot of chatter from the rest of the team, a good sign; people who knew their jobs didn't need to talk a lot. They'd be entering verification codes and required text data. Comparing the launch-sequence plan with what the computer was spitting out.

Singhe, on the Strike circuit. *"Captain? Request permission to send, TLAM make ready."*

The "make ready" command sent engagement plans and mission data to the missiles, which would power up and start the test protocols. Dan clicked his mike. "Granted."

"TLAM make ready, plans sent."

"Missiles pair, all plans."

Standard commands, from drills on the old *Horn.* The combination of familiarity and reality felt weird, the way it always did when he'd had to fight. Like two layers of reality, drill and what was really happening.

Mills murmured, *"Lahav* still on our starboard quarter. No surface or air contacts other than Iranian group fifty miles to the south. No air tracks except for Red Hawk. We'll clear him to the west just before launch. EW reports coastal radars have ceased illuminating."

"Huh," Dan said.

Singhe, on the circuit. *"Missions checked and downloaded. Rounds spinning up."*

"Spinning up, aye." Once in flight, the rounds would navigate by GPS, but for the initial regime they'd depend on gyros to operate their vanes for boost, pitchover, and transition to engine start.

Which was usually where things went to shit. Dan kept wanting to lean forward, say something, but reined himself in. He got up again and was pacing around when the engagement planner called, "Skipper? Ready for onscreen approval."

Dan bent over his shoulder, checking the graphic display. No problem with the flight path. He checked missile type and time data. It all looked good. "Mission 1A1 approved. Send to launch."

Singhe was off the red phone. Dan moved back so she could take her normal seat again. Murmured, "Launch direction."

"OOD, Strike: Verify launch direction clear to port."

Mytsalo verified that the bearing was clear. She warned him not to change course or speed for the next ten minutes, then went back to the countdown. At minus two minutes she picked up the 1MC mike. "All hands. Tomahawk missiles will be launching from forward and aft launchers. All hands remain clear of weather decks while salvo alarm is sounding."

Mills, at his elbow. "Captain? The helo . . . ?"

"Thanks, Matt. Let's get Strafer out of there."

Mills, on the Transmit button. "Red Hawk, Matador. One minute to launch; stand clear to the west."

The pilot rogered up. The salvo warning alarm wailed faintly through steel. Dan closed his eyes, tracking his mental checklist.

"Confirm whip and fan antennas silent."

"Confirm blast exhaust doors open."

"Alignment complete."

"Time to launch: thirty seconds."

His cue. He'd worn the keys around his neck, on the same chain as his Academy-issue dog tags, since they'd left Naples. He stood above the launch console. Lifted beaded steel over his head, and handed the key to Singhe.

"Time to launch, ten seconds."

Singhe plugged her own key in, then Dan's. Glanced at him, the dark eyes passionless, and gave each a half turn.

Everyone looked at him. Dan waited a beat, then nodded. "Batteries released, primary plan."

"Salvo firing commence," Singhe said, and the launch controller hit the Shoot button.

A distant thud, then a shudder: the cell and uptake hatches slamming open.

Someone had focused one of the gun cameras on the forward VLS. Along with the others in CIC, Dan watched a huge ball of flame suddenly burst into existence just aft of the forward five-inch gun. Almost too fast for the eye to follow, the missile flamed up through its rubber waterproofing membrane, then slung suddenly upward from its cell.

Like an Olympic gymnast performing some complex twist while hurtling through the air, it reoriented, surrounded by the glare of the orange flame, and departed, a bright star quickly dwindling. Smoke blasted across the field of view, then thinned in the wind. Hemicylindrical covers tumbled through the air, blown free in the first hundred meters of boost.

The camera tracked jerkily upward, and caught it again. An orange star, red as Mars, still climbing, still shrinking. He'd seen the sequence dozens of times, first during development, then in predeployment testing, then during Prime Needle . . . until it sometimes seemed that the weapon he'd shepherded through its teething was the main way his country interacted with the Arab world. The engine inlet popping open, shedding the dual shrouds protecting the exhaust. Fuselage wing plug covers ejecting. Steering and stabilization fins switchblading out, followed by the wings. Then booster burnout, and the nose dropping.

He held his breath, but there it was, the winkout of the orange spark of the booster, and nearly simultaneously, the black smoke of engine start. . . .

Singhe keyed her red phone. "*Cutlass*, this is *Savo*. Greyhound away. Break. 1A1, transition to cruise. Out."

Dan blinked at the screen. The smoke column looked grayer than he recalled. Had they changed the booster composition? The remaining missiles went out at eleven-second intervals. It was growing dark. Another missile ignited into orange fire, illuminating the forecastle in glaring Halloween light, lofted, dwindled. Then the launch-roar shifted aft as the rounds in the stern magazine woke, ignited, and departed, a squadron of avenging furies.

"Rounds complete," Singhe told him at last. He passed a trembling hand over his forehead and turned away. Shaken, as if his own sinew and muscle had lifted tons of explosives and sent them hurtling over sea and land. But then he had to turn back and take the key she pressed into his hand. Loop it over his neck again, feeling the stainless chain warm from her hands, slick from his own sweat and perhaps hers, too.

He said hoarsely, "I'll be topside when you're ready to send the firing report."

ON the bridge, it was nearing full dark. He brought *Savo* around to clear the submarine's range. If a booster failed, he didn't want to be in the way. Then stood on the wing with his binoculars, watching *Pittsburgh* firing from beneath the dark sea. The big night glasses pulled each missile in close as it leapt free of the waves, ignited with hot red-orange flame, and blowtorched away into suddenly brilliant night. Tangerine glared off onyx crests. Smoke trails glowed like cotton candy, draped across a black starless sky. Every eleven seconds another blasted up from the deep, ignited, and accelerated off. He followed them in the dark double circles of the glasses until they occulted. Youngblood called over the red phone, giving his end-of-salvo report. Cutlass acknowledged and made the launch area cold, but told both shooters to keep the remaining TLAMs powered up until further notice.

Dan checked his watch. His own salvo would be crossing the coast just about now. No doubt the Syrian air defense network, one of the densest in the Mideast, had the hurtling airframes on their screens. Was following an international boundary violating the airspace of the countries on either side? He didn't have a clue.

A hollow thunk as the wing door opened. A shadow in the dark, complete with helmet and life preserver. "Captain?"

"Fahad. What have you got?"

"I reported strike complete. To CTF 60."

"Well . . . I was going to do that. But I guess that's all right." If the Syrians did lash back, the quickest way would be to unleash those C-802s. "They say anything about air cover?"

"No sir."

"Did you ask?"

"No sir."

"XO, what're you doing right now?"

"Supervising the bridge team. Isn't that where you wanted me?"

"Right, right . . . How about getting on the horn and making sure everybody knows to be alert for some kind of retaliation. Most likely, a sea skimmer from the Syrian side." He considered asking him to get with Grissett, tasking him to dig into the sickness issue, but didn't. Right now, they had to be ready to fend off a more immediate threat.

A pale red planet caught his eye, moving slowly south to north. He frowned, then identified it. Deholstered his Hydra. "TAO, CO: We need Red Hawk back between us and the coast. Tell 'em to keep their eyes peeled. Also, ask 60 about that air cover they promised would be on tap."

"You didn't say anything about asking for air cover." The voice from the dark was resentful.

He felt abruptly sick of this whole situation. No matter what he said or did, Almarshadi took offense. "It wasn't a criticism of you, Fahad. Okay? I've just got a lot on my plate right now. We'll sit down and have it out when we're not at Condition Three. Till then, can we just . . . *stuff it?*"

A stiff silence. Then, "Yes sir, we will stuff it. But I'm going to request a reassignment."

"Great, whatever. Now can you do what I asked, and make sure we're scanning for C-802 signatures?" He crossed to the doorway, leaned in, and asked the helo control talker for time remaining to bingo fuel. It wasn't long. He started to hoist himself into his command chair, but failed. Shit, he was too fucking exhausted even to get up into the fucking chair.

"Captain, course from here?"

"What do you recommend, Ensign? Remember, we're going to have to recover the bird shortly."

"I think we ought to . . . head south? Back toward Point Adamantine?"

"Sounds good." He rebraced himself and this time managed to half-jump, half-lever himself up. Coughed hard, then relaxed back into the cool padded leather, like a softball into a well-worn glove, and closed his eyes.

The beep of his Hydra, as he was slipping away. Just as the vividness of dream began to supplant a heaving sea, the whistle of the wind in the antennas, the squeak and murmur of the helm console. He grunted, then resubmerged. The radio beeped again. He fought to the surface like a drowning man, groping for it. "Unh . . . Captain."

"Skipper? TAO here."

"Hey, Cher, you back on already?"

"Afraid so, sir. I'm bringing us to flank and heading south."

"Why? What's going on?"

"Monitoring the chat. Israel's taken enough. That two hundred dead was the last straw. They've decided to retaliate. Just sent us a warning message."

He opened his eyes. For a moment what she'd said didn't make sense. But it must have been just some open circuit in his own brain, because the next moment it did.

All too horrifyingly. The Israelis had shown over and over again they wouldn't take aggression lying down. Entebbe. The Osirak reactor. Lebanon. You could debate whether armed reprisal was a tactic, or a mind-set, that could ever lead to permanent peace. But certainly, striking back in the name of the dead of the Tel Aviv bunker was consistent with their previous policies.

He cleared his throat, still trying to get his head around what it would mean. "Uh—retaliate. Did they say how, Cher?"

Before she could answer, the scarlet bulb strobed above the Navy Red handset. *"Matador, this is Iron Sky. Stand by for flash traffic from Iron Sky actual. Over."*

Iron Sky was CTF 60, the task force to the west. He got it with his left hand while he asked Staurulakis again, on the Hydra fisted in his right, "Retaliate? How? —This is Matador actual. Over."

"There's speculation. A missile counterstrike seems to be the consensus. But of course they don't say. Just warning us to stand by. So we can be ready. For the consequences, I mean."

The Navy Red circuit said, *"Matador actual, this is CTF 60 actual. Flash traffic follows."*

"What kind of missile? —This is *Savo*, uh, Matador, ready to copy." He jerked his head at Van Gogh, at the nav console. "Get this down, Chief."

"They don't say. And no one knows. They have a nuclear capability. Whether this is a case where they'd use it . . ."

"This is CTF 60 actual. Dan, we have a flash notification about Israeli plan to retaliate for the Tel Aviv hit this morning. We need you back in your defender position ASAP."

He gestured again, angrily, to Van Gogh. Snapped into the handset. "This is *Savo*. Copy your flash notification. Coming to flank speed at this time. Uh, just to make clear: I have only two Block 4s remaining. And limited self-defense capability."

"Understand limited capability. Remain alert for counterstrikes. Review your op order. Let me know if you need a frag on your ROEs. Iron Sky, out."

The light died. Decoded, the task force commander had just advised him to be perfectly clear that he understood under what circumstances he could fire first. And to let him know if the rules of engagement seemed too restrictive. Too late, Dan cursed himself; he hadn't brought up the question of air cover, either. They'd be out here naked if the Syrians decided to vector a couple of MiGs his way.

When he went to rub his mouth his hand jerked, and a cup of cold coffee he hadn't even realized in the dark was there tipped and spattered. Damn it! It was happening again. Strike and counterstrike. Reprisal and counterblow, and a steady descent into bloody chaos.

But what should anyone have expected? This was the Middle East. Any fuze you lit was tangled in among a dozen others. And would light them all as it crept toward its own bomb.

Why did it seem like mass killing was the default option for every international quarrel? As if human beings didn't have enough to deal with: . . . No, they still had to throw themselves beneath the entrails-bedecked chariot of Mars. Or was he thinking of some other god, equally bloody-handed? And why did all the gods, it seemed, come from a three-hundred-mile radius around where he rolled through this black sea?

But what he wondered made no difference. His duty, and that of every other man and woman aboard, was plain as if engraved on bronze tablets. The ship reeled. Somewhere steel banged hollowly, and the wind sang in *Savo*'s thirty-eight antennas like a mourning chorus in a Greek tragedy.

18

Oparea Adamantine

WHIRLING *snow, again.*
The booming sea.

They echo through deserted caverns as he feels his way. Un-
sure of any destination. With the white thing, which he'd only
glimpsed from the corner of his eye, following him. Still back
there, somewhere. And only a little air left on his gauge . . .

Then, somehow, Wenck was down in the watery caves with him.
What the hell? "What are you doing here, Donnie?" he asked the
electronics technician.

"How about waking up, Dan? Uh, Skipper?"

He woke with neck cricked, curled awkwardly in his chair. The
air-conditioning made a rushing clatter like a flock of blackbirds
taking wing. Someone coughed, the dry hacking stirring a tickle in
his own scarred trachea. He stirred, gaze pulled to the screens.
"Cher . . . Matt," he croaked. "Where the hell are we?"

"Five miles from the oparea boundary," Staurulakis murmured.
When he glanced over, her face was Wicked Witch green. For a moment he didn't know if he was awake or still dreaming. Then realized she'd only changed the display; the emerald hue was from her
terminal.

Wenck again, murmuring close to his ear. The bright blue, off-
kilter eyes glittered as if he were on some nonregulation chemical,
but that was just Donnie. "We gotta talk a minute, Skip."

"Tell me what you've got, Donnie. It can't be anything Commander
Staurulakis hasn't heard before."

"Maybe so, maybe not. Over in the corner, okay?"

Back in the dark under the comm status displays, Wenck bent to the scuttlebutt. It was seldom used now, since most of the crew bought bottled Aquafina from the soft-drink machines. The water came up under high pressure in a thin stream, almost a spray. He straightened, drops glittering on his cheeks, and wiped his mouth on one sleeve. A heavy book was clamped under his arm. "Sir, I'm reading the backroom chat. That missile hit Tel Aviv? You know they're gonna react to that, right?"

"That's why we're heading back south, Donnie. Wasn't that message in your queue?"

"Sir, don't take this wrong, but by the time you zeros get shit through Radio, it is *long* past the sell-by date. Me and the Terror, we're following the chatter on one of the Israeli nets. Got in through a back door. She's crooked, that girl. Don't let that quiet act spoof you."

"Who—Terranova? Are you serious, Donnie?"

"Serious as shit. Since they approved coordination, we said, we gotta have some way to coordinate, right? Most of it's in some other language, Israeli I guess, but they use English for the technical discussions, and we can see the numbers, and all the code's in Ada. Like, when they're talking about range-gate anomalies, or whatever—I guess Hebrew doesn't have the words, or it's easier because that's what their Patriot manuals are printed in. Anyway, they got the heads-up. Counterstrike. Beth and me worked the target out from the ascent trajectory."

But before he could ask, the chief went on. "It's Baghdad. Baghdad for Tel Aviv. Eye for an eye, I guess."

"What kind of missile? What's the payload?"

Wenck unelbowed the blue-backed copy of *Jane's Missile Systems* Dan remembered seeing racked with the other CIC reference works. "What they call the Jericho. Like our old Pershing. One-ton warhead. Four-thousand-klick range. Nuclear or conventional warhead."

Dan ran his eye down the page. An idea was germinating. But he needed more data. "Couldn't you ask them a question?"

"Who?"

"The guys on this chat you and Terranova're lurking. The Israeli techs."

"We could *ask.* Whether they'd answer . . . What you want to know?"

"Tell them we need to deconflict, too. When do they intend to launch? And what's the payload?"

Wenck snorted. "They're not gonna tell us *that.* I'm not even gonna ask."

"Okay, but we have to know *when*, at least. That's a reasonable request."

The chief went away behind his eyes, gaze vacant. Then bent to the bubbler again. "Okay."

When he left, Dan paced back and forth, took a drink from the scuttlebutt himself. It sprayed his face too. He wiped it with his palms and went to the J-phone on the bulkhead and punched in his own in-port cabin.

"Ammermann here."

"Adam? Dan Lenson. You cooled off any?"

"What choice have I got?"

"Come back up to CIC. I might have a job for you."

"Oh, you need me now? After having your goons haul me out?"

"I'm sure Chief Tausengelt was perfectly respectful, Adam. But get in my face during combat operations, and you get the 'goons,' as you put it. Just stay on your side of the line and we'll get along fine."

A grumpy "Right," and the staffer hung up.

Dan socketed the handset and paced the width of the space, beam to beam, looking at each screen and acknowledging each man or woman at his or her station. A nod, a shoulder pat, an encouraging word. Singhe, by the Aegis console, was doing some kind of yoga pose, one leg held up with an arm behind her back, the other arm extended toward the overhead. She dropped it as he neared, and returned his nod with a cool smile.

On the aft camera Red Hawk was coming in for a hot refuel. Snow—snowing *again?*—drove across the screen like confetti, and beyond it the black waves heaved. Mytsalo had altered course to improve the wind. Strafer would hover five to fifteen feet above the slanting, pitching deck, and tank up through a dangling hose. Dan watched the SH-60 grow larger. It seemed to sway from a string. He didn't envy the pilot. The helo crew had one of the most dangerous jobs on the ship. And if a C-802 came over the horizon, their station put them between it and *Savo Island*. Not a healthy place for a low-flying aircraft squawking a signature mimicking a cruiser.

He ducked into Sonar, where as usual Zotcher and his boys seemed to be doing absolutely nothing, but was back in his chair when Ammermann's wide-cheeked face loomed out of the dim. The staffer caught a stanchion as the deck slanted. Dan pointed to a chair.

The West Winger perched, scowling, dark hair lank over his forehead. "Okay, I'm here. What do you want?"

"First, some advice." Dan described the Iranian task force closing from the southwest. "What do they intend to do up here? Especially now, when we're breaking into the house next door—they've got to mean that as a provocation. If not a threat."

"We'll deal with them next. They've got a WMD program too."

"Okay, whatever, but . . . Are you saying this is their way of warning us off? In case we're thinking exactly what you're saying?"

"I can't speculate on what they think."

Dan frowned. "But that's exactly what we *have* to do, Adam. They can't like having four U.S. divisions and fifteen air wings right across the Shatt al Arab. Which is where the endgame's gonna leave us." Ammermann didn't answer, just scowled at the deckplates. "Okay, you haven't thought about it, but I'm asking you to. Reach back. Find out what the national security adviser—Dr. Szerenci— what his gang thinks they're doing. Because once that task group gets here, I've got to figure out if they're enemies, or just front-row spectators."

"Okay." The staffer sighed. "Is that all?"

"No." Dan coughed hard, feeling like something wanted to come up but couldn't. Christ, he was tired. "Want some coffee?"

"No. What's that noise?"

"That's our helo refueling. And when he's done, he's going to go out again and fly back and forth between us and some Syrian missile batteries that have been shining us. In case they decide to go hot. This is the real deal, Adam. We need you on the team. We've all got to set ego aside."

The staffer grimaced. "Want me to call back? Then give me a phone. Or a circuit. Whatever you call it. What else?"

"We just got word Ariel Sharon's approved a retaliatory missile strike. Apparently, on Baghdad. A population center."

Ammermann paled. "Christ!"

"Correct. I don't need to tell you how hard that's going to make it with our Arab allies, do I? How that's exactly what Saddam hopes Sharon'll do? If you have any pull with Ed Szerenci, or any channel to the president or State, this'd be the time to use it."

"When? When are they planning to—"

"I'm trying to find out. But we don't have long." The hovering helo's engines were the thunder of drums from aft, diminished by steel and Kevlar armor, but perfectly audible. He twisted in the chair. "Matt, tell Branscombe to set Mr. Ammermann here up with hicomm voice to whoever he wants to talk to."

"Got it, Skipper."

Staurulakis stood next to Mills, hands on her hips. Getting ready to take over the watch, apparently. Dan glanced from her to the vertical displays. *Savo* was crossing the northern boundary of Adamantine. Mills was on the line to Main Control, discussing dropping their speed once more. Dan sighed. He didn't have much fuel left, after the sprint north, then south again. They'd have to request a tanker. . . . Maybe Adam could actually do some good. If he had the ear of someone in the White House, they could put the screws to the Israelis, convince them it really wasn't in their best interest to strike back.

He paced the space again, staggering as the slowing ship picked up a corkscrewing roll. Then slid back into his seat and felt for the clipboard with the op order. He read it through again, forcing his eyes through each line of print, forcing his fatigued cerebrum to visualize clearly what every sentence might mean in terms of an engagement. Then zeroed in on the opening paragraph again.

5. (TS/FW-DS) CINC AND NCA GUIDANCE FOR CTG 160: REF C IS DRAFT NCA GUIDANCE REGARDING EMPLOYMENT OF TBMD ASSETS WITHIN A COMBAT THEATER. REF C IN EFFECT AS OF THIS DTG. REVIEW AND COMPLY.

6. (TS/FW-DS) IT IS UNDERSTOOD THAT FOR THE FORESEE-ABLE FUTURE USN TBMD CAPABILITIES WILL BE EXTREMELY CONSTRAINED BY LIMITED NUMBER OF SERVICE-READY BLOCK 4 SM ROUNDS. THEREFORE, IN THE ABSENCE OF MORE

DETAILED GUIDANCE, ASSETS WILL BE EMPLOYED IN THE
FOLLOWING ORDERS OF PRIORITY:

PRIORITY ONE: OFFENSIVE MISSILES TARGETED AGAINST US
OPERATING FORCES AND LOGISTICS BASES.

PRIORITY TWO: OFFENSIVE MISSILES TARGETED AGAINST
FORCES OF US ALLIES.

PRIORITY THREE: OFFENSIVE MISSILES TARGETED AGAINST
CIVILIAN POPULATIONS.

PRIORITY FOUR: TBM INTERCEPTOR PLATFORM (OWN-SHIP
DEFENSE).

7. (TS/FW-DS) IT IS ALSO UNDERSTOOD THAT GIVEN HIGH
SPEEDS OF ENGAGEMENT AND UNCERTAINTIES IN IMPACT
PREDICTION, CO/TAO MAY BE FORCED TO USE BEST JUDG-
MENT IN ASSIGNING PRIORITIES AND ROUNDS AGAINST IN-
COMING WEAPONS. REGARDLESS OF PRIORITY DERIVED FROM
THE INTENDED TARGET, CO/TAO NEED NOT ENGAGE IF COM-
PUTED PROBABILITY OF KILL FALLS BELOW .3 FOR A SINGLE-
ROUND ENGAGEMENT.

8. (TS/FW-DS) CO/TAO WILL TAKE INTO ACCOUNT REMAINING
LOADOUT AND CURRENT THREATS IN ASSIGNING ASSETS.

He contemplated this, forefinger polishing the bridge of his nose.
Own-ship defense was plainly not a high priority. Which was pretty
much consistent with a cruiser's traditional mission. On the other
hand, priority three seemed to have been written very tightly. Once
U.S. forces, logistics bases, and those of allies were covered, his mission clearly included the protection of civilian populations.

Not *friendly civilian populations.*

Not *civilian populations of states not currently engaged in offensive operations against U.S. or Coalition forces.*

Just . . . *civilian populations.*

"Sir, I've relieved Lieutenant Mills as tactical action officer."

"Sir, I have been properly relieved." Mills and Staurulakis stood over him, looking expectant. He harrumphed acquiescence and checked his watch. "Very well. Cheryl, anything I need to know?"

"Within oparea boundaries. Speed five. Course one seven zero. Two SM-2 4As active and green. Aegis at ninety-eight percent in TBM mode. INS *Lahav* three miles due north, following in our wake. Red Hawk 02 refueled and returning to ready station."

"The Iranians?"

"Forty miles southwest. Looks now like they're making for Tartus."

"Uh-huh." Tartus was the Syrian navy's main supply and outfitting port. It hosted the Russians, too, when they made port visits in the Med. Made sense that the Iranians, one of Syria's patrons and suppliers, would also refuel and resupply there. Sending an unmistakable message that they stood behind that regime, if the U.S. decided not to stop at invading Iraq.

For the first time, a glimmer of reason behind the deployment. "That track's gonna take them real close to us here."

"Correct," Mills said.

"So they could still actually be headed for us? Not Tartus?"

Staurulakis's clear gaze turned in some manner opaque, as if an invisible barrier, impervious to X-rays, perhaps, had been slipped behind them. "I know, I know," Dan added hastily. "But I have to consider these possibilities, Cheryl."

"I would think it'd be Tartus, sir," she said.

"Well, I think so too. For the record . . . all I'm saying . . . ah, forget it. —Matt, lay below, get your head down. We've got another long night ahead." He checked his watch again; what exactly was the time? Eight, but 0800 or 2000? Day or night? Losing track wasn't a good sign. Then he remembered the gun cameras, the darkness outside. 2000, then. He'd missed dinner somehow.

"Longley was up about an hour ago," Mills supplied. "You were, um—you had your eyes closed. I told him you probably needed rest more than dinner."

"I'll give the mess decks a call. Have them send up a sandwich," Staurulakis said. Mills lingered for a few seconds, then pirouetted groggily in place before getting his bearings and heading for the aft exit.

Dan stretched, got up, and prowled again, not relishing being nursemaided by his midgrade officers like some dotty old uncle. He remembered how Crazy Ike Sundstrom had napped in his chair, snoring. Had querulously bitched over the most trivial things. And how his staff, including Dan, had all laughed behind their hands.

Now it didn't seem as funny. People didn't bounce back as fast at forty-something as they did at twenty-two. Interrupted sleep night after night, plus heavy Navy chow and no exercise, was no avenue to alertness. He could guzzle all the coffee they could brew, but his brain was working more and more reluctantly, like a garbage grinder designed to run on 220 volts but getting only 120.

He massaged his neck. God, he was getting tight. Wished he could have taken Amarpeet's yoga class. But that wasn't going to happen, the skipper going to the mat with four females in sweat gear. Nuh-uh.

"I'll be out on the weather deck for a couple minutes," he told the space at large. "TAO has my seat." Without waiting for a response, he let himself out.

THE night was heaving outside, the wind a cold bayonet in his throat. He doubled, holding his belly, coughing and coughing. *Savo* was in darken ship, of course; he'd had to fight his way out the weather-decks door through the black canvas screens. When he caught his breath at last he fumbled at his belt to make sure the Hydra was on. The tiny red LED that said so was the only light in the entire world.

He felt his way, one hand outstretched, through a void like that of intergalactic space until his outstretched fingers brushed the life rail. He gripped it like a man adrift grabbing a raft, and hauled himself uphill as the deck rolled, slick under his boots. He didn't want to go over the side. Not in this blackness. He looked aft, searching for *Lahav*, but didn't see her. Probably darkened too.

Crouching there, gripping the cold steel, he reviewed options.

Complicating any decision were three factors. First was "rounds in the shot locker." He had only two more Block 4As. Use them on an Israeli missile, and he'd have none left if Iraq struck again.

He turned his TAG Heuer and checked the luminescent hands. By now his salvo of Tomahawks, and *Pittsburgh*s, would be reaching their targets. But they wouldn't have damage reports for hours, until daylight let drones and satellites get a close look at the Western Complex.

The second factor: What if rounds three and four didn't work? So far his batting average was only .500. And as Roald had said on the red phone, that was already above the test average.

And the third: Wenck and Terranova's backstairs scuttlebutt from the Israeli tech side was welcome, but he couldn't depend on it. He couldn't tell where a ballistic missile was aimed during its boost phase. And this would be a very complicated, risky boost-phase intercept. Their SM-2 would have to perform a tail chase intercept, a mission geometry that, he knew from the test data, had never worked well.

Bottom line: If he fired, he wouldn't have a real good probability of kill. All in all, less than .3. At a guess.

He sucked cold sea air, going downstream on that logic as he searched the darkness. They'd already failed once, on the Tel Aviv hit. What would rolling craps again mean for the Navy? It didn't look appealing. And what if he succeeded? In blocking *both sides* from aggression, would he be committing the U.S. to a role it couldn't really fulfill?

Actually, he thought wryly, starting to shiver now, Dan Lenson wouldn't be committing anyone to anything if he screwed this up. Only himself to a court-martial, disavowal, and being cast into outer darkness forever. The Navy was merciless toward commanders who screwed up. He'd already had a full ration of second chances. As Nick Niles had made abundantly clear.

He was still staring into a darkness his gaze could not penetrate when the Hydra on his belt beeped. He fumbled for it. "CO."

"Sir, TAO here." Her voice was tenser than he'd ever heard it. *"EW reports C-802 lockon from landward. Also, we've got a course alteration on the Iranian task group."*

"What kind of alteration, Cheryl?"

"Directly for us, sir. Stand by . . . EW reports fire-control radar scanning from the west as well. Correlates to Alborz task group."

He lifted his head, cupping the heavy little radio, dense with its thick weight of metal and battery. The darkness was rushing toward him, blustering like the wind that whined in the antennas above. "How about the Jericho launch? Any further word on that?"

"No sir, none I've heard. I'll check with Terranova. Are you coming to Combat?"

He half-smiled, a tight grin that probably would've looked sardonic, or maybe tortured, if anyone had been there to observe it. Something twisted in his gut, sharp-cornered as a masonry trowel. Taking a deep breath, he pressed the Transmit button, fighting it off. Fighting off all emotion. And said, forcing into his voice the firmness and confidence that were the very last things he actually felt, "Yeah, Cher. I'll be right in."

19

I'M glad you're back," Staurulakis murmured, pushing short hair back. For the first time since he'd met her, she seemed on edge. And no wonder, he thought as she outlined the situation. A lock-on from the fire-control radars they'd identified along the coast. Increased activity from the truck-mounted jammers that would make detection of an incoming sea-skimmer much more difficult. Wenck and Slaughenhaupt hovered near the command table, looking grave.

Dan tried to make his face as much like stone as he could, although that blade still twisted in his gut. "You said the *Alborz* group—"

"Turned toward, yes sir." She typed and the display changed. It showed a sharp hook east.

Three ships. Yet only two had turned. "Who's that staying on the original course?"

She typed and the callout strobed. "*Bandar Abbas.*"

"The supply ship?"

"Combined tanker and storeship. Limited self-defense capability, but not a combat unit."

"They're dropping their logistics train."

"Yes sir. Not good news." She rippled the keys again, and they studied the warships headed for them. The primary threat would be from the frigate, but he couldn't ignore the smaller craft, a cruise-missile boat, either. "It's either some kind of overt provocation, or an actual run-in."

"Not necessarily on us," Slaughenhaupt put in.

"Correct, Chief. Could be *Lahav;* or a strike on the coast. But we've got to assume the worst-case scenario. And since we're get-ting illuminated from the east as well, it looks like a coordinated attack developing." Dan shoved back from the desk, skin crawling. It really would be "worst-case." *Savo* was still in BMD mode, and had to stay there. Which meant they were limited to keyhole-peeping with the SPY-1, and not nearly as capable of fending off a below-the-horizon attack.

Yet, despite the pain in his gut, he was starting to feel eager. Any resolution would be better than keeping on with this uncertainty. "Designate *Alborz* and the missile boat to Harpoon. Tell Amy to spin up four TLAMs for those coastal sites. CIWS to automatic. Duckies and chaff to standby."

Staurulakis looked wary. "Sir, we need an MDU for a Tomahawk strike—"

"No we don't, Cher. We can set in the GPS coordinates ourselves. And I'll give you 'red and free.' If they fire, rules of engagement give us a self-defense right to take them out. —Let Red Hawk know what's going on. We'll keep him out to landward, but let him know we may have goblins coming in from *Alborz*'s bearing, too." He nod-ded. "Let's get set, guys. This may be it."

He hoisted himself to his feet, trying to bat away the cobwebs of too little sleep, too much stress, the sheer bone fatigue that set in fighting the slant and lean of a ship in heavy seas day after day. Not to mention trying to guess a way out of the rapidly constricting box *Savo Island* was being trapped in.

He wheeled abruptly down the narrow corridor between the air consoles and the EW stacks. Weariness engraved the faces of those who manned them too. The chill air stank of sweat and ozone and bodies not washed often enough. The edges of the gray steel con-soles were grimed black where wrists had rested for hour after hour, watch after watch, day after day. *Savo* wasn't billeted for continu-ous Condition Three. Her truncated crew had come through man-fully up to now. No, not "manfully"—that would have excluded too many. Staurulakis. Singhe. Terranova, and so many others, from the deckplate engineers to the bridge watchstanders. Who had all, in the words of that traditional Navy accolade, sailed close to the wind.

He was suddenly filled with emotion so overwhelming his eyes stung. He had to clear his throat and scrub a mistiness from his sight. He was proud to lead them. He only hoped he could do as well, when the crunch came.

Which could not be far away now. And the very fact that they were all exhausted, running on empty, meant he had to be more careful than ever. This was when commanders made stupid mistakes, or misjudged the situation. And people died.

"Sir, illuminating from fire-control radar. Bearing one two five."

He wheeled back to the EW stack and cleared his throat again. "You mean two two five?" It must be *Alborz*. Or her smaller, faster consort, trying to nail them from a distance. Strange, though; tactically he'd have expected them to separate, angling for different bearings for a coordinated launch.

"No sir. One two five. K-band radar; correlates with Eilat-class corvette." The petty officer darted him a glance. "It's *Lahav*."

He couldn't help whispering "Crap." What the hell was Gabi Marom doing? "Could they be illuminating *Alborz*? And we're just in the way?"

"Don't think so, sir. I might pick up a side lobe, but . . . no sir, he's locked solid on us."

Dan's fists tightened. The Israeli corvette, which so far had seemed to be escorting him, riding shotgun, from the hints her captain had dropped, was now scanning him with its fire-control radars. Could the Israelis have intuited, guessed, his so-far barely formulated intent? And now were warning him? They were inside *Savo*'s Harpoon range. If they attacked, all he could do was hope to slap down their missiles with Sea Whiz, then take them under fire with his five-inch gun.

He didn't like how this was developing. Coincidental or not, it was becoming all too much like the classic three-point attack, with threats developing from widely spaced bearings all around the horizon. Stretching even the most capable combat suite's ability to detect, track, and respond.

HE was standing by the command desk, unable to decide even whether to sit, when a murmur ran through the space. Cheryl Staurulakis said something under her breath, and gripped his arm like a falcon alighting. He could actually feel her nails. It was so unlike her that he flinched. Glanced at her, then looked where she was staring.

Fahad Almarshadi stood just inside the doorway from aft, beside the dark gray rubberized curtain that partitioned off Sonar. The slight little XO was holding something down close to his leg. Dan frowned. What the hell was going on?

Slaughenhaupt, on the right of the command table, half turned his head. Murmured, "He's got a gun."

Ice ran down through Dan's arms. He sucked a breath and straightened. The motion must have attracted the exec's attention, because his face came around. The thin hawklike visage steadied on him.

Almarshadi took a step toward Dan. Another. Holding his right arm down close to his side. As he advanced, the petty officers scattered, jumping up, backing away, to the far end of CIC. Leaving a cleared space around the command table. Now what the little XO held was visible, pointed muzzle-down alongside his thigh.

Voilà, Dan thought. The mystery of the missing nine-millimeter was solved.

Almarshadi halted. He peered around, then back at Dan. Who'd frozen, bent forward at the waist, half-standing, palms flat on the desk. Beside him, apparently not having noticed anything amiss, Staurulakis was typing away, head down.

Dan cleared his throat. "XO. What's going on? Thought you were on the bridge. This is a real-world contingency. I really need you up there." A reminder of the guy's duty; maybe that would snap him out of whatever this was.

"You should have cleared me."

No, duty wasn't going to work. Dan straightened. If the guy was going to shoot him, he'd take it standing. An image: his own pistol—locked in his weapons safe, in his at-sea cabin, as it so happened. Only about fifty yards away, but as inaccessible as the Andromeda galaxy. "*Cleared* you? Of what, Fahad? I've never charged you with anything."

"They say you were tortured. In Desert Storm. Maybe that's why. I don't know."

Dan lifted a hand, slowly, and smoothed his hair. Trying to get his breath, which was suddenly coming hard through his damaged airway. "I'm not following, Fahad. I had a bad experience. True. But I think I've treated you just as—"

"Shut up." The exec didn't look enraged, or berserk. Just more determined than usual. "This time, *you* listen to *me*. Cher! Stop typing."

Staurulakis flexed her shoulders and glanced over. And only then looked surprised, as if realizing just now that an armed man was in the space. "Move away from him," Almarshadi told her. "This is between the captain and me."

Staurulakis braced herself on the arms of her chair but didn't rise. "Go ahead," Dan told her. "He's right. This is between us." To the exec he said, "How about if we take this out on the weather decks? The two of us? No reason to put anybody else at risk."

"They're all on your side."

Dan cleared his throat, trying for a reasonable tone. "There are no *sides* here, Fahad." A gross oversimplification, his brain commented dryly. But let it stand. He took a step forward, but halted as Almarshadi's weapon rose. He presented his palms. "How about putting that away? Or at least telling me what you want?"

"What I want? It's what I *wanted*. But it's obvious that's beyond what you felt like accommodating." Almarshadi swallowed visibly; the muzzle, though, hardly wavered. "I'm the second-most-experienced officer aboard. I screened for command! But to you, I'm only here for the paperwork. Maintenance documentation. And to dump on when you're pissed off. You don't want me on station when we're alongside. But you call away a shipwide search when you can't find me.

"Face it, Captain Lenson. It isn't Fahad Almarshadi you've got it in for. It's anybody with an Arab name."

Dan glanced aside, to see Amy Singhe crouched tense as a panther five yards away. Unfortunately, one of the ASW consoles, a hulking mass of metal six feet high, was between her and the man with the Beretta. He switched his gaze back quickly, but not without sending her a thought message: *Don't*. He took a step left, and the muzzle followed him. The little open black hole described tiny circles, but never seemed to leave his center of mass.

Dan murmured again, "If that's the case, you don't have a problem with anybody else here. Let's take it outside. Commander Staurulakis?"

She flinched. "Sir?"

"Take my seat." He raised his voice so everyone in the space could hear. "TAO has tactical command. CO and XO are . . . uh . . . offline." For once, naval terminology failed him. The only military term that seemed at all applicable to what was going on seemed to be "mutiny." But it didn't seem politic to throw that word at the sweating, desperate man who stood irresolute a few feet away.

Despite himself, Dan glanced at the vertical displays. And took another quick breath; the tracks of the incoming Iranian contacts had split. They were on diverging courses now, opening their bearings to *Savo*, though still closing the range. Like muggers in an alley, spreading out to confront a cop with one bullet left.

But he had to solve the more immediate problem. "Okay, XO. You're in charge now. Where're we going? Out on the weather decks?"

Almarshadi wavered. He glanced at the screens, then back at Dan. "They're attacking?"

"Doesn't it look like it? You did the TAO course at Newport."

Almarshadi blinked and took another step back toward the door. He frowned at the displays. "Aren't you going to preempt?"

"Not in the ROE, Fahad."

"You're a strange guy, Captain."

"I just follow orders, Fahad." Dan took another breath, but it seemed to be getting harder, as if his throat was closing up again, as it had after the firebombing in Naples. Could the guy be right? That he'd regarded him with suspicion from the first . . . because of his ancestry, and his name? He didn't want to believe that. He didn't *think* it was so. But maybe . . . maybe some of the blame was his.

Hell, he was the CO. *All* the blame was his. No matter what happened outside, on those wet slick decks, in the blackness of winter night. Actually, in the dark, Almarshadi would be vulnerable. And he had to foresee that. So he'd probably shoot when Dan's back would be to him, going through the darken-ship curtains.

But at least no one else would be in the line of fire. The issue Berettas held fifteen rounds: enough to take out most of the men and women around them in CIC. Above all else, Dan had to get him away from them. He forced numb legs into reluctant motion. "Shall we?"

As he took a step forward, Almarshadi took one back. Still holding the gun on him. Still looking both irresolute and past caring.

The gray canvas curtain to Sonar parted. Something small and low to the deck barreled out. A crouched-over Chief Zotcher hit the XO in the midriff, arms extended, grappling for the weapon. The impetus carried them both bodily into the dark corner under the comm readout. The thump and clang as they collided with the scuttlebutt was overlaid by a pistol crack. Confined by the black-painted bulkheads, the low overhead, it was as close and loud as a lightning strike.

Zotcher reeled back and crashed into the outer door as it burst inward. The doorway was suddenly filled with bulky figures in orange float coats and body armor, shouting hoarse commands and pointing shotguns and short-barreled rifles. *Savo*'s intercept and boarding team. Scrambled, Dan had no doubt, by Staurulakis's typed message over the ship's LAN. The lead petty officer crouched low, sweeping the space with his weapon, then caught the pointing fingers and wheeled left.

Almarshadi had the pistol free again, but he wasn't aiming it at anyone. He was just holding it down, along his thigh. Frowning. Looking puzzled. "Don't shoot him!" Dan shouted. "Fahad! Put the gun down!"

"No, there's no point in that," Almarshadi said.

"Put it down, Fahad. Please."

"I'm sorry, Chief," the exec said to Zotcher, who'd slumped to the deckplates and was holding his side, face shocked white. The executive officer lifted his head, and his voice. Looked them all over. "I could shoot somebody else," he said. "But what good would it do? Just confirm what you already think. That Arabs kill."

"Give us the pistol, Fahad," Dan pleaded. "Fahad. Please."

"May God have mercy on me," Almarshadi said. He fingered the sidearm for a moment, groping at the neck of his coveralls with his other hand, while the boarding team kept their carbines on him. Then brought the gun up again, slowly, his gaze locked for once with absolute confidence on Dan's, and pressed it to the side of his own head.

CHIEF Zotcher had taken a bullet in the side. Grissett straightened from the Stokes litter where the sonarman lay. "It missed his kidney, I think. If I can stop the bleeding, he might not be in danger."

Dan was on one knee by the litter. "Can we get him down to sick bay? Is it safe to move him?"

The chief corpsman said it probably was. Dan squeezed Zotcher's hand. Blinked past him to the covered form in the corner. A green nylon bag lay unfolded and unzipped beside it, freshly stripped of plastic packaging; the air smelled of blood and talcum and burnt powder. The pistol lay a few feet away. The chief master-at-arms was bagging it with gloved hands. He glanced up. "Serial matches the one missing from the quarterdeck. Sir."

"All right. —Thanks, Doc." Dan wanted to stay, but couldn't. He laid Zotcher's hand back on his chest, and patted his shoulder. Met his squinted gaze. "Nice work, Chief. You done good."

A grimace, probably meant as a smile. "Not totally a pain in the ass . . . right, Skipper?"

"Not totally. I'll see if I can get you something for this." Dan patted him again, shaking his head, and jerked himself to his feet.

Took two steps, and knelt by the body. Almarshadi lay with his head turned away, which was just as well. Blood and brain matter spattered the cables that ran up the matte black of the bulkhead. The XO's left hand still gripped the cross that had hung from around his neck. Dan put his hand on the motionless chest. *I never*, he thought. *I didn't* . . . His inner voice faded back into the blank hissing rush of fatigue.

He'd mishandled the XO. That was the bottom line. Misread whatever subtext had dictated his bewildering touchiness, his strange mixture of prickliness and eagerness to please.

Just another failure in a long string of them.

"Can I get a shot, sir?" Grissett said, beside him. Holding a camera. "Then we'd better bag him, and get this cleaned up."

"Treat him with respect, Doc."

"Always, sir. Want the pistol back in inventory?"

"I imagine it's evidence, right? The NCIS's gonna want it?"

"Could be. Yeah."

"Then no. Bag it and lock it up."

He pushed the guilt and sadness away and rose, knees protesting after so long on the hard steel.

*   *   *

HE wiped both palms across his face, trying to reorient as Staurula-kis, who'd gone back to her seat as soon as the boarding team had broken in, briefed him in spare sentences. In the minutes the con-frontation with Almarshadi had eaten, the Iranian warships had separated even farther. They were now ten degrees apart in bearing, with their courses still diverging.

"Does that missile boat have to be bow on to us to launch, Cher?"

"Not that class, sir. Not with that missile."

"And *Lahav*—"

"Bearing zero seven five, range fifteen thousand. Course, zero three zero, speed twenty. Opening to the northeast."

A heavy figure in civvies stood at his elbow. "Tell Bart we want full power available," he told Cheryl. "Let's go to general quarters." He nodded absently to Ammermann, his mind caroming around several tracks at once as the 1MC crackled, hissed, and began to bong in that sustained note that always stilled his heart when he heard it. Nothing much would change in CIC; they were already at full battle manning. But the rest of the ship would be dogging doors and hatches, donning helmets and flash gear, manning damage-control teams, weapons, launchers, magazines.

Getting ready for the ultimate test.

Lahav was opening, but she was still between *Savo* and the Syrian radars, the truck-mounted launchers. The Israeli Corvette had ceased illuminating them during the drama with the exec. Which he did not have time to think about any more just now . . . "*Pittsburgh?*"

Cheryl flinched and rattled the keyboard. "Almost forgot about them . . . They're out of torpedo range, but locked on to the missile boat with sub Harpoon."

"Okay, that leaves *Alborz* for us—"

"Can I get a word in?" said the staffer.

Dan forced his tone halfway toward courtesy. For a second he couldn't remember what he'd sent him to do. Then did, and coughed into a fist. "Uh, Adam. Any luck on what I asked you to look into? Intentions of the Iranians? Whether the West Wing can get Israel to hold off striking back?"

"I talked to the national security adviser. Dr. Szerenci said you know each other."

"Uh-huh. He was my professor at George Washington. A long time ago, when we . . . anyway, a long time ago."

"Well, he couldn't give me anything on the Iranians. We don't have a window there, apparently. There are a lot of different factions, too. The regular navy. The Revolutionary Guards. Not a unitary actor. If you know what I'm talking about—"

"Don't talk down to me, Adam. Yes, I know unitary-actor theory."

"Sorry . . . Captain." The staffer shook his head like a boxer shrugging off a hard punch. "He said he'd call Sharon. A personal call—apparently he can do that if it's important enough."

"That's all? He's going to call?"

Ammermann shrugged. Dan stared for a moment longer, then sighed. He'd tried. More and more, it was looking like that was all he was going to be able to do. Just try . . . but fall further and further behind rapidly cascading events.

"That missile boat's a Thondar-class," Staurulakis murmured. "Could be a Guards unit. Like he says."

"It's getting a little late to speculate on who exactly's who," Dan told her. "These guys are in an attack profile. The only question is at what point we hit them. Range?"

"Thirty-four thousand yards."

Outside the warning range from his ROE, but hostile maneuvering trumped range. "Warn them," Dan snapped. "Break off, or I will open fire."

"You said you can't shoot first," Ammermann said.

"I sure as hell can in this situation," Dan told him. "And I will, but I don't really have time to explain it,"

Staurulakis called something from the desk and a man Dan didn't recognize came toward him. Tall, mustached, swarthy, in his mid-thirties, he inclined a long, closely shaven skull with grave politeness.

"Who's this, Commander?"

"This is SK3 Kaghazchi, Captain. A native Iranian speaker."

The man's large eyes were burning, unsettling. Where had this guy been until now? Dan didn't remember seeing him about the ship. SK meant storekeeper, one of Hermelinda's people. He probably worked in some tiny office. It did seem that whatever language you needed, someone in your crew could be found to speak it. Still, he thought he'd met everyone aboard. "Excellent. Okay, Kag . . . Kag*haz*-chi, right? Where are you from, Petty Officer?"

"Sanandaj, sir. In the west." He had an astonishingly deep voice, almost an operatic bass. Good, they'd sound authoritative as hell going out over ship-to-ship.

"And what exactly do you speak? I know several languages are current in Iran—"

"Farsi, that is my father's language. And some Urdu as well. From my mother."

"I see. Well, I know you're in Supply, but consider yourself under the commander's orders now. Convey what she tells you, but use your head. I'd rather avoid a confrontation than have to win one."

"I understand, Captain. I will attempt to do that."

Ammermann said, "Are you sure about this, Dan?"

"My ROEs are pretty clear in this situation," Dan told him mildly. "So's the LOAC."

LOAC was the law of armed conflict. The staffer started to expostulate further, but Dan waved him to silence and leaned back, listening as their warning went out, first in English, then in the staccato notes of Farsi. It sounded familiar to him from repeated deployments in the Gulf, though he knew only "hello" and "thank you" himself. He doubted words would have much effect if whoever was commanding the task group had orders to clobber him, or somehow thought this would be a good time to try. But in this case, for once, as he'd told Ammermann, his rules were clear. He had the right to defend his ship in the face of attack, imminent attack, or demonstrated hostile intent. The maneuver he was seeing constituted that. But first he had to issue a warning. "If they don't cease illuminating and don't open the range, I'm taking *Alborz* out with Harpoon," he told Staurulakis.

"Warning shot, sir?"

"Not at this range. If we have to hit, hit hard."

"Copy that, sir. Three-round engagement?"

"Set it up. Make sure *Pittsburgh* gets that word." He coughed and ran his gaze over the displays again. A cup clanked down next to his elbow. He sucked the black scalding liquid down almost in one breath. Hot and thick, the strong dark blood the Navy ran on. As long as they had fuel, ordnance, and coffee, they could stay on station forever. For whatever reason, adrenaline, caffeine, the confrontation with Almarshadi, the abruptly cut-off note of the GQ alarm, all the displays glared more brightly. His brain seemed to have shifted into high gear.

When Ammermann cleared his throat Dan remembered him. "Uh, Adam, find yourself a seat if you want. Chief? Chief Slaughenhaupt? Need a helmet here. And flash gear."

"On it, sir."

"Are you serious?" Ammermann gaped. "I thought this was armored—"

"Just wear it, Adam."

"Uh . . . okay. Can I smoke now?" He had the pack out already, was tapping a cig out with trembling amber-stained fingers.

"No. So, no joy from Jerusalem?"

"Tel Aviv. I told you, Ed's calling Sharon."

Dan bet it wouldn't be "Ed" if the junior staffer were face-to-face with Dr. Edward Szerenci. The guy had been nothing to trifle with even back when he'd been a professor in defense analysis at George Washington, moonlighting from the War College. Szerenci was a hard-liner, a numbers man, dealing in megadeaths as coolly as Dr. Strangelove.

Dan was opening his mouth with some sort of joke about Szerenci when a chime sounded from over by the Aegis console. The same high insistent note as once before. All speech in CIC ceased. Someone had turned on audio from the SPY-1: a familiar crackle, like popping popcorn. The beam going out, five times a second.

"Sir, we have cuing from Obsidian Glint," Donnie Wenck called. "Suspected launch."

Next to Dan, Staurulakis riffed the keyboard, bringing up the radar output on the large-screen display. The spokelike beam yawed, then switchbladed back toward the coast. The Terror was shifting to the location the satellite had just downloaded to them. It locked into its new position and clicked back and forth, the spectral amber fans tracing ancient mountains like a blind man fingering a face. They all stared up, skin sallow and corpselike in the nectarine light.

Dan squinted. "I don't see anything."

Then he did.

A white dot had blinked on in the center of the screen. The hook darted in and snagged it. A callout flickered on. Terranova said, loud enough so everyone could hear, "Profile plot, Meteor Echo: altitude, angels thirty. Climbing at angels five per second." Already well into boost phase, then. Possibly even post–first stage separation.

"Matches alert script on the Jericho," Wenck called. The symbology was already a red caret, but he added, "Designate hostile?"

Dan nodded. "Designate hostile."

"That's an Israeli missile?" Ammermann murmured.

"Correct," Staurulakis snapped when Dan didn't answer.

He was watching the horizontal velocity on the callout. So far, it was nearly zero. But wouldn't this be the best time to take it? Nearly a dead-on angle? The P-sub-K numbers in the tests had dropped fast with a negative velocity vector. He eyed the screens again, and decided. It would put her stern to the Iranians, but *Savo*'s close-in stingers, her canister-mounted Harpoons, were canted up back aft.

He hit the worn lever on the 21MC. "Bridge, come to course zero nine zero. Speed fifteen. Set Circle William. Launch-warning bell aft." He snapped the dial to Helo Control. "To Red Hawk: Reposition to the north. Stand by on flares and jamming. Remain alert for 802s from northwest, west, and northeast." Two seats away, Slaughenhaupt was readying the ship for self-defense with chaff and decoys.

Dan groped into the neckline of his coveralls and came up with the firing key. "Cher? Take Meteor Echo. Two-round salvo."

Ammermann reached for his arm. "Captain! This is crazy. You can't do this."

"It's what my orders specify, Adam."

"Not taking out a friendly missile!"

Dan turned his head. Sweat sparkled on the staffer's bulging brow. A lock of dark hair hung over his forehead. He looked more frightened than when an Iraqi Al-Husayn had had them boresighted. "Adam," he murmured, "there's no such thing as a 'friendly' ballistic missile. Not when it's targeted at a city."

Beside him Staurulakis was continuing the litany, gaze welded to her screen, chanting like an acolyte in a liturgy as the responses came back. "Launchers to operate mode. . . . Set up to take Meteor

Echo . . . two-round salvo. I say again, two-round salvo. Sound warning alarm aft. Deselect safeties and interlocks. Stand by to fire. On CO's command."

"You can't mean to actually . . ." Ammermann's outrage-swollen visage hung in front of him, then turned away. He straightened and raised his voice, addressing the others. "Listen to me! I'm counter-manding that order! You—you people can't *let* him! Don't you under-stand what he's doing?"

Amy Singhe, behind them. "Sir? Shall I call the master-at-arms again?"

Dan shook his head, very slightly, gaze averted. He was holding back, reviewing exactly what he was doing and why. He was going to use up the last two shots in his locker, taking down the Israeli counterstrike against an enemy that had struck first, and struck grievously. Nearly two hundred dead. Women and children.

No. He was executing his orders. Priority Three: *Offensive missiles targeted against civilian populations.*

He couldn't say he was sure this was the right course of action. He really wasn't.

But that was why there *was* a captain. To make the decisions that had to be made, under whatever conditions of stress and uncer-tainty, deep in the murky swamp of war and politics.

Then paying the piper, if that decision turned out to have been the wrong one.

He spared a quick glance around, trying to read body language. It was rare anyone openly contradicted a skipper, but if he was too far off track, that could give you a clue. Staurulakis, Slaughenhaupt, Singhe, Wenck, Terranova, Kaghazchi, were all looking at him, but their expressions varied. Some looked horrified; others, inspired. Donnie Wenck was smiling, blue eyes crazy, mashing down a cow-lick of spiky blond hair. *Go for it, Skipper*, he mouthed.

"*Don't*," groaned Ammermann. "I'm warning you—"

"To hell with it," Dan whispered under his breath. He fitted the key. Hooked a nail under the clear plastic cover of the switch, flicked it up, and snapped the toggle to the Fire position.

* * *

ONCE again, that agonizingly stretched-out pause, no more than three seconds, but seemingly without end. The vent dampers *whun-k*ed shut. The ventilation sighed to a stop, and *Savo* moaned and popped as she rolled, the turbines thrumming through the steel and rubber beneath his feet like distant war drums.

A thunder from aft. Brightness like a welding arc burned on the cameras. "Bird one away. Stand by . . . bird two away."

The bright symbols left *Savo*'s circle-and-cross, quickly blinking into blue semicircles as they tracked east. Dan said, "TAO, inform Iron Sky we've fired our last two TBM-capable rounds against a presumed Jericho launched from northern Israel. Add that we're now engaging two Iranian surface units executing an attack profile. Warnings were issued." His gaze nailed the Iranian-American, who stood holding a mike near the Aegis console. "That's right, isn't it, Petty Officer Kaghazchi? We warned them, on bridge-to-bridge?"

"*Baleh, agha* . . . yes sir. But they never answered, Captain."

"Transmitting loud and clear," Slaughenhaupt said. "Confirmed with Radio. They heard us, all right."

"Good, Chief. Thanks for the backstop."

"No problem, sir."

Terranova chanted, "Stand by for Block 4 intercept, Meteor Echo. . . . Stand by. . . ."

"Seeker profile on X-band!" the EW operator yelled, and Dan winced. "Bearing . . . bearing two six four. Seeker correlates with C-802 terminal radar seeker. Designate Goblin Alfa."

He nodded. What he'd half expected, and would have preempted, given thirty more seconds. But the other side had thrown the first punch, after all. Muffled thuds came from outside. In the cameras, smoke trails smeared the sky, tipped with flame-hot pinpoints. "Chaff away," someone reported. "Duckies deployed."

Dan put his hand between Staurulakis's thin delicate shoulder blades. The cotton of her coveralls was damp and hot. "Take 'em, Cher."

"Stand by on Harpoon. Three-round engagement, target *Alborz*, salvo fire, *batteries released*."

"Stand by for intercept on Meteor Echo . . . *now*," called Wenck.

Dan jerked his gaze up to the display as the blue and the red callouts merged. The brackets locked on the hurtling missile. Jerked, tracked back. Then hunted back and forth, as if unclear what they were supposed to be looking for. They slewed away, then hunted again, at the same moment as a roar rattled the deckplates and the helo-deck cameras went the off-white of booster smoke.

"Radar return getting mushy . . . may be body separation—"

"Sir, we can't wait on this incoming—"

He tore his gaze away. Blinked. "Got it, Cher. Secure from TBMD mode! Shift SPY-1 to self-defense. Sea Whiz released. Standard released. Take incoming Goblin with birds."

"Self-defense mode, aye. Salvo alarm, aft and forward." She sounded relieved, and a wave of commands and responses moved away down the consoles, along with buckling and adjustments as flash gear got tightened.

The picture on the rightmost vertical screen blinked. Then the pie wedge, the closed fan, suddenly spread, opening like the Argus-eyed tail of a peacock. The amber traces probed outward, 360 degrees, clicking deliberately yet with wonderful rapidity all around the horizon. Shorelines and islands, contacts and callouts, sprang up. *Savo*'s awareness was suddenly total, a godlike gaze of perfect knowledge within a three-hundred-mile radius. Some contacts were red and blinking, others amber, yet others green. Two were the red vertical carets of hostile missiles, jumping rapidly inward at near-supersonic velocities. With the next sweep, another popped up, this one closing from the east.

But, that suddenly, he could see. He could fight. It felt like being underwater, wound tightly in heavy chains, and feeling them fall away. As the helo controller reported Red Hawk dumping chaff and flares, Dan cycled the Fire Auth switch, leaving it in the up position. Called back to Singhe's team, "Strike, stand by for TLAM mission. Salvo of four. Where we marked those truck-mounted launchers." He reached for his helmet, and found himself face-to-face with Ammermann.

"That was a stupid move," the staffer said in a low voice. "And believe me, you'll pay for it."

Dan felt for the lever and reclined his seat. Cleared his throat. "You do actually understand what's going on, Adam? Right?"

"Oh yeah, I do. You just shot down—"

"No. Forget that. What I mean is, we've got mail. Three inbound antiship missiles. An 802 from the Syrian coast. Two 801s, the ship-to-ship version, from seaward. Over a thousand pounds of high-energy armor-penetrating warheads on the way, at .8 mach, fifteen feet above the water. The first one, roughly two minutes out." He lifted his eyebrows. "So maybe I won't have to worry about justifying myself. Or paying for anything."

A commanding officer got a lot of practice masking his emotions. But the staffer obviously hadn't. His mouth sagged; he looked terrified. Dan himself felt tense, yet eager, even vengeful, here at the end. When it would all come down to whether all their shit worked, and how fast he could make decisions. Not to mention how deep their magazines would prove, compared to those who'd just declared themselves America's enemy.

He gave Ammermann one last tight smile, and patted his arm. Said, teeth bared in mock politeness, "Excuse me, Jars. Right now, I seem to have a battle to fight."

20

AN hour after dawn the lookouts reported black smoke far to the west. Dan made up on it cautiously, electronic ears pricked, studying what gradually rose into view over the sawtoothed horizon with gun cameras at full magnification. He kept calling, on international distress, bridge to bridge. And on what intel said was an Iranian navy freq like the old USN Fleet Common. No answer. Not a peep. The other attacker, the missile boat, had disappeared from radar. *Pittsburgh*'s periscope check had found scattered debris, nothing more. He asked her to clear to the south and stand by, just in case.

The battle proper, last night, had lasted for no more than twenty minutes. A close-in, all-out knife fight that at its height had forced him to switch Aegis into full-auto self-preservation mode. At near-supersonic speeds, with multiple incoming threats, human beings could no longer react swiftly enough to fight.

Gradually, decade by decade, war—like manufacturing—was becoming the province of the robot.

However, people were still doing the dying. He hove to a mile off and studied the hulk for a long time through his 7x50s, bracing his elbows on the varnish of the bridge coaming. The wind remained keenly cold, but the sky was brighter, if still overcast. Only an occasional flake of snow blew past. The situation brought back uncomfortable memories. Of another ship, in the South China Sea, doomed and sinking. Of oil-smeared, helpless arms raised for help; of desperate voices pleading, far away on the wind.

He shivered. And then came another, even deeper memory, nearly three decades back now: of the disastrous night a superannuated destroyer had died in the Irish Sea, when he himself had had to jump into a raging ocean; and no one had come to their rescue.

No. He wasn't going to steam away again.

Mytsalo cleared his throat beside him. Under the helmet, chest bulky with flak jacket, the ensign didn't look as pink-cheeked and boyish as at the start of their cruise. He was thinner, his cheeks sunken. Dan met his eyes, and didn't like the haunting in them. God willing, he'd not impose on this boy what had been imposed on him.

He'd reported to Jen Roald on high-side chat around 0400. She'd made supportive noises, but so far, everyone above her was silent. No reaction yet. No official comment at all. Though he'd made sure to info absolutely everyone he could think of. They wouldn't be able to reproach him for an attempted cover-up, at any rate.

He sucked a breath, let it out. In the face of what they looked out on, it seemed petty to worry about whether he'd be left in command, or summarily relieved. But still. "What you got, Max?"

"Captain, Radio's picking up something on one-fifty-six five. Channel Ten."

Dan took the offered handset. Looked across again to where the gray ship rolled, inky smoke still streaming up from aft, then thinning to a brazen haze against the lightening sky as it blew away downwind. He told the officer of the deck, "Man the portside thirties and fifties. No—both port and starboard. Sea Whiz in local control. But keep weapons tight."

The frigate's mast and antennas were wrecks, bent, twisted, scorched. Cables swung to a slow roll. Fragment-gashes gleamed here and there, and all the windows in her pilothouse were broken. At least one missile had guided in for a mission kill on her sensors. The other, or others, must've impacted farther aft. Including, Dan was pretty sure, at least one of the four 802s fired from Syria, but spoofed away from *Savo* and redirected by some electronic sleight-of-hand Donnie Wenck had explained twice, but Dan still didn't fully understand. As they drifted downwind the changing angle was gradually revealing the Iranian's stern. It looked as if she'd caught a missile there, too. An explosion had caved in the helo pad, and the hangar was still burning, streaming up that oily black smoke that towered like a beacon above the sea-horizon. Threatening whatever fuel storage they had back there, no doubt.

Which explained, of course, both the lack of comms, and being dead in the water. But he didn't see anyone fighting the fire, or really any activity at all. Lying doggo? Playing dead, to sucker him in close? He didn't like to think in those terms, but he and this ship had encountered each other before. And he'd come close to dying then.

He angled the radio to his lips. "INS *Alborz*, this is USS *Savo Island, Savo Island*. Off your starboard beam. Over." He snapped to the OOD, "Petty Officer Kaghazchi to the bridge, please."

The blast of Nuckols's pipe over the 1MC. *"Now Petty Officer Kaghazchi, lay to the pilothouse. On the double."*

Dan moved a few feet forward to give the M60 crew room. The gunner dropped the wing 7.62 onto its mount with a thunk. His assistant snapped open the loading gate and draped a belt of cartridges into it. The gunner racked the bolt and swiveled the muzzle to cover the slowly nearing, ominously deserted wreck as Dan depressed the transmit button again. "INS *Alborz*, INS *Alborz*. This is USS *Savo Island, Savo Island*. Over."

The voice was scratchy, lagging, faint. *"This is INS Alborz. Over."*

"This is USS *Savo Island*. U.S. Navy cruiser, off your starboard side. About a kilometer away. Do you require assistance?"

A short pause. Then, heavily accented, *"We . . . do not . . . ask help."*

Dan kept watching the bridge, but they were either under cover, or the pilothouse was abandoned. "This is *Savo* actual. This is the captain. Request speak to your commanding officer direct. If possible. Over."

A new voice came up about a minute later. *"This is captain of . . . of Iranian ship. Do you require assistance? Over."*

"Ha-ha. Nice one," said Mills, beside him. The TAO was in a green nylon foul-weather jacket, the collar snugged up. He held another coat out to Dan. "Thanks," Dan said. He *was* getting chilled.

He shrugged into it as he considered how best to play this. When he glanced into his own pilothouse the petty officers were at the consoles that operated the 25mm chain guns, gripping the game-type toggles. Red lights and lit screens told him both guns were live. Down on the bow, the long tapered barrel of *Savo*'s forward five-inch rose and fell, correcting for the roll, pointed at the smoking wreck that now heaved slowly only a few hundred yards away. On the wing, the machine gunners were sharing a cigarette, hunkered below the coaming. They looked unconcerned, as if none of this was their business.

He said into the heavy little radio, "This is *Savo Island*. Thank you for your offer. We were attacked during the night by missiles from shore. I do not require assistance. However, I see you are fighting a fire. It is a tradition of the sea to offer help to other mariners in distress. Do *you* require assistance?"

Another long pause. Finally the other voice, a rough lagging one he assumed was her CO's, came back. *"We too were attacked by missiles from the shore. They were Israeli. Assistance is not required. I repeat, not required. However, if you wish, close on my starboard side and help fight the fire."*

"He's doing us a favor. Letting us help," said Mills, straight-faced.

"Whatever," Dan said. The guy was trying to save his ship and his men the best way he could, given a regime that was by all accounts ruthless with anyone who stepped over its fundamentalist, anti-American line. He straightened, noticing their own Iranian, or rather Iranian speaker, waiting just inside the wing door. Muster the damage-control teams aft. Fire hoses, laid out on the port quarter. He probably won't let us board, but we can lay some A-triple-F into that smoke. Petty Officer Kaghazchi, just stand by, please; the other side seems to speak English."

Dan let the ensign take her alongside. Mytsalo brought her in at a shallow angle until they were a quarter mile astern, then eased off to three knots. The frigate was beam to the seas, which meant *Savo* started to roll hard too as she lined up.

Mytsalo kept reducing power, until they were edging up at about half the speed of smell. Dan started to tell him to goose it, get on in there, and to use his screws to keep her twisted into the wind. But closed his teeth on it. The only way you learned shiphandling was by doing it. And too slow was better than too fast. What was that old tin-can saying . . . oh, yes. "Try to avoid situations that call for excellent shiphandling."

He smiled and coughed into a fist as Nuckols lifted the stainless coffee urn and his eyebrows at the same time. Dan held up thumb and forefinger an inch apart, remembering when someone else coughed too that he'd promised to get back to Grissett about the men in sick bay. The results of the tests on Goodroe's body . . . but now wasn't the time. Not a hundred yards away from an enemy with whom they'd traded deadly blows. *Hard* blows. Keep your mind right, Lenson. Game's not over yet.

They were sliding into the slot. Dan tensed. It looked awfully close. He started to say, "—"

"Engines stop," Mytsalo called.

The helmsman: "Engines stop aye. Both engines stopped."

Dan closed his mouth and went out on the wing again.

Looked down on from fifty yards away, the damage was much worse. The smoke blowing down on *Savo* smelled like a burning refinery. In the hangar the tail of a small helicopter lay twisted like a scrap of aluminum foil tossed into a recycle bin. He coughed again, scarred throat closing, and retreated into the pilothouse. Started to call for the XO, then remembered.

"Want the senior watch officer, sir?" Mills asked him.

"No, you can do it, Matt. Leave Cher in Combat. . . . Keep an eye on Max. He's doing good, but we need somebody senior to an ensign in charge. Oh, and call Adam Ammermann up here. I want him to get eyes on this from close aboard."

"Aye aye, sir. And you'll be—?"

"I'm going aft, get some foam on that fire."

THEY were alongside for two hours, pumping fifteen thousand gallons of firefighting foam that smelled like curdled blood onto the hangar and helo deck. Meanwhile the wind blew steadily harder, laying streaks of foam like detergent suds across the wine-dark waves. Snow blew down now and then from clouds dark as cast lead. The frigate's crew came out from behind the superstructure—where they had, apparently, been hiding—and resumed their own damage-control efforts. Perhaps they'd feared being machine-gunned as the cruiser approached. Dan offered the loan of portable pumps, a firefighting team, but was brusquely turned down. The Iranian commander had at last emerged into sight, and gazed stone-faced across from his bridge wing. By 09 local the fire was out, but he still didn't see any sign of power being restored. Actually, you could hear whether a ship had power, and this one, clearly, still didn't.

Savo was slowly drifting away, the black disturbed water between them widening. Fifty yards. A couple minutes later, sixty. She'd done that all morning; her sail area was larger than the frigate's, giving the wind more purchase. The increasingly violent seas didn't help. He'd approached from downwind for that very reason—hadn't wanted to be pinned against the other hull—but it necessitated continual screw and rudder orders, jockeying to stay close enough to fight the fire while not actually colliding.

"Noodge her in there again, Max," Dan told Mytsalo. He snugged the foul-weather jacket to his neck, screwed on his combination cap, with the gold braid on the brim, more tightly, and went back out onto the wing.

The other captain was still at half attention, gripping his binoculars, pointedly looking away from *Savo*. Dan leaned against the coaming until they came abreast, then shouted across, "D'you have power yet?"

The Persian's black eyebrows, so heavy they were one dark line, contracted. He shook his head slightly. In his forties, at a guess. Mustached, not exactly clean-shaven, but not bearded, either. The black stubble was trimmed around the jawline, as if to fit a gas mask. Above it, a hawk-beak of a nose. A dark, foreboding glare, sort of like a male Singhe's. Dan figured him for a regular, most likely from the shah's old navy, trained as an ensign in San Diego or Newport.

"Propulsion?"

Another negative wag. He lifted the binoculars and focused them somewhere past Dan. "We will take it soon, though."

"Uh-huh. Where are you headed?"

No answer. "Syria?" Dan prompted. "Tartus?"

The faintest motion of the shoulders; otherwise, perfect immobility. A figure moved behind the commander, just inside one of the smashed-out windows, and Dan saw one reason why he might not be that forthcoming. Someone was listening, from inside. Holding out . . . a microphone? Was everything he said being recorded?

"We will regain powers very shortly," the captain muttered through tight lips.

"Yeah? Well, look. Fleet Weather says this is gonna get ugly again.

Forty-knot winds. Fifteen-foot seas. I don't know how bad that port-side damage is, but you want to get into shelter before it puts too much stress on your hull girder. Right?"

"I will reach port," the guy said. Obviously hating every word he had to exchange with this enemy, this foreigner, this infidel. Yet also thinking about how he was going to save his ship, and his men. Not a bad skipper. Probably a pretty good one. And if he was like the Iranian destroyerman Dan had faced in the Gulf a few years before, a competent and dogged seaman.

"I can put a line over," Dan called over the rising wind. "Provide a tow. Get you part of the way there, at least. Until you get your shafts turning."

The guy was obviously struggling with himself. "You will wait," he said at last, and ducked into the pilothouse. Figures moved back and forth in the semidarkness. Dan couldn't see what was going on, so he went to the radar and checked it, his boots sliding as *Savo* rolled. He called down to Staurulakis for an update and to make sure she was passing everything that was going on to Higher via chat.

When he socketed the J-phone Van Gogh said, "Sir, we can't stay alongside much longer. We're really starting to pick up motion, and this close—"

"Yeah, Chief, I know. Make sure it gets logged, that we offered a tow."

"Logging it all, sir. From the minute we sighted them. Chief Grissett's back on the signal bridge getting photos, too."

Document everything—that was apparently going to be the Navy's watchword from now on. Dan nodded and told him to lay out a course to Tartus. He paced to the starboard side, ran his eyes around the horizon, though the machine-gun crew and the junior officer of the deck were both out there, and paced back. Out to the port wing again.

"We will accept tow," the other captain called, still not looking at him. "Until we have engine powers again. But no one comes aboard."

Dan nodded. "Got it. How's your hull damage?"

"We are keeping up," he said, and Dan caught the unspoken message: It wasn't good.

"Do you have a towing hawser? A special rope for towing?"

The other nodded. "Towing hawser. Yes."

"I'll need it bent onto twenty fathoms—sorry, forty meters—of your anchor chain. Make sure to rig chafing gear. Lock your propellers if you can. And put your rudder amidships." The guy nodded, looking even more pissed off. Dan started to turn away, preoccupied already with the mechanics of towing eleven hundred tons in a heavy seaway, then pivoted back. "Tartus?"

The Iranian squinted, obviously hating what he had to do. But forced to answer. "Yes. Tartus."

Dan was turning away once more, assuming the conversation was finished, when the man spoke again. "You are Lenson. Yes?"

"I'm sorry—I didn't catch that?" Although he had, all too clearly; but he needed a second to process the question. Or rather, what the asking of it meant.

"Commander Lenson. The one who stole our submarine. And who sank our sister ship. I must . . . thank you for the assistance. But I hope we will meet again."

Dan returned his saturnine stare, but could muster no appropriate response. Very suddenly, he felt deeply apprehensive. The Iranian's smile seemed to say he knew something Dan didn't, and wouldn't like.

"Keep your forward gun turned aft," he called over the widening sea to the Iranian, trying to make his own expression equally remorseless. "To protect it from damage, of course. But I just want you to know. If you turn it toward me, I will sink you."

HE pondered that as he paced the bridge, that they knew him by name; then worried about the weather, which was a more immediate threat. Towing was never a routine evolution, and towing in heavy seas could be a bear—exacting, tiring. And, if you screwed up or got unlucky, dangerous.

It took a while to rig aft, then longer to reposition upwind and float a buoyed messenger line down. The Iranians, in green camo and bright red life preservers, lashed a heavier line to it, which *Savo*'s deck gang hauled back. Then came the towed ship's hawser. This turned out to be brand-new twelve-strand polyester with a stout thimble. *Savo*'s deck seamen bolted the cruiser's own hawser to the thimble, then paid both lines back out until they had a good two hundred fathoms catenaried between them, from chain through *Savo*'s stern pad eye to black-painted anchor chain dropped from the frigate's bow chock.

When the first lieutenant reported they were rigged to tow, Dan passed the word aft to make fast and stand clear, but also to have a big guy standing by with a sledge in case they had to trip the pelican hook. By noon they were under way at five knots, plodding north, more or less crosswind. A hundred and thirty-two miles, Van Gogh said.

The wind kept increasing, howling in their antennas and snapping their flags. Dan couldn't believe how cold it was getting. How long this front was lingering. The seas swept in from off the bow, burst against their sides, rolled *Savo* far over before she came back again. Belted into his command chair, he watched spray fly up, trail across the flat banks of hatches on the forecastle, blow aft and rattle against the pilothouse windows.

Savo screeched and groaned as she plunged and climbed, not nearly so violently as the ships he'd grown to manhood on—FRAM destroyers, Knox-class frigates, Perrys—but more ponderously. And, given her top-heaviness, sometimes frighteningly. Still, he felt confident in her. It would be a shame to have to leave her.

But he had to face the possibility.

Staurulakis checked in on the Hydra. Dan told her to stay at Condition Three. The Tomahawks they'd fired the night before had sent a message, but he wasn't sure how the Syrians would react. As for further BMD missions, there was no point continuing to scan. Their magazines were empty of anything that would take out another Al-Husayn. "Anything on the chats about us, Cheryl? Any reaction at all yet to our after-action report? And that we're towing this guy in?"

"*An acknowledgment from ComSixthFleet. 'Your message date-time-group yada-yada received.' That's all.*"

Strange that Ogawa wouldn't have provided orders. So the jury up at Higher was still out . . . or the hot potato was being bucked upstairs. Dan called sick bay to check on Zotcher. The sonarman was stable. Grissett had done a sonogram, located the bullet, and extracted it; it had missed the kidney; he sounded optimistic. Dan told him to tell Zotcher he'd called. "And tell him he probably saved all our lives in CIC. I'm putting him in for as high a decoration as I can swing."

Next he called Ammermann and asked him to come up to the bridge. He made sure the staffer had seen the damage to the Iranian, and that he'd make a report too, including the results of the night action and the disappearance of the missile boat.

He went down to his sea cabin and checked his message file, checked a couple of chat rooms, and sent an e-mail to Blair.

He sighed and eyed his bunk, wavering to its siren call. But . . . no. Not while they were towing. Not still in range of the Syrians. He sighed and climbed slowly back up to the bridge. Each boot he lifted was strapped with heavy iron.

THEY towed through the afternoon as the wind built to thirty to thirty-five, gusts to forty. *Alborz* yawed occasionally, but her CO wasn't taking Dan's rudder-centerlining command literally; was seaman enough not to. She came back around and although the catenary dipped, making the first lieutenant clear the fantail, never put too much strain on the towline. Dan drowsed in his chair, snapping awake from time to time. Breathing fast, throat sore, sweat itching under his coveralls. He kept dreaming about the white thing. Each time he woke he checked with whoever was on watch, but they still hadn't gotten any steaming orders by the time dark fell.

When Longley brought up a covered tray with Dan's evening meal they were eighty miles off Tartus. Dan napped in his chair through the night. At 0109 a message came in directing him to drop the tow off the coast, and under no circumstances to enter Syrian territorial waters. This seemed wise, and he sent a brief acknowledgment, underlining his depleted magazines and fuel and asking for orders.

At dawn the purple mountains of the Levant glowed like backlit transparencies on the horizon. He shaded his eyes, watching those far peaks for a long time. The seas were still ten to twelve feet, rushing in hollowed and belligerent to collide with the bow like semitruckloads of wet shining gravel. *Savo* bulled her way through them like some armored cataphract through ranks of the Seleucid infantry Freya Stark had described in her book.

Back then, Syria had been a Roman colony, and one of the most loyal and civilized. A lot had changed in this corner of the world since. Including the lock-on a number of Russian-made fire-control radars had maintained on *Savo Island* for the last few hours. The mountains pushed upward slowly as they plodded on, growing sharper, darker against the climbing sun. Here and there plumes of thin smoke rose. Trash fires, or maybe burning off fields; they didn't seem heavy enough to be signs of war.

Another message came in, giving him a rendezvous position with a tug at the head of what looked like the lead-in channel for the port. Van Gogh plotted it and they altered course gradually, dragging their charge around at the end of the towline. Making the last few miles directly into the prevailing sea, which made the wind seem twice as strong and converted their roll into a plunge and lift that set metal clanking around the bridge. The mountains kept growing, the land imperceptibly closing, until he could make out small settlements and villages through the binoculars. They passed no fishing boats, which didn't surprise him. Not in winter, in seas this heavy.

Nuckols struck eight bells. 0800. Tartus crept into view, an open roadstead that at first didn't look like it would offer much shelter, until long stone breakwaters gradually coalesced from the beach. Dan went up to the flying bridge to use the Big Eyes. He inspected the shore for a long time through the huge stand-mounted binoculars, and decided at last that if the tug didn't show, he wasn't going in. He'd drop the frigate at the outer anchorage, and let the Syrians and Iranians sort things out. But not long after, CIC reported a contact leaving the harbor. It hove into view as a speck, then slowly became a small craft. As the three ships labored toward a meeting, Dan passed the word to stand by to bring in the hawser.

The tug ranged alongside, unexpectedly small, more like a harbor tug than a salvage type, low, battered, with rusty patches like red lichen along her dented-in sides. Waves broke over her rear deck, which hardly showed, at times, above them. But the crew knew what they were doing. A gun cracked. A bright green projectile angled across, curving in the wind, and draped a line fluttering down across their bow. First Division hustled it aft and pulled across a heavier line, this one bent to the end shackle of the frigate's hawser. The boatswains on the three ships seemed to be doing fine with hand signals, so Dan left them to it. He kept looking aft, studying the pilothouse with his binoculars, but didn't see the Iranian captain again.

A whistle shrilled. The tug hoisted the black diamond shape that meant craft in tow. The phone talker said, "Fantail reports: Dropped the tow, sir."

"Very well." It looked like a damn small tug to handle something as large as that frigate, but it wasn't his responsibility any longer. They still didn't have any orders as to where to go from here, but this wasn't a good place to linger. "Restow all gear and secure. OOD, let's go to two-six-zero and fifteen, get clear of Syrian waters."

They didn't get a message responding to their after-action report until that afternoon. Iron Sky directed them back to a rendezvous with the main body of Task Force 60. A Naval Criminal Investigative Service team would be on its way shortly by helo. On rendezvous, Dan would crossdeck to *Theodore Roosevelt*, to appear before Admiral Ogawa. A senior O-6 from Ogawa's staff would take temporary command of *Savo Island*.

Almost as an afterthought, it mentioned that defense counsel had been appointed for Captain Daniel V. Lenson, USN.

The Afterimage:
USS *Theodore Roosevelt,*
CVN-71

IT felt all too familiar. Being led like a sacrifice through labyrinthine corridors smelling of latex paint and lubricating oil and stale refrigerated air. Stepping over an endless recession of knee-knockers, the oval openings of frame doors stretching away as if reflected in endlessly fleeing mirrors. The snapping to attention of flawlessly turned-out Marines in dress Charlies and white cap covers, complete with aiguillettes and holstered pistols. Then being ushered into a low-overheaded flag wardroom, cleared for the occasion of dishes and cutlery and idle junior officers. But the familiarity didn't make him feel any less nauseated.

Oh, yeah. He'd been here before.

A court of inquiry. The faces that turned toward him, then quickly away, from a knot of service dress blue at the far end of the space told him that much. As had his counsel, a young woman also in dress blues. Dan himself was still in three-days-unwashed khakis, the best uniform he could muster. Her advice had been singularly unhelpful. Be forthcoming. Lay it all out. Tell the truth. It's not a trial, just an inquiry.

Nothing he hadn't heard before. Not that it had helped much then.

He drifted to the sideboard and found coffee. When the cup clattered as he poured, he leaned against the bulkhead, closing his eyes. He kneaded the bone and flesh around them until phosphenes coruscated digital patterns in the twin displays of his optic nerves. When he released the pressure a deep scarlet rushed around him, like a whirlpool of blood. When he opened his eyes the whirlwind was still there, just not completely red. The murmurs from the far end of the wardroom continued. No one came his way, no one approached to welcome or condole.

His mouth twisted in a crooked, humorless smile. He remembered a corridor floored in Italian marble, and a shaken-looking man with silver at his temples like the chromium eagles on his collar. And a bleak thousand-yard stare. The previous CO of USS *Savo Island*.

They needed a scapegoat. Make sure you're not the next one.

Now he stood in the shoes of the dishonored captain he'd relieved. A strange turnabout, a full-circle return.

If he went out in the passageway, started opening doors, would his own relief look up, startled and abashed at being discovered, waiting in another room?

BUT half an hour passed. The moment stretched, stretched out. He finished that cup of joe and had another. He kept wondering how Chief Zotcher was doing, down in the carrier's operating suite. How *Savo*'s crew were taking the loss of their second captain in a row.

He breathed deep and slow, trying to put regret, and a sorrow almost like losing a loved one, behind him. For Dan Lenson, USS *Savo Island* was history. Let it fall astern in the wake, grow tiny, rising on the last swell between him and the horizon. And vanish forever . . . At least he'd saved some lives. He tried to comfort himself with that. Enemy lives, Iraqi civilians, but saved nonetheless. It helped about as much as a maintenance aspirin on an amputation.

He had half a doughnut, then a third cup, and finished the doughnut up. He arrested his hand in the act of reaching for another pastry. Sugar wasn't the way to shed the shakes. Damn, if he only could have gotten some sleep. More than the half hour's nap on the helo that had left him groggy and nasty-mouthed. If only he'd brought the Freya Stark book with him. He'd left it aboard; would never finish it now.

What the hell. He knew how it ended: Rome fell. He paced around, noting how even as he ghosted past, ten feet away, not one of the men and women around the low table set with months-old copies of *AFJ* and *Defense News* and *Approach* acknowledged his existence.

But these men and women were not his shipmates. To judge by those carefully averted gazes, they weren't even in the same navy.

He sighed and checked his watch. Nearly an hour now . . .

"Gentlemen?" An immaculately uniformed lieutenant (junior grade), blank-faced as a robot, at the door. The aiguillette proclaimed him a flag aide. "There's going to be a slight delay. Please stand easy. —Captain Lenson?"

"That's me. Yeah."

"The admiral would like to see you privately."

Hmm. *This* was not routine. The lifted eyebrows around the coffee table attested to that. The convening officer was supposed to stand clear of the proceedings of a court of inquiry. No, wait; he was supposed to stand clear of the *members*. Did that include the defendant? Maybe . . . or maybe not.

"This way, Captain." The jaygee held the door open carefully, even solicitously, as if Dan were an eighty-year-old Mafia don.

CTF 60, the battle group commander—"Iron Sky"—was a rear admiral Dan hadn't met before. He introduced himself, but didn't shake hands. Perhaps he feared whatever Dan had might be catching. There was no mention of admiration for his Medal of Honor, or anything else. Just a blank "Good to see you. Let's step into my office."

The adjoining room was set up for videoteleconferencing. Two dead screens faced a padded chair. The one-star didn't introduce an enlisted man sitting to one side. He pulled a second seat up to his own station for Dan. The petty officer addressed himself to a keyboard, and a ruby LED blinked on over a tiny camera pointed at them. Both screens lit, one after the other. The leftmost illuminated a brilliant noon-sky blue, but without video feed. Whoever was on it didn't care to be seen. The right one came on to reveal Admiral Ogawa, Commander, Sixth Fleet, head lowered, reading something. Dan could make out the beginning of a bald patch on the top of Ogawa's skull.

"Good morning, Admiral," the rear admiral said. "I have Captain Lenson here with me."

"Thanks, Sly. You have his billet taken care of?"

"I sent one of my staff captains over. Temporary fill." The rear admiral hesitated. Cleared his throat. "Pending the outcome of the inquiry."

"Right. Morning, Captain Lenson." A curt nod.

Dan said, "Good morning, Admiral Ogawa."

Ogawa handed whatever he'd been reading to someone off-camera and turned his attention their way. Responding to some unseen signal, the enlisted man set his keyboard aside and glided out, easing the door shut on them.

Ogawa opened. "Dan, I'm sorry to see you in this position. As far as I'm concerned, *Savo's* answered all bells. Nick said you could turn her around, and you did. And the night action—we're going to have to look at that in detail, but it seems plain the other side fired first. And after that, you fought your ship effectively. Despite a very unfortunate . . . incident with your exec. Which is also going to be looked at in detail, by the NCIS."

On the screen, Ogawa's look turned frostier. "But your other actions, your decision to intercept a friendly TBM, then offering a tow to a defeated enemy . . . I admit to grave doubts. Especially as to the former. My JAG here looked over your orders. I grant you, a literal interpretation supports the action. But there have been repercussions. A formal diplomatic protest."

Dan didn't say anything. Maybe he could have. Ogawa had paused, after all—for an explanation, an apology? To hear any extenuating circumstances? If that was what he was waiting for, Dan didn't have one. He'd shot down an Israeli retaliatory strike. If the repercussions and protests were from Tel Aviv, then that was far above both their pay grades. A matter for the national security adviser, the State Department, the West Wing.

. . . The West Wing. He cleared his throat. "Sir, you may know this, but we had an executive branch staffer on board during that action. Mr. Adam Ammermann."

Ogawa turned his head slightly, as if to listen to someone off-screen. He nodded. "We're aware of Mr. Ammermann's presence aboard. Are you saying he ordered, or perhaps advised, you to intercept that launch?"

"Ah, no sir. No. In fact, he counseled against it."

"Oh." The admiral's face fell. Grasping, no doubt, that Dan had just foreclosed the Navy's chance of offloading any blame onto the administration. "You're certain of that?"

"Yes sir."

"Then why bring his name up? I'm not sure I understand what you're driving at, Captain. Surely you can't be proposing he shares responsibility."

"No sir, I didn't mean that. The decision was entirely mine. Just pointing out that he was aboard and in CIC when it was made. If what happened was wrong, I take full responsibility." He gave it a beat, then added, "If the decision was correct . . . he was still in CIC."

Ogawa nodded slowly, and Dan watched him process the point. He'd phrased it subtly, but one didn't make admiral without being able to read between the lines. Ogawa cocked an ear again to whoever was speaking to him off-camera; shook his head, and leaned forward again. "Well, let's not be too hasty. Either way. The fact is— do you know Bankey Talmadge?"

"Senator Talmadge? My wife does," Dan said cautiously. "She used to work for him, for the Armed Services Committee staff, before she went to the SecDef's office—"

"I see. Well, he's adumbrated what he calls the 'Lenson Doctrine.'" Ogawa made a distasteful face. "Defined roughly as follows: that if a U.S. theater commander finds himself in a position to stop the delivery of a weapon of mass destruction, even if by someone the U.S. is not at war with, even by an ally . . . he has not only the legal right, but a moral obligation to do so."

"That's . . . a significant departure from current doctrine," said Iron Sky, from beside Dan.

"No shit, Sly! It also imposes a much higher threshold of requirement. Which I'm not at all sure we're ready to step up to. Certainly not with the force level we currently have."

"But the point is, right now, the issue's in play. This senator's even talking about calling him—Lenson, I mean—to testify. And the CNO's weighed in too."

"The CNO? On which side?"

"Not on any *side*, but it's been . . . oh, *made plain* to me that if they're even thinking of adding this to our mission requirements, there's going to have to be a concomitant increase in operating funding. We may have to bring forward the conversion of the Burke-class Aegis suite to full ballistic missile defense capability."

The flag officers fell silent. Dan sat quietly too, trying to sort through considerable anger. That it was Senator Talmadge defending him made it perfectly clear. Blair was riding to the rescue. Pulling strings behind the scene, to bump the question up to where it couldn't be handled just as a Navy issue. Or, put another way, to where the Navy could see pitching what he'd done as a way to increase its funding.

"So, on this end," Iron Sky prompted.

"Right. On your end, we can't exactly hose your captain for doing what might very soon become doctrine. Whether or not we think he exceeded his rules of engagement. And I need *Savo Island* in the Arabian Sea. Back at state one readiness."

Dan lifted his head. No one had mentioned this. "The IO, sir?"

"Possibly . . . or even farther east." Ogawa leaned again, listened to the murmured voice, nodded. "We have two carrier groups tied up at the north end of the Gulf. In view of . . . other current developments, we definitely need a TBMD-capable unit on station close to Iran and Pakistan."

Dan put his surprise to one side. "Sir, our readiness is significantly degraded. *Savo*'s magazines are empty. We need stores, fuel, and repairs. We're down one DPD, need chassis and parts. We need a software patch on ALIS. Plus, we had significant fire and water damage to the aft vertical launch system. We managed to jury-rig those last two Block 4s back in operation, but—"

"I read your opreps, Captain." Ogawa sounded more tired than annoyed, but annoyance was there too. "Your next stop'll be Crete. A contractor team, a new VLS cell, and a full rearm of Block 4A Standards are en route to NSA Suda Bay. What else do you need?"

He was trying to think. But the fog of fatigue, the red hissing whirlwind, made it hard to concentrate. "Uh, some outside training assistance—a casualty assistance team—a personnel augment. A new XO—no, actually I'd like permission to fleet up my ops officer to exec. A replacement sonar chief. I need a medical team, too, there's something—"

"Put it in a message. I want you back at full mission readiness as soon as possible. Report daily. I'm not making any promises, Lenson."

None. At all. But as of right now . . . Sly, this is your call, really. But it might be advisable to suspend his court of inquiry, pending further developments."

"Yes sir," Iron Sky said. "My thoughts too. Consider it done. Restore to command?"

"He never left it. But the court isn't called off, either. Only postponed. Due to operational commitments."

Which meant, Dan understood, that he still might face the green table one day soon, depending on which way the debate went on intercept doctrine. As well as whether someone might have to be thrown to the wolves, to placate the Israelis.

But for now, at any rate, he'd be going back to his ship.

The blue screen to the left, which had been audio-silent this whole time, flickered and went black. It must have done so at Ogawa's location, too, because the admiral seemed to unbend. He murmured, "Good luck, Lenson."

"Thank you, sir," Dan said.

"Sly, let's go to flag chat. Signing off."

The right screen flickered and blanked too. "Any questions?" the one-star asked him.

Dan blinked at the overhead. He had dozens. They had to rearm, replace a VLS cell in a foreign yard, and get ready to redeploy south. The Arabian Sea. The Indian Ocean. What was going on, that they needed a tired ship so badly?

But it seemed he was still in command. At least for now.

WHEN the aide escorted him back the wardroom was empty, except for a kid in a white paper mess attendant's cap, running a vacuum over the carpet where the putative board members had gathered. Dan stood watching the young man for a while, mind as blank as a deprogrammed RAM.

Things that had to be done surged up into his consciousness, then faded. He tried to be angry at Blair, then couldn't be. He'd always told her not to meddle. To please leave the Navy alone. But he was where he still was because of her, or at least partially because of her. The blue screen—that had to have been the deputy CNO, Barry "Nick" Niles himself.

Thanks to the two of them, and the fact that the sea service might actually gain from his act, he was still in the CO's seat. And, from the sound of things, in line for a follow-on mission.

Leaning against the sideboard, he pressed the heels of his palms deep into his face. Tired as if he hadn't rested for a hundred years. The yoke of command was settling back on his shoulders. *Savo Island* didn't just need voyage repairs. She needed an overhaul, new software, a better missile; his crew had kept falling ill and no one knew why. She was ready to go home, not to extend her deployment.

Instead, he had to take her back to sea.

Had he screwed up, or done the right thing? Not only did he not know, it didn't seem anyone else did either. From his own command chair in CIC, all the way up to the Oval Office.

What hadn't gone away, it seemed, was the threat. Defeat it here, and it reared its head elsewhere. Crush it in Iraq, and its bloody jaws snarled again from farther south and east.

But this, too, was nothing new under the sun. It had been the same for the soldiers of Caesar, of Constantine, of Julian. No matter what those at home thought, the legionaries had understood.

The border had to be held. Or all would dissolve back into chaos. All.

He straightened, forcing iron into his weary back. What mattered was not what lay within a man. What mattered was what he did.

Perhaps the cruise of USS *Savo Island* had only begun.

ACKNOWLEDGMENTS

EX nihilo nihil fit. For this book I owe thanks to Antonio Cobb, John Cordle, Callie Ferrari, Francisco Galvan, Sylvia Landis, Emily Merritt, Christopher Moton, Gail Nicula, Rick Potter, Sarah Self-Kyler, Robert Titcomb, and many others who preferred anonymity. Thanks also to Charle Ricci of the Eastern Shore Public Library; the Joint Forces Staff College Library; the Office of the Chief of Naval Information; the Naval History and Heritage Command; the Library of Virginia; Commander, Naval Surface Forces Atlantic, and his staff; the Naval Criminal Investigative Service; and very much to the crew, chiefs, and officers of USS *San Jacinto*, CG-56, who welcomed me to sail with them. They resemble the crew of USS *Savo Island* only in the positive ways!

I write from a complex braiding of memory, imagination, and research. For this book, I used maps, charts, and advice from a meeting with the very helpful Port Ops crew in Naples. Aegis facts and intercept scenarios were spliced from articles in the January 2012 *Proceedings* by Kevin Eyer and Jim Kilby, interviews aboard USS *San Jacinto*, and input from Mark "Dusty" Durstewitz and Mark Moore, who both commented on several drafts. They put a great deal of time into helping me! On cracks in the superstructure, see Christopher P. Cavas, *Navy Times*, December 9, 2010. The information about infections and the death scene were developed with the help of Dr. Frances Williams. The discussion of EMI is from OPNAVINST 3120.32C. That of TLE download difficulty is from an unclassified BMD 3.6 Bulletin article. The fire in the VLS scene began with a tour and briefing by Pablo Yepez.

The data on jammers is from open sources, mainly an *Air Power Australia* open posting by Dr. Carlo Kopp, April 2012. The power-out figure is from mostlymissiledefense.com.

Chapter 15 is mostly from my *San Jacinto* embark, plus a 2003 article in *Lifeline* magazine. Insight into a sometimes prickly relationship is from "US-Israeli Missile Defense," http://www.jewishvirtuallibrary.org/jsource/US-Israel/missile_defense.html. Bill Hunteman helped with the Tomahawk launch scene. The info on force levels is from "CRS Report for Congress, Iraq: US Military Operations," July 2007. The discussion of ROEs is based on *Rules of Engagement Handbook*, U.S. Naval War College. Missile specifications are from various open sources.

Joe Leonard read large parts of the book and supplied invaluable perspective from the points of view of a cruiser captain and a squadron commander.

Let's emphasize that all these sources were consulted for the purposes of *fiction*. I'm *not* saying that anything in these references leads to the conclusions my characters reach or voice. Likewise, the specifics of personalities, tactics, and procedures, and the units and locales described, are employed as the materials of fiction, not as reportage. Some details have been altered to protect classified capabilities and procedures.

My most grateful thanks to George Witte, editor and friend of long standing, without whom this series would not exist; to Sally Richardson, Matt Shear, Kenneth J. Silver, Kate Ottaviano, and Sara Thwaite at St. Martin's; and to Lenore Hart, anchor on lee shores and my North Star when skies are clear.

As always, all errors and deficiencies are my own.